CW00515512

To Angus,

There are worlds within!

Richard Dillan

THE STEALER OF WORLDS

RICHARD **DILLAN**

The right of Richard Dillan to be identified
as the Author of this Work has been asserted
by him in accordance with the Copyright,
Designs and Patents Act 1998

This book is a work of fiction. Names, characters,
places and incidents are products of the author's
imagination or are used fictitiously.

Copyright © 2013 Richard Dillan

All rights reserved.

ISBN-13: 978-1483977249
ISBN-10: 1483977242

This book is sold subject to the condition that it
shall not, by way of trade or otherwise, be lent,
resold, hired out, or otherwise circulated without
the publisher's prior consent in any form of
binding or cover other than that in which it is
published and without a similar condition
including this condition being imposed on the
subsequent publisher.

GLASS MOLLUSC *Hemphillia vitrum*

... The nightmare of living flesh was over ten feet long, shaped like a cross between a slug and a worm; long and thick, its body covered in large bulbs of flesh. The whole creature was almost completely see through, its lumpy skin resembling the frosted windows people put in their bathrooms...

Identification: Approximately cigar shape, exhibiting longitudinal symmetry the Glass Mollusc bears a passing resemblance to other invertebrates such as slugs. They are however much larger; an average sized adult Mollusc of seven feet is not unusual, with one sighting (Bracuti 2010) providing photographic evidence of an individual of over twelve feet in length with an estimated weight of 600-700 kilograms.
The Glass Mollusc is an aggressive predatory species of unknown origin. As their common and scientific name suggest the Mollusc is almost completely transparent - analogues with deep water jellyfish lead one researcher (Nel 2010) to postulate that they evolved in a sunless or otherwise poorly lit environment, although no firm evidence has been provided. This is mainly due to the extremely hazardous nature of contact with the Molluscs.
No Mollusc observed has been seen to possess visible sensory organs; exactly how they locate their prey is still a mystery.

Habitat: Left unchecked, a population of Glass Molluscs will devastate an area, ablating all organic matter, especially plant and animal life, leaving a wasteland where little can grow. In extreme circumstances, where plant or animal life may be scarce a Mollusc can even absorb the nutrients in the topsoil as it passes over it. Infestation of a Mollusc population can rapidly lead to an area being turned into a lifeless desert in a matter of months or just a few years.

Therefore, if discovered a Mollusc should always be reported to the relevant authorities.

Range: Molluscs have been observed in a wide variety of habitats, ranging from near desert to rainforest (although any Mollusc population would rapidly scour away the lush jungle). The only environment where they have never been observed has been the extreme cold wastelands of the polar tundra. Whether this is due to the extreme cold or the remoteness of these areas has yet to be determined.

Feeding: The Glass Mollusc is truly a remarkable creature. It is capable of transmuting almost any organic matter into food for energy, by direct contact with its flesh. This is achieved by a digestive system that is spread throughout the creature's body that tapers to microscopic pores on its outer surface through which pass extremely powerful acids. The extreme flexibility of the Mollusc's body therefore allows it to partially alter its shape and form to engulf relatively large prey within itself. Molluscs have been observed feeding on both living prey ranging in size from a dog up to a bison and inanimate objects such as bushes and even coal. Theoretically, a sufficiently large Mollusc could engulf an elephant.

Life-cycle: Little is known of the life-cycle of the Glass Mollusc. There are none in captivity and mating and birthing have never been witnessed in the wild. One theory (Follows 2011) is that the Mollusc reproduces asexually, much like snails etc. Certainly there is little evidence of any distinct genders in the species to contradict this.

Notes: Glass Molluscs seem impervious to minor and medium physical damage, their soft, malleable bodies capable of sustaining cuts, lacerations and blunt force trauma that would incapacitate or kill a mammal of similar mass.

Molluscs can also tolerate limited direct exposure to extreme heat and cold with little or no ill effects. Severe prolonged contact to a concentrated source of either could, in theory, cause death. There is no evidence either way on the effects that exposure to radiation would have on a Mollusc, but given that the Mollusc is comprised of living organic cells it can be relatively safely inferred that such exposure would only be deleterious.

It is noted that while the Mollusc cannot swim it also cannot traverse great distances underwater. It is hypothesised that this is due to Mollusc respiration occurring through some as yet undiscovered breathing organ. One researcher (Venning 2011) has advocated that the Glass Mollusc draws breath through the entirety of its external surface as well as being able to absorb nutrients this way. Whatever the reason for the Mollusc's inability to traverse large bodies of water, it is noted that this is a useful method of escaping their pursuit.

Warning: It would be reckless of the author not to issue one final warning to anyone who wishes to conduct field studies of Hemphillia Vitrum. Do not underestimate their speed or aggressiveness. Several well respected and renowned practical scientists have been lost, presumed consumed by the Mollusc they had set out to observe, the only signs that they had ever been in the area being a metal tie-pin or other such indigestibles encased in the Mollusc's crystalline scatological remains.

For Sarah

The inspiration behind all the
good ideas contained within

100% TAKEN...

1

School's Out

When the water stopped coming out of the taps, Robert realised he was in serious trouble. Looking back on it now, from the vantage point of three days later, he realised how naive he had been just seventy-two hours earlier in thinking that everyone on Earth would somehow reappear, as mysteriously as they had vanished, while he had been asleep that night. Hindsight being twenty-twenty, he now knew that the first, wasted day should have been spent in preparation. He should have been finding food and water supplies to see him through what was looking to be the rest of his life alone on Earth, with no way of knowing what had happened to his Dad or Elisabeth, let alone the rest of the world.

He had decided, in the effort to conserve what water he had managed to store, to stop bathing. With only Catanooga for company, and he didn't seem to mind if Robert smelled, or at least not so long as he opened a tin of food every morning, there wasn't much point in wasting fresh water.

Still, the electricity continued to work, so he was at least able to heat and light his house. Robert half-laughed, more to stop himself crying at the thought. He supposed it *was* his house now. His one last link to his missing Dad and big sister.

Swivelling his desk chair round, he flicked on the flat-screen monitor of his computer, and for the seventh time that day checked his inbox for any replies to the hundreds of email SOSes he had set the computer up to send. Nothing. The same nothing that had greeted him for three days now. He tried not to slump in his seat.

'C'mon Robert,' he said in an effort to lift himself. 'Get a grip.' Unconsciously, he pressed his hand to his heart and felt the reassuring lump of metal under his clothes. She was still with him, even if she had been pulled away from him just over a year ago. He straightened his posture, imagining his Mum telling him to do so, recalling her softly accented voice which he had not really picked up, and she had not really ever lost. Calling up his blog, YouTube, Facebook, and the dozens of other networking sites he had joined in the past couple of days, Robert diligently added another day's worth of SOSes to each of them, so in case there was someone, anyone else out there they'd know he was here.

Job done, Robert picked up Catanooga from where he had been cleaning himself and stroked his pet cat, the warmth of another living thing reassuring in his hands, the soft ginger fur smooth under his fingers. Catanooga for his part tolerated his master's attention for a few minutes, before making it plain that he had had enough for now, and jumped back down to the floor with a soft thud.

'Fair enough, Cat,' said Robert, realising that in any battle of wills with his pet cat, he would most likely not be the winner, and anyway, he didn't want Cat ignoring him. Not now.

Elsewhere

A long way away from Robert and Catanooga, the man in an impeccably tailored sand-coloured suit with a crisp white shirt underneath it, stood looking at the block of glass that acted as his safe. The glass was lit from above by a single spotlight, and as the man moved towards it the bright light glinted off the hard edges, rainbows prisming out in every direction.

Inside, suspended like a fly in amber, lay the Plan that the man guarded with his life. Currently, the Plan resembled a computer printed report, a wad of A4 paper bound together by a spiral of black plastic. Such a plain and ordinary covering for something so monumental. However, the Plan had not always looked like this.

Over the course of its existence, from the time the man first devised and formulated the Plan to the present day, it had variously been etched in wax, scratched into clay tablets, scribbled onto reed papyrus, carved into the atoms of the crystal lattices of diamond, germanium and silicon, as well as taking on a hundred hundred other different forms, each one directly related to the latest stage. It had even, for a brief time, been encoded in a continually circulating loop of red light, wavelength 680 nanometres. And all through its long history and many forms the Plan had resided in its glass container.

The man stood before the clear slab, his face hidden in the shadows cast by the high spotlight. Long years of familiarity allowed him to approach it this closely with complete safety.

In fact, no-one other than the man had ever seen the safe for longer than a minute. Once, a lifetime ago someone had tried to steal the Plan, to know the man's designs, and had got as far as making it into the room the man now stood in. But one of the thousands of booby-traps that peppered the room and the glass had taken care of him, and his life as he knew it up to that point ended. How he spent the remainder of his days was a matter of great speculation amongst his acquaintances, but he was never seen by any of them again. Well, not in a form that they recognised anyway.

The man valued the Plan's safety very highly.

He reached out to the glass and gently touched its surface,

running his powerful fingers along its edges as if in anticipation. *Soon,* he told himself, counselling patience. He had been waiting several lifetimes for this to come to pass, for a world large enough to progress the Plan to the next phase. And now he had secured it. Ten earth days, or rather more accurately, his days now, was not too great a time to wait for the culmination of his boldest endeavour yet. And the seven billion lives it would cost were trivial compared to the scale of his ambition.

The man turned from the glass slab and walked back to the preparations for the next stage.

Ten days. Soon enough.

The next day was the turning point for Robert, in more ways than one. He had woken from a fitful sleep, to find Cat reassuringly curled up on his bed by his feet, a lump of warmth, just the way he had been that first morning. It had been Cat's presence there that brought all the memories of the last four days to mind, and Robert realised he needed to write them down while he still had them fresh in his head.

He called up his blog and began typing.

He started with the memories that were strongest, the ones formed when he thought everything was still normal. He remembered waking up with Catanooga's heaviness blocking his exit from his bed just as he did every morning. The bathroom had miraculously been a big-sister free zone he remembered thinking at the time. Elisabeth had started spending more than the occasional night out round at friends' houses, but not enough to ensure Robert could assume he'd always find the bathroom empty. He'd still tried the handle carefully, self-preservation a strong survival instinct in a boy with a seventeen year old half-sister. Bathroom business done, he'd gone down stairs to the kitchen but had found that empty also, with no Dad around getting his family ready for school. Everything was where it should be, but no Dad.

Robert remembered how he'd assumed his Dad had had

to pull another all-nighter, the burden of single-parenthood taking its toll on the Cotts family in a thousand different ways, leaving Robert no stranger to sometimes making his own breakfast. He'd reheated a couple of dosas (Mum's recipe, Dad's cooking) and scoffed them down hungrily.

Robert paused at the memory of the dosas. Despite his insistence that his Dad teach him the recipe, Robert knew that any he made now would never be the same. Before, they represented, to him anyway, a link with his late Mum through his Dad. Now though, they were spoilt forever.

He remembered cleaning his teeth and as he looked at his light brown face and deep brown eyes in the bathroom mirror he told himself to ignore Jonesy today, despite what he might call him, or do to him. He had not wanted to get goaded into another fight. Instead he had tried to think of something clever to say to Erica, the girl with the large brown eyes and long, straight dark brown hair who made Robert blush uncomfortably whenever they accidentally-on-purpose caught one of each other's sideways glances with one of their own. Finally, he tousled some wax into his fine black hair, but gave it up as a lost cause.

Next had been his best friend Henry's house, and the short bike ride to it. How could he have not suspected something was wrong at this point, he wondered? The journey to Henry's had been very quiet, almost unheard of on the estate they lived on. In fact there had been no cars at all on the roads, and Robert remembered although it had felt strangely quiet, for the most part he'd just enjoyed the freedom of a ride free from fumes and the near-death-experience-by-4x4 that constituted an average day's journey.

Henry was also not home, as after a couple of minutes patient, then slightly more impatient knocking on the front, then back door failed to yield the usual being ushered in by Henry's Mum, Robert was left standing outside on his own. He recalled picking up his bike feeling slightly dejected and more than a little isolated, having seen no-one else for nearly two hours by then.

Robert paused and grimaced at that last sentence. What were a couple of hours on your own weighed against the rest of your life? *No, don't think like that.* He began typing again.

School was the next largest memory of this time, after the slightly strange journey to it. He didn't pass anyone on the pavement, and while there were cars parked in the drives and on the side of the road, there didn't seem to be any driving around. The tyres of his bike slish-slish-slished along the wet paving stones in rhythm with his pedalling feet. All in all it was a disquieting silence that hung heavily in the air all around him. The noisy refuge of the bustle of delivery vans, postmen, commuters, school-runners, buses and everybody else who had to be somewhere by nine o' clock was absent. He was the single living person in this unconventional calm.

School turned out to be no better. Instead of its normal barely-controlled pandemonium, his form room sat quiet and vacant, row after row of unoccupied desks and not a single classmate. Robert was never first to school so was not used to seeing the room empty. Even if he had been, *this* would still have felt wrong. The empty desks stared back at him in their ranks and files like a squad of soldiers waiting for the orders to relieve them that, fatefully, would never come.

Like the journey to it, the school at this time of day should have been awash with noise: chatter between the cliques of girls, a knot of boys discussing football, an altercation that could spiral into a fight, the bell indicating that other concerns be suspended; and above it all the teachers trying to focus everyone enough to learn. The school was missing the busy lives of its young occupants who energised it and gave it purpose. Without the squawks, cries and bustle of the pupils it was hollowed out, sapped of vitality, enervated.

And wrong.

Bewildered and skittish, and more than a little nervous-frustrated, Robert turned round in the doorway intending to search the school for someone, anyone else.

Back out in the corridor, the search began at a brisk walking pace. Arms initially swung confidently in time with the strides, full of purpose. It couldn't last. The children that normally coursed along the corridor, making it buzz with noise and life were missing. The teachers trying to maintain order absent too, leaving the school too quiet.

Too quiet and too big.

Jogging now, three classrooms later, all equally lifeless as the first. Fighting back the primal urge to run away, a scared and frightened animal, the school building overwhelming in its sterile quiet.

Four more identical rooms and jogging was a memory.

Running. Flat out between rooms. Each empty one pressing more and more on him, but him having to keep looking. He had to find someone here. He just had to!

The search of the second floor was a flight from classroom to classroom of desperate footfalls and banging doors. Shouts of rising panic that no-one answered.

Now at the point of angry courage he meant to check the staff room and the Headmistress' office, consequences be damned. The staff room was as empty as all the classrooms had been, the only thing in there being the persistent stale smell that always hung heavily in the air. Stifling a cough Robert flung the door closed with a shout.

'For fffffs sake! Where. The. *Hell!* Is. Everyone?' His exclamation sounded all wrong. Too high and desperate as it carried far along the echoey corridors. He breathed in deeply through his nose in an effort to calm the storm that was rising inside him. He *had* to find someone and losing the plot in the middle of the empty school wasn't going to help at all.

An empty staff room left only the Headmistress' office to try.

Robert paused again. He wasn't exactly proud of what he had done next, but given the circumstances, it might have just about been justified. Either way there was no way he was going to admit to losing his temper, hurling his school bag across the Headmistress' office and almost taking out the expensive flat-screen monitor that sat on her desk.

Deciding that whoever might read this one day had probably had enough of his school day, Robert went on to document his fruitless journey to his Dad's office to tell him, only to find it locked and deserted; then the shocking scene at the traffic junction where he had been stopped in his tracks and stood open mouthed for minutes at what lay before him. Everywhere he had looked, abandonment. Nothing but a chaos of deserted traffic pointing in every direction. A breeze picked up the pages of a newspaper and they blew past him down the street, colliding with and swirling over the dead cars.

It had been like something from a science fiction film! Except that in the Hollywood movie there would be the high incessant drone of a car horn, and he would go to it and rescue the person slumped unconscious on the steering wheel and, and…

But even that noise was absent. The whole scene was silent.

He wrote about his hurried return home to the house and watching the news in the hope of some information, but there was none forthcoming. How he found he could not stay in the empty house, its hollowed out interior of missing family pushing him back out on to the street and onto the police station where even the cells had been empty; his ride back home once more as it began to get dark, the orange sodium lights coming on, pushing away the deepening gloom of the winter night and casting everything in long, dark shadows. At least the nighttime had partly obscured the truth of the abandoned cars for his ride back, although he could have done without the caw-caw of a group of crows roosting nearby as he passed by.

Back home he had turned the television on, in the hope of catching a news update, something that would shed some light on what was happening, only for him to discover that he was watching exactly the same news.

And that was when it dawned on him, late in the evening on that first day, when the news was exactly the same, even down to the small slip made by the presenter. If there was no one to write and present new news, who was left?

There was no new news for exactly the same reason that there had been no one at school that morning, or no one at his Dad's office, and the abandoned cars and empty police station. Realisation crashed on Robert with the weight of the world that he now knew he was the last person left on.

Robert scanned what he had written and wondered if he should be telling people all these things, all the small secrets and thoughts that went in part to making him who he was. Probably not, he reasoned, and scrubbed everything but the bare facts from his account.

Satisfied that he had at least documented his situation so far for posterity, he started on an email to his Facebook friend Peter in Hong Kong, more for something to distract him than anything, when the computer switched itself off in front of him.

No, not that as well. Not now. Please! Surely it can last longer than that!?

Robert prodded the on switch on the front of his computer, but nothing happened. Still almost not wanting to believe what deep down he knew must have happened, he flicked the light switch. Nothing. The electricity had stopped.

Robert shivered, and not just from the deepening cold of his house as the evening darkened into night. He had lit as many candles as he could find, but their light did little to lift him. The enormity of his situation was too much for him to face in the near dark; it threatened to overwhelm him, and Robert felt the panic from that first day beginning to return.

If he'd been living the movie version of the events, there would be others like him left in the world, and he'd meet up with them, and there'd be adults who were there to run things until they found a way of getting everybody else back. And there would be other kids for him to hang around with (maybe even his Dad and Elisabeth would be there!) and everything would work out OK in the end.

But this wasn't the Hollywood-happy version of things. This was real life, his real life. As far as he could tell everyone, every Mum or Dad, every big sister or little brother, every son or daughter, everybody in fact was gone, and he had been forgotten, left behind somehow, for some reason.

There'd been no warning that this was going to happen. No mysterious lights in the sky, or reports of something in space, or news of a disease. Nothing.

'Get a grip,' he told himself out loud, addressing the persistent night as much as himself. It felt good to hear a human voice, even if it was his own, so he spoke again, this time with a little more determination in his self-administered order. 'Don't lose the plot, not now.' Robert held his necklace, his Mum's former mangalsutra with both hands. His Mum had gifted it to him before she had died, and it was Robert's most treasured possession. He never ever took it off. Ever.

Robert willingly paid the price of the teasing about his masculinity for his necklace. It had been his Mum's and now it was his. Apart from his memories it was all Robert had left of her. The sensation of the cold metal between his fingers re-assured him and calmed him down a little. 'I'm not losing them too Mum. I'll get them back somehow, I promise.'

Speaking out loud and making his promise to his Mum, Robert felt the rising panic ebb out of his consciousness, and calmness and rationality begin to creep slowly back in, until after a good fifteen minutes of talking to both the darkness and his Mum telling her he'd do whatever it took to get Dad and Elisabeth back, Robert fell asleep in his chair, exhausted.

Outside, in the cold night air, a pair of eyes watched

Robert's house patiently, carefully. They had been watching his house for several hours now, ever since they had seen the candle light spill out of the windows. The man who owned the eyes stood waiting for something to happen, for someone to emerge from the house but no one did. Over the next few hours the light slowly dimmed and eventually went out completely.

The man considered his options. He did not know enough about the place he had arrived at a few hours before, and needed more information before he made his move. He could find himself facing one or a dozen people in that house.

How many other houses therefore could be occupied? It was too risky to break into one and find out; he had learnt not to blunder into situations without knowing as much as possible. Checking the device that had brought him to this planet, he saw it had enough power to keep him warm for the next few hours.

He'd wait until the morning. Then his first priority would be to check out the house with the light.

Nine days left. . . . .

2

King For A Day

Sleeping as he had done meant that Robert woke in quite possibly the most uncomfortable position he could imagine. One whole side had gone numb, and he gently tried not to move it too much while the pins and needles danced up and down his leg. Eventually he was able to use both his feet again as well as feel the fingers in his left hand. 'Remind me not to do that again, Cat,' he addressed Catanooga who had come looking for food.

Remembering his promise to his Mum, Robert decided he needed to do something, anything to somehow get his family back. Washing and changing out of his clothes for the first time since putting them on, Robert swapped his school uniform for something a little more sensible. His favourite top wasn't available, as it sat, still damp in the washing machine, where it had been for four days now, along with Elisabeth's far too strappy for college as far as Dad was concerned clothes.

Feeling stronger and more capable of facing the outside than he had been since that first day of revelation, Robert stepped out of his house into the chilly, grey morning. Picking his bike up off the lawn where he had abandoned it three nights ago (well, who was around to steal it anyway),

Robert headed off back into town as the first part of his making-it-up-as-he-went-along plan to get his family back.

He had barely got as far as the first junction when he became sure he was being observed from somewhere. He slewed his bike to a stop with a squeak of the brakes, and stood, straddling the crossbar, in the middle of the road.

'Hello!' he called out to the empty street. 'Hello!' he tried once more.

Nothing. Just the same emptiness he had been hiding from for three days.

Shaking his head, Robert stood on the pedals and was off again.

The man who had watched Robert's house all night waiting for someone to emerge, saw the door open, and a young lad, perhaps not even a teenager, depart on his bike. *What? It was only a boy. How had this happened?*

The man weighed the significance of this new information. Should he confront the boy? He was not sure. The one thing he was sure of however was that he needed to find some clothes. With it obviously being winter on this planet, standing naked in the frigid outside, especially during the long nights was not a viable option, even if he did have the means to warm himself.

When he was sure the boy on the bike was well out of sight, the man broke cover from his hiding place and made for Robert's house, letting himself in through the unlocked front door.

After a pointless half day trying to find someone, Robert, after grabbing a couple of bottles of mineral water from a deserted shop, headed home.

Once back at his house he noticed with alarm that he had left the door unlocked. He remembered his feelings of being watched from that morning, and the unease he had experienced then came back to him now, only more so. He was convinced there was someone in there.

Leaning his bike against the wall as quietly as he could, he frantically scanned around for anything he could use as a weapon. All the garden tools were safely locked in the shed, and the only thing to hand was the heavy lock from his bike.

What should he do? It wasn't like there were any police to call or anything!

Reaching for the lock as his only option for defence, Robert decided that no one was going to take his Dad's house from him, and gently as to be as silent as possible, he pushed the door open.

Immediately he heard a voice calling from the kitchen. 'Robert? Is that you?'

Robert did not recognise the man's voice as either one of his teachers or any of his Dad's friends. He stayed still. And quiet.

'Robert?' the voice called again. 'It must be you, this is your house isn't it? Please don't be afraid, as I'm not here to hurt you. You have my word on that.'

Robert took a gamble. 'Who are you?' his voice cracking a little, he took a deep breath before continuing. 'If you're not here to hurt me, what's your name? You know who I am, so what are you called?'

'Fair enough, I suppose. Look, I'm going to come there OK, so don't panic please. And my name is Tairn. I'm kind of like you in a way.'

Huh?

But Robert did not have any longer to wonder what this man called Tairn meant. He heard footfalls leaving the kitchen and when he judged the owner of them was right by him, he swung the bike lock as hard as he could at where he hoped this Tairn would be.

'Uuufff!'

Robert stepped from his hiding place to see Tairn holding his midriff in obvious discomfort. 'Ow! Mollusc Pellets Robert! I said I wouldn't hurt you, didn't I?' Tairn gasped.

Robert took a step back as the man before him straightened up a little stiffly. He was enormous, and the clothes he had on barely did up, and in places were stretching to splitting point.

Robert realised his mistake and that he was hopelessly outmatched should Tairn want to cause trouble. 'Sorry, I thought you wanted to hurt me,' was all he could manage in the way of an explanation.

Tairn nodded his patient understanding. 'Well, I don't, so please don't hit me again.'

Then Robert realised something. 'Why are you wearing my Dad's clothes?' he asked. He had meant to carry on acting all indignant and as threatening as possible, brandishing the bike lock as menacingly as he could, but the sight of this man who was built like a heavyweight boxer standing there in a pair of jeans that almost came up to his knees and a t-shirt that barely contained his muscular frame and asking not to be hit again struck him as so incongruous that it was the most logical thing to say.

'Uh, yeah.' Tairn, for his part looked a little embarrassed at his state of dress. 'It looks like I don't take the same size as your Dad. Still, better than having to wear one of your sister's skirts eh?'

Tairn immediately realised his misjudged attempt at humour, as, at the mention of Elisabeth, Robert immediately raised the bike lock again, waving it vaguely in his direction still needing convincing of Tairn's passivity. 'How the hell do you know so much about me and my family? Who are you to come breaking in to my house anyway!'

Whatever answer Robert was expecting, the one that Tairn gave came as a complete surprise. 'I told you, I'm kind of like you, Robert. You see, I had my world stolen from me over twenty years ago, when I was a little older than you are now.'

Robert gawked.

'Can we sit down, and I'll try and explain?' Tairn asked, rubbing absently at his middle.

'But why are you wearing my Dad's clothes?'

Fifteen minutes later Robert and Tairn sat in Robert's living room, Tairn taking one of the armchairs, and Robert sitting holding Cat on the sofa. After apologising for reading Elisabeth's diary, 'I needed to find out things quickly,' he had offered in the way of an explanation as to how he knew all about Robert and his family, the conversation had turned to Tairn's arrival.

'Well, it's kind of embarrassing really. You see, I didn't have the energy to bring my clothes with me. All I had left in me was enough to jump to the last planet he stole.'

'He? Who? Who's taken my family?'

'His name is Ballisargon. He stole all the people of my world, much like yours, but I managed to escape and I've been running and hiding ever since.'

'Bal-iss-argun?' Robert stumbled over the unfamiliar name.

'Ballisargon. All one word,' prompted Tairn.

'And you've been running for how long?'

'Ever since I was fourteen. I usually hide out on recently emptied planets, as there's always plenty of resources left and there's only one of me.'

I am not becoming that, thought Robert as Tairn continued.

'Normally they were pretty scarcely populated, but highly advanced worlds, but this one looks different. Like there were a lot more people around than the worlds he normally steals. How many people lived here Robert?'

'About seven billion. Why?'

Tairn whistled to himself. 'Wow. He must be planning something very big indeed to need that many people.'

'What? What is he going to do with them? With my Dad and sister?'

'I'm sorry Robert, I don't know,'

'Well I know I want them back. Tell me how to find him.'

'What? Are you mad? You don't want to go looking for him!'

'Yes I do,' stated Robert, matter-of-factly. 'If he's taken

everyone from Earth, then he has my family, and I want them back. I will go and, I don't know, ask him if he will send them back.'

'Ask him! ASK HIM! Hahahaha!' Tairn's deep voice boomed loud in Robert's living room.

'Don't laugh at me.' There was a shard of flint in Robert's voice that did not go unnoticed by Tairn.

'Ha-heh uh, um. You're really serious about that, aren't you? Yes, you are I can see it in your eyes.'

Robert said nothing in reply. He just stared at Tairn, which made Tairn uncomfortable. There was something in the boy's eyes that he found unsettling. Something primal and noble. Tairn decided that although the threat from Ballisargon was ever present, it was for the time being very remote, whereas the threat from this boy, although much less terrible was much more immediate.

'I tell you what,' Tairn offered in as a conciliatory tone as he could. 'If you help me here on this world, I'll see what I can do,' the last part whispered as if someone very specific might overhear.

'Good. What can you do?'

Tairn motioned for Robert to move closer to him. He began to whisper, almost conspiratorially, 'I can send you to his lands. The farthest distance from his stronghold, you understand. I can't risk him knowing it was me that helped you.'

'Fair enough. What help do you need in return?'

'Some new clothes would be a good start.'

One hour and one forced lock later, Tairn stood clad in what Robert could best describe as a Hell's Angel outfit. Boots, jeans, heavy shirt and a leather jacket rounded off by the large unkempt beard Tairn wore certainly made him look like someone you really wanted on your side in a fight. Tairn scrutinised his reflection. 'Nice,' was all he had to say.

'You know, I've been thinking about why you're helping

me,' offered Robert.

Tairn said nothing.

'You want me off the Earth don't you? It makes it safer for you if I'm not here. I mean this Ballisargon won't come back if he gets me will he? That will leave you the whole planet.'

Tairn turned to Robert, flexing his fingers into huge fists, before breaking out into a wide smile. 'Very smart, Robert. And even if he doesn't get you, I think it's best if I stay away from you in general. So, do you still want to go?'

Robert didn't miss a beat. 'Yes.'

'OK, no time like the present.'

'What, now? But I've got stuff to get from my house.'

But Tairn was no longer paying attention to Robert. He had fished something that looked like a mobile out of the leather jacket and was worrying away at the buttons and dials on it. When he had finished, he turned back to Robert. 'Ready?'

'What? No, I mean, yes, I mean, wait.'

But it was too late. Whatever Tairn had been doing was done. Robert found it harder and harder to see the shop all around him, as darkness began to creep in around the edges until it seemed he was looking down a tube at a picture of where he was standing.

'What do you mean you want to 'stay away from me in general'?' Robert had to shout his question, as he could hardly hear or see Tairn through the darkness. 'I only want to find my family...'

He barely heard Tairn's reply. 'You know, Robert, I think you'll do a lot more than that...'

As Robert vanished from the Earth, two very unique individuals were waiting and talking about him. They were called Pradeep and Vidya, and they were brother and sister. While they weren't twins, they did share a number of similar physical characteristics.

Presently they were sitting on a sand dune, underneath a rust-red sky. They had been there for several days now, ever since everything had changed. When that had happened, they left the business that was occupying them, and headed off to wait.

Pradeep was the more accomplished waiter of the pair; he sat casually on the sand, his legs crossed out in front of him, while Vidya paced around on the spot a small distance away. He was about to answer the question his sister had posed when he sensed something.

He caught her green eyes with a flick of his own. 'He's coming.'

3

Road To Nowhere

The tunnel zoomed back out. The sight that greeted Robert was not the shop he and Tairn had just been in; he was somewhere else, somewhere very different indeed.

In fact he was not even inside anymore. Stretching off in every direction and all around him as far as he could see was dark red-brown sand. There was no grass or trees, or flowers or any kind of plant life that Robert could see. All there was was the red sand. Dry, dead and lifeless. Robert strained hard to hear even the tiniest of sounds: insects, animals, anything, but there was nothing.

Oh that's just bloody marvellous. I've been dumped in the middle of the… He looked up while thinking the word 'Sahara' when he saw the sky. *What the..? This isn't Earth!*

Instead of the safe and familiar deep azure that the sky should have been it was rusty red, the colour of dried blood. There was no sun that he could see but there was a kind of daylight that didn't seem to cast any shadows. Dark grey clouds scudded overhead, driven by winds high in the atmosphere.

Where the hell am I? Mars?

Then, *How did he do that?*

Robert shivered involuntarily at the thought of having been sent so easily to another planet, even though it felt ludicrous when he imagined it. Then he had another feeling, as he realised what he now faced. He was alone, most likely stuck, on another *somewhere* with no means of either locating his family or getting them back home.

He kicked ineffectually at the sand in frustration at Tairn for sending him here without any plan or any anything other than the clothes he was standing up in.

The sand puffed away from his trainer before settling to the ground.

He kicked it again. 'Dammit! You could have let me bring…' Nothing came readily to mind, which made him even angrier.

OK, got to keep it together.

But how? How was he supposed to do that? He didn't know where he was, which way he was supposed to go, even how far away from home he was. The one thing he was sure of was that his family was here, and they needed him. He needed a plan, even if for the time being that amounted to finding a useful looking direction to head in. He'd work the rest out on the way.

In the hazy distance Robert could make out what looked to be a dark strip in the desert. It was almost dead straight, meaning it was unlikely to be natural.

At least he had found his direction to head in.

Pradeep and Vidya had been walking for several hours, in the direction indicated by Pradeep. As the journey had worn on Vidya had begun to grow restless. Her nature was not her brother's, and she felt she needed to be doing more than just walking. She was edgy. 'What if he gets lost?'

'He isn't. We're about an hour away.'

Vidya gazed hard at the horizon, seemingly not comforted by her brother's confidence. Pradeep decided he needed to change the subject. 'What do you think we should tell him? I mean, we're going to be a bit of a shock.'

Vidya paused. Pradeep was too good at knowing what she was thinking, and was always able to distract her from herself. She thought before replying. 'Well, with everything he's likely to have experienced in the past few days I would say he'll probably cope admirably.'

'You mean it's not like we're wild animals?' her brother replied with a smile.

Vidya shook her head in mock annoyance. 'Be serious Pradeep. You know what I mean.'

'Yeah, I guess I do. But what about everything else? He's going to have questions that we're not equipped to answer,' he hinted at what he was thinking.

His sister replied curtly. 'No. Not after what happened.'

The strip was indeed artificial. Two straight lines of metal side by side, a few centimetres apart with a channel in the ground between them, sat between a wide concrete path that looked to reach to the horizon. It wasn't much, but at least it proved that there was, or at the very least, had been, civilisation here.

After an hour of walking, Robert began to see a shape in the distance, something dark silhouetted against the red sky. As he neared it, keeping his gaze more or less permanently fixed on it, it became a collection of buildings of some sort. The walking became a slow jog.

Closer still he could see that it was quite a few buildings, a small city of some kind? At this distance each building looked no more than two or three storeys and seemed to be made from some sort of white stone, so that as Robert drew near the outskirts, they stood out quite distinctly from the red sand all around.

Robert couldn't help but break out into a run. However once at the bounds of the city his enthusiasm died as he saw the ruins he had been heading toward. Every single structure over a certain height, without exception as far as he could see, had been decapitated at the third floor level. It looked as if someone had sliced a giant knife through the air and taken the tops off all the buildings, leaving great piles of rubble scattered at the bases of most of the structures.

What the hell had happened here?

Despite himself, he padded toward the nearest most intact looking building. At the entrance his foot stubbed against something half buried in the sand. Stopping, he bent down to see what it was. Next to his trainer was a lump of clear something. Robert excavated it, and saw it was a solid, smooth and heavy looking crystal of some kind, about the size of a cricket or tennis ball. He picked it up to find that it weighed something like a bag of sugar. The crystal was semi-transparent and turned the colour of oil on water as he rolled it over in his hands. The edges, though slightly dulled were still very pronounced, and each facet was only slightly scratched from its exposure to however long it had been out here.

Robert carefully put the crystal to his nose and sniffed gently. It did not seem to have any odour that he could tell. *What was it?* Looking around he could see more lumps covered by sand scattered all around him. Whatever they were there seemed to be a lot of them.

'Hello? Is there anybody there?' He called into the open doorway. His voice echoed loudly round the empty property, and for a second he had a vivid déjà vu of his time in the school.

Shaking the memories and feelings away he crossed the threshold. The interior of the building was gloomy, and it took Robert's eyes a few moments to adjust.

When they had, he realised that he was standing in what had once been a dining room on this world, but was now devoid of any life.

Robert went to pick up a piece of what looked like a vegetable sitting on one of the abandoned plates. As soon as his fingers touched it, it fell apart in his hand, crumbling between his fingers and onto the plate. It had turned to sand, it had been here that long.

This place had been dead for decades. It was a tomb, and he was the only living thing in it.

Unable to stop himself, he hurled the crystal he still had in his hands against the nearest wall, where, much to his surprise, it went straight through, leaving a neat hole the size of his fist. He was no better off here than he had been on Earth! At least there he knew where everything was. Here, he didn't have a clue.

The anger made him feel stronger, braver somehow. But it was a selfish confidence. While he may have felt able, in those moments of extremis, of taking on the whole world in a fight, he would only have to answer for the consequences of any rash actions he undertook. It was easier to lash out, to react rather than to think, and while some situations demanded action, others did not. The anger was almost a refuge; a safe place to hide when things got difficult or when it felt like the world was ganging up on him.

But…

While here he did not have to worry about being punished, the consequences of ill thought actions were far greater. At least on Earth he had the luxury of knowing that someone (his Dad, usually) would pick up the pieces he left scattered after an outburst. Here he had no such comfort. Losing it big time here could, and probably would, be fatal.

Robert tried to breathe slowly and deeply. He tip-toed to the hole in the wall and looked through it. He could see the crystal out in the street again, a few metres away. He cringed, just glad that no-one had seen him vandalise what was obviously an abandoned house.

Pradeep and Vidya stood at a corner of one of the abandoned buildings not too far from Robert. Pradeep sighed at his sister's reply. They were going to have this argument again. And it still wasn't settled.

'But the Engineer is in the best position to tell him and teach him,' he stated, matter-of-factly.

'Pradeep, I said no. I won't take him there. I can't be held responsible for my actions if I have to speak with the Engineer.' Vidya headed off, ahead of her brother, this time with a barely controlled anger.

'And who else do you think can explain everything to him?' Pradeep called after her. 'And I know you too well. You're still hurting too much to talk to him impartially.'

Vidya ignored him, so he changed tack, catching up with her once more so they were level, shoulder by shoulder. 'We don't know enough about how the world works, about Ballisargon, about the Move, about why things change or even the... them,' he finished, swallowing hard, uncomfortable at whatever it was he couldn't name.

'I mean,' he continued, his point coming back to him, 'I know *how* to Move. I've been doing it all my life, but I'll be damned if I could teach it to someone else. And Ballisargon. How much do we really know about him? We've never even seen him, and I've never met another person aside from the Engineer who has.'

Vidya stopped again. She knew Pradeep was right, she just didn't want him to be right in *that* way.

Seeing her pause, her brother pressed his argument as much as he dared. She might have been his sister, but he did not want to rile her. An angry Vidya he could do without. 'The Engineer was there, remember. First hand knowledge.

If we want to help Robert then the very least we can do is to make sure he knows what he's doing.'

Vidya could not deny that her brother's argument had merit. The Engineer was the best person to equip Robert with the knowledge she and Pradeep would struggle to impart. And if she was serious about helping Robert, then she owed him every chance and advantage she could give him. But that meant...

Vidya broke her long silence. 'And how do we go about looking like we want to help without *looking* like we're helping?'

Pradeep let his original point drop for the moment. At least she was talking to him again. He looked thoughtful, pulling his large expressive mouth one way, then the other. 'You know, I really don't know. I guess we'll just have to play it cool, and try to answer his questions honestly, but be careful at the same time.'

'I'm not lying to him Pradeep.'

'I'm not asking you to. But if we tell him everything all at once, it might be too much for him. I don't know how I'd cope finding all that out in one hit.'

'But what if he asks something awkward?'

'Then the Engineer would be the perfect person to answer him without the risk. I know what you think about the Engineer. Hell, most of the planet heard about your falling out. You weren't exactly… discrete. I just hope we're still welcome on the Bridge.'

Pradeep had steered the conversation back to what Vidya did not want to talk about and it was obvious he was not going to let the matter drop. Vidya knew that her brother felt the same way about Robert as she did, he just expressed it differently. She was itching to get going, but once again he urged caution and preparation. So, she had two choices. Swallow her pride and do something she swore to herself she would never do again, or not take Robert to speak with the Engineer. So really only one choice. Two of the three promises she had ever made in her life were now in conflict and it was obvious to Vidya which one she had to break.

The one she had made to herself.

'OK. We'll take him to the Engineer.'

'Thanks.' he said solemnly. This was not the time for a joke.

'So, how do we explain our presence here to him then?'

'We'll just have to play dumb for a while. It'll be easier to keep an eye on him then if he doesn't suspect too much anyway. Huge coincidences do sometimes just happen,' he finished with a smile.

'Bumping into us here is pretty huge Pradeep.'

'Not really. After all, it was sat on the main hub-way so it's logical for him to follow that here, and as it is really the only remaining set of buildings between here and the Bridge, why shouldn't we be here?'

'I don't know, it's a pretty big chance you're taking.'

'Me? When have you ever known me risk anything? Look, I'm sure this is where he is. Sit down Vidya, please?'

Robert looked guiltily through the new hole in the wall he had been responsible for, then glanced around. Now feeling like he was trespassing he went back outside and inspected the crystal. It was virtually unharmed. Deciding it was too heavy to take with him, he left it lying on the sand.

He looked at the ruined buildings all around him. The city was dead and lifeless. Its living heart of people who should be crowding the squares, pumping through its streets and alleys all gone. Stripped of the reason for its existence, the vacant city felt aimless and purposeless. A monument to nothing.

Disquieted in a way he would have found difficult to articulate, but knowing that it was not a pleasant feeling,

Robert suspected that whatever fate had befallen Earth had happened here too. What was it Tairn had said? 'He cleans worlds,' or something. Robert shuddered.

He could spend all day, days even, wandering round this empty mausoleum of a city looking for people who no longer lived here. He had to come up with something else, and soon. What that something else was, however, Robert did not have the faintest idea.

It was then that he heard the voices. Faint and indistinct, but still voices. He did not need any further encouragement. He was off at a sprint in a second.

Once he had made it to the back of the building he thought the voices were coming from, he paused, listening, trying to determine if they were friendly or hostile.

'...ook, I'm sure this is where he is. Sit down Vidya, please?' said a male voice. It had a deep sonorous tone to it, and an accent Robert found familiar.

'I'm going to look for him,' came the female reply. The voice had the same cultured resonance to it, and for some reason Robert felt reassured at hearing it.

'If we want to see the Engineer, then we're going to have to wait for him to arrive. He'll be here. Trust me.'

'I never said I wanted to see the Engineer, Pradeep.' The male voice gave a small sigh, but the female voice continued. 'I'm only agreeing with you because you think it is a good idea.

So they were waiting for a man called the Engineer, and it didn't sound like he had arrived yet.

Robert carried on listening to try and find out more; he was still not sure if the people on the other side of the building were friendly or not, regardless of how posh they sounded.

The female voice continued, 'It's just that it's not too safe out here. Maybe we should go and look for him. He may have got lost. Or worse.'

'You worry too much,' said the male voice as if stating a

fact. 'He'll be fine.'

Robert got the sense that the female voice was not quite convinced by this, and as if to confirm his suspicions, the male voice re-assured, 'Alright, we'll give him another ten minutes. If there's no sign of him by then, then you should go and look for him, while I stay here and wait. Agreed?'

'Agreed.'

Well they don't sound hostile. And maybe I can tell them that I've not seen anyone on the way I came from, so they won't have to waste their time looking that way, thought Robert. He decided to introduce himself to the owners of the voices.

He stepped round from his hiding place to find himself not looking at two people as he had expected, but at two tigers, sitting sphinx-like on the sand. Two tigers. Two fully-grown tigers! Heads bigger than his whole chest, enormous paws the size of his face, long, sleek ochre and black bodies that seemed large enough to contain him whole.

TIGERS! Ohmygod! I'm dead!

Robert's eyes went wide when one of the tigers looked languorously over its shoulder at him. He fumbled for his necklace. When the second tiger joined its companion and turned its head at him, he took a small step back, very carefully. But when they both got up off their haunches and began to walk toward him, he broke out into a run.

'Hey! Stop. We won't hurt you.'

Robert was round the corner and nearly twenty metres away when he heard the call that stopped him dead in his tracks. *It had been them!*

Robert stood his ground as the tiger pair slinked round the corner and stood facing him. One looked at the other, seemed to see a 'you go first' look from its companion and cleared its throat. 'Sorry we startled you. Please, we're not going to attack you, if that's what you're worried about.'

Robert stood there a mix of shock and disbelief. They could talk. 'You can talk,' he echoed his thoughts, despite the obviousness of his observation. Then: 'Pleasedonteatme!'

The tigers shared a look. Then the male one said to his companion, 'Apparently, Vidya, he does not want to be eaten.'

Vidya, if that was her name replied to the male tiger. 'Pradeep. Please be serious.' Then directed back at Robert she said, 'Of course we won't eat you. Why would we want to do that?' She sounded almost aghast at the notion of eating someone, especially a lost boy from Earth.

Robert looked sceptical, but the male tiger picked up where the female one had left off. 'Now, since we've got that out of the way, I think introductions are in order,' he said. 'I am Pradeep, and this is my sister, Vidya.' He pointed with a paw at the other tiger.

Vidya raised her paw in greeting, and waved it gently at Robert. He saw, that unlike Pradeep, Vidya's paw, and the rest of her right front leg was pure white. There was no hint of the deep orange that she had on her other limb, and all the black stripes were missing too. Robert found himself beginning to stare, and checked himself. He hoped Vidya had not noticed. He did not want to seem rude.

'What are you doing out here in the Lyr?' asked Vidya seemingly unaware of Robert's attention to her leg.

'I'm looking for my family,' replied Robert, glad that the conversation had continued. He deliberately tried to focus his eyes anywhere but Vidya's forepaw. 'I woke up a few days ago to find they had disappeared. Well, everyone had disappeared, but I'm here to get my Dad and sister back. On Earth I met a man called Tairn, who told me that someone called Ballisargon had taken everyone, and he sent me here somehow. So here I am.'

The nervous energy from seeing two tigers caused Robert to say whatever came into his head. If he kept them talking maybe they would keep their promise and not want to eat him. 'Tairn said he'd send me as far from this Ballisargon's stronghold as he could. He didn't seem to want Ballisargon to know it was him who helped me,' he continued.

Pradeep looked up at the sky, which had grown considerably darker in the time they had been waiting for Robert, and his arrival. 'It's quite a journey to Ballisargon's Keep, so we'd bet...' he began, before trailing off, seemingly losing the thread of what he was going to say next. Then he narrowed his eyes, and his large ears twitched as if hearing something a very long way away.

'What is it, Pradeep?' his sister asked.

But Pradeep did not answer. He was concentrating hard. Then his head jerked round and he looked at the horizon.

Robert followed Pradeep's gaze. He could make out a darkness in the sky some distance away. It looked like a large indistinct dark red-brown mass in front of the grey clouds. He tried to tell what it was. It *looked* like a cloud; it was too large and densely packed to be a flock of birds, and was too irregularly shaped to be anything artificial.

Even in the short space of time it had taken Robert to work this out, the cloud-thing had grown larger and nearer in the sky. Now he was able to see that there were trails of some sort hanging underneath it, making it look like a giant jellyfish hanging in the air. The whole thing reminded him of something, but he could not place where he had seen it before.

He did not have time to work out why it seemed familiar, because Pradeep was shouting something.

'Run! For pity's sake run, Robert! Follow us! Now!'

Shaken from his reverie by the tiger, Robert saw the pair of them bound off. Vidya paused, turned her head and called him. 'Come on, Robert. It's bad. Really!'

Robert did not want to hang around and find out what caused two tigers to turn tail. In a second he was off, running after them as fast as his feet could carry him.

He turned a corner, following the tigers. Behind him he could hear the storm approaching. He glanced over his shoulder as he ran. The storm seemed to be made of the desert itself, the sand-cloud-tentacles hissing like rain as they struck the ground.

In a minute the storm was upon him, and the tigers just ahead of him, sweeping them all up in its roar. In less than a second he lost sight of them both; they seemed to merge with the sand the storm was made of. Another second later Robert lost all sense of direction in the swirling tumult. His world disappeared into a haze of dark noise, the sand blocking what little light there was and shutting out all other sounds.

He slowed to a walk for fear of smacking into the wall of a building. He pulled the hood of his top up, but it did no good. Within no time at all he found his mouth and nose clogging with the fine dry sand. He coughed, but this only served to fill his mouth with more sand. He could feel, even with his eyes closed, the sand scratching at his eyeballs, clogging his tear ducts. He stumbled forward, blindly, his arms flailing ahead of him, reaching for anything he could shelter in. He shouted a cry for help. Then it all went black.

The man in the suit looked up from the current stage of his preparations. A few hours ago, a tickling sensation had started at the base of his skull, inside his spine where he could not reach. It had persisted for a while, until the man had been able to ignore it and concentrate on his work. Now it was gone as suddenly as it had arrived.

This was unusual, and the man did not like things that happened out of the ordinary. His discomfiture was such that he turned from his work, leaving it half-finished. He angled his head as if into the direction a faint sound was emanating from and closed his eyes in concentration. Underneath his eyelids his eyes flicked back and forth, looking into the darkness.

Then they stopped moving and the man in the sand

coloured suit opened them again, but only a fraction. His expression hardened.

He would despatch something to investigate.

4

Silent All These Years

A very long way away from the tigers and the man in the suit, on a distant world orbiting a bright blue sun, another sandstorm battered the thin silk screen of a shelter. Inside, huddled around a weak lamp, Jaan, the leader of the Judaki tribe hid from the maelstrom outside.

Safe from the raging winds, Jaan was grateful that Jana, heiress to her position, was safe with her grandmother. She did not want to risk her daughter getting lost in the slip-storm outside, which to judge by the ferocity of the winds, must be attempting to rebalance the passing between worlds of something very large indeed. It was vital she did not touch it, otherwise she risked being lost herself.

The cry from outside was so quiet, hidden under the roar of winds that Jaan was initially not sure that she had heard correctly. Then it came again. She pitied the poor soul caught out there.

A minute passed during which she thought of nothing but the cry she had heard. What if it was one of her friends? Then they were on their own. But what if it were Jana? Immediately realising her failing, disgusted at herself for being driven to be so selfish, Jaan wrapped her scarf over her nose and mouth, grabbed the lamp and pushed her way out through the silk screen and into the storm.

Outside was a blizzard of noise, and every gust threatened to knock her off her feet. She stared hard into the tumult, sweeping the lamp in front of her, when she saw the figure stumbling ahead. Bracing against the winds she forged over to whoever she had seen, only to find it was a young boy, perhaps no older than her daughter, dressed in strange looking clothing.

She took hold of him and shouted through the deafening roar. 'Who are you? What are you doing in the storm?'

But the boy said nothing. He seemed to stare straight through her, his eyes seeing things that were perhaps not there, or more accurately were elsewhere.

Jaan tried to pull on his arm to take him to her shelter, but he stood fast, holding both hands up to his chest, as if cradling something. 'Come on!' she screamed at him, and pulled his arm again. This time it came free, and Jaan saw for the briefest second a flash of gold about his neck. *No, it couldn't be.*

Now unconcerned about staying in the storm, Jaan carefully held the lamp up to the boy's face, seeing his brown eyes and gentle features for the first time. She lowered the lamp slightly to his chest and saw there the upturned triangle of gold and ruby that he wore. She fingered the identical necklace around her own neck.

It was him, there was no doubt of that. The boy had to be him. Before he grew up and became the origin of all their troubles.

She hesitated, unsure how to proceed. If she intervened, the problems here on Iosod could be solved. No, more than solved, they would never happen. But in doing so, she knew she would be condemning millions, billions of strangers to a worse fate. Her failure to act sooner when she first heard the cry shamed her now. She knew what she had to do.

'You cannot be here now; you should be elsewhere! You are here too early!' Jaan shouted at the boy, but he seemed not to hear her. So, taking him gently by the arm, she led him out to where the storm seemed strongest. She did not have much time, the storm was losing power rapidly. Sand was starting to fall from the sky and settle to the ground.

When she was confident that the boy would be returned to where he should be, she leant over and kissed him lightly on the cheek.

'Farewell Robert. We shall meet again.'

Jaan turned her back on Robert and headed back to her shelter, which she hoped was still standing.

Eight days left. . . . .

Morning broke in the red desert and over the deserted city. The sun did not rise, for there was no sun. There had not been a sun for almost as long as anyone could remember. Only the old ones recalled the time when a sun had lit the sky and warmed their faces, and they were fewer and fewer in number with every passing decade. Soon there would only be a handful of individuals who had ever seen the dawn break or a sunset. That number would eventually dwindle to one, the longest lived inhabitant of the land, surviving on stolen life, the land altered almost irrevocably by his will.

Some things however were beyond changing, and even the power that ruled the land so totally could not stop night turning into day. So even though there was no sun to rise, it did get lighter; the dark grey of the night giving way to a pale red dawn, that slowly brightened to the same flat light of the previous day and an almost innumerable number of previous days before it.

The slip-storm had passed several hours earlier leaving everything it had not shifted between worlds covered in a heavy layer of the sand it had been composed of. Very little was recognisable under the coating of desert; strange lumps and bumps lay silently amongst the greater flat plain of sand. Individual details were impossible to determine, smoothed and ablated away.

As the day wore on, two of the lumps in the sand began to move. Slowly at first, sloughing off the coat of dust as they shifted, before enlivening and eventually coming to an upright position.

The tigers coughed as they stood up, shaking sand out of their ears and clearing it from their eyes and noses. Immediately they scanned around them, looking for Robert, but he was nowhere to be seen.

Robert woke lying prone on the desert floor, his clothes filled with sand. He opened his eyes, coughed once then checked he still had his necklace. His fingers closed around the reassuring presence of cool metal, its configuration well known to him. He felt along every intimately known bump and etch, his fingers moving from memory along the hard edges. Reassured by that at least, he stood up and took stock of his situation.

He remembered fleeing from the sandstorm, following the tigers through the city. The tigers. Where were they? Robert span round. In every direction he turned there was nothing but sand and the empty city. No tigers.

So, I've lost them too, he thought, shivering. He suddenly felt more alone than he had done in his entire life, including those last days on earth.

Then he realised that he did not recognise the part of the city he was standing in. When he had met the tigers he had been wandering side streets and alleys. Now he found himself in a large open plaza, with oddly proportioned statuary dotted around it. Not only had he lost the tigers, the only living things he had seen on wherever it was he was, but he had lost where he had been.

Despair crept in, just for a second, and Robert slumped

where he was standing. He remembered his promise to his mum. *This was not going to be easy was it?* Straightening himself Robert decided he had better try and find the tigers; after all they had seemed friendly enough, and hadn't Pradeep indicated that he might know where Ballisargon's stronghold was?

Then he was struck by another thought. He realised that in the time he had been here, wherever here was, he did not seem to be getting hungry, or even thirsty. His feet ached and his joints were stiff from the exercise, but his stomach still felt full and his throat wasn't dry. *Odd.*

Just as he was thinking this, his ears caught the faintest hint of a sound in the distance, coming from somewhere behind him. Robert jerked his head up at the noise. After the almost complete silence of the past few days Robert had become sensitive to even the quietest whisper. He closed his eyes to concentrate on using his ears.

For a few moments nothing, then just as he was beginning to think he had imagined it, he heard it again. A low noise, alien to the desert environment. He strained to work out what it was, even holding his breath, so the sound of his breathing did not interfere with his attempt to hear.

The sound came again, and again, only this time a little louder, and a little more clearly.

It sounded like voices. Low, keening noises, distorted and softened by the desert for sure, but voices nonetheless! The tigers! The voices were too far away to make out any individual words, but they were growing louder all the time.

Robert wasted no time in heading off in the direction the sound had come from.

Almost straight away he could see shapes in the hazy distance. Silhouetted against the edge of the plaza, dark against the white buildings, he could make out a small group of people pulling or dragging something large through the sand. *OK, so not the tigers, but maybe they would know where they might be*, he thought to himself as he strode toward them.

The gap between Robert and the strangers narrowed rapidly, his excitement and eagerness to see someone else overcoming the ache in his feet and legs. As he got closer to them, the group of strangers resolved itself into three thin individuals, and the large shape behind them seemed to be a handcart of some sort piled up with something he could not make out.

They had been too far away initially to see any details and only now, as he approached the figures did he become aware of something very wrong with them.

At the distance he was away from them Robert could see that the three figures were extremely thin, almost unnaturally so; he was reminded of photographs of famine victims or concentration camp survivors. But it was not the thinness that disturbed him. Nor was it the clothing that they wore, although clothing seemed too grand a word for the scraps of fabric that clung round the their midriffs and shoulders, and which was torn and shredded to almost nothing. Even rags would have provided more protection. Nor was it the almost continuous noise they seemed to be making; a low, moaning sound in place of speech, empty of any emotion except sorrow, keening its way across the desert to his ears.

While any of these would have been bad enough on their own, combined they were almost too dreadful. But there was one thing worse than their thinness, clothing or moaning.

The aspect of the figures that unsettled Robert so profoundly was that their heads were not where they should have been. On each of the three the head hung upside down on the figure's back so that, as Robert realised to his horror, they were actually walking backwards but still looking forward. They looked as if something had swept their heads back so hard and so fast that their spines had shattered with the force of the blow. As the three shambled forward (backward?) each head rocked from side to side across the figure's back.

Wah?! Oh my God!

Robert stopped dead in his tracks when he realised what he was seeing. The sight of the shuffling trio shook him in a way he had never felt before. An overpowering urge to run and hide before they spotted him rushed through him. Frantically he looked round for something to conceal himself behind, but in the wide-open and featureless expanse of the plaza there was nothing.

Robert looked at the figures to decide which way to go. But it was too late. They seemed to have sensed his presence, because they had stopped moving. Robert stood motionless, his feet felt rooted to the ground with cold dread. The figures in the group swayed slightly, still moaning, but the timbre of their low susurration had changed subtly. What this indicated Robert could not know, but he still felt deathly afraid.

He called out to them. 'Hey!'

The group of figures seemed to take this as their cue to resume their journey, and began shuffling along their path toward Robert leaving the handcart behind.

Reasonably sure that he could outpace them even at only a moderate walking pace, he took a single, cautiously hesitant step back when they began to advance again.

The time it took Robert to take that single pace backwards was all it took for the group of figures with the broken necks to cover the distance between themselves and him. In less than a heartbeat they had surrounded him. He hadn't even seen them move. In one blink they had gone from *there* to *here* and ensured Robert was incapable of escape.

'Wha!' he screamed and closed his eyes in panic and surprise, covering his head with his arms, expecting at that moment to be attacked.

When the fatal blow did not arrive after a few seconds, Robert nervously opened one eye, then the other and peered through his arms.

Up close the three were even worse than they had been at a distance. Robert was now able to see that they were women (or had been women, once), but they had obviously been a long time walking the desert.

Their heads now all hung forwards on their chests; what hair they had was thin and grey, hanging in lank knots from any remaining patches of skin. Their limbs were stick figure thin, but the joints were monstrously swollen; large fat patches of flesh that looked too soft were wrapped around their knees and elbows like overripe fruit. They had only the barest strips of cloth around their middles, and none on their torsos, and on their feet they wore what had once, decades previously, been sandals of some sort, but were now torn and almost non-existent, held together by the same tattered fabric they wore elsewhere.

But the worst thing of all was their skin. Blistered and blackened by countless years of exposure to the elements, it hung loosely on frames that no longer had enough muscle to be contained by so much covering. In places it was peeling away, in others it had gone completely leaving dried flesh and exposed bone. Robert was just grateful he could not see their faces; he did not want to imagine what they looked like.

Robert turned his head, trying to avert his eyes, but something in him compelled him to look. It was like staring at death; you wanted to look away in case it noticed you, but felt this was your only opportunity to learn as much as you could about it.

Robert blinked away the tears that had formed at the corners of his eyes. The area of his skull directly behind his eyes ached as he forced himself to focus on the women. It was difficult, as looking at them this close up caused the blood to pump hard round his skull, setting up a thumping in his head.

Then the low moaning noises the three women had been making stopped.

'Boy/Son/More/of/than/Adam/that!'

Red-hot needles stabbed into his skull through his ears at their words. The pitch and volume of the three women speaking in unison forced Robert to put his hands over his ears, and close his eyes against the pain. He was not sure what they had said; all three of them spoke as one, but they all said different things, the resulting jumble being an almost unintelligible cacophony of noise and pain.

'Who... who are you? Please?' Robert asked, carefully opening his eyes again, but still very afraid.

Immediately he regretted his question, as the three women began speaking again, all at once.

'Travel not/Stay well/Nothing good/this path/away from/can come/or way/here/of it,' they shrieked in unison. Robert felt like his head was being pressed on all sides. It was as if he was hearing without using his ears, and the women were putting the sounds directly into his brain.

He did not want them to speak again, but he had to try and find out who they were and if they could help him in any way. Bracing himself for the assault on his senses he knew would come when he posed his question, Robert implored again, 'Please, tell me who you are?'

Even with his hands clamped firmly over his ears the reply caused Robert to grimace in pain. The women's speech, however was slightly slower this time, and Robert was able to catch the barest sense of meaning in it.

'...three sisters...forever...' and '...transgressed,' were all he could make out from the din that shook inside his skull.

'You're sisters?' he asked, then before they could answer, 'What did you transgress against?'

Once again, the three women spoke in a deliberate effort to make Robert understand. This time he was able to hear '...lord...' and '...punishment...' amongst the jumble of language filling his head.

Robert, feeling that if they were going to kill him they would have done so by now, grew slightly bolder. 'You mean Ballisargon?' he asked. 'You transgressed against Ballisargon, and he punished you?'

The resulting scream from the women caused Robert to sink to his knees in agony. He felt his teeth were about to explode from the pressure, and his bones throbbed. His muscles knotted, and he was sure his eardrums were going to burst. The scream seemed to go on forever and ever, and Robert was on the verge of passing out with the pain when it died away.

The women once again spoke together, but this time they were all saying the same thing, and the tone they used was gentle and almost melodic.

'Tyger tyger burning bright
In the forests of the night
What immortal hand or eye
Could frame thy fearful symmetry?'

Their chorus came to an end, and the three women parted to allow Robert to leave.

Robert rose unsteadily to his feet. He noticed a small patch of darker red on the desert floor where he had been curled up, and put his hand carefully to his nose. Looking at his fingers he could see he had a nosebleed, no doubt caused by the women's screams.

'You said 'tiger'. Do you mean Pradeep and Vidya?' he asked the women.

'Go. Away from us. Leave us boy, son of Adam, more than that. Go!' they all said to him.

'But...' he pressed, but the three women stood silent and immobile. Whatever they had intended to do was obviously done, their business complete.

Robert took one hesitant step forward to leave, and as soon as his foot touched the sand in front of him he was alone again. The women, and their cart had disappeared. It seemed he was safe.

But how had they moved so quickly? He was sure he had enough distance between himself and them when he had called to them, but they had surrounded him in an instant. But, nosebleed aside, they had not seemed to want to harm him.

However, the fact that they had been able to traverse the

gap so quickly made Robert wary of drawing the attention of anything else he might run into, just in case they were not so benign, until he met up with the tigers again. Encountering the three strange women like that had unsettled him. Despite them not hurting him he had been completely vulnerable to any attack they might have chosen to make. He realised that for some reason, even when running from the sandstorm, when he had been with the tigers he had felt secure somehow.

The man in the suit sat back in his chair. While he could no longer feel the tickle in his mind, he felt happier having despatched one of his agents to search for the source of it. If it was not a threat, then the patrol would report back as such. And if it was, then at least it would provide some sport for the thing he had sent out before it killed whatever it found.

'Where the hell is he Pradeep?' asked Vidya, as if blaming her brother for somehow losing Robert. 'He was right behind us.'

Pradeep looked lost for an answer. 'I don't know,' was all he could manage. 'I can't hear or smell him anywhere. He's not here.'

'That's not possible. We've been circling around where we lost him for half a day. He has to be here.'

The tigers had indeed spent most of the day looking for Robert. While the day before they had been led by Pradeep's powerful nose and ears, today they were proving useless. It was as if Robert had vanished, like all the people on Earth had. But they had come here, so where had he gone?

Vidya drew in a slow, deep and deliberate lungful of air. 'So if he's not here, is anyone else?' she asked patiently.

Pradeep frowned as he smelt the air, listened to the breeze. 'The Betrothed. Half an hour that way and moving away.' He indicated with an outstretched paw.

'Let's go find them,' replied his sister.

Just as they knew it would, the three women's presence had been sensed by the tigers. They led them toward Robert, then transported themselves off round the other side of the planet. Once they had gone, Pradeep had no problem in picking up Robert's location, and within minutes, they were crossing the square at a run towards him, while he was running at full pelt at them.

The tigers had to stop themselves nuzzling up to Robert, and instead contented themselves with a mildly admonishing 'There you are.' in the way of a reunion. Robert, for his part, not wanting to look soft, tried to play down his relief at finding his new friends again with a nonchalant 'I was OK.'

He recalled his meeting with the three women, and tested his nosebleed again. It seemed to have stopped, however he was left with a thick feeling in his head, where his blood had clotted. It was not the only reminder of the women. Their words still echoed in his head, more persistent than any physical sensation. Part of what they had told him had registered with him on some deep emotional level that he was not fully able to work out. He felt they had been trying to help him in their own way, and maybe it had been him who had not listened hard enough. *What had they meant, and who were they?*

He asked the tigers.

'They were Ballisargon's brides,' answered Pradeep. 'He scoured a dozen worlds looking for three very particular women, and when he had found them, he made them his chief lieutenants, his 'brides'. They all had a particular aspect to them that made them special somehow, and they did his bidding for over a half a century, until one day something changed. He raged against them, and in his anger he broke their necks so that they could never again see the world straight and true, and cursed them to wander the Lyr.'

Robert shuddered. If he hadn't liked the sound of Ballisargon before, this new revelation hardly helped. 'What happened to make him so angry?'

'They attempted to leave his servitude. They were sick of the things they were forced to do, so they rebelled. Whatever it was that made them special to him they took away. They refused to be his pawns any longer. That was what made him so angry.'

'How do you know all this?' Robert asked.

'Tigers just know,' replied Pradeep.

'Oh, right,' said Robert. 'Anyway, it doesn't matter who the women are or whether they can be trusted or even if they did tell Ballisargon to go and take a running jump. I just want to get my family back. I'm not interested in anything else.'

Pradeep and Vidya exchanged a glance that Robert did not see. In that instant of unspoken communication between them they knew that maybe, just maybe the three women had been right all along.

By the time the tigers' explanation of the women and their connection to Ballisargon had come to an end, Robert saw that it was growing dark. With no sun in the sky there were no lengthening shadows. The sky just grew darker and darker in its unnatural dusk, the red light fading until Robert could no longer see the clouds that still passed silently overhead.

Pradeep looked up at Robert. 'Hmm, you won't make it to Ballisargon's Keep today, Robert,' he said indicating the deepening gloom around them with a huge forepaw. 'Better you spend the night here with us.'

Robert, his jaw set firm, stared into the deepening night. He had no idea what else might be out in the desert. If the tigers counselled resting for the night, who was he to argue with two such formidable guards? He settled down with them and eventually fell asleep curled up against Pradeep's extensive tummy fur, which was softer and warmer than any bed he had slept in.

His dreams were filled with tigers.

5

Someone Saved My Life Tonight

The green of the limitless jungle sprawled before him. In every direction he looked it was heavy with trees, every square metre filled with a wild variety of plant life. Vines, branches, voracious ivy, moss-covered trunks and the jungle floor barely visible through the thick covering of ground plants.

From above, the lush canopy rolled like a thick green carpet beneath the bright blue of the clear sky. From below it was a chaotic maze of branches, stalks, stems and leaves where even the smallest plants fought hard to catch fleeting rays of sunlight.

Sleek and smooth, his massive frame was barely encumbered by the abundant life all around. He cut an easy path through the jungle, the briefest glimpse of orange all that was ever seen of him. He was master of the jungle, and servant to no one.

Seven days left. . . . . .

The dawn came too quickly for Robert. He was adrift in a world of green and orange, and his mind was reluctant to abandon sleep completely. His body too, was thoroughly tired; the long solitary days on Earth followed by the time in the desert had tested him physically more than he could remember.

Therefore it was with great reluctance from both Robert's mind and body that he woke up. His head hurt and his legs ached, everything tired and strained by exertions of the past few days. He opened his eyes, blinking against the light, to see Pradeep standing over him, watching him with interest.

'Ah, good. You're awake. Finally,' said the male tiger.

'Don't tease him Pradeep,' admonished Vidya gently to her brother. 'I am sure Robert was quite tired after his adventures so far. After all, how many other eleven-year-olds have you ever met who have made it from Earth to the Lyr.'

Robert just mumbled, and rubbed his bleary eyes, blinking away the bright spots. He was sure he had heard Vidya say something, a word maybe, he had not heard before (or maybe they had used it yesterday?) but was too tired to try and work out what it was. Instead he just stretched himself out, arching the stiffness from his spine with a large yawn.

'Pradeep and I have been talking about your situation,' continued the tigress, 'and we are going to help you out. We are going to come with you to help you find your family.'

'What? Why?' Robert asked, slowly waking up.

'Well,' said Pradeep, 'we don't really like the idea of you wandering round the Lyr all on your own.'

There it was again. The Lyr. This time Robert's mind latched onto the strange new word. He sat up, now wide awake, 'Is that what this place is called then? The Lyr?'

'Mm-hm. That or the Lyr desert, the Lyr plain or half a dozen other names. Mostly we call it The Lyr for simplicity,' replied Vidya.

'Where is it?' Robert asked.

'Well, in purely geographical terms the Lyr is a vast desert on a vaster planet, which itself is almost all desert these days, in orbit around a massive sun…'

Robert stood up and looked up at the sky. In the previous

day in the Lyr he could not remember seeing the sun. He opened his mouth to say as much when Pradeep raised a paw to silence his unspoken question.

'Yes, there is a sun, but no, Vidya and I have never seen it. In fact since Ballisargon's dominion of the Lyr no-one has. Anyway, where was I? From what I understand the Lyr is roughly seven hundred light years from Earth.'

'Seven hundred light years!' Robert repeated. 'You're saying I'm… halfway across the galaxy?' Robert tried to take in what Pradeep was telling him. If this were true how the hell was he going to get his family back home now?

Vidya saw the look on his face and padded over to him. 'Are you alright?'

Robert stared back at the tigers while his mind fought to maintain control in the face of this new and seemingly overwhelming setback. 'It. It just feels too big now. How am I supposed to get myself back seven hundred light years, let alone my family!'

Sensing Robert's rising emotions Vidya said gently, 'Well, Pradeep and I have been talking about your situation and we are going to take you too see an… acquaintance of ours, called the Engineer, who is very knowledgeable about everything in the Lyr and can certainly answer your questions.'

Pradeep flicked his orange eyes over at Vidya at her use of the word *acquaintance*, and tried to sound a little more enthusiastic. 'And after you've spoken to the Engineer, we are going to help you out. We are going to come with you to help you find your family. Look at yesterday. You'd barely been here a day before you encountered the Betrothed.'

'The who? Oh, Ballisargon's wives,' Robert realised. Then he added, 'How do you know all this?'

'Tigers just know,' replied Vidya confidently. 'And who knows what trouble you are going to find yourself in without a couple of experienced, and dare I say it, formidable guides at your side.'

Robert thought for a moment. Maybe the tigers were telling the truth, and this Engineer *could* help him. He certainly had no idea how to travel through space to get back home. 'Well, I suppose I could use a little help,' Robert admitted, echoing his thoughts and remembering how defenceless he had felt the previous day. Then, as if deciding he said, 'Alright. Deal.' A couple of tigers as companions could come in really useful. 'Where does the Engineer live then? Is he near?'

'Just over a day's walk, AwayKeep of here, on a structure called the Bridge,' replied Pradeep. 'The terrain is pretty easy going for the most part, so we shouldn't have too much difficulty. It's certainly no harder than the last couple of days walking you've done.'

'AwayKeep? What's that?'

'Hmph,' grunted Vidya. 'Since Ballisargon's arrival, and dominance of the Lyr, its inhabitants have come to refer to the direction they are travelling in with regard to Ballisargon's Keep. Very few creatures voluntarily travel in the direction *popularly* known as Keepward,' she said with barely controlled contempt.

Robert couldn't work out exactly who she was angry with, herself, the other people or Ballisargon. Thinking that an angry tiger was perhaps not the best travelling companion he tried to change the subject. 'Well, I don't care which direction it's in, so long as this Engineer can help me get my family back. Hang on, did you say another day's walk?' Robert's heart sank as he remembered the already exhausting time in the desert so far. He wasn't sure he had it in him again.

''Fraid so,' replied Pradeep. 'But at least this time you'll know you're going in the right direction to get them back.'

Pradeep and Vidya exchanged glances that seemed to Robert, to say: Well, we're ready, let's get going then. They both turned to Robert, who shrugged his agreement and followed the tigers away from the plaza, out of the city and back out into the red desert.

For the first few kilometres Robert asked the tigers dozens of questions about the Lyr, themselves, the Betrothed and Ballisargon. The tigers, for their part tried to reply as fully as they could, but qualified almost every answer they gave him with something like: 'The Engineer will be able to explain it better than we can,' or 'That's really something the Engineer knows more about.' Robert was beginning to suspect that either the tigers knew very little about anything, or that they were not telling him everything, and Robert really did not believe that the tigers were stupid. Eventually he gave up asking questions, and settled into a sullen silence, plodding along a metre or so behind them, lost in his own thoughts.

After what felt like a long time walking Robert checked his watch. It was still working, and seemed to show the time as nearly midday. Robert looked up at the sky. Overhead the clouds still passed silently by. He reckoned that it was about midday on this world; the sky had been lightening for most of what must have been the morning, and now, the strange light seemed to be at its strongest if what he remembered from the previous day was correct. He couldn't work out why the day should be the same length as the one on Earth. *Surely the rotation of the two planets couldn't be exactly the same?* He asked the tigers about it.

Pradeep and Vidya looked at each other, as puzzled as Robert was. It was Vidya that spoke, 'Robert, we don't understand either, but I think that…'

'…the Engineer will be able to explain.' Robert finished her sentence for her. 'You've been saying that to almost everything I ask for ages now. Don't you two know anything?' he asked, immediately regretting his sarcastic tone. 'Sorry, I didn't mean it like that,' he added before either of them had a chance to reply. 'It's just that all you keep saying is that the Engineer can explain it, whatever I ask.'

Pradeep thought carefully for a second before answering, 'Robert, the Engineer is perhaps the cleverest person in the whole of the Lyr, who knows far more than we do about almost everything that happens. You are going to have to trust us that we are doing the right thing for you.'

Robert hesitated.

'You do trust us, don't you?' Vidya's question was genuine. She really wanted to know that Robert had confidence in them.

Robert heard something in Vidya's voice; a tone he recognised from somewhere. For some reason, he realised that he *did* trust the tigers. He had been rude to them when they were trying their best and he felt guilty for it.

'Yes, I do,' was all he could manage, humbly.

'Ah, don't feel too bad Robert,' said Pradeep. 'You didn't upset us, if that's what you are worried about.'

'Really?' he asked, brightening.

'Really,' replied Vidya solidly. 'It takes a lot more than that to make us angry.'

'Oh, OK then. But I still don't understand what is wrong with my watch,' Robert said as he resumed his march across the sand, the two tigers leading the way once more.

After the small confrontation, and its mutual resolution, the conversation was much easier between the three companions. Robert wisely kept his questions to a minimum, while the tigers in turn began asking him more and more. They seemed very keen to know about Earth, and how tigers there were treated. When Robert told them that for the most part tigers were either an endangered species or kept in zoos Pradeep and Vidya were horrified.

'Why don't they complain?' Pradeep asked indignantly.

'Um, well, uh,' Robert prevaricated, not wanting to break bad news to his new friends. 'It's just that, uh, on Earth tigers can't talk.'

'Oh,' replied the tiger, slightly taken aback.

'Well, like none of the animals on Earth can talk,' Robert added hoping it would explain the situation.

'You can talk,' Pradeep said.

'Well, yeah, people can talk,' ventured Robert.

'And you're just another animal,' Pradeep countered.

'I s'pose…' said Robert, not sure where this was going.

'Well then, it's just not fair. After all, you're no better than a tiger, or a bear, or any other animal. Just because they can't *tell* you not to put them in cages or shoot them, doesn't mean you should, does it?' Pradeep sounded irate and stalked off ahead, his tail swishing from side to side against the back of his legs.

Vidya stayed by Robert's side. 'Don't worry too much about Pradeep. I think it's just been a bit of a surprise to him that things are not the same on all worlds. Almost all the animals in the Lyr can talk. At least those of a certain size anyway. I guess he expected it to be the same on Earth.'

'It's not my fault,' bemoaned Robert. 'I can't make the world right, I'm just one boy.'

For the next couple of hours all three walked in silence, the mood dampened by Robert's revelations about what most people on Earth thought of animals. Robert had tried to explain that not everyone thought the same way, and that there were loads of people who thought that animals were great. There were even some who didn't even eat them, to which Pradeep had made a sarcastic quip about 'tiger burgers' which Vidya had chided him for, but Pradeep was still uncommunicative, so Robert gave up, at least until the tiger had stopped sulking. They plodded along that way until Pradeep looked up, paused and narrowed his eyes as if trying to see something far away.

Robert, who had been trying to think of something to say to Pradeep to cheer him up, almost bumped into the male tiger's rump as Pradeep stopped. He tried to see what it was that Pradeep was looking at. Narrowing his eyes too, he squinted into the distance, but all he could see was the empty horizon stretching away on both sides, seemingly endless. Whatever Pradeep could see was too far away for Robert's eyes.

Looking down Robert could see Pradeep was deep in thought. 'What is it? I can't see anything.'

'Nemorus,' replied Pradeep. 'It's up ahead, about another hour's walk. Our grandparents used to live there. Pradeep shook his head with regret. 'Well, we've got to go through it sometime so we might as well get going. We'll make camp there tonight. It's better than being out in the open desert.'

Pradeep's predicted journey time was accurate to the minute. Nemorus turned out not to be a town as Robert had been assuming, but the edge of a jungle. Or rather more accurately what had once been a jungle.

Robert initially glimpsed it as a small dark patch on the horizon after only a few more minutes of walking. At that distance it was little more than a smudge of grey against the dark red of the desert, but as he and the tigers closed the gap between themselves and the dark blot, it grew slowly in size and complexity.

Once the jungle had got close enough to identify individual trees, Robert could see there were no living plants left. Each tree was petrified; stark lines and hard shapes where flowing curves and rounded trunks should be. Everything was bare, the dense foliage long gone leaving naked branches clawing at the sky.

'Are we really going in there?' Robert asked Pradeep as they stood at the edge of the tree line.

'Yes, it is the fastest way to the Bridge. Skirting round would add at least another day to our journey and you did seem keen to get there.'

Robert peered ahead, trying to see into the jungle. Lacking leaves, what was left was not as dark as the ones he had seen on Earth but it was still dense, the remains of the trees packed closely together. Robert could not see much further than ten metres or so. 'Does anything live in there?' he asked nervously.

'Not any more,' replied Vidya. 'Nothing has lived here for many years. It is quite dead.'

Vidya's words brought to Robert's mind the dead city and its lack of life. Had Ballisargon destroyed everything on this world?

'We'll walk for another hour or so, then make camp,' said Pradeep, stepping forward.

Vidya followed her brother, pausing only to beckon the stationary Robert with a nod of her head and a 'Come on, Robert.'

Robert, still unsure that this was a good idea, paused for a second. *But then the tigers had asked him if he trusted them, and he did.* Putting his doubts aside, and his faith in the rightness of Pradeep's decisions Robert followed the two tigers into the belly of the jungle.

His hesitation at the boundary meant that Vidya had got a little way ahead of him, and Pradeep still further ahead. More than once he lost sight of them, only to see a flash of orange weaving between the grey remnants of tree trunks as the tigers pushed their way forward.

Afraid that he would get lost if he fell too far behind, Robert picked up his pace to a quick walk. He caught a glimpse of ochre flank off to his right, and reckoned he could narrow the gap between himself and the tigers by cutting across the path. He veered off the course he had been following and began to jog, taking care not to snag his clothes on the sharp barbs of twigs. Trying to catch the tigers up meant that Robert was not taking as much care as to where he was putting his feet as he could have been, and he did not see the slight depression in the sand as he approached it.

The instant his striding foot hit the dip he sank in it up to the middle of his thigh, throwing all his weight forward and tipping him heavily onto the floor, knocking the breath out of his body. He called out in surprise and fright as he fell, only to have his cry silenced by the force of the impact with the ground.

Coughing hard, wheezing and gasping for breath Robert felt himself starting to sink into the sand. Frantically he tried to struggle free, but his leg was in too deep for him to get any leverage, and the ground underneath offered no resistance to his efforts to push himself out. His other leg sank beneath the surface of the sand, leaving only his upper body sticking out of the forest floor.

He called out to the tigers for help, but was only able to manage a small croak. He tried again, but it was no good. All he achieved was a coughing fit as his body tried to get some oxygen back into him. By now he had sunk up to his chest. He spread his arms out either side of him to try and slow his inexorable descent but it did no good. In a few seconds his shoulders were underneath the ground and that all that could be seen of him was his head.

He felt the sand reach his chin. In panic he cried out again, this time managing a feeble 'HELP!' before the sand rushed into his open mouth. He coughed and spat, clamping his mouth shut. He felt the sand creep up over his mouth and up into his nostrils. Breathing rapidly Robert blew up little puffs of sand before his nose sank below the surface.

The sand flooded into his ears, and reached his eyes, which he was forced to close. Deaf and blind as well as mute now. Finally the jungle floor closed over the top of his head, and Robert disappeared from sight. He could not see or hear a thing except the pattern of lights behind his eyes and the sound of his blood rushing in his ears.

He realised was going to die now, in a silent dark world where he could not even speak. Without any visual clues Robert could not tell if he was still sinking or not. He felt suspended in the crushing body of sand that surrounded him, and which would kill him.

He fought hard to control his breathing, his body

demanding he try to draw breath. He lost the battle with himself and reflexively opened his mouth a crack to breathe in. But it was no good. There was no air in this dark place, deep under the ground. Only sand. Endless, lifeless sand. The final irony of the situation occurred to him as he slipped into peaceful unconsciousness. He was going to drown on a desert planet.

Pradeep stopped. His ears flicked picking up the smallest sound in the petrified jungle. In a heartbeat he had turned and was running, running as fast as his legs could carry him. He whipped past Vidya. 'Robert's in trouble.' It was all she needed to hear before she was running with her brother through the dead trees.

Vidya galloped hard, pulling ahead of Pradeep in their flight toward Robert, desperate to be in time to save him. 'Which way?' she called as she passed him.

'Just keep going straight,' the male tiger called back. 'About another hundred metres.'

Both tigers put on a spurt, paying no heed to the trees in their way. The sharp branches tore at their sides and faces, pieces of the long dead wood snapping off and embedding themselves in their bodies as the tigers powered through the trees, shattering and scattering everything that lay between them and Robert.

They reached the shallow dip in seconds. Vidya skidded to a stop, Pradeep halting himself next to her. Numerous sharp fragments of the trees stuck out of them, but the tigers were oblivious to the pain of their wounds. Pradeep sniffed the air in one long inhalation, then pointing a paw said, 'In there.'

The tigers moved as one. Pradeep took hold of Vidya's long tail in his powerful jaws, braced himself and watched his sister dive headlong into the ground. She vanished almost instantly up to the base of her tail, drilled into the sand by her powerful back legs. Pradeep slid forward to the very edge of the pit before he managed to stop himself being pulled in too, sand piling up under his broad paws as he struggled to gain purchase on ground reluctant to grant it. He felt Vidya kick with her back legs and a further metre of her tail disappeared into the ground. Pradeep could feel his sister deep under the surface, her weight doubled by the sand on top and all around her.

Breathless seconds passed. Pradeep dared not move, not even breathe till his sister gave him the signal.

More seconds passed in which time almost the rest of Vidya's tail vanished into the sand. Pradeep's head was now flush with the ground, his pink nose scraping the surface. He continued to hold his breath.

Vidya had been underground for nearly a minute now, and Pradeep was becoming worried, when suddenly he felt Vidya twitch her tail, the tip of it tickling the side of his mouth.

Immediately he pulled, his muscular back legs digging into the soft floor, his neck taught with the strain of his sister, and he hoped, Robert. His massive frame edged back a few centimetres, which slowly grew to become half a metre, then a metre. As he retreated from the edge of the pit he saw the base of Vidya's tail, which became her back legs then her broad shoulders and neck. He heaved again, his legs hurting, his jaw muscles trembling with the effort, either or both of them threatening to give way any second. Vidya's ears poked up through the sand followed by the rest of her head and one of her forelegs. The other, the pale white one, was still underground though.

Vidya took some of the strain, Pradeep still holding her so she did not sink back in. She pulled hard, her shoulders bunching as she strained with her burden. Robert's head emerged from the surface, his hair filled with sand, his eyes closed.

Vidya pulled again, and Robert surfaced from his would be grave, her sharp claws snagged in his clothing. Vidya dragged Robert's unconscious body away from the pit onto more solid ground, Pradeep only letting go of her tail when both she and

Robert were safe.

Robert lay very still. Pradeep put his snout next to Robert's face and held his breath. The tiger was rewarded with a sensation of air passing over his sensitive nose. Robert was still breathing. He told his sister, who was busy snorting the sand out from her own nose like puffs of smoke.

'Good… we were…in time,' was all she could manage between large gasps, her huge chest ballooning out as she heaved in lungfuls of air.

Pradeep remained by Robert's side, carefully brushing the sand away from his face with the back of paw the size of a dinner plate. 'He really does look like her, doesn't he Vid,' he said as Robert's features became visible again.

Vidya wobbled over to Pradeep on unsteady legs. 'Yes, I thought we'd recognise him when we saw him, but I did not expect the resemblance to be so striking. I hope we didn't give anything away. As you said, it is too much for him to take in right now.'

'I hope the Engineer can answer his questions for him, although I think he may be in for a surprise when they meet,' Pradeep said with one eyebrow raised to his sister

'Indeed,' Vidya confirmed. 'Mind you, he nearly guessed earlier, didn't he, when he got angry with us?'

'I think so. Still, we'll be at the Bridge by this time tomorrow, so we won't have to keep up the pretence much longer. It will be easier when he knows. Ah, look he's coming round.'

Pradeep returned his attention to Robert, who had started moving. He blinked and coughed his way back into life. Pradeep gave him a gentle pat on the back to help clear his blocked airways, and Robert spat out a mouthful of red sand.

'Thank…you,' he gasped between coughing fits. 'I thought… I was going… to die.'

Vidya looked into Robert's eyes and shook her head. 'I… that is, *we* would never let you be hurt.'

Robert was too concerned with breathing to properly hear

what Vidya had said. All he could think to do was to say thank you again.

'We'll make camp here for the night. Well, a little way away from the quicksand,' Pradeep said once it was obvious that Robert was going to be all right. 'I think we've all been through enough for one day.'

Robert was now cogent enough to take stock of his and the tiger's situation, and the first thing he noticed was that his companions had a number of the stone twigs sticking out of their fur. Pradeep had one large piece poking out of his cheek, which to Robert looked extremely sore, while Vidya's white foreleg was streaked red with blood seeping from half a dozen little wounds. 'Oh my God, you're hurt!'

The tigers noticed their injuries for the first time. Pradeep winced as he pulled the long stone stick out of his cheek, while Vidya showed a little less discomfort as she removed the six or so smaller fragments from her leg. Pradeep flicked his long tongue over the small hole that had been left, while Vidya lapped at her leg. Soon enough the bleeding had stopped on both tigers, and Robert could not apologise enough.

'I'msorryI'msorryI'msorryI'msorry,' was all he could say.

'No need to blame yourself Robert,' said Pradeep carefully, trying not to open up his wound again. 'We didn't know that Nemorus has quicksand in it either. We'd all better be careful from now on.'

'But you hurt yourselves saving me.'

'This?' asked Vidya, waving her leg and flexing her paw.

She was about to say something else, but before she could Pradeep interjected, 'OK, so you may not be able to play the piano again…' then without missing a beat the male tiger finished the punchline, 'But then again, you never could.' Pradeep laughed at his own joke, his humour tempered slightly by a grimace from his wound. Vidya raised her eyes skywards in mild despair but Robert just looked puzzled. These tigers, he decided, were definitely not your normal run-of-the-mill variety.

'Oh look,' said Vidya pointing at Robert's left leg. 'You've lost a shoe.'

Robert looked down at himself. He had been too concerned with the tigers to notice that he had indeed lost the trainer off his left foot. 'Aw…' he almost swore. 'I can't walk another day like this? What'll we do?'

'Well, you can take turns in riding on our backs when your feet get too sore. You don't weigh that much, so us carrying you shouldn't slow us down, should it?' Vidya directed the question at her brother.

'No, I don't think so. We should still get to the Bridge before dusk. All the same, I think it would be better if we tried to make an early start, especially if we've got to be careful on our way through here. C'mon, let's get our heads down. I don't know about you two, but I'm exhausted. One rescue a day is my limit.'

Robert and the tigers found a suitable spot to spend the night, well away from anything that looked even remotely like a quicksand pit. All three of them were totally spent from the exertions of the rescue, and three pairs of eyes, brown, green and orange all closed quickly as the sunless dusk set in, and gave way to the dark, starless night of the Lyr.

Elsewhere in the Lyr, quite unconcerned by quicksand pits, the agents of Ballisargon went about their business. They had been abroad in the desert for over a day now without rest or nutrition of any kind, their single-minded determination borne of their total subjugation to the will that controlled them. They would continue to search until they could no longer sustain themselves if that was what Ballisargon desired. They were after all only tools to serve a higher purpose; they existed to do his bidding. And right now that meant finding anything that should not be out and about in the Lyr. If such a thing existed, Ballisargon was determined to find it.

Six days left. . . . . .

6

Fight Like A Brave

Robert did not remember dreaming that night. His sleep had been long and deep and he barely moved from the position he originally laid down in. The two tigers slept almost as heavily, rousing themselves only minutes before Robert woke.

He turned to Pradeep and asked how much further it was to the Bridge.

'We should see it well before dusk, but I am afraid it will mean another day of walking. Vidya and I will take turns in carrying you for brief periods, but you will have to put in some legwork. It's probably best if you take your other trainer and your socks off as well. That way you'll at least be even when you're walking.'

'Why aren't I getting hungry or thirsty?' he asked as he plopped down onto the sand. 'After all, I've been here,' he paused while he counted 'two days now. I should be almost dying of thirst, surely.'

'There is a theory about that,' said Vidya. 'It is the Engineer's belief that the Lyr affects its inhabitants as much as they affect it; a kind of mutual interdependence, not unlike a symbiotic relationship. As there is nothing left in the way of food or drink, the Lyr has had the effect of rendering its population resistant to the ravages of hunger or thirst. The Engineer really understands more about the Lyr than almost anyone else in it, perhaps even more than…' Vidya tailed off.

'Ballisargon?' Robert ventured, worrying at the laces on his trainer. They loosened under his attentions, and he slipped the shoe off his foot.

'Yes, perhaps even more than Ballisargon.' Pradeep was impressed with Robert's intuition. 'I think you're going to enjoy speaking with the Engineer when we get to the Bridge.'

'I am? Why?'

'Because I believe you'll understand more than you think you will,' he said with a knowing smile.

Not for the first time in his conversations with the tigers, and he was sure it would not be the last time, Robert had lost the meaning of what they were saying. He opened his mouth as if to reply then thought better of it. Better to wait till he had spoken to the Engineer before asking stupid questions.

'And you won't get to talk at all unless we get going,' Pradeep urged.

Robert got to his feet, trainer in hand and followed the tigers through the rest of the stone jungle, Pradeep navigating them around several more quicksand pits before they finally reached the edge some two hours later.

Three hours more walking later, Pradeep stopped dead. He lifted his muzzle to the air and sniffed. Cocking his head to one side he closed his eyes and listened.

'What is it?' Robert asked.

'Shh,' whispered Vidya gently.

'What's going on? Why have we stopped here?' he asked more quietly.

'Pradeep has sensed something. Look.' Her brother looked ill at ease; something serious was troubling him.

Pradeep's senses were the keenest of anyone, man or animal, in the whole of the Lyr. Those senses, his hearing and his smell, had detected something. Something hostile lay nearly two kilometres away across the vast open desert, and was heading their way.

Pradeep looked at Vidya and Robert, and indicated the direction he wanted them to go with a nod of his orange head. Robert looked over his shoulder toward a steep rising dune they had skirted round a few moments before. Vidya did not need to be instructed twice and joined her brother in pacing around to the rear of the dune.

As the tigers walked in silence, Robert looked over his shoulder to see them brushing away their footprints with their long, furry tails, carefully and deliberately removing all signs of their presence. Robert couldn't imagine what could be so dangerous that two adult tigers would go to these lengths to conceal themselves from it.

He gulped when he realised that perhaps, he did not want to know.

Once safely in the lee of the dune Pradeep made a gentle patting motion with a paw and lay himself down. Vidya and Robert dropped to the desert floor too. Robert lay as flat as he could on the ground, hoping the dune would conceal them all from whatever it was that Pradeep had sensed. He held himself rigid, hardly daring to breathe in case it was detected by the as yet unknown danger.

For a whole hour they stayed behind the dune, the tigers stock still and Robert shifting only the slightest body part to allay cramp. The last thing Robert thought he needed was to call out in discomfort. During that long, silent hour Robert's thoughts turned over and over in his head. He remembered the lonely days on Earth and in the desert before he met the tigers, and how alone he had felt. Now, in their presence he felt safer and more secure than he had done for nearly a week, even with whatever it was out there right now.

The Lyr was a strange and hostile place; it had nearly claimed him twice, and he was glad he had companions in his search. The tigers themselves seemed willing to do whatever they could to help and protect him, and in a strange way, Robert felt that he would be willing to do the same.

His thoughts were interrupted by Pradeep who said quietly, 'You can talk again now if you like, but we can't move on for another hour I am afraid.'

'What happened? Why did we stop?' Robert asked Vidya.

'A servant of Ballisargon. A Glass Mollusc sent to look for something,' she replied.

'Or some*one*?' Robert asked nervously, remembering his unease at the tigers' earlier covering of their tracks.

'Now we don't know that for sure,' said Pradeep. 'Glass Molluscs patrol the majority of the land between here and Ballisargon's Keep. They are wide ranging beasts, roaming far across the Lyr. At any one time there may be as many as a dozen or so of them abroad, depending on Ballisargon's mood.'

'Mood?'

'The Molluscs are Ballisargon's beasts. They are held in thrall to him by powerful means. It's almost as if they're a direct extension of his will. If he is determined enough about something then there will be a legion of them patrolling the Lyr. Fortunately for us it is some distance away, and we are safely out of range of its senses,' explained Vidya.

'Our father,' Pradeep indicated to himself and Vidya, 'told us a tale in our youth of a Glass Mollusc that caught a cub when he himself was young. He said that he had been at play with a friend when they had strayed across a resting Mollusc. Knowing about them from their parents they tried to retreat, but the Mollusc knew they were there. Our father said that he saw it move, far too fast for something so obviously large and cumbersome. In an instant it was upon his friend. It engulfed her. He did not know how else to describe it. She was *engulfed* by the Mollusc. He could see her trapped inside the thing's transparent body, struggling to escape, clawing at the clear flesh all around her. But it was all in vain. Slowly the Mollusc began to absorb her. He saw her liquefied by the thing's powerful digestive system.'

Robert shivered at the image of the tiger cub caught in this huge, *something*.

Pradeep continued, 'He bolted and ran. He ran in terror till his legs were giving out. He kept running until he found his father. Three adults went out to where the cubs had been, but by then the Mollusc had had its fill and had resumed patrol. They found no trace of her. Not even a single tooth or claw. It had all been consumed with no waste.

'He never saw one again in his many long years, but he told us enough for us to be wary of them...' Pradeep trailed off. 'They are powerful beasts Robert and great care should be exercised, even when one is several kilometres away. It is a brave creature indeed that engages one in single combat.' He was looking directly at Vidya with fierce pride shining brightly in his eyes.

Robert saw the look. 'You've fought one?' he almost gasped to the tigress.

Vidya said nothing in reply. She stared down at the sand directly in front of her, not moving her head, her face expressionless, emotionless. She closed her eyes and remembered. Remembered the savagery and violence of her encounter with the Mollusc. The ripping and tearing of cold hard flesh with her teeth and claws. She remembered how she had found the wounded Pradeep unconscious, with the Mollusc bearing down upon him, ready to inflict the killing strike, and how she had thrown herself at it in a blind rage, not caring for own safety.

She remembered the first swipe of her right paw, the feeling of her strong foreleg clashing with the smooth hardness of the Mollusc's body, and how its flesh had given way and her leg sunk inside it up to her shoulder. Almost immediately she felt burning agony all along her leg, and saw the colour leach from her fur. Nearly unconscious with pain she had torn herself free, and smashed her paw immediately back at the Mollusc, only this time her razor sharp claws connected with the Mollusc's outer skin and took hold. She heaved back her leg, the muscles in her shoulders straining as a hunk of Mollusc flesh came loose.

The Mollusc bucked her off, but now that its attentions were focussed on her, and not Pradeep she leapt back at it roaring a full-throated howl of anger and determination. In the end it had been her fury that had saved both tigers. The Mollusc was unprepared for an attack of such violence from an adolescent tiger; four paws full of claws and a mouth full of teeth biting and tearing and gouging and ripping as it fell in one short minute, lifeless pieces of it strewn around.

When her senses returned, Vidya looked around at the destruction she had wrought upon another living thing. What was left was barely recognisable as having ever been alive, let alone having any sense of what it once was.

Pradeep however was whole and living. Vidya had done what was necessary of her to save her brother. It was all any tiger would do; what was needed of it.

Vidya opened her eyes, shaken by the force of the memories. 'Yes Robert, I have fought one. It was the toughest creature I have ever faced in battle and killed. But I cannot say I am proud of it.'

'How can you not be proud of killing something that awful?' Robert sounded confused.

'It's not the killing I am ashamed of. Nor the fact I was forced to take its life; it was about to kill Pradeep and I could not let that happen. It was the way I fought that I cannot forgive myself for. It was if I was watching myself taking it apart, piece by piece. I could not stop myself, even after it was obvious that the Mollusc was no longer a threat. I just kept on attacking until there was nothing left.

There are levels to your being that you are unaware are there until you are sorely pressed; you may very well act in a way that you thought you never could or never would, and sometimes those actions may not be truly honourable. And to this day I carry the reminder of my actions. I am both proud I was able to save Pradeep, and yet I can never forget how I let myself lose control. Never again. You may not understand but it is all a matter of control. Knowing what you're capable of but using that to control it.'

Robert still did not really understand what Vidya had said, but knew that she was not going to say any more about it. He didn't press her, and was about to change the subject when Vidya beat him to it, 'Pradeep, can we talk about something else please? Tell Robert about the old jungle we passed through yesterday.'

Pradeep was more than glad to talk about something else. While he owed Vidya his life for her defeat of the Mollusc, he also knew how much she had lost for it, and it was a debt he had not yet repaid. He was unsure how, if ever he was going to be able to restore the balance in her soul, but he knew that he would die trying if he had to.

Pradeep cleared the knot from his throat with a discrete cough, and began telling Robert the stories his father had told him about the days when expansive forests grew over vast areas of the Lyr. When there had been many many more tigers and bears and wolves and birds and people in the Lyr. When the sun had shone bright in the deep blue sky and rivers had run, and when hunting was a pleasure. The thrill of the chase as your prey slowly realised that its time had come.

Listening to her brother talk, Vidya was there with Pradeep, leaping through the forest in pursuit of her prey, gloriously alive with the thrill of the hunt, the blood pounding in her ears driven by the powerful heart beating in her chest. It must have been a good life before Ballisargon, and the Molluscs, and she wished to see it for herself. Maybe, just maybe, she thought to herself as she looked over at Robert.

When Pradeep had finished Robert asked him, 'How much further to the Bridge?'

'Another half day's walk now the danger's passed,' Pradeep replied. 'We had been making good progress so we're not too far behind schedule due to this little stop.'

'I've got a question for you both,' Robert stated.

The tigers both looked at him, and in unison said, 'Yes?'

'Well, when I first found you, I overheard you talking about waiting to meet someone.'

'And?'

'And I was wondering if it was the Engineer you were meeting?'

Pradeep and Vidya both began speaking, then both stopped as they realised they were talking over each other, then both began again before Vidya said, 'You first Pradeep.'

'Uh, well, yes, yes it was. We were supposed to be meeting the Engineer when you found us, and we were going to uh...' he trailed off.

'We were going to see if we could find anybody in the city you had been in,' finished Vidya.

'Oh. Right,' said Robert. 'Well, if the danger's passed we can get going again, can't we?'

'Oh, yes, certainly,' said Pradeep leaping to his feet. 'Come on then you two, we can't hang about here all day, can we.'

Vidya got to her feet a little too quickly too.

Robert stood up and followed the tigers. *Why did they lie?* By now Robert had tons of questions, and he hoped the Engineer could answer them.

In fact the Glass Mollusc had sensed Robert, but its self-preservation kept it from intervening directly. It may have been under Ballisargon's control but it still had enough of its own mind not to try and engage two adult tigers in a fight. If the odds had been more in its favour then perhaps, but it was suicide without reinforcements. Instead the Mollusc headed back to Ballisargon's Keep where it would report back what it had discovered.

7

Stairway To Heaven

Across the whole of the Lyr there were just two structures which stood taller than the few storeys of the ruined cities. One was Ballisargon's Keep, his stronghold and place of power, which every living thing that could think for itself tried its best to avoid. Some of the more superstitious inhabitants of the Lyr never even turned and faced in its direction. Decades of hiding from him had taken its toll on their psyches, and they were a scared and scarred set of individuals. The rest of the Lyr avoided it, both in conversation and in deed, and were content that they drew Ballisargon's wrath no more.

The other building of roughly equal magnitude, but viewed far more benignly, was the Bridge of the Engineer. If Ballisargon's Keep represented everything that had ruined the Lyr, then the Bridge in its own strange way, represented everything about the Lyr that its population had lost. Sober, sombre people knew it as a place of sanctuary and safety where anyone was welcome to make their home; while the desperate and broken people claimed that the Bridge was the recruiting and training ground for the vast and powerful army the Engineer had been raising since Ballisargon had arrived on their world, and that one day this army would rise up and overthrow him. But these people were the fractured and damaged ones, stripped of all hope save a few folk tales they warmed themselves with when the winter arrived with its savage cold that caused their bones to ache.

Thus the Bridge drew people to itself, the opposite pole to Ballisargon's dark magnet of a building. People came to the Bridge voluntarily, whereas no-one sought out Ballisargon's Keep.

The Engineer had not intended to build the Bridge (as everyone in the Lyr called it, although it had never been formally granted that title by its designer and builder) and had certainly, not initially anyway, intended it to become the sanctuary it now was. The Bridge had been designed and built as a temporary measure against the almost ceaseless incursions of the Glass Molluscs.

In the century since the first massive stone had reached skywards the Bridge had become home to almost every remnant of Lyr society that had been left. Dozens became hundreds, which in their time became thousands, and existence for them became almost living again. Social structure and cohesion re-emerged as family networks were created and community bonds re-formed.

For the most part, it worked; the people of the Lyr had had centuries of prosperity before Ballisargon's arrival and that had engendered in them, for the most part, a sense of tolerance and respect for each other. It was this tolerance that allowed them to all remain living, in relative harmony, on the crowded bustle of the Bridge.

However, only a fool would have mistaken pragmatic tolerance for willing acceptance of their fate. There was not a man, woman or child on the Bridge who had not lost an immediate family member to Ballisargon; most of them having lost everybody in their extended set of relatives save themselves. Therefore the survivors were bound together in a common hatred of the man who had destroyed their lives, and given the opportunity most, if not almost all of them, would gladly trade their own existence to restore the Lyr to what it once was.

For the next hour or so Robert had great difficulty not looking at Pradeep and especially Vidya with a mixture of awe and apprehension. Of course, deep down he *knew* that they were capable of killing; they were tigers after all and it was part of their nature. It was just that he had pushed those particular thoughts to the back of his mind; Pradeep and Vidya had been nothing but friendly towards him, but it still unsettled him to be reminded that, at a moment's notice, he could end up just as dead as the Glass Mollusc had.

While Vidya's eyesight was no match for Pradeep's, it was keen enough, and Robert's furtive sideways glances had not gone unnoticed. After all a tiger could never be too aware of its surroundings. The glances, coupled with Robert's nervous body language caused her to speak. 'You don't have to worry, you know. We won't hurt you,' she said in as reassuring a tone as possible. 'What I did to the Glass Mollusc was to protect Pradeep. We would never hurt you, you are...' she trailed off.

'I'm what?' Robert asked.

'Nothing,' said Pradeep, giving Vidya a stern look. 'It is nothing important. Anyway, we're here.' He pointed a forepaw.

Robert gazed out along Pradeep's outstretched limb to see the most incongruous sight he had yet seen since arriving in Ballisargon's realm. It was a lake in the middle of the vast red desert. However, it was not the lake that was the unusual thing. What was different about this lake was that there was what appeared to be a structure standing in the middle of it.

The Bridge (and it *had* to be the Bridge that the tigers had mentioned) lay some way off, so Robert could see all of it in its entirety. Even at this distance he could tell it was massive. Two tall white pillars, wide at the bottom and tapering gradually as they rose upwards, reached from the surface of the water until they seemed to touch the sky. At their tops they met to form a wide arch upon which rested a flat platform that formed the top of the Bridge. Due to the immense height of the pillars, the top of the Bridge was partly obscured by the clouds that passed by, so that Robert could only glimpse the barest fragment of detail between the gaps in them. He saw what appeared to be a wall on either side of the Bridge, and thought he could make out some sort of structure, a small house perhaps, but he could not be sure.

While a bridge in the middle of the desert would have been odd enough, this bridge did not even seem to go anywhere; as far as Robert could tell, both ends of the Bridge jutted out into empty sky, seemingly unfinished. The whole thing looked more like a segment of a bridge waiting patiently for others to join it and make it go somewhere.

The lake, the Bridge and its apparent uselessness as a bridge did not make any sense to Robert, but then not a great deal had made sense for the past few days now, so he just accepted it as it was.

'How do we get to it?' he asked.

'Well, first we have to swim to the base of the left pillar.' Pradeep pointed at the nearer of the two legs, 'then there is a set of steps inside the leg leading to the top. But I am afraid that you are going to wait at the bottom of the staircase while Vidya and I go and speak with the Engineer. It's been a few years since we've been here and, well just say that we could have all parted on better terms.' He flicked a glance over at Vidya who made a 'My fault?' face.

'So, what, like he won't see me or something if I'm with you two?'

'No, not that. It's just that when I last saw the Engineer I said a few things I need to apologise for,' replied Vidya. 'And Prad… we, think it is better to go and smooth things out a bit first. The Engineer has been on their own for quite some time now, and the last we heard had become something of a recluse. We just need to check that everything is OK. That's all.'

Robert looked sceptical.

'No, really. The Engineer really is the one who can answer almost all your questions about Ballisargon and the Lyr. The Engineer has been around for decades and knows more about this world than anyone else on it. And we just need to make sure that how we left things is not going to interfere.'

'So I guess I just hang around the bottom of the pillar for, what half an hour or so?'

Vidya looked rueful. 'Better make it an hour. The Engineer may not initially accept my apology.'

Robert gaped. He couldn't think of anything that anyone could say to him that an hour of sincere apologising wouldn't have made him forgive them for. 'O…K…' he said slowly. Then he remembered. 'Hang on, you said *swim*? I'm not sure I'm too keen on that. Can't I just ride on one of your back's like earlier?'

'No, we all have to swim I am afraid.' Pradeep said matter-of-factly. 'Can't you swim then?'

'Uh, it's not that, I uh... I just thought that with you being cats and all that, that you wouldn't like, uh *like* swimming.' Robert realised that sounded lame, even to himself. It was a pretty feeble excuse, and he knew it.

'Tigers are excellent swimmers, ' said Vidya. 'In fact we quite like having a dip from time to time. We find it helps us relax.' Vidya smiled a large, cat smile. 'Come on, we both know you can swim. Why don't you want to?'

'It's just that I uh... I uh...'

'Get teased in school?' Pradeep asked kindly.

'Yes,' Robert replied in small voice. 'They make fun of my... me because of my necklace.' He looked down at his feet.

'Well, we're not cruel little boys and girls who don't understand what it means to you, are we Vidya? We know that your Mum gave it to you, and...' Pradeep went very quiet, very quickly.

Now it was Vidya's turn to shoot a consternated look at Pradeep.

'I never told you that.' Robert observed.

'Come on, stop stalling and let's get to the stairs. It'll be night-time soon, and we don't want to have to do the swim in the dark,' Vidya said.

That was twice now, thought Robert to himself, as he followed Pradeep and Vidya down to the shore of the lake.

As he approached the Bridge and its lake, both grew slowly in his vision until he and the tigers were at the water's edge. He looked up again at the Bridge, which although had looked tall only a few minutes ago now felt huge. It seemed to shoot up into the red sky in defiance of gravity, and Robert had to lean right back till he nearly fell over to see to the very top. The massively tall arch stretched upwards above him, the apex scraped by the ever-moving clouds. *Must be chilly up there.*

He put one foot carefully in the water then quickly pulled it out. *Chilly in here!* he thought. Just his luck; not only had he met two tigers who enjoyed swimming more than he did but the water he had to swim in was freezing cold!

He was about to ask Vidya if it was really necessary to see the Engineer, when he saw Pradeep bounding toward the lake, a flurry of orange fur. In a second the male tiger was airborne, and Robert could have sworn he saw him curl up into a ball before he hit the water, with an almighty splash. For a moment Robert watched the slowly widening circle of ripples the tiger had left when he entered the water. The concentric rings reached the shore and bounced back on themselves, merging and interfering with each other. Pradeep surfaced, his huge head now seemingly tiny against the vast flat body of water he swam in.

'Come ON Robert,' shouted Pradeep from the water, turning to look over his shoulder. Vidya looked over at Robert with a 'go on then' on her face before she too entered the lake, only with a much more graceful set of steps than her brother.

Thinking it was probably best to get the entrance to the lake over and done with as quickly as possible Robert backed up a little way then ran. At the lake's edge he launched himself at the water, colliding with its glassy surface and plunging into it.

He surfaced with a whoop, and after shaking his head to clear his eyes, stroked out to where Vidya and Pradeep were obviously heading. Practicing life saving in school (the one time he had not been teased as he was able to hide his necklace under his clothes) he was used to swimming in clothes, even though they were heavy with water, and pulled at his body. He was a stronger swimmer than he gave himself credit for, and had soon caught up with the tigers. Through the crystal clear water he could see their legs swim-walking with powerful grace, and together the three of them made for the base of the Bridge in slow, even strokes.

At the very bottom of the enormous white pillar Robert could see a low platform rising slightly out of the water. He swam over and grabbed hold of it. He pulled himself out of the water, which poured from his clothes as he stood up. He shook himself as best he could, taking off his top and wringing it out. He squeezed his jeans against his legs to try to expel what water he could only to discover, when he looked at his feet that he had lost his other trainer in the swim to the bridge.

'You need to get yourself some pads,' Pradeep joked, flexing a paw out of the water in demonstration. What good are those shoe things if they are just going to fall off all the time? Ah, never mind, Vidya and I will see if the Engineer has got anything in your size.'

The tigers hauled themselves out of the lake. Even with their fur matted down by the water Robert could see they were still formidably large creatures. Unlike some animals that seemed to be all fur and no body who seemed to disappear when they got wet, the tigers were almost as massive wet or dry. Robert shivered, partly from the cold of the water and partly from their physical presence.

The tigers shook the excess water from themselves before disappearing into the belly of the pillar. Robert could hear them talking for a minute or so, but could not make out the words of their conversation before the sound died and he was left alone again.

Only this time he wasn't quite alone. He had met someone (well, two someones) who had offered to help him, and while they might have been tigers, and talking tigers at that, they seemed genuinely friendly. He wasn't sure that they were being completely honest with him, but about what he couldn't be sure. They had proved themselves by doing everything that they said they would do: accompanying him, looking out for him and now leading him to the Engineer, but he still knew they were lying to him sometimes.

Well, OK, not *lying* exactly, but certainly (what was his Dad's expression?) being economical with the truth. But about what he couldn't tell yet. He tried convincing himself that maybe it was something private to them, but that didn't feel right. The tigers seemed incredibly open about most things, and only got shifty when he talked about… Maybe once he'd spoken to the Engineer he could ask the tigers a few more questions and try to understand them a little better.

He looked down at his feet and sighed at the loss of his footwear. The Lyr was proving to be almost as dangerous a place to be a trainer in as it was to be an eleven and a half year old boy. He turned and looked at the opening in the stone pillar in front of him. Inside he could just make out a set of steps, spiralling upwards. He checked his watch; it had been nearly an hour, more than enough time for the tigers to speak with the Engineer and smooth out whatever it was that had caused the animosity between them surely?

Anyway I can't sit here forever. And it's not like there's anywhere else to go is there? And with that thought he headed off into the belly of the pillar.

The ascent was not easy and Robert stumbled more than once on the worn steps, stubbing his unprotected toes on the rise in front of him. He decided to take his socks off as to get a better grip on the stone. Stuffing them into his pockets he resumed his climb.

As he climbed, Robert became aware of a low noise at the very edge of his hearing. It was so quiet that for a time he was not sure he was even hearing anything; the inside of the pillar muffled every sound so effectively that Robert thought his ears were playing tricks on him to compensate for the silence. But as he climbed higher he was sure he *could* hear something. A bassy electrical hum, like the sound of a stereo turned right up when nothing was playing. The hum seemed to have a rhythm to it; rising and dropping in pitch ever so slightly like a giant slow heartbeat.

He stopped his ascent and felt the stone through his naked feet. There was a definite vibration there, tingling at his soles. He set off again, upwards.

Robert found himself involuntarily stepping up the stone stairs in time to this pulsing noise, his footfalls measured against the backdrop of sound that grew in volume the higher he walked. Walking this way seemed somehow easier, as if the hum and thrum gave his steps a purpose they had lacked previously, and Robert realised that he was less tired than he should be, considering the height he estimated he had so far climbed.

Robert had no idea quite how far he had come, or how far he had to go. All he had was the constant step-stepping beat of his feet against the steps to measure his progress.

After a while, Robert realised that the regular pulse of the sound was growing quieter, and with it he felt his energy seep from his muscles. Now, as he climbed and the sound grew fainter he became acutely aware of the aches in his calves and thighs and the soreness of the soles of his feet. Each step grew more difficult than the last until Robert had to take a rest.

Sitting himself down on the steps facing downwards, Robert paused to catch his breath. It was then that he noticed for the first time a gap in the stone, like an arrow slit in a castle wall. He pressed his right eye up to it, closing the left one for better clarity.

He was rewarded with a view of the Lyr stretching away now underneath him, and the sky with its clouds seemingly only a few metres above him. *Just how high is this thing?* Straining his view downwards he could just about make out the edge of the lake and the pencil thin line in the sand that was his and the tiger's path that led to it. *I must be nearly there by now, surely.*

Inspired that he was indeed very near his goal Robert got to his feet and attacked the staircase with the renewed vigour that came from knowing that his goal was in sight.

8

On A Plain

Barely twenty more steps upward, Robert emerged into the twilight that had fallen during his long ascent inside the pillar. After the brightly lit interior, the deepening dusk of the outside appeared darker than it was, and Robert struggled to make out any shapes in the gloom. He waited a few moments for his eyes to adjust, which they did seemingly faster than normal, and the vista at the top of the Bridge came sharply into focus.

Pradeep and Vidya sat sphinx-like just off to one side. He looked over at them, and while Pradeep nodded, Vidya just looked sad, as she closed her eyes and dropped her head slightly. Whatever had taken place between her and the Engineer obviously still troubled her. And for some reason, maybe it had been the way she had looked at him, or the things she had said, Robert could not shake the itch in his head that told him he was part of it somehow.

Pradeep gestured with his head. Robert looked and saw a slender figure standing some distance away from him, looking out over the edge of the Bridge into the distance, leaning heavily on a cane. He was sure that this was the Engineer he had been brought all this way to meet.

Robert began to approach, but wary after his encounter

with the Betrothed, tried to stay as close to the staircase as possible.

'Hello. Are you the Engineer?'

The Engineer turned and took one awkward pace forward, the cane obviously bearing the greater part of their weight. Robert decided that he had better be the one to close the distance. After all, he *had* come all this way to meet this person, who appeared to offer no threat to him, so a few more metres should be no problem.

No sooner had he thought this particular thought than, with a rushing of air passing over him, he found himself standing in front of the Engineer, who was still where Robert remembered. This time, it was *Robert* that had moved like the three women.

'Whoa!'

Then two things happened in rapid succession.

The first was that Robert realised he had been wrong when he'd assumed the Engineer was a man.

The second was that the woman he now stood before suddenly started shouting at him, for no apparent reason.

'No! This was a mistake. I should never have listened to them. I'm not getting involved again!'

Robert took a half step back in case she started beating him with her cane or something. 'I'm sorry. What was a mistake? What did I do wrong?'

'You. You can Move, so you don't need my help. It'll only end wrong again. No, I won't do it. Now. Go!'

The Engineer raised her arm, the one with the cane, and Robert flinched, lifting his arms to protect his head and face. He could not help closing his eyes, when he felt the same whooshing for the briefest moment. When it ceased he sensed that the Engineer was no longer standing next to him, and he carefully opened his eyes.

He was standing at the edge of the lake again, the Bridge towering up over him!

Huh? How the…?

Before he had the chance to wonder what had happened he saw Vidya waving to him from the base of the pillar, just at the entrance to the staircase.

'Wait there,' he heard the tigress call. 'I'm coming over.'

Robert expected Vidya to jump back in the water, but she didn't. There was a fragile blur in the air next to him for a split second then Vidya was standing right by him.

Robert fell over onto his bum with the surprise.

'Sorry,' said Vidya honestly.

'You could have warned me, you were going to do... What exactly *did* you just do? It was like just like the Betrothed when they...' he trailed off shaking his head in disbelief. 'And how did I get back down here? And where's Pradeep?' Robert got to his feet.

'My guess is that he is talking to the Engineer. Trying to persuade her not to *do that* again.'

'Do what? What are you talking about?'

Vidya looked back up at the Bridge for a moment, then as if deciding something, addressed Robert. 'It's called the Rook's Move. It is a means to travel distances in a heartbeat. I never thought she'd Move you off the Bridge like that.'

'But why? I thought you said she'd help. Doesn't look to me like she's going to. Perhaps I'd be better off not bothering with her. Stupid bloody woman, nearly hitting me with that stick anyway.' Robert turned to walk away from the Bridge back into the Lyr.

'Robert, no! I mean, please stop and wait. Come back with me and let me speak to her. Perhaps Pradeep and I can make her change her mind.'

Robert paused, one foot off the ground in a half step. Did he really need the Engineer's help? After all he had got this far more or less on his own. He may have only been eleven but he was sure as hell not going to put up with being treated like *that* without a damn good reason. To Hell with her.

His foot hit the ground and he began walking again. Away from the Bridge, and certainly away from the Engineer.

'Whatever, Vidya. I'm not putting up with that. I don't care if she is your friend.'

Vidya bounded after the retreating Robert, and ran in front of him. 'Please wait.'

'Get out of my way Vidya.' He didn't care if he made her angry now.

Vidya, who although faster to anger than her brother, was still much more controlled than Robert. And besides she knew first hand what the Engineer could be like. She refused to rise to Robert's challenge. 'Please Robert. Stop and *think*. I know you're sore from her rudeness. Believe me, I know what she's like but I, and I mean *me* here, not Pradeep and I, but me, *I* really do think that you need to speak to her. Really.' Vidya scanned Robert's face for a sign that he was going to change his mind while Robert scanned Vidya's with the desire to believe what she said.

The tigress continued. 'I. I made a promise to myself, a long time ago that I would have no more dealings with her. She… took something away from me a long time ago and I swore then that that would be the only time I would allow her to have that effect on me. But with you here now, in the Lyr in need of more than my help, I am going to forget that I ever made that promise.

'I know your pride has been injured and I know you just want to walk away and forget it ever happened, but sometimes some things are bigger than yourself, and personal pride. Remember why you're here. Remember who you've come to get back.'

Dad.

Elisabeth.

Something in Vidya's voice brought their images to mind more vividly than if he had just thought about them himself. They were after all the whole reason he was here. Did he *really* need the Engineer's help? He may have got this far on his own, but that had been mostly though luck. If the Engineer was as knowledgeable as the tigers had been making out, then there was only one answer to this question.

'OK,' he said slowly, 'But you'd better make sure she doesn't wave the stick in my face again,' he said with a grimness that actually made Vidya worry for the Engineer in case she did.

'Let me worry about that cane. You just listen to what she says. Please?'

Robert nodded.

'Now, let's get back. I think Pradeep may have had some success in calming her down.'

'No, I can't do it, don't you understand? The cost is too high. I won't get involved again,' said the Engineer as she sat awkwardly down in the armchair. She had walked heavily from the door where she had greeted a wary Robert with a tentative handshake (which he refused), leaning the greater portion of her weight onto her cane as she moved.

Now, in the better light of the Engineer's living room, Robert could see her properly for the first time. She looked to be a woman in her mid-forties (even though Vidya had told him that she was much older than she looked), dressed smartly in a trouser suit. Her silvering-black hair came halfway down her back, and was tied in a neat and practical ponytail at the top of her neck. Her face rarely changed expression, even when it was obvious she was in physical discomfort as she shuffled in her seat, frequently adjusting her sitting position around her midriff in an obviously futile attempt to be at ease. Only her eyes ever betrayed her thoughts, and only then very occasionally when she looked extremely sad before the look vanished and her mask of control re-appeared. This Engineer was a world away from the shouting, mad and angry individual he had met earlier.

'But why?' asked Robert. I need you to teach me about the Move and the Molluscs and Ballisargon and everything.'

The Engineer regarded Robert for a long time before she spoke again. She had indeed calmed down, but while she may have no longer been shouting or waving her cane at him, she still refused to help.

Why couldn't the boy see her point of view? Or at least respect her decision in the matter. She had seen too much over the long years of conflict with Ballisargon, sacrificed too many friends and…

'Look, Robert. I apologise for over-reacting earlier, and Moving you from the Bridge was the very height of bad manners for which I am sincerely sorry. You are of course welcome to stay on the Bridge for as long as you desire. I offer sanctuary from Ballisargon to all who want and need it. But in the other matter, I will not help you. I cannot.'

Robert opened his mouth to start saying something in his defence when Vidya rested her white paw on his knee. 'Robert, could you step outside for a moment please? I want to speak to the Engineer in private,' she requested gently.

Robert huffed his way to the door followed by Pradeep who knew his sister would not want him to hear what she was about to say.

Once they were out of earshot the tigress turned to the Engineer. 'Look, I'm not going to beg you to help, and despite what you might be thinking I'm not going to threaten you either.' The Engineer relaxed visibly at this. Vidya was nothing if not a creature of her word. 'Remember what Pradeep and I promised her when you helped her leave. You owe me for that, and we, *I* need your help in keeping Robert safe while he is here in the Lyr. He needs to learn how to Move, what the Molluscs are and what Ballisargon is capable of. You're the only person I know who knows all that.'

The Engineer sat back and thought to herself for a moment. Could she teach Robert enough to keep him safe, or would he end up as just another casualty in the conflict that had raged for nearly a century now? She didn't know. The last thing she wanted was another pointless death on her conscience. She had already lost so much. Too much.

But the alternative was worse. She'd seen the

determination in Robert's eyes. He was going to confront Ballisargon whether she helped or not. Only a fool would stand in the path of this eleven-year-old boy. Better he knew what he was doing then. If he was intent on rescuing his family then he should at least have every advantage he could. But then surely all that would do would give him false hope, which was worse than no hope. Robert would fall just like all the others before him had done. The Engineer said as much to Vidya.

'We have faith in him. I know he can do what everyone has failed to.'

The Engineer looked at the tigress with suspicion. 'Why? What aren't you telling me Vidya?'

And Vidya told her.

'Hello Robert,' said the Engineer. 'What say we start over?' The Engineer held out her hand to him once more.

Robert rose from the armchair he had been seated in and stepped forward. Vidya had told him that The Engineer wanted to speak to him in private. He took the Engineer's hand and accepted her handshake with one of his own. 'OK, but don't point that,' he indicated her cane with his head, 'at me again. It wasn't nice of you.'

The Engineer looked down at her support and nodded ruefully. 'No, you're right, it wasn't right of me. Again, I apologise. I won't do it again. And anyway, if I tried to strike you with it I'd probably just fall over. I'm none too steady on my legs these days,' she added with what she hoped sounded like good humour.

Robert's smile indicated that their relationship was warming.

'Vidya has …more fully explained your situation to me and I have agreed to help you in whatever way I can. I expect you have lots of questions, and I will answer them as fully as I am able. Firstly, I imagine you're wondering why I'm not a man?'

'It had crossed my mind, yes.'

The Engineer smiled at him and gave a small laugh to herself. 'I appreciate that I've not been quite what you were expecting.' she stated gently. 'I suppose the title is a little confusing. How about you call me Eirian instead, if that makes it easier for you? OK?'

Robert nodded. 'How did I do...the thing, what did Vidya call it?'

'The Rook's Move?' Robert nodded, and Eirian continued. 'I remember learning to use it. It can be quite disorientating the first few times you do it, but once you get used to it, it is quite simply the most exhilarating way to travel.'

'But hang on, weren't you supposed to... No wait, they definitely said 'he'. It *was* me they were waiting for,' Robert said more to himself than to Eirian. 'They lied to me.'

'Yes, yes they did. They have their reasons, at least for the time being, but suffice to say that they have your complete safety at heart. They would do anything to protect you.'

Robert remembered the quicksand pit. 'Why?'

'Because they are tigers, and they act according to their nature,' replied Eirian. 'Now, I understand that you are here to get your family back from Ballisargon.'

Robert tried a joke of his own. 'I'm certainly not here sight-seeing. There's nothing but desert for miles!'

Eirian looked over him and out of the large window that showed the vastness of the Lyr. Robert felt his cheeks redden as he realised he had said something very out of place. 'Sorry,' was all he could mumble.

'No, you're right. There's precious little to see any more, even from all the way up here.' Eirian indicated with her cane and the pair of them stood before the pane of glass; the desert stretched as far as the twilight would allow his eyes to see in all directions.

'Has it always been like this? So empty?'

'No, not always. Only since Ballisargon arrived and brought the Molluscs with him. They have consumed almost everything and left us a barren existence. No forests, no birds, no laughter or songs. We've been brought to our lowest point...' Eirian trailed off.

'I'm sorry,' was all Robert could think to say.

'It's not your fault. You're here to find your family, and we'd better make sure you are equipped to do so.' She reached behind her back and with a flourish produced a pair of trainers. Eirian glanced at Robert's bare feet. 'I think they should be your size.'

Robert looked puzzled. How had she done that? Still, he did need something to wear on his feet. Robert began to put his new trainers on, getting the damp socks out of his pockets, when Eirian stopped him. 'Best we get those clothes dry first, eh?' Eirian said. 'My house has a modest bathroom where you can wash, and there are a couple of spare bedrooms for you and the tigers.'

As if that was their cue, Robert spied the orange and black flanks of Vidya and Pradeep push their way back in through the door.

The tigers padded over to where Robert and the Engineer were standing. Seeing Robert's new footwear Pradeep remarked, 'Let's hope this pair stay on this time.'

Robert smiled at the joke, while it was the Engineer's turn to look puzzled.

The tigers padded off to a room almost as if they knew where to go, while Robert was directed to a room where he was assured he could clean himself up and where he would find a change of clothes that Eirian guaranteed would fit.

Robert had a shower, taking great pleasure in feeling clean for the first time since arriving in the Lyr. He washed the sand out of his hair and from between his toes and from his ears. For a time he just stood under the warm water, letting the soothing heat seep into his aching bones and muscles. He cleaned off the debris of the past few days and watched as it swirled and gurgled away down the plughole. Then he cleaned his teeth; his mouth felt really rough on the inside and he did not want to imagine what his breath smelt like.

Robert chose a set of clothes remarkably similar to what he had already been wearing (jeans, t-shirt and a hooded top); the clothes smelt new and fresh, as if they'd been made and washed the day before.

Robert met Pradeep and Vidya in the hallway. The tigers looked cleaned and presentable, their fur positively fluffy and their fangs shining. Robert idly wondered how tigers cleaned their teeth; did they make tiger sized toothbrushes? Their wounds from the jungle looked cleaned as well, and appeared to be healing well. Robert was pleased at this, as he still felt guilty for causing the tigers to be hurt in their rescue of him.

'My my, don't you scrub up well,' Pradeep joked when he saw Robert in his new clothes. 'Come on, let's go talk to the Engineer.'

Back in the sitting room the Engineer stood staring out of the window.

Robert gave a discreet cough, and she turned. 'Ah there you are. The clothes fit, I hope?' she asked with a smile, sounding fairly sure that they did, and not really expecting a reply. 'Please sit down,' she gestured toward the sofas indicating that Robert could sit where he liked.

Robert made himself comfortable on one of the sofas across from the chair the Engineer lowered herself into. The tigers sat on the floor, Pradeep by the Engineer and Vidya next to the sofa Robert was on.

'Right, you need to know about Ballisargon. What he is capable of, and what he does.'

'I know he steals worlds,' said Robert, remembering what Tairn had told him and how there seemed to be no one left on Earth.

'Yes, he does.' The Engineer looked pleased but not

surprised at Robert's knowledge. 'He removes everyone from a planet and then uses them as power.'

'What, in mines or something?'

She gave a small shake of her head. 'No, Ballisargon has no use of physical items. What he craves is power. Power in its rawest form. He connects the populations he captures to giant generators, then uses that energy to fuel his further conquests. What he expects to do with all that power is beyond me.'

'Anyway,' the Engineer continued, 'maybe he knows why he is doing it. I certainly don't.'

'How do you know about the generators?' asked Robert. 'Were you a prisoner in them or something?'

'Because, Robert, I built them for him.' There was no sense of pride in her voice, only bitterness and regret. 'I was, still am I suppose, this world's greatest builder of things. Ballisargon arrived here over a century ago and ...abducted my husband. I was forced to build those monstrous machines from Ballisargon's own designs in payment for his safe return. Those machines hum and crackle with the stolen power from many worlds of people. Eventually I escaped here to the wilderness, and built the Bridge as my haven. I shuffle it from place to place every few days using the Move, along with the lake to keep out of Ballisargon's reach.'

'What happened to your husband? Did Ballisargon return him?'

The Engineer fell silent. She looked away from Robert and back out of the window into the darkness of the night and the clouds which still passed by outside. It was some moments before she returned her gaze to him, during which time Robert felt immensely uncomfortable. He looked at Vidya, but she was looking at Pradeep. Robert looked at Pradeep, but Pradeep had his eyes closed. Robert got the distinct feeling he had overstepped some unspoken boundary and was about to apologise when the Engineer spoke again in a cracked voice, 'I suppose you're wondering how you moved across the Bridge so quickly?'

Gratefully welcoming the change of subject Robert wholeheartedly agreed. 'Yes. I saw The Betrothed do it a couple of days ago as well. You called it the Rook's Move. How does it work?'

'It allows you to go from *here* to *there* in a heartbeat,' the Engineer began, the strength returning to her voice. 'All creatures in the Lyr can do it, some to a greater extent than others.'

'What about Pradeep and Vidya? Can they do it?'

'Of course. They live here; they can make use of the Lyr's unique geography.'

'What about the Glass Molluscs?' Robert remembered how scared he had been when one passed them by on the way to the Bridge. 'Can they do it?'

'Only in the most limited of ways,' the Engineer continued. 'Ballisargon's control prevents them from utilising too much of their own intellect, so they are unable to Move more than a few metres, no more than a handful before they become exhausted. Luckily for us.'

'Us?'

'Everyone else. All the inhabitants of the Lyr desert. We call ourselves The Lyrne. There are isolated pockets of people still living in the desert, while the rest... Well, you'll see tomorrow.'

'Tomorrow? Why tomorrow?'

'You'll see,' the Engineer replied.

'Will you teach me about the Move, and Ballisargon, and the Molluscs? I want to know as much as I can about everything.'

'Of course. You don't expect me to allow you to wander the Lyr without being prepared do you? I'll teach you how to control the Move. How to make it work for you. The Rook's Move is a lifesaver. Without a working knowledge of it you would be defenceless in the Lyr.'

'But what about Pradeep and Vidya, couldn't they protect

me?'

'From one solitary Mollusc, of course, but Ballisargon has hundreds to command. When you've learnt to use the Move it will save your life, I guarantee that.'

Hundreds, thought Robert, remembering how anxious Pradeep had been at the thought of just one. Maybe he should spend some time learning this Rook's Move, but he had to get on with rescuing his family, especially now he knew they were connected up to some sort of energy generator.

'How long will it take to learn the Move?' he asked, realising that he sounded a little desperate (but then he was). 'It's just that I don't want to get to Ballisargon's Keep only to find that my family are already...' he struggled over the last word, as if it saying out loud would bring it about.

'A day or two,' replied the Engineer, then qualified her statement, 'Don't worry, Ballisargon's generators would take months, if not years to exhaust a population as large as the one from Earth. It is the single largest body of individuals I have ever heard of him Moving at once, and his need for power has grown considerable over the last few years. He must be planning something very large scale to need all that energy. Even so, the generators work at a finite pace and no faster, regardless what Ballisargon may want. Remember, I built them; I know how they work. Your family will not be used up quickly, I promise. You will do them more good by learning the Move. Patience Robert.'

Robert did not like the Engineer's use of the phrase 'used up'. It brought to mind images too unpleasant to think about for very long, so Robert didn't. 'OK,' he replied slowly. 'I'll learn the Move and anything else you think I need to know. I want to get my family back, but appreciate I'm not going to do that if I am completely unprepared.'

Pradeep and Vidya looked at each other and nodded their consent. In their opinion Robert was rapidly becoming a very shrewd boy.

By now it was getting late, nearly midnight and Robert felt

the lateness of the hour and the effects of the climb. He tried to stifle a yawn, but it was no good. The Engineer and the tigers sensed Robert's tiredness without needing to see him yawn, and she announced that it was better to continue the conversation the next day, after everyone, herself, tigers and eleven year old boy had had a good night's sleep.

Eirian showed Robert to a bedroom before retiring to her own quarters. Robert's head had barely touched the pillow before he was sound asleep. It had been a very long, exhausting day indeed.

What Robert did not know was that tomorrow was going to be even longer.

9

In Dreams

Eirian raises her head from her work at the sound of the reminder bell. She had set it some hours before, having known full well that she would get absorbed in her work and forget completely and miss her appointment. She shakes her head, partly at herself for once again becoming lost in the task at hand and partly at the speed in which the time passed; there never seemed to be enough hours to complete everything.

Zinan, her beloved husband of many years walks into her study-laboratory-workshop already dressed for the occasion. He wears a finely pressed, immaculate dress suit complete with top hat, brushed cotton gloves and a cane, topped with a silver orb gripped by claw or paw of some sort. To her eye he looks as fine and elegant as he ever has; the man she loves and has loved for nearly twenty years.

Realising that unless she makes haste, she too will be late, Eirian reluctantly leaves the plans for the structure she has been commissioned to design and build and hurries to change.

Later they both sit as guests at the table of the Annual-President, laughing and talking with the others at the dinner. Every strata of the Lyr is there, from the current kings and queens (chosen bi-annually, and whose titles are passed around and swapped like stories), to the priests and devotees of the numerous religions who manage to convince some amongst the population that they have a message that speaks to them.

Everywhere throughout the Lyr, similar gatherings and celebrations are happening. After all, there is a lot to be thankful for. War and poverty, starvation and intolerance have all but been eliminated. For countless decades every person has had enough to eat, somewhere to live and a peaceful life. In every town and city on the planet there is a party like this; a population-wide celebration of the rewards of the decades of temperance and restraint that saw the Lyrne through the darkest period in their lives, and out the other side, a stronger, but more careful people. They celebrate the sacrifice of their forebears in bringing them to this, their golden age.

One of the athletes leads a toast to the loser of the bout; offering her sincere appreciation of the effort and determination he had shown, and wishing him a better outcome next time. People applaud and the victor shakes her fellow runner's hand. Now it is the turn of the runner to choose someone to congratulate. He rises to his feet and offers a toast to Eirian, who blushes at the attention of the room now focussed on her. The runner talks of the golden domes sparkling like fire in the sunlight; about temples for the priests of the land, whose spires reach up to the heavens and seem to touch the stars themselves; about slender and elegant bridges that span vast valleys almost too wide for anything to cross them; and about the tunnels that ran under the oceans ferrying travellers along to their destinations.

Her work, he says, has touched the lives of everyone on their world somewhere, somehow. She is speechless at the toast. She rises to her feet to reply that he is too kind and she only wants to serve the people of the world, when the gathering falls silent. All conversation and laughter stops as the room suddenly seems too full with people. It is as if everyone is there, the whole world has come to hear her speak.

Eirian looks around at the massed faces before her. In front of her eyes they become the ghosts of the world, their accusing stares on her, their words blaming her. She is the builder no more; she is the architect of their ruin. She is responsible for the machines that destroyed them. Their accusations pile on her, the weight crushing her. She turns to Zinan for support and comfort, but he is no longer there. In his place sits an empty set of clothing. The condemnations continue to grow. She covers her ears, but it is no good. The long-dead ghosts' denunciations of her work echo in her head. She is gasping for breath. Cannot breath, must get out, must escape.

Pradeep is in the jungles of old Lyr, chasing down his prey. Leaping and bounding through the tangle of roots and branches, revelling in the thrill of the hunt. The green whips past him, leaves slapping his muzzle harmlessly with the pace of his run, his legs a blur of motion propelling him forward. He can hear the pounding of his blood in his ears, and his heart sings as he clears a fallen tree. He can sense his prey, very near now and he closes in for the kill.

But there is no sign of it in the clearing he finds himself in. Instead it is a dead end, a thick wall of plants all around. The jungle seems to loom too large, the space feeling too small, the green closing in on him. He turns to leave only to see the Glass Mollusc of his youth barring the way out. He remembers the fight he could not win. He tries to dodge left, then right, but the Mollusc keeps pace with his efforts, matching him move for move. Then, suddenly it moves, too fast to dodge and it is upon him. All around he feels the cold hard flesh pressing on him, smothering him, squeezing the breath from his body. Pradeep feels himself begin to fall into darkness.

Vidya moves silently nearer her prey. Across the room she can see Pradeep echoing her movements, a mirror image of her stealthy approach. She pads softly and deliberately closer until she and Pradeep are within striking distance of the man. He seems completely unaware of their presence, his attention focussed on the screens in front of him. This was their only chance, to take him unawares and off guard. Any hint of their presence and the whole endeavour would be over.

Patience is the key, Vidya thinks as she plants a paw silently on the floor in front of her. She arches her back in deliberate readiness, her hindquarters tense, like coiled springs waiting to release.

Huge muscles power her and Pradeep forward into the air at the man, who, at the very last instant before impact raises his arms either side of him, catching the tigers in mid pounce, freezing them in space.

The man flings his right arm across his chest hurling Pradeep at the wall. Vidya hears her brother's bones break as the man smashes him into the hard stone, Pradeep falling to the ground in a shattered and bleeding heap. Vidya is impotent and powerless to save her brother from harm.

She barely has time to register what has happened to him before she feels herself propelled upwards, far too fast towards the high ceiling of the room. Instinctively she closes her eyes and tries to avert her head as the hard flatness of the roof rushes at her.

Vidya feels herself crash into the ceiling, which steadfastly refuses to give even an inch under the force of her impact, offering her no cushion at all. Somehow through the pain of broken limbs she remains aware, the respite of unconsciousness denied her.

She turns her head against the force holding her in place to see the man looking up at her, smiling like the devil. He pushes his already raised hand up higher, and Vidya feels herself crushed even further into the ceiling. It is getting harder and harder to breath as her body is slowly and painfully flattened, each breath more and more difficult to draw than the last, until eventually the pressure becomes too great.

Robert is out with his Mum, at the funfair together. Children run and shout in pleasure around them. The stalls offering goldfish in bags, the candy floss, the rides. The rides! Robert points to the Ferris wheel, looking up at his Mum imploringly. She nods gently in agreement. She pays the man the money and they get on. The ride starts and the carriage lifts off and up into the sky, the horizon falling away from them. Round and round on the wheel they travel, the falling and rising sensation in their stomachs making them call out in delight.

The wheel stops, their carriage at the very top, rocking gently under the remains of its momentum. Robert looks down. The ground seems so very far away. Surely they are too high up? He begins to feel short of breath, gasping for air. He feels his Mum's squeeze his hand, and he looks at her. She smiles to him, then seeming to address the sky itself says, 'You will not harm him. Not while I watch over him.'

Five days left. . . . .

10

There's More To Life Than This

Robert woke with a violent jolt. For a moment he was sure he was high up somewhere, in danger of falling. He put his hand out behind himself, as much to be sure he was not going to fall as to steady himself. Then his surroundings slid into place, the memory images of the dream slowly fading to be replaced by the reality of the bed, the room and the Bridge. He drew in a long deep breath. His heart was beating hard in his chest, he was sweating and he realised that his hands were shaking.

He struggled to recall the dream, remembering only that he had been in trouble and his Mum had helped him somehow. *What had happened?* He was sure he did not know, but for now he seemed to be alright.

Forcing himself to calm down, Robert noticed the animal noises coming from the somewhere in the Engineer's dwelling. Loud, deep animal noises like two cats fighting; two *large* cats fighting.

The tigers!

Robert bounded off the bed and into the sitting room to see Pradeep and Vidya both curled up into tight balls of orange. The tigers were jerking violently, their heads twitching back and forth, their legs spasming as if fighting some unseen foe. Their tails were thumping into the rug they lay on, beating out a rhythmless tempo, while their mouths were pulled back hard, exposing sharp white teeth and bright pink gums. They looked like they were both having the worst nightmare of their lives.

Cautiously, Robert made his way to them, creeping between their twitching paws, and the deadly razors that flicked and threatened to tear Robert's bare feet to ribbons. He crouched behind Pradeep's shoulder and, taking a deep breath of courage, shook it as gently as he could.

Pradeep was on his feet faster than Robert could blink. He fell back in part surprise and part terror as the huge form of Pradeep bowled him over. Animal instinct caused him to curl up into a ball.

'ROWR!' Pradeep roared as he shook the bad dreams out of his head, then seeing Robert huddled in panic took a deep breath. 'It's OK Robert,' he said gently. 'I'm awake now. You're safe.'

Robert pulled his hands away from his face, 'Are… are you alright?'

'Yes, I'm fine now,' the tiger replied. 'But it looks like Vidya isn't. You'd better stand back, her reactions are somewhat sharper than mine.'

Robert scooted backwards on his bum until he was behind the sofa he had been sitting on the night before. 'OK,' he called in a quiet voice from his hiding place.

Robert only heard Vidya waking from her nightmare, but that was more than enough to make his skin prickle. There was a blood-chilling roar, followed by a whipping noise before Pradeep said, 'Careful there, you nearly had my eye out.'

There was a pause for a few moments, then Robert heard Vidya ask where he was.

'He's fine,' replied Pradeep, 'He woke me up first, luckily, or you could have gutted him with that swipe.' Robert's eyes went wide.

He cautiously stood up from behind the settee and waved at Vidya weakly. 'Uh, are you OK?'

'Yes I'm fine. Thank you for waking us. I suppose I should go and check on the Engineer. Please excuse me for a moment.' Vidya padded out of the sitting room as if nothing had happened.

'You really don't want to surprise her if you can help it. She's got lightning reflexes. I tell you though, one day she's going to be too fast for me,' Pradeep said with a smile.

Robert laughed nervously. He was still shaken by Pradeep's reactions and was just glad he had not chosen to rouse Vidya first.

A few moments later both Vidya and the Engineer emerged from the latter's bedroom. 'Well, that was a thoroughly unpleasant experience, I must say,' the Engineer said almost nonchalantly as she lowered herself into her armchair. 'It's been quite a while since I had a nightmare that bad. Most unsettling. How about you lot, any bad dreams?'

Pradeep and Vidya looked at each other, then down at the floor in unison. 'Mm,' was the most they seemed willing to volunteer.

'What about you Robert? Any nightmares?'

'I dreamt something about my Mum. Something bad was going to happen, but she looked after me. I wouldn't say it was a nightmare though,' replied Robert.

'Hmm, interesting. Who woke up first?'

'Well, Pradeep woke me, and said that Robert had woken him, so I guess he did,' said Vidya, now more communicative.

'Hmm, interesting,' the Engineer said again. 'This is all very, very interesting, if not wholly unexpected.' She sounded almost excited.

'Thank you for waking us Robert. I expect most of the inhabitants of the Lyr are currently having some of the worst dreams of their lives. Ballisargon is trying to put on a show of force. That Glass Mollusc you lot almost ran into yesterday must have reported something he didn't like, and he's trying to put the frighteners on everyone.'

'My Mum said bad dreams can't hurt you.'

'Your Mum sounds like she was a very astute woman. It was what saved you from the worst of Ballisargon's attack. Now, let me get washed and out of these,' she indicated her nightclothes and dressing gown, 'and I'll see what I can do about teaching you what I know today. I suggest you do the same; you'll get mighty chilly standing out on the Bridge in just your pyjamas all day.'

With that the Engineer rose carefully from her chair and slowly made her way back to her bedroom. Robert looked at the tigers, who just shrugged. They didn't need to get dressed after all. Robert plodded to his room to put on his clothes.

Thirty minutes later, the Engineer emerged from her bedroom fully clothed. She sat in the armchair waiting for Robert, who emerged a few minutes later in his jeans, trainers and hooded sweatshirt.

'There you are. I hope you're ready for a few surprises today. Shall we step outside?' the Engineer said lifting herself from the chair and motioning with her cane.

Dawn was breaking over AlongKeep, its pale red light slowly replacing the dark grey. Eirian turned and faced Robert. 'I am going to teach you how to use the Rook's Move today.'

Robert remembered Eirian saying something about the Lyr's geography and it being responsible for the Rook's Move. He asked her about it.

'Well remembered. I won't bore you with too many details, but suffice to say that the Lyr has a particular quantum signature, which when brought together with the conscious mind of a living being, such as yourself, gives one the ability to flex the space around you and shift your body through the resultant narrowing of distance.

'Basically you are able to bend space, or Fold it, until you can make two points touch. You are then able to slip between these two points, and once space is unfolded again you find yourself in the second of the two.'

'Oh, you mean like teleporting?' asked Robert.

'Well,' Eirian started, 'I have never seen the technology to actually *teleport* someone or something, but the Move is a credible analogue. All you need is the willpower, intelligence and strength to do it. That is why the Move is such a good defence against the Molluscs; they are fairly witless creatures, not possessed of a high degree of reasoning capability whereas you, me or the tigers, being more clever, are able to Move far further, and with a greater degree of accuracy. Watch.' And with that Eirian vanished, only to re-appear one metre to her left almost instantaneously. 'Good, eh?'

'Cool,' said Robert. 'I so want to be able to do that.'

Eirian frowned at Robert's odd expression. 'And you so shall,' she said, trying to imitate Robert's turn of phrase.

'Rocking! Wait till I show the kids in school.'

'Ah, as far as I know, the Move doesn't work on other planets, so no, you won't be able to show your friends in school. Sorry.'

Robert thought about this for a moment, and decided that, upon reflection he would only have to show everyone else how to do it and then it wouldn't be special. Here, it was.

'So, how does it work then? How do I do it, how do I Move? How do I fold space?' he asked brightly.

'Well the mathematics behind it is…' but Eirian got no further with his sentence before Robert groaned.

'Maths? I can't do maths. Even with a calculator I'm pants at it.'

Eirian narrowed her eyes at him.

'It's just that maths and I seem to be happier when we don't bother each other, that's all.' Robert ventured in the way of an explanation.

'Stuff and nonsense.' Eirian reproached him fairly sternly. Then more gently, 'It might help if you try thinking about it this way. Imagine you are standing on a flat plain.'

Robert sighed. Eirian obviously wasn't going to let this

drop, so he guessed he'd better do as she asked. After the past few days in the desert the image she'd asked him to conjure up was easy for him to visualise. In his mind he saw the flat sand stretched out on all sides.

'Now, imagine what you would look like to someone looking at you from a few metres away.'

Robert closed his eyes and pictured the scene as if viewed through a camera looking at a young boy some distance away. 'OK, I think,' he said.

'Good. Now imagine that you are looking at this scene from above as well as a from the side.'

Now that Robert had his imaginary camera switched on and focussed in his mind's eye, he could rotate and zoom in and out on the figure before him at will. He found this part fairly easy. 'Got it,' he said with increasing certainty in his voice.

'Excellent. I want you to try and pull back so you can see more of the desert on all sides. Say a hundred metres?'

In his mind, Robert did a zoom out until the small boy stood in the centre of a patch of sand roughly the right size. 'I think I'm getting the hang of this,' he said.

'Now, here is a tricky part. Imagine that the desert is flat, like a piece of paper, and as you pull back further and further you are able to see the underneath and all four sides of the paper, and you are standing at one end of it.'

'Looks lonely,' Robert said, not meaning to articulate his thoughts so loudly as he pictured his avatar no larger than an ant on a sheet of A4.

'Now, slowly *fold* the paper in half until the far end touches the end you are standing on.'

The imaginary piece of paper began to flex in Robert's mind, the far end curling up and over onto the end with the ant sized boy. For some reason Robert felt himself begin to get warm, his hands sweating and his feet tingling in his trainers. His eyes twitched under their lids and his forehead had deep furrows of concentration in it.

In his mind the ends of the paper touched.

Eirian smiled. Robert was doing it, she was sure of it. He was Folding space in his head. All that was needed now was the release.

'Now, unfold the paper Robert.'

Robert let the paper go in his mind. It sprang back with a suddenness he was not expecting and dragged him with it. He blinked out of existence.

Eirian followed Robert's first conscious Move with her mind and worked out the re-entry point.

With a slight popping noise Robert materialised exactly where she had imagined he would. He was breathing hard, but had a look of total enjoyment on his face, like he had stepped off the best rollercoaster in the world.

'Wow,' was all he could say before falling over.

Eirian Moved over to him to check he was alright.

'Just wasn't expecting it to be so quick,' said Robert, sitting on the Bridge. 'I was off balance when I re-appeared, that's all.'

'Are you ready to try again?' asked Eirian. 'We can take a short rest if you like?'

'No way. I want to do it again,' said Robert enthusiastically. 'That was *brilliant.* It's like falling from really high up, but not scary at all. And when you land it doesn't hurt, it tingles all over. I've just got to remember to keep my balance when the paper unfolds.' Robert got to his feet and dusted himself down.

'This time, try imagining yourself on the *Bridge* instead of on a piece of paper. Visualise the surface you're standing on then Fold the two points you want to Move between. Don't try too far too soon, just a couple of metres again.'

Robert closed his eyes in concentration. He imagined what he must look like standing on the Bridge. Then he moved his imaginary camera back a few metres until he could see where he wanted to Move to. This time he imagined the Bridge folding, not a piece of paper.

Eirian followed Robert's efforts with her mind and saw his Fold begin. She watched as Robert's force of will bent the space that the Bridge occupied until…

Robert vanished.

Then re-appeared exactly where he had thought he would. This time he did not fall over.

'Excellent!' Eirian exclaimed. 'You've got the hang of the basics very well indeed. Let's practice.'

For the next hour Robert, under Eirian's patient and careful tutelage, learnt how to Move. He learnt to control his body and mind, so that each successive Move was less tiring than his first, until Robert could perform half a dozen or so Moves in rapid succession before tiring. It was during these sessions that Robert thought he spotted something unusual. He had been Moving ever so slightly further and further each time, imagining more and more of the top of the Bridge until on the final Move he thought he had 'seen' something. It looked indistinct and fuzzy, but it was definitely there. A kind of shimmering wall in his mind's eye running right across the width of the Bridge some metres away from where he was.

When he re-appeared, he asked Eirian about it, in between catching his breath.

'Ah, yes. I did say you'd find out today.'

'What is it,' Robert asked again.

'What does it look like? Look with your eyes, then with your mind,' Eirian continued as she walked along the Bridge towards the Keepward facing edge. As she did so Robert thought he was looking through a heat-haze; Eirian seemed to shimmer slightly around the edges.

Robert closed his eyes to look with his mind as she had instructed. He brought the mental representation of the Bridge to his mind's eye, then zoomed his imaginary camera back. He saw the shimmering wall clearly now. He pulled his view back further to see another wall behind him, roughly the same distance away. As Robert drew further and further away from where he was standing he began to make out the true shape of the Bridge. Wall after wall ran between the two edges along almost the full length of the Bridge, all of them meeting in an archway. On top of these walls lay another platform, and on top of this platform more walls and arches. The Bridge had tier upon tier stacked up for a hundred metres or more, dozens of them, easily doubling the height of the Bridge.

Robert opened his eyes to speak to Eirian. 'But why are they invisible?' he asked.

'The Bridge has more secrets than Ballisargon knows about,' she replied. 'I have kept the true scale of it hidden from him for nearly a century. He believes me now to be almost a solitary recluse, a hermit on my Bridge, and while he thinks that we are safe.'

'We?'

'The inhabitants of the Bridge. I am far from alone here, Robert. Look.'

Eirian tapped her cane on the surface of the Bridge. Slowly, as if emerging from a mist, the massive invisible stone walls and tiers faded into view all around them. Robert felt the walls appear in his head, like when he Folded space, but this time it was different, stronger, more powerful. He could feel a vibration through the soles of his feet, and the air all around became tight, pressing on his chest. Where Robert was standing was cast into dark shadow by the tier above his head. He could not help but look up at the huge archway he now stood under. He wondered what was up there.

Too late she felt what Robert was doing. From behind the wall Eirian sensed a Fold occurring, but it seemed too large and in the wrong direction for Robert to be making. But she was wrong. Robert had decided to visit one of the tiers and was busy creating an upwards Fold, which completed just as Eirian worked out what was happening.

She ran through the archway in the tier, but it was too late. Robert had vanished.

Robert arrived in the middle of what appeared to be a meeting place. People of all sizes and colours and dressed in a variety of sturdy, if well worn, clothes shuffled and pushed past each other, some standing listening to public speakers, others just trying to escape the throng. Robert decided to stop and listen.

He approached a small crowd gathered round a tall, slender man in his mid forties. He wore a loose fitting shirt and trousers of plain design, and a dark blue headdress. His skin was weathered, but he had bright blue eyes that shone as he spoke.

'The dreams were a warning!' he exclaimed. 'Take heed, Ballisargon is abroad and he seeks us. Our only hope is to give him a tithe of our bodies and spare the remainder from the Molluscs!'

Robert shuffled between the legs of the crowd trying to get to the front when he was grabbed by the arm. A voice whispered in his ear, 'No lad, don't let him see you.'

Robert looked round into the bearded face of a man also apparently in his mid-forties. 'He means you harm.'

'What? Why? He doesn't know me,' he protested. 'And anyway, *you're* hurting my arm,' he finished.

'My apologies,' said the stranger before releasing Robert. 'I meant only to stop you. Please, come with me,' he urged.

Robert was about to say no thank you very much, but something in the stranger's voice made him stop. The sense of immediacy gave Robert pause. Robert instinctively felt that this man did not intend to hurt him. 'OK,' he said warily, 'I'll come, but the first sign of you turning funny and I'm out of here. I know how to Move and won't hesitate in vanishing in a second,' he qualified.

'I'm sure you won't. I am called Roen.'

'Robert,' replied Robert.

Roen led Robert from the thronging bustle. He kept looking over his shoulder the whole time in a way that made Robert slightly nervous. They arrived at what Robert took to be Roen's house, a modest low rise dwelling slightly set apart from the rest.

Inside it was cool and dark. Roen gestured for Robert to sit down while he lit a candle. The weak sputtering light did not help illuminate the small room. 'Sorry about the lack of light. It's bad for them.'

'Them? Who?' Robert asked

'The last of the flies.'

'Pardon? Did you say flies?

'Yes, they cannot tolerate too much light when they are this young,' he replied. Roen reached for a large glass container, like a bell jar. He held it up for Robert to inspect.

Inside Robert could see several dozen small shapes flitting about, constantly moving and changing direction. Occasionally one would alight on the inside of the glass and Robert could see that it was indeed a tiny fly. 'Oh yeah,' he said. 'What are you doing with them?'

'I am their custodian. They are the last of the flies that remain on the whole of the Lyr. The Molluscs have seen to it that almost everything else living has either been destroyed or rendered homeless. When the Molluscs came to our town decades ago, I fled bearing the flies to safety. Since then I have not seen any more flies here or anywhere else in the Lyr. So now I guard them for the time when Ballisargon will be gone and life can return to the Lyr.'

'But they're just flies,' said Robert. 'What good can they do even if you do get to release them? I mean it's not like anyone likes flies.'

'They were all I could save in the time I had. No one asked me to rescue them and no one is forcing me to guard them. I do it because it felt the correct thing to do at the time and still feels the correct thing to do. They may be small, but they are alive, and on this world that counts for everything. I would defend the flies with my very existence.'

'Well, I don't know about saving flies, I'm just here to rescue my family,' Robert said.

'Your family? Why, are they in danger from the Hecatomb? Are they to be sacrificed to the Molluscs?'

'The hecawhat?' Robert asked.

'The man you saw earlier, Verun, is their Mahatma. The Hecatomb, lad. How can you live on the Bridge and not have heard of them?'

'But I don't live on the Bridge,' said Robert. 'I come from Earth.'

Suddenly there was a knock on the door.

Roen's eyes widened and he jerked his head toward the door. 'In that case Robert, you cannot stay here any longer. If Verun were to find out that an outsider was here you would certainly be taken for tithe,' he said urgently.

The knock came again, this time more forceful.

'You must go, now.'

The person on the other side of the door knocked again, and this time called out quietly, 'Robert, are you in there?'

Robert recognised Eirian's voice, as did Roen, who rose to open the door.

'There you are. I have been looking on all the tiers for you.' The Engineer sounded angry and worried at the same time. 'Luckily Roen found you before Verun did.' The Engineer paused, realising that perhaps she was being too harsh with him. 'No matter, you are safe. Come on, we have to get back to the base level where you'll be safer. Thank you for taking him in Roen. Now I am in your debt.'

'Never, Madam,' replied Roen. 'You saved my life.'

'And you may very well have saved his. Now come on Robert, we cannot tarry here any longer. Can you visualise the lowest level?'

Robert looked with his mind, 'Yes,' he said meekly.

'Good, then we bid you farewell, Roen,' said the Engineer before disappearing.

'Bye, and thanks for letting me see the flies,' said Robert, before he Moved back to Eirian's level of the Bridge.

When Robert arrived back he found the Engineer and the

tigers waiting for him.

'I am sorry for getting angry with you, Robert, it is just that the upper levels of the Bridge are... well, not exactly dangerous, but certainly not safe for the inexperienced. If you had said you wanted to visit them then I would have been happy to go with you, as I have no doubt Pradeep or Vidya would have done.'

'Indeed,' said Vidya. 'We are here to protect you until you can find your family, and if you still wish to see the upper levels then we will accompany you.'

Robert looked down at his new trainers. He had been a little reckless in going off on his own. 'I'm sorry,' was all he could mumble.

'Don't be silly Robert,' said Pradeep, 'You have nothing to apologise for, you were just curious,'

'And curiosity killed the cat?' Robert asked.

'Ha! Hardly,' exclaimed Vidya, 'Her claws kept her safe, as we prefer to say.'

'We'll show you round tomorrow morning, if you would like that,' said Pradeep. 'All the way up to the top of the Bridge.' He looked at the Engineer who nodded her approval.

'OK,' said Robert, 'we'll go tomorrow.'

'That's settled then, ' said the Engineer. 'Right, back to the training.'

And for the rest of the day Robert was taught the finer points of the Rook's Move by the three of them. He learnt how to time his Moves to maximum effect, allowing greater distances to be covered in three shorter Moves than could be done in two long ones. He learnt how to control vertical Moves, being made aware of ensuring you did not materialise in the middle of the floor. He learnt how to sense other creature's Moves with his mind, seeing the Fold in space before it was complete: 'a genuine lifesaver', Vidya had called that particular skill. And Robert also learnt how to tell if there was anything else currently occupying the space he would Move into; 'very messy if you get *that* wrong', Pradeep had joked.

By the end of it all, Robert's head was spinning and his body ached all over. He retired for the night, exhausted, and if Ballisargon sent out any bad dreams that night he was too tired to experience them, as he slept solidly until the next day.

Four days left. . . .

11

Burden In My Hand

CRASH!

The spherical stone smacked into the surface of the Bridge. Eirian looked at it with mixture of mild disdain and gentle frustration. It was the sixth time that Robert had tried to perform a Rook's Move while carrying the boulder, and it was the sixth time it had hit the ground where Robert had been standing when he had started the Move.

Robert appeared a couple of metres away, his empty hands cupped where the weight had been resting on his chest. He spied the boulder rolling gently toward him until it touched his trainer.

He kicked at it hard, angry and frustrated, oblivious to the pain it caused his foot.

Eirian started at the violence. 'What are doing?' she asked in a mixture of shock, confusion and concern as she rushed over to try and stop him.

Robert looked at Eirian, almost not seeing her through his anger, until he took a deep breath and looked down at the stone a few metres away. 'I…' he began calming down. 'Sorry. I just get angry at things sometimes and I can't help myself.'

'But that's no reason to *injure* yourself, surely? What good does that serve?'

Robert paused before answering. 'It just makes me feel better when I can't cope,' he said.

Eirian was troubled by Robert's anger. It had been many years since she had seen anyone display such a level of emotion, and having to deal with the aftermath of it was unfamiliar to her. 'Maybe we should try something...' Eirian began before Robert cut her off.

'What, smaller?' he snapped back, sounding sarcastic. 'I'm not a baby, you know. I don't need a *training* boulder. I know how important this is; you explained it all to me. I do know, you know. It's not like I'm not trying, if that's what you're saying.'

'She was saying nothing of the kind, Robert,' said Pradeep gently. Robert had not sensed the tigers' approach, and hoped they had not seen him losing it.

'Indeed,' said the Engineer remaining calm. 'What I was about to say was 'Maybe we should try something different for a while', at least until you get your mind focussed again.'

'Oh,' said Robert. He had been trying for nearly an hour now. He could not understand why it was proving so difficult and the repeated lack of success now was getting to him. The Engineer had explained how the only way to get his family out would be to use the Move, as they would most likely be unconscious once Robert freed them from the generators.

'Maybe now is as good a time as any to have a better look around the upper tiers. What do you think?'

Robert thought about it for a moment. He was tired, and he was getting nowhere here, so maybe a break was the best thing to do. He could certainly do with a rest and a chance to clear his head. 'OK,' he agreed.

Eirian privately cautioned Robert that some of the people who lived on the Bridge's upper levels were extremely private. 'I must ask that you act with courtesy and dignity while you away from here. Please?'

'OK,' he said quietly. 'I think I understand.'

He checked that the tigers were ready to go. Pradeep and Vidya nodded their readiness. 'We'll go to some friends of ours first, as we would very much like you to see them again, if that is alright?' asked Vidya.

'Sure,' said Robert. 'Let's get going.'

Robert followed the tigers' Move to appear outside a small, low house, much like Roen's. Vidya padded up to her door, and rapped on it softly with her white forepaw. The door was opened and a woman carrying a small child.

'Hello Telain,' said Vidya.

'Well, bless me,' replied Telain. 'I had no idea you two were back in this area. The last word I heard was that you had gone into seclusion after Kshama left.'

Unnoticed by Robert who was busy smiling (and trying to be the right mix of friendly but not unfriendly looking) Pradeep blanched at the mention of the name and Vidya was just glad that Robert could not see her face, as an expression of some alarm involuntarily crossed it. 'Yes, well,' she recovered her composure as much as she could. 'That was a long time ago, and much has changed since then. We are here with this young man and were hoping to spend a little time with you?' She hoped Telain would pick up on the hint.

'Hello. I'm…' she started as she looked properly at Robert for the first time and saw… Now it was Telain's turn to blush. 'Oh my…' she began, her hand moving unconsciously to her mouth, then quickly, 'Of course, of course. Please come in. I would be honoured.'

Robert, feeling slightly bemused, followed the tigers into Telain's living area. The inside of the house was very similar to the dwellings he had been exploring in the dead city, both in terms of layout and dimensions. It gave Robert a strange sense of déjà vu.

'Robert is here from Earth, the latest planet whose population Ballisargon has taken,' explained Pradeep.

Telain looked as if this was in no way news to her, but offered her sympathies instead. 'Oh Robert, I'm so sorry that you had to experience what we've gone through here.'

'That's OK,' he replied. 'As a matter of fact I'm here to get my family back from him.' Robert sounded sure of himself. 'Eirian has been teaching me the Rook's Move.'

'On first name terms with the Engineer eh? I cannot think of anyone I know who addresses her by anything other than her title. You are honoured Robert. She must regard you very highly indeed. How is the Move going?'

'I started out OK yesterday, but today I've been having some trouble.'

'Really? How so?'

'I can't get the hang of Moving something else with me. Not even a small rock.'

Telain paused for a moment, then said, 'When you Move, do your clothes stay behind? After all, *they* cannot Move, can they?' he said.

'Well, no of course not, that would be silly,' replied Robert.

'Why?'

'Well, it just makes sense that they'd come along with you. Otherwise you'd be naked every time you tried to Move anywhere.'

'And do you think that Moving something else is silly, or sensible then?'

Robert paused.

'OK, let's try something.' Telain went to a shelf and picked a small piece of wood. 'Right, take this and put it in your pocket.'

Robert took hold of the carved wood and turned it over in his hands. It was hexagonal, with two triangles facing in opposite directions carved onto one side, and three lines that ran from opposite corners forming a star on the other. 'What is it?' he asked?

'It's the Te piece,' Telain said. 'It is the piece of self awareness in the game of Ur.'

'Oh,' said Robert as he put it in his pocket. He wasn't

sure exactly where this was going, but was happy enough to co-operate.

'Now, Move one metre to your left.'

Robert looked over his left shoulder to see Pradeep sitting there. Pradeep looked up at Robert, then over at Telain. 'Oh, *I'll* get up then, shall I?' he said.

'If you wouldn't mind,' said Vidya. 'After all, you've just been sitting there the whole time.'

Pradeep made a show of getting up and sat down elsewhere. Then Robert performed the Move.

'Now, see what's in your pocket,' instructed Telain.

Robert was in no way surprised when he felt the small, flat piece of wood there. 'Of course it would be there,' he said to Telain. 'After all it was in my pocket.'

'And what if it had been in your fist, what then?'

'Well, it would have come with me also,' Robert replied.

'And what about if it was just resting on your outstretched palm? Would it have still Moved with you then?'

Robert opened his mouth to start to say something, but then realised that *he did not know*.

Telain saw Robert's puzzlement, and said, 'I'll leave you to work out the rest, I think. Now, if you three don't mind, I have three children I need to find.'

Feeling that the time with Telain was indeed over, Robert turned to leave, before remembering the Te piece in his pocket. He fished it out and held it out to Telain.

'Keep it. Maybe it will help you perfect the Move.'

'Thank you,' said Robert.

'It was my honour,' replied Telain, and when Robert and the tigers had left, with the door safely closed and Robert well out of earshot she said, quietly to herself, 'Make her proud Robert.'

Standing outside Telain's house the tigers asked Robert what he wanted to do next. There were plenty more levels of the Bridge, and the tigers had friends on quite a few of them.

However, Robert was eager now to return to his practice.

'I don't want to spend all day talking to people I don't know when I should be practising the Move.'

'Fair enough,' said Vidya. 'If that's what you feel you should do, then we'll do it. Guests first,' she indicated with a paw. Robert obligingly disappeared, followed by the two tigers.

Back on the lowest level of the Bridge Robert remembered something he had meant to ask Telain and the tigers. 'Who's Kshama that Telain mentioned?'

'She was a very dear friend of ours,' replied Pradeep, this time not missing a beat. 'She decided to leave the Lyr many years ago, and Vidya and myself missed her deeply for a great deal of those years.'

'Wow, she must have been a really good friend,' said Robert.

'The very best,' said Vidya. 'Kshama was… a unique being. Kind and gentle, yet fiercely protective of what she considered to be correct.'

Hearing Vidya talk about this woman called Kshama made Robert want to reach out and… he realised wasn't sure what he wanted to do. He was struck by an urge to either pat or stroke the tigers somehow, but wasn't sure they'd appreciate being treated like, well, cats he guessed. Instead he just stood there, conflicted, impotent and uncomfortable. He has little experience with handling the emotions that being around the tigers aroused in him. Their lives were so much more complicated than his; their victories and defeats, their loves and losses and their vastly complex reasons for doing things. Robert struggled to understand them at times, and this was one of them.

His discomfiture was mercifully cut short by the re-appearance of the Engineer, who had sensed the three of them returning. She walked as quickly as her uncomfortable gait would allow, swinging her cane ahead of her in high spirits with each step, a broad smile on her face. 'There you are,' she beamed as she saw Robert. 'Ready to get back to it?'

'Yes, I am. Telain gave me some help with the Move, and I want to practice some more.'

'Excellent. Excellent,' said the Engineer. 'I have to admit, I was at a loss on how to help you. What did she tell you?'

'I've got a series of experiments I want to try before I go back to using the rock.'

'Certainly, certainly.'

'Can I try them now?' asked Robert.

'Of course, of course.'

Was Eirian going to say everything twice? He explained the experiments Telain had set out for him; the Te piece in his pocket, then in his fist and finally resting on his outstretched palm.

'Good, good,' said the Engineer, continuing her newfound habit of repeating herself. 'Try it out, and we'll watch,' she said with genuine encouragement.

Robert felt in his pocket, and his fingers touched the small hexagon of wood that Telain had gifted him. He withdrew his hand, secure in the knowledge that he still had the Te piece on him. Then he Moved.

Re-appearing a few metres away, he reached into his pocket and withdrew the Te piece. He scrutinised it intently for a minute before closing his fist tightly around it. And he Moved again.

The Engineer watched Robert's Moves intently. *He was doing it, even if he did not fully understand what he was doing.*

Robert popped back into existence, his fist still closed. He unfurled his fingers slowly, like a flower opening into bloom. The Te piece was still there.

Now, standing there with his hand out in front of him he closed his eyes and concentrated. He concentrated on the feeling of the small playing piece resting in the bowl of his palm, the cool smoothness of the wood, the grooves cut into the flatness of the side, the points where the hard lines of the edges met. All of it, the piece in its entirety. He imagined the difference between it in his pocket or his fist and now, resting on his hand, and realised that in fact there was no material difference. It was still part of him, the way his clothes and his shoes were, connected to him by physical contact, capable of being Moved.

Robert Moved.

The Engineer looked round, searching for Robert's entry point. Where had he gone? Seconds went by, with no sign of him. Even more seconds elapsed. And more. By now a whole minute had passed and still no Robert. The tigers were getting worried, their ears flat against their heads. 'Where is he?' Pradeep asked.

'I don't kn…' began the Engineer before Robert re-appeared right next to her, causing her to start.

The Engineer looked at Robert with concern. In his outstretched hand lay the small piece of wood, still where it had been when he had Moved. Robert was smiling broadly.

'What…' she began. Then, 'Where, I mean how...' She started again. 'Where *were* you? You took so long to re-appear. We were worried.'

'I wanted to make sure I was carrying it,' he said nonchalantly. 'Why, was I gone a long time?'

'Over a minute,' said Vidya, the concern in her voice obvious.

'Really? It didn't feel that long. In fact it didn't feel any longer than a normal Move.'

'I don't understand, ' said the Engineer, 'it shouldn't have happened like that. Maybe we should stop for a while, while I think about this?'

'No way, I want to try something larger while I'm on a roll,' said Robert, turning and casually heading over to where he had left the boulder earlier that morning.

The Engineer watched him intently. He sensed her gaze, and turned to her, still curious about one thing. 'Where did they all come from? All the people who live on your Bridge.'

'They are the Lyr's inhabitants; its native population, or what is left of them anyway after the Molluscs' incursions into the Lyr's cities, towns, forests and plains.'

'But that still doesn't explain how they came to be *here*, on the Bridge.

'I rescued them. And now they live here on the Bridge's upper levels. When the Molluscs first began taking people we had nothing to fight them with. Ballisargon was too powerful. After the first few waves of attacks from the Molluscs so many people had been taken that whole communities were in peril of extinction. I had to act and Ballisargon never counted on me retaliating in the only way I could; by building a sanctuary, the Bridge.

'The first months were the worst, the hardest. But I had two of the best guards I could have hoped for.' Eirian looked over at the two tigers who by now were playing a game of cat and, cat, guessed Robert.

'You mean Pradeep and Vidya? I thought this was over a hundred years ago? They're not old enough, surely?'

She smiled. 'No, not Vidya or Pradeep. Their grandparents. Two of the finest and most noble creatures I have ever had the pleasure to know. They were good friends and valuable allies in those early days. Never for one moment did I think that the Bridge would become home to so many for so long. However, even the best of intentions can have unforeseen consequences. Frustrated by my protection of the Lyrne, Ballisargon turned his attentions elsewhere. Other worlds, unprepared for him and unprotected from the Molluscs. He re-configured the machines to Move whole cities in one go, then countries, continents and now entire worlds at once.'

'How many worlds has he stolen?' asked Robert.

'To tell you the truth I have lost count over the century. Ballisargon tests handfuls of a population first. No doubt your world has stories of people inexplicably going missing; abandoned boats or somesuch?'

'Yeah, loads of them in the Bermuda Triangle,' said Robert. 'And the Marie Celeste.'

'Well, I've no doubt that was Ballisargon stealing people from Earth.'

'But people have been going missing there for years and years; the Earth got stolen only a few days ago.'

'Ballisargon is nothing if not patient and diligent,' Eirian replied. 'The generators are finely balanced and attuned to only work with compatible people, and it can take him years to be sure that his chosen targets are of the correct kind.'

It was horrible. Now Robert was more determined than ever to get his family out.

He paced back to the boulder. This time he would do it. Squatting over the heavy stone, he gripped it with both hands, and stood up straightly. There was not even the vaguest hint of a wobble in his posture as he came to his standing position. He felt the boulder cupped in his fingers, which were part of his hands, which connected to his arms, which ran to his shoulders into his chest, which the boulder lay across, pressing onto him. No not onto him, INTO him, the way the Te piece had been part of him earlier. This time the boulder was connected to him, he was sure of it. He closed his eyes, took a deep breath and steadied his mind the way he had steadied his body.

He Moved.

The boulder did not crash to the ground. Instead it Moved with him, and when he reappeared he was holding it above his head, triumphantly. He had a determined grimace on his face.

He could do it.

12

Since You've Been Gone

Robert retired to bed early that night, well before the red-brown dusk had deepened into the dark black starless night across the Lyr desert. He was fatigued from the repetitive practice, but by the end of it he had been Moving with the load as if it were second nature.

Pradeep and Vidya had also turned in early; they were cats after all, and had categorically stated that they were seriously sleep-deprived, having had only eight hours or so each for the past few nights. They had curled up together in their room with explicit instructions not to wake them for at least twelve hours.

This left Eirian alone with her thoughts in her living area. She could not sleep, even if she had wanted to. Her mind was buzzing with conflicting emotions and reasoning. Seeing Robert's bright, youthful determination to get his family back had woken something deep inside her; something she had thought long since dead and buried in the recesses of her subconscious.

She paced back and forth, talking under her breath to herself.

'But what if it goes wrong again?

'It won't, you've seen him, you know who he is.'

'But I can't get involved again, I won't let it happen again.'

'But he could do it, all he needs is your explicit help.'

'No, it's too big a risk, I've already exposed myself too much.'

'Aha, so you admit you've gotten involved again.'

'No, it's just that he can't go against Ballisargon completely unprepared.'

'There you go then, you'll have to finish what you've started. After all, do you really want one more death on your hands?'

Eirian continued her frantic pacing for many more hours, slowly, ever so slowly talking herself out of the views that she had held fast to for nearly a century. It was a slow process, arguing with herself that the vow she had taken to be the cause of no more misery should be challenged. But as the hours rolled by and night gave way to dawn, Eirian realised that she had been grievously wrong all those years.

Three days left. . .

Robert opened his eyes after a good night's sleep, unaware of the moral wrangling Eirian had gone through over the course of the night. He trotted happily into the living area, hopping as he tried to put on his trainer on the move, before conceding defeat against his foot and stopping to bend down to do the job properly. 'Hi,' he said breezily to Eirian. 'What do we do today? More Moving, this time something bigger?'

She turned to face Robert who stood there, confidence shining out of him. In that instant she knew her sleepless night had not been in vain.

'No, something different today, I hope,' she replied.

'Cool. What?'

'Please, sit down. I have something extremely important to discuss with you.' Eirian motioned with her cane as Robert plonked himself down on one of the armchairs. 'Robert, when you arrived on my Bridge I was confident that

I could assist you without directly involving myself. For many years I have adopted a policy of tacit non-interference with the events of the Lyr. While I am happy, if not grateful to accept any refugees who make their way to the Bridge, I no longer go in search of them. I see now that Ballisargon had broken me into a position of utter submission. I told myself it was a stalemate, but it was not. He had won decades ago, leaving me to pick up the pieces of the destruction he had wrought. So, when you turned up I talked myself into thinking that by teaching you the Move I was giving you enough to protect yourself.

'But I was not. You see the Bridge is more than just a sanctuary; it is a gateway. The only way into Ballisargon's stronghold undetected is by using the Bridge's ability to enhance your Move potential. However, the Bridge is currently out of range of the Keep, for obvious safety reasons and cannot be Moved into Ballisargon's territory without a new set of instructions for its information processing matrix.' Eirian hoped Robert grasped what she was telling him.

'So you're talking about a software upgrade then?' replied Robert.

Eirian smiled at Robert. Once again she had underestimated the young boy from Earth. 'Yes Robert,' she said shaking her head at herself.

'Right, so what, do you need my help or something? I'm not too bad with computers; I've helped my Dad install stuff on his Mac before.'

'If only it were that simple,' she said. 'The software I need is located on your home planet.'

'Pardon? You mean Earth?'

'Yes.'

'But…' began Robert. 'I mean… How can it be on Earth when you built the Bridge years, *decades* before we even invented computers?'

'It's a little complicated, but the *essence* of the Lyr is dependent on the predominant technology, ethos, culture and standards of the population that is powering the generators. You see, everything in the Lyr is controlled, no that's the wrong word, is *influenced* by the thoughts and lives of the people harnessed to those machines. Hence my attire and your clothes.' Robert looked down at his hooded top and jeans. 'Earth languages, all of it influenced by your people. This influence extends to our technology as well. People from Earth are the principal driver for the computers that power the Bridge, so it is on Earth that you will find the necessary technology to upgrade the Bridge's systems.

'Now, this is the part where I need to ask you a favour.' Robert nodded for Eirian to continue. 'I need you to go to Earth and retrieve the software.'

Robert sat in silence for some moments before replying. 'Where on the Earth is it?' he said giving Eirian every indication that he was willing to go.

For her part, Eirian had expected more opposition from Robert; after all he was here to find his family not go back to Earth empty handed. Robert for his part had already worked out that this was the most expedient way to get his family back and just wanted to get on with it.

'Well, I've spent some time plotting the most likely areas of your planet, based on technological advancement, population intelligence, wealth and history of innovation, where the software is likely to have been developed etcetera, and have come up with two areas with a number of hotspots each. The first, with three likely hotspots is around the western seaboard of the United States; I believe it is called Silicon Valley.'

'Yeah, they do loads of computing stuff out there,' Robert interjected.

'The second is Tokyo, with eight.'

'Tokyo then,' said Robert without missing a beat. 'I've always wanted to try sushi,' he joked. 'When do we get going?'

'I'm not coming with you. I've got to prepare the Bridge's

systems for the upgrade.'

'I didn't mean you, I meant the tigers. Me and the tigers. After all, they'd probably insist on coming anyway. Come to think of it, where are they?'

'Oh, they gave instructions not to be disturbed; I think they need their beauty sleep,' Eirian joked back with a wink. 'Still, I think they've had enough now,' she said looking at her watch. Eirian got up and walked over to the closed door behind which the tigers were sleeping. Carefully and quietly opening the door, she leant inside the room. Putting her fingers to her mouth she whistled as hard as she could.

Robert heard the commotion, the roaring and snarling followed by a loud thump. Eirian turned to Robert with a mischievous grin on her face. 'There, that should have done it,' she said as she made her way back to Robert. 'Quick Robert, sit down as if nothing has happened.'

Robert flicked his eyes quickly over to the open door as the tigers emerged, then back to the Engineer. Pradeep made his way to where Robert and the Engineer were sitting, and took a posture of righteous indignity.

'And who, precisely, did that?' he asked in as calm a voice as he could manage.

'I'm sorry,' said the Engineer, turning her head as nonchalantly as she could, 'Did *what* exactly?'

Pradeep turned his attention to Robert. 'Robert, what about you? Do you know anything about that rather uncalled for interruption to our sleep?'

'I'm sure I don't...' Robert began, but looking at Pradeep sitting there on his back legs with his head tilted to one side he could not contain his mirth any longer. He burst out laughing, which prompted the Engineer to do the same. Pradeep just sat there for nearly a minute while Robert and the Engineer struggled to regain their composure. Eventually, after a number of false starts the Engineer managed to gasp out that it was she who had woken them both up rather unexpectedly, but that time was very much of the essence.

And anyway, she finished, they slept far too much.

'So you see,' she summarised, 'Robert needs to go back to Earth in order to retrieve a vital piece of software for the Bridge, and he wishes you both to go with him.'

'That's right,' explained Robert, 'I would feel much happier, not to mention safer, if I knew you were both with me. Even with no people around we'd still be going to places I don't know, so three brains have got to be better than one. And with your senses, and Vidya's fighting skills I'm sure we could be there and back in under a day. What do you say?' Robert knew the last part was complete flattery, but then Pradeep and Vidya were both cats, and not immune to having their egos massaged, even if it was by an eleven-year-old boy.

'Well,' Vidya began, 'since you put it like that, I am sure we can overlook this morning's... intrusion. And anyway, we promised to look after you, and we will.'

'Excellent, that's settled then,' said the Engineer. 'I'll erect a Gate using the Bridge. Shouldn't take much more than an hour to work out the co-ordinates for Tokyo. I'll try and drop the three of you as close to the most hotspots as possible, give you a fighting chance of getting the stuff quickly and get back here.' Robert wasn't sure if the Engineer was talking to them or herself. A bit of both he suspected.

'What's a Gate?' he asked.

'Oh, it's like a semi-permanent Fold. Allows two way traffic between points in space. Very useful, but extremely heavy on the power consumption. Still, I should have enough reserves to keep one open for over a full day if needs be. Failing that, I'll shut it down, then periodically open it up again every hour for five minutes or so. We don't want you getting stranded back on Earth, do we?'

'I guess not,' said Robert. He had not expected to be going home so soon, and if the truth was to be told he was quite looking forward to it. The Lyr was a strange place and Robert was feeling the need to see a blue sky again.

Robert was informed by Eirian that she would need to concentrate on constructing the Gate, yes it would take something round about an hour and that no, there was nothing Robert could really do to help. Eirian suggested that maybe Robert would like to thank Telain for her help while she was busy with the Bridge's computers.

Robert thought that this was not such a bad idea, and within ten minutes was standing chatting to Telain on the lowest level of the Bridge, just outside the Engineer's house. He was telling her about how he had managed to perfect the Move, when a group of figures appeared a few metres away from them, near the entrance to the staircase. They were all dressed in blue headdresses, the same as Verun.

'Look at them, the fools,' said Telain her voice flat and hard with real hostility. 'I did not realise that the time of the tithe had come around again.'

Robert remembered Roen mentioning the tithe and asked Telain about it.

'They call themselves the Hecatomb,' she began. 'They're a sect of people led by Verun who believe that the only way to exist now is to try to win favour from Ballisargon. Every half year they try to gather converts to their beliefs to pay the tithe, as they call it. A blood sacrifice to the Molluscs and Ballisargon of ten of them. They believe that this keeps the rest of them safe. They're a bunch of idiots, punishing themselves and us for Ballisargon's evil.'

'But why?' asked Robert. 'Surely they must know that all Ballisargon will do is take them and give them nothing in return.'

'Strong beliefs can be blinding as well as enlightening,' replied Telain. 'And Verun is *very* persuasive, I can tell you. He believes to the exclusion of all else that Ballisargon is a punishment on this world, and all worlds for the 'excessive' freedom we used to enjoy. If he had his way we'd all be lined up and given to Ballisargon. Look, there they go.' She pointed at the ten figures who had lined up in front of the doorway to the stairs, before they began a low moaning chant as they started their descent down the hundreds and hundreds of steps to the lake. Telain shook her head and muttered 'Mollusc fodder,' under her breath as the tithe headed off to sacrifice themselves.

High above Robert and Telain, on the next tier unseen by them, Verun looked over the low wall that ran along the length of the Bridge. He watched the tithe head off down the staircase, and smiled to himself, satisfied that the sacrifice would be worth it. He was about to lean back and set about his business when he noticed the two figures chatting near the Engineer's house.

Telain he recognised from her failed initiation into the Hecatomb, but the smaller figure next to her was a mystery. It looked like a young boy. Verun thought he knew every child on the Bridge; you could never tell when a new initiate would come along, but this boy was unknown to him. Then he remembered the rumours of a visitor from Earth who was supposed to be on the Bridge. He had dismissed them as folly when he had first heard them; after all Ballisargon missed no-one. He was not given to mistakes. But Verun could not doubt the evidence of his own eyes. There did indeed seem to be a little boy from Earth here in the Lyr. *Maybe there could be eleven sacrifices this time*, Verun thought to himself.

By the time the Hecatomb had reached the bottom of the stairs several events had been set in motion. The Engineer had finished determining and loading the co-ordinates for the Earth end of the Gate in Tokyo; Robert had finished his conversation with Telain and had roused the tigers (who had been cat-napping after their rude awakening that morning) in preparation for their departure; Verun had decided that the sacrifice of the last person from Earth would greatly enhance his sect's chances of survival; and Roen, who had spies in the Hecatomb had been informed of Verun's plan.

The Engineer found Robert sitting in her living room thumbing through a small booklet he had found on one of her shelves. It was a set of essays and thought-experiments that the Engineer had written over the course of the preceding century. They described a detailed explanation of the physics and meta-physics underpinning the Move, notes and ideas on how to improve the Bridge's defences, and most worrying for Robert the most recent entry was a collection of ideas on what Ballisargon planned to do with all the power the population of Earth would generate. Robert put the book down when he saw the Engineer come in, a broad smile on her face. 'There, done it,' she announced to the three figures. 'You can leave any time you like.'

Robert looked at the tigers who looked back at him as if to say: *No time like the present.* 'Let's get going then,' Robert said to all three of them. The tigers nodded their heads once in approval.

The Engineer gestured for Robert and the tigers to follow her. She led them into a room that would have put NASA to shame. Stacked up on every wall, from floor to ceiling was bank after bank of computers; a rack of silver smooth, hi-tech servers stood against one wall. On another wall sat a group of sixteen monitors in a four by four square arrangement, each one showing a different aspect of the outside of the Bridge; the lake, the legs, underneath the great arch that joined them and the Lyr desert stretching off in all directions. Against the third wall sat three monitors, all in a row with two keyboards, one above the other sitting beneath them. On the final wall there was the door they had all come in.

'Wow,' Robert whistled in amazement at the array of technology in the room.

'Not bad, eh?' said the Engineer. 'From here I can control all I need to. She pressed a key on the uppermost keyboard and the centre monitor glowed into life. A picture of the Earth appeared in the middle of the screen. The Engineer pressed another key and the view of the Earth zoomed in until it had settled above Tokyo. Eight red dots appeared on the screen, each one connected to a set of scrolling hieroglyphs to its right. 'There,' she said, indicating a point between five of the red dots, 'is where I think you should arrive. It gives you efficient access to the most locations the software could be at.' She reached across her desk, and handed Robert a small plastic case. Popping it open revealed a pair of contact lenses. 'Here, put these in.'

Robert looked nonplussed at the Engineer's request, but she answered his unspoken question for him. 'You'll need a map. Also, I am guessing your Japanese is likely to be a little rusty?'

Robert could hardly disagree. He may have known how to say a few words of Mandarin thanks to Peter but that was not going to help him here. He took the small discs of plastic from the Engineer, and with a lot of blinking, slipped them over his pupils. Immediately his vision was overwhelmed with graphics; lines and text popping up over everything he looked at.

'What do they do?' he asked, a little disorientated by the flood of data in front of him.

The Engineer broke into a smile. 'Three-D overlay mapping combined with realtime aug data on anything you look at. I've loaded as much information about Tokyo as I could on the lenses, and also installed a translation app for you. Just look anything you happen to need to translate and the screens will do the rest. Blink twice to switch between the datafeeds and the map, so you can find your way around.'

Wow!

The Engineer then reached across to one of the many servers and pressed an area on the outside of it. A section of the machine opened up to reveal a bank of I/O ports. The Engineer picked up a memory stick, as shiny and polished as the rest of her hardware, plugged it in for a second until the LED on it flashed green, then retrieved it and handed it to Robert.

'Keep that safe Robert. It is the mechanism to retrieve the software upgrade. Locate a computer in one of the hotspots and insert the stick. The software contained on it will do the rest. If the upgrades I need are anywhere on network in the vicinity, then the software will find it. It will flash green once it has the data I need.'

Something about the plan sounded wrong to Robert as he took possession of the slender electronics. He was convinced it would not work but could not think why. Then he realised. 'There was no electricity on Earth when I left,' he said. 'I think the power stations had run out.'

The Engineer thought for a moment, then disappeared out of her control room, only to return a few moments later carrying a compact rucksack and small black box with plug prongs sticking out of one end of it. 'That should sort out the power temporarily. Just plug it into any socket you find in the building and it will energise the whole loop for you.'

Robert stuffed the black power box into the rucksack, and tucked the memory stick into one of its zip pockets. 'OK, I guess I'm ready.'

'Right, stand back,' said the Engineer. She leaned over and jabbed a key on the frontmost keyboard.

Robert became aware of something going on in the room. The air seemed to wobble and glow a strange purplish colour. He felt the hairs on his head and arms begin to prickle. Pradeep started to growl, a low unhappy sound. Robert looked down at the tigers to see their fur standing on end.

'Nearly there,' called the Engineer. The purple light grew brighter until Robert was forced to close his eyes. He realised that his arms and head were no longer tingling, and opened his eyes. In front of him, hovering above the floor was a thin dark line in the air.

Robert walked around the line, inspecting it from all sides. It sat a few centimetres off the ground and ran to a height of nearly two metres, and it looked like a line no matter which angle Robert viewed it from. Baffled, he began to say something, but could not find the words.

The Engineer vocalised his thoughts for him. 'What you're looking at is the result of the semi-permanent Fold in space. When you hold a Fold closed, the space along it creases until the Fold is released, creating a Gate. To move through it just touch it, and you will be transported to the other end.'

Robert looked over at the tigers, both of whom looked extremely uncomfortable at the prospect. They viewed the Gate with some suspicion; they were tigers and were used to being in the Lyr. They had defined territories, they knew where the landmarks were and knew where the dangers could come from. The thought of leaving the Lyr for Earth made them uncomfortable; they would be out of their element in an unknown and possibly hostile land. Pradeep vocalised both his and Vidya's thoughts, 'Are you sure it's safe?'

'Of course it is, Pradeep,' said the Engineer. 'After all you don't think I'd send you through anything dangerous to anywhere where you weren't likely to succeed do you? With all the humans gone from Earth you should be perfectly alright. And Tokyo is very heavily built up so the chances of running into anything hostile in the way of local fauna is vanishingly remote.'

'Alright then,' Vidya said slowly, still wary as she and Pradeep joined Robert next to the Gate.

All three of them raised a limb, Robert his right arm, the tigers a forepaw each, and reached out. Try as he might Robert could not fight the urge to shut his eyes as he moved his fingers closer and closer, until finally they hesitatingly made contact with the Gate.

Robert and the tigers disappeared.

13

Another One Bites The Dust

The woman with the cane approaches the man as stealthily as possible. Either side, the tigers pad softly and deliberately closer, until they are within striking distance of him. He seems completely unaware of their presence his attention focussed on the screens in front of him. This was their only chance, to take him unawares and off guard. Any hint of their presence and the whole endeavour would be over.

Patient.

A large paw is put gently down on the floor.

Silent.

Backs arch in readiness.

Deliberate.

Hindquarters tense, filling with energy.

Purposeful.

Huge muscles power the tigers forward into the air, flying at the man whose attention is still elsewhere. A heartbeat from impact the man raises his arms either side of him, the tigers caught in mid pounce frozen in space. He turns to face her, the tigers turning with him.

'Naughty.'

Her heart sinks, crushed at the sight of him overpowering

her allies so effortlessly.

'Why?' She screams the question at him.

'Because I can.' He lifts his arms up and the tigers move with them.

She rushes at him, pulling the sword from the cane and swings it hard at him.

Surprised by this the man flinches backward, losing control for a single heartbeat, but long enough to drop the tigers and too long to stop the tip of the rapier sharp point digging a deep scratch in his cheek.

The tigers don't waste their second chance. As soon as they hit the ground they jump back up at the man, claws out meaning to stop him.

Despite the burning in his face the man is collected enough to stop one of the tigers again, this time throwing it forcefully against a wall. Bones break inside the animal as it smashes into the hard stone, and it falls in a heap on the ground. But its companion is too quick for the man and claws connect with flesh, removing all the fingers from the hand as they swipe past, scattering the digits over the floor.

The man sways from the attack. He looks at his ruined hand, an idiot expression of disbelief on his face as the tiger leaps up again. This time he is fast enough to stop the sharp fury as it flies toward him. He catches the second tiger centimetres from his face and cups his remaining hand, holding the tiger, now completely frozen and motionless in mid-air. The man returns his gaze to the woman with the sword-cane.

'There. Am I enough like him for you now? Have I done enough yet?'

She can't think of anything to say that will un-make what she has done, so she stays silent, but keeps her gaze, full of hatred and longing upon him.

'It was an easy choice, to take control, you know. After all, it seemed to be what you wanted, or at least what I had come to believe. But then maybe that is why you went to him? For the power he commanded? You must have known what he was planning, surely? So why then, Eirian? Why? Why him?' The man's expression and body language change, soften almost, as he remembers.

'I...' she begins. 'He was so different then, or at least he pretended well enough for me not to know the difference. I thought he wanted to help the world, and I wanted to be part of that. He was so seductive. I suppose it *was* his power. I did not plan on... I mean it was an accident that I...'

'An accident?' The woman realises that she has made a terrible error for the second time. 'You threw our partnership, our marriage away *accidentally*?' He spits the term back at her.

'I didn't want you to do this. Not to become this. I never meant to hurt you!' she pleads desperately appealing to whatever remaining shred of what he had once been.

'Hurt? Me? You haven't hurt me, you've liberated me. I am free to act as I will, and I have the power now to do so. And if you truly want to see hurt,' he continues, 'just take a look at your friend here.'

With that he thrusts his hand upwards, fast and hard. The tiger's immobile form reacts similarly, propelled upward, toward the hard ceiling as if shot from a gun. There is a sickening wet crunching noise as the tiger crashes into the ceiling.

The woman raises the sword above her head to strike again. He smirks as he shakes his head at her. 'Strike me and your friend will surely fall to its death.'

The woman with the sword hesitates, unsure. She has to stop him, but can't sacrifice her friend. She has lost so much already. The sword wobbles in her hand, her grip on it suddenly not so sure.

'Weak.'

She can't do it.

'Pathetic.'

'BASTARD!' she retorts.

He shrugs.

She looks across at the broken form of her friend, blood oozing from its eyes and ears, then up at the paralysed, impotent animal in the air. 'Do. It.' is all the frozen tiger can whisper.

With a scream of fury and sorrow the woman slashes at the man's hand, neatly removing it from his arm.

The force holding the tiger in the air vanishes and the woman barely has time to throw herself underneath the falling animal and break its fall with her own body. There is a hard, dull crack as they collide, but neither of them dies.

An echo of the cracking noise repeated itself several times before Eirian realised that she had been remembering. The noise came again and again and it took her several seconds to locate the source of it as her door.

As her fingers closed around the pommel of her cane she closed her eyes and gave a small, determined shake of her head. She let the cane fall from her grip and tried to rise. She had not got a metre from the sofa when the pain shot through her from her hip, causing her to cry out. She tried to take another step, but as soon as her weight shifted the pain came again. It was all she could do to not fall over as, lip bitten hard, she returned to her prop. Angry and defeated she crossed her living area, leaning the whole time on the thin wooden support, wiping away the moisture at the edges of her eyes as she went. The knocking was still insistent and wasn't going to stop until its demands were met. The Engineer peered through the small spyhole in the door. Standing outside, still rapping his knuckles on the door was Verun.

Dammit! Not him, not now.

Gathering her wits and shaking the final remnants of her memories from her mind, the Engineer opened the door. 'Hello Mahatma. What can I do for you today?' she asked as pleasantly as she could, using Verun's self-appointed title.

The Engineer and Verun existed in an uneasy truce, her morals compelling her to tolerate Verun's excessive outbursts, and he enduring the inherently large bias toward the Engineer amongst the vast majority of the refugees. It was a relationship that was repeatedly strained, mostly by Verun and especially around the time of tithe.

'Architect,' he replied with a curt nod of his head, using a title that the Engineer had at one time been celebrated and respected for, but now came equipped with barbs. It was a deliberate wound, and both knew it. The Engineer for her part did not flinch. Verun had been calling her that for decades, and while it still stung her she was damned if she was ever going to give him the satisfaction of seeing it in her eyes. Instead, she invited him in.

'I presume you wish to consult with me on some matter?' she asked as matter-of-factly as she could. Verun's intellect was quick and sharp and he never did anything without a purpose. She would have to be careful; she could not afford the luxury of allowing herself to get angry with Verun, not now with events unfolding the way they were. 'Please sit,' she indicated with an open hand.

'If it all the same to you, I will remain standing. What I have to say will not take long. I understand that we have a visitor to the Bridge.' Verun stood with his arms folded behind his back.

The Engineer said nothing. Instead she sat down on the armchair facing Verun, put her cane to one side and crossed her legs. She had been half expecting this conversation would take place ever since Robert's arrival. She was just glad that he was safely out of the way on Earth for the time being. She was not about to prompt Verun; whatever he had to say he would say.

'I also understand that this visitor is under your protection.'

'Everyone on the Bridge is under my protection,' replied the Engineer. 'Even you.' She nodded in Verun's direction, indicating her desire not to be confrontational.

'I am further led to believe that two of Akash's children are accompanying him.'

'A great many people come and go from the Bridge, most of their own volition. You know I grant free sanctuary to any who desire it.'

'You did not answer my questions.' Verun uncrossed his arms from behind himself and re-folded them over his chest.

'I was not aware you had been asking questions. You are merely stating what you believe you know.' The Engineer chose her words carefully, as not to give Verun any more information than he had already worked out himself.

'Very well. Let me state something else. When Ballisargon discovers this… singleton he will not be happy. I imagine he will attack the Bridge, our home.'

Verun obviously had something in mind regarding Robert and was not going to volunteer the information if she remained so affable. She decided to push the direction of the conversation, deliberately goading him, but keeping her tone even. 'You speak for him now Mahatma? I did not realise your relationship with him had grown so …cordial.'

Verun blistered at the remark and spat his reply at her. 'Listen to me *Architect.* Ballisargon will discover the missing boy whether you are hiding him or not, and when he does-'

'And when he does,' the Engineer cut in, 'he will do what exactly? Send his pets? Inflict more nightmares on us? The Bridge is sanctuary, we are all quite safe here. You have my word on that. Now I feel that I have taken enough of your time. I have matters to attend to and would not wish to detain you further while I deal with them.'

Verun stood silently for a moment. He had failed to gain any more information about Robert and he was angry with himself for it. 'This is not the end of this matter,' he said, jabbing a finger at the Engineer as he Moved back to one of the upper tiers.

Rude to the last. What bothered Eirian more though was

that Verun was probably correct.

For several hours Eirian sat in solitude playing the meeting over and over in her head, looking for any hidden meaning in what Verun had said. She found she was forced to take him at his word. If he hadn't already, Ballisargon would eventually find out that Robert was missing from the population of the Earth. That something was amiss, Eirian had no doubt that Ballisargon was aware of, but the *what* exactly he was most likely still in the dark. *I must proceed as if he knows anyway.* Eirian was not looking forward to Ballisargon realising that someone, especially Robert, had slipped past him.

Eirian checked her timepiece. Robert had been gone nearly twelve hours. She was mildly surprised that he had been gone that long. He must have checked out over half the potential locations by now; after all, the Gate was placed well within walking distance of five of them. It would be unfortunate, but not outside the bounds of possibility that the software was located in one of the other three. *Patience,* she counselled herself. *He'll be fine. He has the tigers with him, and is currently well out of the reach of Ballisargon.*

During the next twelve hours Eirian variously slept lightly and fitfully. She could not relax easily knowing that Robert was still on Earth. He had been gone longer than she had expected, and she was becoming increasingly worried that something had gone wrong.

She was struck by inspiration. While it would be impossible to locate Robert for the same reason that Ballisargon had missed him, the tigers would show up in much the same way as a human would; they were after all self-aware and therefore should be easy enough to find.

Back in the control room she typed in a couple of commands, and the top-down view of the Tokyo cityscape scrolled left, then down before moving right and back up to its starting place. Eirian waited while her systems interpreted the data. She was rewarded by two faint green spots near the third likely site.

Two questions struck her at once: *Why were the tiger's signals a lot weaker than she was expecting?* and *Why after twenty-four hours was Robert only at the third site?*

What could be the cause of that?

She pondered over this for a few minutes, hypothesising and discarding various explanations before a thought entered her head. She turned the thought over in her mind, examining it from all possible angles and points of view. With a sense of mounting horror Eirian realised that she had the answer to both her questions.

She had made a very very big mistake, and urgently needed to put it right.

Verun had been furious from his conversation with the soft-minded Architect. He rose from his private chamber, and stepped out into the communal room that the rest of the Hecatomb lived in. 'Has there been any word from the other tiers? Any more sightings of the boy?' he barked.

The quiet murmurs of conversation died away at his words. It was clear to the devotees that their Mahatma was still very angry, and none of them wished to incur his wrath.

'Well?' he shouted.

A slightly built teenager, little older than Robert, approached him timidly, his head low in supplication. 'No, Mahatma, there have been no more sightings of the boy. We can find no trace of him anywhere. It is as if he has vanished.' The boy cowered, fully expecting to be punished for brining the Mahatma such bad news.

Something the neophyte said stuck in Verun's mind. *Vanished.* 'What about his companions, the tigers?' he asked.

'It would appear that the tigers have also not been sighted since the boy was last seen. It is as if they had, all three of them, disappeared.'

Verun paused. *So, the tigers were also missing.*

He rose to his feet. 'I am leaving you for a time,' he said to his followers. 'I expect to be gone only half a day at the most. I expect you all to continue your duties in my absence. Pytr here is to be considered my right arm while I am gone.' He indicated to the young boy, who looked startled at his rather rapid promotion.

Verun left the room with a Move, leaving the Hecatomb looking at Pytr for direction. He looked as bewildered as the rest of them as to what had just happened.

Verun calculated that he had perhaps two hours to reach the tithe before the Molluscs had taken them all. He had better be quick.

Appearing at the lakeshore he set off along the well-trodden path, to the site of the tithe offering.

Roen spoke to the Engineer in his dimly lit living area after she had arrived seeking his counsel on the Hecatomb.

'My sources in the Hecatomb indicate that Verun has set off somewhere, less than half a day's travel. I believe he is rendezvousing with the tithe. To what end I do not know, but I know of his interest in Robert, so fear that this action is directly related to him.'

The Engineer nodded hesitantly, her expression blank. 'Yes,' she half-muttered to herself. Then more confidently, 'Dear friend, I cannot leave the Bridge. My presence is required to keep the Gate open should Robert return. I almost don't want to ask you...'

Roen lifted his chin from its resting place on his clenched hands. 'Nonsense. You more than anyone have every right to seek any assistance that anyone on the Bridge can provide.'

'Thank you Roen. I am afraid I must return to my vigil. Do not underestimate the Molluscs. If there is any sign of them return immediately. We don't need another pointless death.'

After the Engineer had left, Roen Moved to a dozen

different locations around the Bridge's upper tiers, speaking to and searching for a number of his friends. Once he had explained the situation almost all of them, man or woman agreed with him in his plan to try and stop Verun. If Ballisargon learnt of Robert's existence, or more importantly where he currently was, then Robert would almost certainly be defenceless. Time was very much of the essence as they set off into the desert.

Verun arrived at the site of the tithe to find the sacrifice about to take place. Still tired from the repeated Moves to cover the distance from the Bridge, he did little to intervene while his followers were taken, one by one by the Molluscs.

Ballisargon had despatched three Molluscs to take the tithe, and they wasted little time in surrounding them in a triangular formation. The majority of them stood almost hypnotised by the presence of the Molluscs. Two of them fell to their knees, weeping and begging for mercy, claiming that there had been a mistake. Another tried to run and break through the barrier the Molluscs had made with their bodies. Verun felt a stab of disgust at this overt display of weakness from his followers; he would have to be firmer with his discipline when he returned to the Bridge.

The woman that tried to run attempted to vault over one of the tapering ends of the Mollusc that barred her way. But the Mollusc flexed its body upward, catching her in its flesh and pulling her into its body. Then she started to scream.

Their fugue broken by the high-pitched howl, the remaining members of the tithe tried to run. Most of them collided blindly with each other, ricocheting off into the unyielding hardness of the Molluscs, where they too shared the fate of their companion; drawn into the living body of the creature only to slowly disappear in screaming agony as the Molluscs ingested them.

Two of the tithe managed to get out and past the Molluscs, but their efforts were for naught too. Verun watched as two of the Molluscs pursued the remainder of his followers into the desert. The last he heard of them was a high-pitched scream, not a woman's, then silence.

Content that the tithe had been taken, the remaining Mollusc set off Keepward. Verun approached the beast from what he took to be its rear. He had never seen a Mollusc at close range before and was revulsed and awed in equal measure. The Mollusc stopped its movement as it sensed his presence. Instead of turning around, it flowed back toward him, seeming to move through its own body. Verun stumbled backwards afraid for himself as the Mollusc approached.

'Wait,' he shouted at it while holding both arms up in front of him in a gesture of supplication, hoping it would understand. 'I have news of the missing boy.'

The Mollusc acted as if it had not heard him, or was ignoring him, and continued to draw nearer. By now Verun could smell it; for a moment the scent was unfamiliar to him. It was a rancid sweet smell and it made Verun gag, his body convulsed with dry retches. His sense of panic mounted as he collapsed on the desert floor, doubled up from the spasms in his stomach. He realised that he was about to die, alone and afraid in the desert at the hands of the man he had spent decades of his life trying to placate.

The Mollusc flowed over him, and Verun felt its cold hard flesh cover his body completely. It crushed him from all sides, smothering him, pressing hard and heavy against his fragile frame. Verun felt his bones begin to break inside himself. The first to go were his delicate ribs. Then his arms and legs broke, twisted and torn in different directions within the Mollusc's powerful body. The instant the Mollusc touched his skin and clothing its powerful digestive enzymes set to work absorbing him. The result for Verun was an agony of tearing through his entire being; the protection his clothing offered neutralised after being absorbed almost instantly.

He opened his mouth partly to scream and partly to try and draw in one final breath. All he was rewarded with was the Mollusc's body flowing into his mouth, blocking his airway completely. Now the searing came from inside as well.

Amid the pain that was now Verun's entire world he became dimly aware of a sensation in his skull. The Mollusc's digestive system had reached his brain, and was beginning to absorb that. His memories and knowledge were drained from him and into the Mollusc.

As he lost consciousness, he realised that the Mollusc now knew what he had known and that Ballisargon cared not for the sacrifices he had offered him. Verun too had now given himself pointlessly to the Molluscs, and Ballisargon.

Almost exactly twenty-four hours earlier Robert, along with the tigers arrived on Earth through the Gate, completely unaware of the events that would unfold around him back in the Lyr due to his disappearance from the Bridge. He was also unaware as to the very real danger he would face on Earth from a very unexpected source during the next day.

Even if Robert had been aware of all that was to occur in his absence, he was far more concerned as to why there was a heavy covering of fine red sand over everything he could see in front of him.

14

Welcome To The Jungle

'Are you sure this is the right place?' Vidya asked, surveying the scene that lay before her, Pradeep and Robert.

Robert looked around; everywhere there was red sand. It was heaped up against the tall steel and glass buildings, reaching up their sides for a few metres, making the tower blocks appear to be growing out of it; it covered the construction vehicles that were parked beside some earthworks, like snow on a particularly strange winter's day; it dusted the now dark, dead neon signs obscuring the colours beneath; and it piled into small dunes where the streets widened at intersections. It was if the Lyr had followed them.

'I don't understand,' said Robert. 'I've never been to Japan, but I'm pretty sure it shouldn't look like this.' He knelt on the ground and brushed at the sand with his hand, sweeping it away until he found the tarmac of the road beneath it. The sand was nearly ten centimetres deep. The Earth he was expecting was still there, underneath its desert coating.

Robert blinked twice, and the map scrolled around in front of him, zooming in and out until it had located where he and the tigers were. After a few seconds of looking up and round, then back at his surroundings, Robert reckoned he had it figured out. 'I think we go that way.' He pointed down a street.

Checking the rucksack was secure, Robert stood still and tried to make a Fold with is mind. He pictured the area on the map he wanted to go to and concentrated on it. However, when he tried to bring *there* to his *here* he found that he had not Moved a centimetre.

'What?' he started, then checking himself, 'Oh yeah, it doesn't work here does it.'

'What doesn't?' asked Pradeep.

'Uh nothing. Forget I said anything,' Robert said feeling slightly foolish at his mistake. 'I guess we're walking then.' Robert set off, leading the way down along the sand-carpeted street. Pradeep looked over at Vidya, who just shrugged. Both tigers set off following Robert a slight distance behind, their eyes constantly scanning one way then the next, their ears standing to attention on their large heads. The tigers had never seen so many structures as large as the dozens and dozens of skyscrapers that sat on either side of the wide street, and at every intersection they came to.

'How do you people manage in somewhere like this,' Pradeep said. 'You can hardly see the sky; I mean it's just a strip of blue in all this grey. And you can only really see in one direction at once; how are you supposed to use your peripheral vision when you can't see more than five metres on either side? There's almost no point in having it if you can't use it. And there's nowhere to hide; how are you supposed to sneak up on prey with all these hard, reflective surfaces? They'd see you coming a mile off. It's like being at the bottom of a well!'

'Have you never been in a city before then? What about the one I was in in the Lyr?'

'We were born after that and all the other cities were razed by Ballisargon. He destroyed all of the previous civilisation when he rose to power. The Lyr as a wilderness is all we've ever known.'

Robert thought about what Pradeep had said. He supposed that to the tigers Tokyo, or for that matter London, New York or any other large city would be a totally alien environment. 'I guess you're not meant to live in cities,' he said.

'I'm not sure that it does you humans much good either,' said Pradeep. 'All crushed in on top of each other, no space to run or be free.'

'Some people like it,' defended Robert.

'Maybe,' replied Pradeep sounding none too convinced. He was a tiger and tigers were not given to large gatherings of their kind, so he struggled to see Robert's point of view. He looked at Vidya for backup, but her expression was unreadable. He opened his maw to say something, but Vidya's look gave him pause. Instead he changed the subject, not wanting to irritate Robert further. 'How are we doing? Nearly at the first location?'

Robert welcomed the chance not to have to defend the way people did things. Sure, he wasn't happy with everything people did, especially wars and famine and all the bad things they did to each other, but was feeling he had to defend his species as best he could. 'I think it's that building on the left,' he said scrutinising the map which hung in his vision, then pointing out the glass edifice that stood a little way off from them.

'Fair enough,' replied the tiger. 'You're the Earth expert after all.'

The offices of Kokoro-Tek were the first location on the map. Robert leant on the brass handle of the heavy glass doors that led into the reception area. As the door slid open the sand that was piled up against it cascaded in to the foyer. 'Good job there's no-one around to see us make all this mess,' he said guiltily as he walked into the lobby, treading sand into the fine carpet. He held the door open for the tigers, who obligingly slunk in through the gap.

Robert looked at the boards above the reception desk for a clue as to where to go. It was unsurprisingly, all in Japanese.

'Can you read that?' asked Pradeep, indicating the signage that Robert was looking at with a tilt of his head.

'No. Let's hope what the Engineer gave me,' he pointed to his eyes, 'is up to the job.' Robert blinked twice again and looked at the notice board. The Japanese script seemed to wobble for a moment before it changed. To Robert's eyes it was the same sign, but now it was in English. *Double wow!* 'It looks like we need the twenty-seventh floor. That's where the research lab is.'

'Twenty-seven!' said Pradeep. While he was physically very fit he did not relish the thought of walking up that many stairs. 'What do you think Vidya?' he asked his sister.

Vidya turned to her brother and shook her head and made a face.

Robert wasn't looking forward to walking all that way either, so he bounded over to the lifts. As soon as he had pressed the button he realised that it was not going to work. 'There's no electricity,' he said sheepishly. 'Look's like were walking after all.'

Forty minutes, twenty-seven flights of stairs and three rest stops later, Robert and the tigers reached the right floor. Pushing their way through the fire door that closed off the stairwell Pradeep said, 'Let's hope this is the right place. I don't much fancy doing *that* seven more times.'

On the other side lay a high-tech laboratory of computers that almost made the Engineer's control room back on the Bridge look outdated. Silver desk after silver desk filled the room, while the walls were pristine white. Every desk had at least three huge flat screen monitors on it, almost enclosing the working space. Sat between the monitors was a sleek keyboard and wireless mouse.

'Wow,' said Robert. Immediately he set to work. Retrieving the power supply unit from the rucksack, he pulled the nearest plug out of the wall and swapped the power unit for it. Nothing happened. 'I thought the lights might come on or something,' he said.

'Try one of the computers,' volunteered Pradeep.

Robert wasted no time in plonking himself on one of the chairs. He pushed the ON button and waited. The LED on the front of the computer obligingly came on, as did the keyboard light. 'We have power,' he said.

Fishing the memory stick out of the rucksack he waited for the computer to fully power up. Once he was presented with a log on screen (the lens-screens still translating the Japanese on the display) he plugged the small piece of electronics the Engineer had given him into the machine, and waited.

The computer read the contents of the memory stick, and suddenly reacted as if it was in pain; the screen flashed on and off rapidly, while strange characters (certainly not Japanese or English) were displayed in seemingly random clumps and collections all over the display. Lines, squiggles and blocks of colour all appeared and disappeared amid the chaos and turmoil in the PC. After a minute or so of this the computer settled down, displaying, this time in English, a message:

>>> Scanning local computer. Please wait...

Then the message was replaced with:

>>> Software not located. Extending scan...

At this point every other computer in the lab switched itself on. The sudden increase in activity in the room caught all three off guard. Robert felt that someone was going to walk in and catch them stealing from the lab. But no-one came and the computer carried on with its quiet scan. Eventually the message on the screen said:

>>> Software not present at this location

Robert sighed a little, trying to hide his disappointment, and pulled the memory stick, which was quite hot, from the socket, popped the cap back on it, then dropped it back into the rucksack. 'Strike one,' he said to the tigers.

'Oh well,' said Pradeep. 'Maybe we'll be lucky with the next place. What do you think Vidya?'

Vidya sat there quietly.

'Are you OK?' asked Robert. 'I noticed that you haven't said anything since we got here. Earth I mean.'

Vidya looked at Robert, slightly blankly before replying, 'I can't explain it, but something has been bothering me for a while now. I think I feel hungry.'

Over twenty-four hours after Vidya had her first hunger pangs, Roen and his group had reached the area where the Molluscs normally came to collect the tithe. The scene was not heartening. Scattered here and there lay the remnants of the tithe; a scrap of clothing, a torn piece of cloth or a single sandal. Where one of the tithe had been wearing or carrying a brooch or something else indigestible to the Molluscs, it sat on the desert floor, discarded inside a crystalline solid, like a fly in amber.

Roen surveyed the scene. It was obvious that the Molluscs had been and gone, the tithe taken effortlessly. But had Verun been here at the time? Roen paced round, kicking up the tattered rags, turning over the sand in the hunt for something. His foot kicked something hard, buried just under the sand. He worked it loose with the front of his shoe. It was a Mollusc pellet, like the many others that were lying on the sand.

Roen knelt down and freed the crystal from the sand. He picked it up and peered at it. Something glinted inside. He reached for his knife, and within a minute had opened a fissure in the crystal, and in another minute later he had his prize.

In his palm sat the gold pin that Verun used to fasten his headdress. They were too late.

Hours before Roen made his unwelcome discovery, the Mollusc that had taken Verun had made its way back to Ballisargon's Keep. Once there its master had interrogated it heavily with the device constructed for extracting information held within the Mollusc's memory. It was not a gentle process, and always resulted in death for the Mollusc concerned; the knowledge dragged from the living tissue and cells of the creature.

Strapped and chained down, in a room specially secured against the Mollusc's limited ability to Move, Ballisargon attached the sensors to the creature. Barbed needles sunk into its flesh, connected via a system of wires to the device that Ballisargon now strapped to his own head. The needles threaded out thin filaments of metal into the body of the Mollusc, snaking through its flesh, marbling the Mollusc like veins in blue cheese.

Ballisargon sat down in a sturdily built heavy wooden chair. He strapped his legs in place with the solid steel clasps set into the legs of the chair and then secured his left arm with his right. He placed the bit between his back teeth, holding his jaw apart. Picking up the controller for the knowledge transfer device, he clamped his right arm into the time-delayed restraint and pressed the button to activate the machine.

Power shot through the needles and into the Mollusc, which bucked wildly against its restraints. It thrashed and shook as the electrical signals from the thin metal threads bit into its cells and began reading the knowledge stored within them. The process was far from swift.

For the only time in its life the Mollusc vocalised a sound, the stress of the process forcing a noise from the otherwise mute creature. 'UUWWHH!' was the Mollusc's first and last utterance before it expired from the shock.

The knowledge wave hit Ballisargon. Insertion was not an easy process. His body forced itself against the restraints as his mind burnt with downloaded knowledge. If not for the bit in his mouth he would have bitten his tongue in half. For nearly a minute the memories of the Mollusc flooded into his mind before abruptly they stopped.

Ballisargon slumped forward against the metal hoops holding him in place. The bit fell from between his jaws as his head fell forward. A long trail of saliva hung from the corner of his mouth, and pooled on the floor in front of him.

Slowly he regained consciousness as the time-delayed restraint activated and freed his right arm. Groggily he punched the release mechanism on his left arm, then he freed his legs. Swaying slightly he waited for his vision to come back into focus before he attempted to stand.

Ballisargon did not think twice about the sacrifice of one of his Molluscs. They were merely tools to do a job; discardable when their usefulness was at an end. It was unfortunate that one had to be used up in such a way but it was an inevitability of the process. The limited intelligence capacity of the Mollusc coupled with the primitive structure of its mind meant that such measures were necessary. On more advanced creatures Ballisargon had more refined and subtle methods of retrieving information.

Rising unsteadily to his feet he accessed the twice stolen memories. *So that's where the boy was.*

'What do you mean, hungry?' asked Pradeep.

'Don't be dense Pradeep. You remember what feeling hungry is like don't you?'

'Well of course, but I've not felt it for years.'

'It's this place, this planet. I think it's affecting me.'

'What do you mean, affecting you?'

Robert listened to the back and forth of the tigers' conversation. It was the most he'd heard Vidya speak since they had all arrived on Earth a few hours ago. Suddenly he heard his name. '…about you Robert?'

'Sorry Pradeep, what did you say?'

'I asked if you were feeling the same.'

Robert closed his eyes and concentrated on his own stomach. It had been days since he had eaten but he had been in the Lyr the whole time. 'Yes. Only a little, but it's definitely there.'

'Well,' said Pradeep, 'let's see if we can find something to eat on the way to the next site. I am sure twenty-seven flights of stairs gave us all an appetite.' He padded off to the door to the stairwell. 'Coming?'

Robert retrieved the power supply unit from the wall. All the computers in the room died simultaneously, the screens going blank in unison. 'Come on Vidya,' he urged the female tiger.

Vidya sat there as if she had not heard Robert for a second, then she jerked back to alertness. 'Sorry, I was miles away,' she said as she followed Robert and her brother down the long flight of steps to the lobby and then outside to the street.

'Where next?' asked Pradeep.

Robert indicated where he intended to go to next. It was the nearest of the four red dots they had not visited, and Pradeep agreed that it was the next logical choice.

As they walked, Pradeep padded up to Robert's side, leaving Vidya some small distance behind. 'I'm concerned about Vidya. She's becoming …distant somehow.' The tiger struggled for the words. 'I can't put my paw on it but she seems distracted by something. What, I don't know, but she is definitely acting strangely for her. Can we try talking to her a bit more? Try to keep her mind focussed on the here and now?'

'Sure,' replied Robert. He walked over to Vidya who was staring absently at a point somewhere in the middle distance. Robert looked at where he thought she was looking but could see nothing that should distract her. He shook her gently by the shoulder with a friendly, 'Hey, Vidya what about…' but that was as far as he got.

Vidya whipped round a massive paw which caught Robert full in the chest. He flew backwards onto the ground, sprawling in the sand. Fortunately for him she had not had her claws out at the time, but Robert was still knocked off his feet and heavily winded.

Vidya sprang to all fours and approached Robert's prone form purposefully, her eyes narrowing to focus on him.

Pradeep was between them in an instant. 'Vidya!' he yelled. 'What in blazes do you think you're doing?'

Hearing her brother Vidya looked up, then realising what she had been doing stopped walking immediately. 'Robert… I'm sorry, I don't know… I…' was all she was able to stutter out.

Pradeep, without taking his eyes off his sister asked, 'Robert, are you alright?'

Robert put a hand to his chest. It was sore where Vidya's paw had connected with him and he would have a large bruise there, but he was otherwise intact. He winced as he tried to sit up and in between coughs and gasps said, 'I think so.' He leaned over to one side to look round Pradeep at Vidya. She had sat back down on her hind legs, her tail curled round in front of her.

'Back up Robert. Put a little distance between us,' Pradeep advised.

Robert did as he was asked and not taking his eyes of Vidya got unsteadily to his feet and backed away a couple of metres. Not too far though that he couldn't hear what the tigers were saying to each other.

'I don't know Pradeep. When Robert touched me I

couldn't stop myself. It was like I was watching me from the outside somehow. I knew I was going to do it, but couldn't stop it.'

'You could have killed him!'

'It was all I could do to not extend my claws.'

'Luckily for him.'

'Let me apologise. I feel terrible.'

'Try to stay focussed. Please.' Pradeep moved aside and let Vidya pass.

Vidya padded deliberately slowly and as unthreateningly as she could toward Robert. When she had walked past her brother, Robert unconsciously took a step backward and reached for his necklace. Vidya stopped. 'I'm sorry Robert. I don't know why I did that. I really don't.' Her head was bowed; she was visibly torn up at having injured him.

Robert was still shaken badly by Vidya's attack but took a hesitant step forward, in a deliberate show of forgiveness. 'That's OK,' he said nervously. 'I shouldn't have startled you like that. I was only going to ask you what you thought about the next location to check.'

'Can I come over there?' she asked. Vidya's attack on Robert had left her feeling she had shattered the bond of trust between them, and she needed it to be strong. She would do nothing that made Robert uncomfortable.

'Sure,' Robert replied, nodding gently. He was dusting down his jeans as Vidya drew up alongside him.

'So, where are we going next?' she asked meekly.

'I reckon here,' Robert replied, pointing in the air to the next location displayed on the map.

'If you think so, then OK.'

'Do you still want to find something to eat on the way there?'

'If you wouldn't mind. I seem to be getting hungrier all the time. And I'm sure Pradeep is feeling the same by now.'

Even though it was not a long walk to the next site they passed nothing in the way of a butcher's shop, a restaurant or even a pet food store where Robert could have found the tigers something to eat. Even Robert's stomach was beginning to rumble by the time they had found the building they were looking for. This time it was a much more modest affair than the grand steel and glass building of Kokoro-Tek. It was a small electrical hardware store, the grilled windows chock full of old hi-fi's, radios, computers, portable televisions and numerous other items.

'Are you sure this is the place?' asked Pradeep.

'I think so,' replied Robert, a little unsure. 'Let's have a look inside.'

Inside the shop there was a glass counter, also stuffed to near bursting point with gadgets. Tall display cases stood on the floor, watches and handheld computers sitting on the now stationary turntables. Behind the counter, running from floor to ceiling were boxes upon boxes of every conceivable electrical item imaginable. All in all it was a tight squeeze for one boy and two fully-grown tigers.

Still feeling guilty Vidya offered to stay outside to give Robert a bit more room to work in.

Robert did not want Vidya to feel excluded in any way, but had to agree that there was not enough room in the shop for the three of them, and he was uncomfortable with the thought of Pradeep being outside while he was in here on his own with Vidya. He felt terrible for feeling that way, but in the end common sense prevailed and he reluctantly acquiesced to Vidya's request.

She walked out of the shop and sat on the sand covered pavement outside. Robert could see the back of her head and shoulders through the glass door. He turned to Pradeep. 'I can't believe this can be the right place. I mean, look at it, it's just a shop. The last place was really advanced, this place is nothing. I can't even see a computer, just the till.'

'Maybe there's a back room?'

Robert looked around. There was a door leading out of the back of the shop, but he had assumed it led to a storeroom. 'Let's have a look then.' He pushed his way through the door into what turned out to be a storeroom after all. Boxed televisions stood stacked up alongside DVD players and video recorders. 'I'm not unboxing a computer,' Robert moaned. 'There must be one plugged in here somewhere.'

He and Pradeep searched the storeroom for a few more minutes before Pradeep found something. 'Over here Robert. Behind this pile of boxes, look, there's a door.'

Robert looked where Pradeep was indicating. Hidden behind a tall pile of cardboard boxes WAS a door, its outline barely visible. 'Shall we?' Pradeep asked, tilting his head toward the boxes.

Pradeep put his shoulder and Robert leant his hands against the boxes and pushed. The pile was lighter than they had expected and the boxes slid easily out of the way to reveal the door. However there was no handle. 'How do we get in?' asked Robert.

Pradeep lifted a paw to the door and knocked on it gently. It sounded hollow. 'Easy,' he said. Pradeep backed up a couple of metres and sprang at the door, his shoulder slamming into it. The door was no match for a tiger colliding with it and flew inwards off its hinges, clattering noisily on the floor. 'Ta-da!' said Pradeep, feigning a bow.

'Show off,' joked Robert as he stepped through to the dark room on the other side of the now empty doorway. 'Can you see anything in here?' he called to Pradeep.

'Off to your right. There's a desk with a computer sitting on it. Underneath there is a spare power socket.'

Robert made his way in the dark room, his hands out in front of him until he collided gently with the desk Pradeep had mentioned. He fumbled in the rucksack for the power unit, then under the desk, searching for the power socket Pradeep had mentioned.

'There. No right a bit, there. No, left a touch. Up, there,' Pradeep said.

Robert scraped the power unit against the wall left, right up and down until the pins sank into matching holes. Immediately the computer on the desk came to life.

'There, you've got it,' Pradeep called from outside the room.

Robert picked himself up off the floor, and now that the computer was on there was a little more light in the room. He repeated his actions from Kokoro-Tek with the memory stick, only to be rewarded with the same message on the screen.

He extracted it from the computer and put it back in the rucksack. Once again as he retrieved the power unit the computer died. 'Strike two,' was all he said as he left the room and walked past Pradeep.

Pradeep followed Robert out of the storeroom back into the main shop. He looked out through the glass door and frowned. He could no longer see the orange and black back of his sister. 'Wait here,' he said to Robert as he pushed out of the shop door into the street.

Robert, unsure as to what was happening waited. Presently Pradeep came back in to the shop, a hunted look on his large face. 'Vidya's gone missing.'

Ballisargon cleaned himself up on the way to his version of the Engineer's control room. It had been built by Eirian over a century ago, and was every bit as advanced as its counterpart on the Bridge. From his control room Ballisargon managed the Moves that shifted the populations of planets from their homeworlds and into his generators. He did not completely understand its inner workings, but Eirian had performed her duties well and the technology that powered the generators was more than capable of self-repair in the event of wear and tear. One thing Ballisargon had learnt however was to re-program some of the systems to perform tasks they had not been designed for. Like opening and closing a Gate for instance.

He sat at one of the desks and slipped his hands into the control mechanism he had had her construct. Each of his fingers and thumbs slid into a solid metal ring; every one made of a different, highly radioactive, heavy element. Ballisargon had long been immune to their radiation; another thank you he owed Eirian, if Ballisargon had been the kind of person to say thank you which he was not. The rings toxicity made them unusable to anyone but him.

He could of course have had a simpler process for controlling the systems of his Keep, but the mechanism of finger twitches and flicks he had to execute while using the rings was both deliberately complicated and ostentatious. The rings fitted him perfectly, both physically and intellectually.

Lifting his hands and the rings free of their resting place, Ballisargon turned to a monitor, and flicked his left hand up then across. A view of the Earth glowed into life on it. Turning his hands over and over, while gently twitching his fingers, the image of the Earth spun round on the screen. Ballisargon stared intently at the representation of Robert's home planet, feeling through his fingers for the signals he was seeking.

After a few minutes he had a potential location. Zooming in on the north Pacific he targeted the islands of Japan, then spent another five minutes pinpointing where exactly the life signs were coming from. He was rewarded with two fairly bright green spots, moving slowly through the streets of Tokyo, stopping occasionally in seemingly specific locations. *Why were there two signals?* Ballisargon had not been expecting to find one signal let alone two, after all the boy had been missed first time around so there would be no reason to expect him to show up again. But two, that was puzzling.

He searched Verun's memories. *The tigers.* Ballisargon postulated that it was most likely Eirian had sent them with the boy. It certainly fitted in with how she thought. So there were three of them on Earth. It made no matter to him.

He thought about Moving the two signals he could see directly into the generators, then dismissed it. He did not want the unbalance of a couple of tigers, not when he had finally acquired a population large enough for the first stage of the Plan. He thought some more and the vaguest hint of smile crept over his face. He had a much better way of dealing with them all.

He reasoned that they would have got to Earth using a Gate; Eirian liked to play it safe so she would not have risked trying to locate and Move them back, so a Gate was the most logical thing open to her.

Flexing both his index fingers caused the display to alter. The two green signals disappeared, replaced by a sea of colours, like a depth chart on a map. Swirling blobs sat one inside the other, shifting and moving, like oil on water. Ballisargon curled and uncurled the little finger on his right hand and the display zoomed in on one dark spot in the sea of colour. *There. That was it. Time to have some fun.*

Ballisargon moved his hand in front of the spot, and clenched it into a fist. Immediately the dark spot began to waver, before disappearing altogether. It reappeared a second later, but was significantly smaller and weaker than it had been before. He clenched his fist over it again. Once more it disappeared, only this time it did not come back.

Openly smiling now, he spread the fingers of his left hand wide, and a separate dark patch appeared where the first had been. As far as the boy and his pets would be concerned it was exactly the same Gate as the one they had come through originally.

Ballisargon's smile broke into a broad grin when he thought about what would be waiting for the little boy and his bodyguards when they stepped back through the Gate. He began to chuckle to himself and wished he could be there to see them when they arrived back in the Lyr. Then inspiration struck him. Why should he wait for them to stumble into his trap when he could send them a little surprise at the same time? The answer was of course that he shouldn't.

Ballisargon turned back to the monitor with its image of Tokyo on it. Reaching out with his left hand he turned it over then clenched his fist. There was an almost imperceptible rumble throughout the Keep as something large and transparent was Moved from the Lyr to Earth.

Up on the screen, near the two green spots now appeared a third one. Much larger, slightly fainter than the other two, but definitely there.

Turning away from the screens Ballisargon slipped the control rings back into their resting place and walked out of his control room, still chuckling to himself as he headed back to his throne room.

The party that had set out to search for Verun, having failed, headed back to the Bridge to inform the Engineer that it was most likely that he had been taken by the Molluscs.

They Moved rapidly, driven principally by fear that the Molluscs would return, until they reached the edge of the lake. By then they barely had enough energy left to make the Move across the water to the base of the giant staircase that spiralled upwards inside the great stone pillar.

Once at the top of the staircase Roen told the rest of the party that he would speak to the Engineer alone, and thanked them for their assistance. For their part the rest of the group were relieved to be safely back home.

Roen knocked on the door to the Engineer's living quarters and waited. No response came so he knocked again. This time the Engineer replied. Roen was struck by the harried countenance she presented when the door was opened. The Engineer's normally well presented appearance was replaced by someone who looked like they had not had enough sleep. She was missing her suit jacket, and her blouse was partly untucked from the matching trousers.

'What's wrong?'

'The Gate,' she began, then, 'You'd better come in and see this.' The Engineer directed Roen into her house and ushered him through the living area to her control room muttering under her breath to herself the whole time. Roen only caught snatches of what she was saying, 'Should never have…' and 'How does he know…' and 'What if he's…' They reached the control room. 'Look,' the Engineer said directing Roen's gaze at the monitors.

Roen looked, but could not see what she was indicating. His knowledge of the Engineer's systems was patchy at best, and his grasp of remote interstellar scrying was even patchier. To him the screen just showed a collection of slowly swirling and undulating blobs of colour, some overlapping and overlaying each other. 'What am I seeing?' he asked.

The Engineer looked at Roen with disbelief. 'There!' she pointed at a darker patch on the screen. 'There man! Can't you see it?'

Roen looked again. There was a slightly indistinct dark smudge just left of centre on the screen. It was so small that it was easily lost in the greater mass of colour. 'What is it?' He felt foolish having to ask, but he did not know what information it was he was supposed to be gleaning from the image he was being shown.

The Engineer grabbed Roen hard by the shoulders and opened her mouth as if to shout at him, before she realised what she was doing. Her demeanour changed and softened as her rationality came back to her. She looked guiltily at her hands about Roen and, with a jerk, released her grip on her friend. 'I am sorry, Roen,' she said. 'I fear the worst for Robert. My thoughts are not as balanced as they could be.'

'Why? What has happened?'

'You see the dark patch, there on the display?'

Roen nodded.

'It is a Gate.'

'And? Didn't Robert go to Earth through the Gate?'

'He went to Earth through the Gate I set up, and that Gate was closed minutes ago by an external power source. The one you see there wasn't opened by me.'

The insinuation sank in to Roen. 'When you say external, you mean…'

'Who else in the Lyr has the technology to open a Gate? What I don't understand though is how he found out where Robert was. His totem should be shielding him. In fact I know it is, as I can only ever see Pradeep and Vidya's signals from Earth.'

'Verun,' was all Roen had to say and instantly the Engineer understood.

'You were too late.' It was a statement, not a question, to which Roen silently nodded his reply.

'Very well then, we must deal with the situation as it is,' said the Engineer finding new determination in the inevitability of the circumstances. 'We must try and find a way to aid Robert.'

'What about blocking Ballisargon's Gate, and re-opening your own?'

'I was trying that when you arrived but was not getting very far. He seems to be able to interfere with my attempts at re-establishing my Gate and his is too powerful for me to counter. His resources are too great, and my power supplies too limited.'

'Then Move me to Earth. I can find Robert, and allow you to locate him.'

'That is not possible either. He is blocking all off-planet Moves. I have been trying to find a way round it, but it does not look…' the Engineer trailed off as something caught her eye on the display.

Roen, momentarily puzzled by her distraction, also turned his attention to the screen when he realised that something more important than their current discussion was occurring on Earth.

Both watched the monitor as a further green signal

appeared next to the Gate. It was not as bright as a tiger's or a human's, but it was significantly larger. There was only one thing it could be.

15

Emergency On Planet Earth

Pradeep insisted that Robert stay in the shop (after locking the door) until he was satisfied that Vidya was nowhere in the immediate vicinity. Robert spent a breathless fifteen minutes peering nervously out through the wire mesh which covered the glass door and windows. He did this despite Pradeep's caution that the flimsy metal grille might stop petty criminals, but would do little to prevent a determined tiger attack. Eventually Robert was rewarded with the sight of Pradeep returning unaccompanied. The tiger knocked on the door, which rattled in its frame under the force of Pradeep's paw.

Robert crept round from behind the counter, unlocked the door and joined Pradeep outside the shop. 'What's the news?'

'Well, I've circled the area around here for four streets in each direction twice, and there is no sign of her anywhere. And if you look at the direction she headed off in,' Pradeep indicated the tracks in the sand left by his sister, 'you can see that she has gone in a direction *away* from the next location.'

Robert looked at the trail in the sand. Vidya's paw prints, each one as large as a plate, snaked off away from the shop in the direction that they had already come in. He felt his chest twinge where she had hit him.

'I'm guessing her instincts are driving her to where she feels safe,' said Pradeep.

'Instincts?'

'Yes, I think Vidya is no longer in conscious control of her actions, the way you or I are. I think she was right when she said that this place, this world is affecting us. You remember what you said about Earth tigers not being able to talk?'

'Yes,'

'Well, I think the longer we spend here the more like Earth tigers we become.'

Robert looked at Pradeep, who saw the concern and apprehension in his eyes. 'Yes, I think it will affect me also. I don't exactly know why Vidya succumbed so quickly, or why I still seem cogent, but I do think it is just a matter of time before you will have to fear me also.'

'But there must be something we can do?'

'There is. We find the software before I lose control, find Vidya and get her, you and me through the Gate the Engineer set up. I think once we're back in the Lyr she'll be OK again.'

'You make it sound easy,' said Robert depressively. 'How are we going to do that?!'

'I don't know just yet. I was hoping you had some bright ideas.'

'Well, I think we can do the first part of your plan, if we can get to the next location.'

It was a little way to the third potential site so while Robert and Pradeep initially set off in silence, both concerned with Vidya, it was a silence that could not last the duration of the journey. Until Robert broke the hush the only noise was the dry crunch of his trainers on the sand, Pradeep's paws making no discernible sound. 'What do the Glass Molluscs look like, Pradeep?' he asked. 'I mean, I've heard all these things about them, like how dangerous they are and stuff, but nobody's ever described one to me. How will I recognise one if I ever see it?'

Pradeep gave a half laugh at Robert's question, to which Robert asked, 'What?'

'Nothing,' replied Pradeep. 'It's just I've never heard of anyone *want* to know more about the Glass Molluscs. Most people feel they know enough with the understanding that they are dangerous. But you, you always want to know more my young friend.'

Robert was struck by the tiger's use of the word friend. He wasn't sure what, if anything this signified, but it made him feel better all the same. Suddenly being the last boy on Earth did not seem such a daunting prospect. He reached out and tickled Pradeep just behind the ear, just like he did with Catanooga occasionally. The tiger chuffed appreciatively. 'What was that for?'

'Oh… nothing,' Robert said somewhat embarrassedly at his overt display of affection toward the tiger. 'You were going to tell me about the Mollusc?' he said changing the subject to hide his blushes.

'Yes, right,' replied Pradeep, a glint of good humour in his eyes. 'What does a Mollusc look like,' he asked rhetorically. 'Well, they're kind of like a giant slug, but more segmented like a worm. Of course they are almost completely transparent, hence the name, but have no visible sensory organs. We do not know where they originated from, they certainly aren't native to the Lyr; until Ballisargon's arrival we knew nothing of the terror they inspire.'

'So basically I'll know one if I see it?'

'You certainly will. And my advice would be to Move as fast…' Pradeep trailed off in mid-sentence as a familiar, if long unsmelled scent, caught his attention. Instinctively he turned his head toward it. In the still air of the silent city aromas carried far, unimpeded by the normally overpowering presence of its human population, and Pradeep's keen nose had picked up on something.

In a second he was off, unable to stop himself from deserting Robert. He had to obey his senses no matter what.

Robert shouted after the tiger as he watched the large cat turn and bound off up a side street that was definitely not on the route.

In just a few moments Robert was standing alone on a sand covered street in Tokyo, one wild tiger and one errant tiger being the only other living creatures for several miles. His previous feeling of a favourable outcome to the situation rapidly deserted him. He looked around himself, nervously starting at every imagined noise or half-glimpsed movement of shadow. It took him all of three seconds before he was running after Pradeep.

Blood pumping, adrenaline coursing through his veins, Robert pushed his legs as fast as he could after the trail of paw prints Pradeep was leaving in the sand. Even running flat out Robert could not match Pradeep's massive stride, the distance between the tiger's footfalls nearly twice what Robert was able to manage with his own legs. He ran for over a minute before he began to become tired, but Pradeep's tracks kept on going.

Eventually, after another couple of minutes of somewhat slower running Robert finally caught up with Pradeep. He saw the fuzzy black tip of the tiger's tail disappear into a small shop just up ahead. It was only when Robert got near to the building that Pradeep had gone into did it begin to make sense to him.

In the window of the shop was a plastic model of a cow, stood above large pieces of marbled steak. It was a butcher's shop. Pradeep's extra sensitive nose had picked out the smell from the better part of a kilometre away.

Robert carefully approached the door, and put his ear to it. Inside he could hear snarls and growls punctuated with moist tearing sounds of what could only be Pradeep gorging himself. He wasn't sure he wanted to interrupt the tiger in the middle of his meal, so he spent a nervous few minutes stood outside the butcher's shop door scanning the streets for any sign of Vidya. More than once he was convinced he saw a blur of orange, distorted and reflected in the glass sides of the monolithic buildings all around him. He felt his heart quicken and his fingers tingle as he struggled to keep control of his breathing. He became acutely aware of feeling trapped on all sides and the creeping death that Vidya now represented stalking him, the greens of a living jungle replaced with the greys and steel-blues of its concrete namesake.

When the sounds inside died down, Robert poked his head round the door. On the floor lay Pradeep, his muzzle coated in fresh red blood, licking his chops in satisfaction.

'Pradeep?' he whispered.

There was no response from the tiger. He continued to lap at his maw, the massive rough pink tongue making quick work of cleaning away the last of his repast before it caked his fur.

Robert tried again, this time a little louder and he gave a cough just for good measure.

The tiger noticed Robert for the first time. He jerked his head round at the sound and looked extremely guilty at the sight of himself sprawled on the floor, bones and ragged chunks of meat lying strewn around him. 'Ah, uh, oh, uh, Robert. This isn't... I mean, what this looks like is... uh,' was all the tiger could manage in his defence. 'I just couldn't help myself,' he said eventually. 'I caught the scent of the meat, and it's been so long since I have eaten anything, let alone anything that smelled as good as this.' Pradeep swept a forepaw around to indicate the remnants of his feast. 'I had to come here, and once I got here I had to eat.'

Robert wondered just how long Pradeep had left before the Earth affected him again, and more importantly would he come back again? Pushing the uncomfortable thoughts away Robert said, 'C'mon, we can't hang around here. We've got to find this stuff for the Engineer.'

Robert and the tiger stepped out of the butcher's shop into the street. 'Lucky all this sand is around,' said Robert. 'Otherwise I'd never be able to find our way back to where we were. I got all turned around chasing you here.'

'Here, hop on and I'll carry you back. I can run far faster than you can and we need to make up lost time,' said Pradeep dropping down on the floor. Robert straddled his legs over the tiger's shoulders, and wobbled slightly as Pradeep stood up. 'You OK up there?' the tiger asked turning his head to check that Robert was secure. Almost before Robert had a chance to nod his affirmation Pradeep was off, bounding through the city streets.

The wind whipped past Robert as the tiger powered along underneath him. For the first time Robert understood what it could be like to be a tiger. The power in your body, your muscles taught and strong from years of hard exercise, the mobility and speed you were capable of, raw strength there for you. But there was more to it than just power. Every one of Pradeep's huge strides was perfectly placed, his pawfalls landing in exactly the same place as they had done on the outward run. While there was a huge amount of power in Pradeep's frame it was rigorously controlled, working for him as efficiently as possible, not one jot wasted. That was what it was to be a tiger. The strength you had came at a price, and the cost was control. Control of your claws and teeth, used only when needed.

In less than a minute they had covered the distance back to where they had split up. Pradeep powered down slightly as he approached the main street again to make the turn. 'Which way at the next junction?'

Robert struggled to try and read the map while bouncing up and down on Pradeep's back. 'Uh, left,' he said. 'Then straight on then third right and we should be there,' he blurted out as quickly as he could for fear of losing his balance. And Pradeep was off again at full pelt.

The tiger slowed and came to gentle stop at the place indicated by Robert. He lay down again to allow Robert to disembark. Robert was struck by the fact that Pradeep wasn't even breathing hard, whereas he was puffing and panting, more from the exhilaration than the exertion of the run.

Pradeep raised his nose to the air, inhaled deeply and frowned, to which Robert said, 'No! No more running off. I don't care what you smell, even if it is Kobe beef again. We've got to get this software. Now come on.' Robert strode ahead of him into the building.

As Pradeep shook his head in a 'it's probably nothing' gesture and followed Robert into the building, a pair of green eyes glided silently from behind the steel and glass tower across the street. They watched the orange and black striped Pradeep disappear inside, moving only once the tip of his tail had vanished from sight. Then and only then did Vidya emerge from her hiding place and follow her brother and Robert into the tower block.

Once inside the building, seemingly another software house like the first, Robert, now a master at finding out where they needed to go, located the computer lab. This time it was on the tenth floor. 'At least we won't have to walk as far this time,' Pradeep commented when he remembered that the lifts would be out of commission again.

Robert was glad that the walk up the inside of the building was only just over one hundred and sixty steps this time rather than the marathon climb of the previous location. Even so, he was still breathing hard when he reached the top of the staircase and leant his weight onto the door into the computer lab.

Ten storeys below them Vidya stood at the base of the staircase. She could smell the human, the prey, and she was very very hungry.

Inside the lab was an arrangement much like the first place they had been; row upon row of desks of monitors and computers. Robert wasted no time in plugging the power unit in, and this time all the PCs in the lab leapt into life.

Robert selected the one nearest to him; he wanted to be done here as quickly as possible. The memory stick slotted into place in the computer, and once again the screen flashed and the now familiar jumble of characters and colours blinked on and off.

>>> Scanning network...
>>> Software located
>>> Copying to backup media. Please wait...

Robert turned to Pradeep and shouted, 'It's here! It's here!'

His jubilation died in an instant as he saw the door open behind Pradeep and the familiar face of Vidya emerge from behind it, her eyes focussed dead on him.

Pradeep saw the look of dawning terror on Robert's face and in a second worked out what he must be looking at. He also worked out that she must be looking at Robert. Pradeep turned his head slowly and saw his sister carefully and deliberately moving into the room, all her attention on Robert. He had one chance to do this properly; he was no match for Vidya in a straight fight so he had to get the upper hand swiftly by surprise.

Robert began to shake in his seat. He could no longer control his fingers properly and had to clench his hands into fists to stop them from flailing around. Even then his arms began to quiver as his nerves shredded under Vidya's relentless gaze. *Do something Pradeep!* he willed the male tiger. *SOON!*

Pradeep rose almost painfully slowly from his sitting position, his attention focussed on his sister. She still paid him no heed. He tensed his back legs. Vidya was nearly level with him now, and still seemingly oblivious to him. He crouched, flexing every muscle and sinew in his body. Her head passed his, then her shoulders then her flank…

Pradeep sprang forward, bowling into Vidya with the full weight of his body. She was knocked sideways nearly five metres by the impact, chairs and desks scattering as the two tigers ploughed through them.

Both tigers were up on their feet in a second. Now Vidya turned to face her brother. 'Don't make me do this,' he implored her. 'Think Vidya, remember why we're here…' Vidya slammed into him, Pradeep narrowly avoiding losing an eye only by moving his head at the last moment. This time it was Pradeep who took the brunt of the impact with the furniture, but he was on his feet again as fast as his sister.

'GET THE SOFTWARE!' he shouted, shaking his head. Robert checked the screen. It still said it was copying the files. He shook the monitor in frustration.

Once again the tigers faced each other. 'Please Vidya,' Pradeep begged, jumping out of the way of Vidya's next lunge as she crashed into the wall, leaving a sizeable dent in the thin partition. She rose groggily to her feet and turned to Pradeep, swaying in pain and confusion. Pradeep began to find it difficult to think coherently on the task in hand. He knew he had to protect someone from something, but what was it? *He had to… He had to…* Vidya crashed into him again, and this time he lashed out with his paw, smashing it into Vidya's flank. *What am I doing?* he thought as he drew his limb back. *Nearly hurt her… Must stop her hunting… must stop hunt… must protect Robert… nearly hurt… stop… hurt… hunt… must… Robert… must hurt… must hunt… must hunt… must hunt Robert.*

And with that Pradeep lost his rational control, the stress of the conflict with his sister waking his animal self completely. He shrugged off Vidya, and turned his attention to the human prey sitting unprotected at the desk.

Robert had watched in shock as the two tigers tumbled and thumped into each other before the fight eventually died down. 'Oh, Pradeep, thank goodness you're alright…' was all he managed to get out before he realised what had happened. Pradeep now looked at him in the same way that Vidya had done when she first entered the lab.

The computer next to him beeped, and the memory stick blinked green, oblivious to the titanic struggle that had been fought and lost while it went about its business. Robert's first instinct was to run, but the tigers just stood there weighing him up. He slowly moved a trembling hand to the computer. His fingers touched the edge of the memory stick's smooth metal cover, but were shaking too hard for him to be able to grip it properly. It felt like it was glued in place; it half slid out only for Robert's fingers to slip off before it came fully loose. He took a deep breath, flexed and unflexed his fingers and tried again, only this time more slowly.

Now he was successful, and the memory stick came away from the computer in his fingers. Not taking his eyes off the tigers he tremulously put the cap back on it and slipped it into the rucksack. The tigers stayed put, as if waiting for him to make his move.

Tense seconds passed as Robert and the tigers stared at each other across the divide of awareness. Until he could get them back to the Lyr Robert's friends were lost to him; caught in a state where all they knew was hunter and prey. And Robert was the prey.

He chanced a flick of his eyes around the room. He caught the briefest glimpse of a door out of his peripheral vision to his left, and it looked open! His eyes saccaded back to the tigers. They decided to push the situation and began advancing toward him. It was now or never.

Robert leapt out of his seat, deliberately sending it skidding across the smooth office floor toward the tigers, and bolted for the door. Unsure if the thing speeding toward them was attacking or not caused the tigers to hesitate, giving Robert the half-second he needed to reach the door.

He slammed it closed just as one of the tigers (he couldn't tell which one) thudded heavily into it, the door frame creaking but holding under the force of three hundred kilograms of large cat. Robert scanned the door for a lock; there wasn't one. He was running before the second attack on the door even happened.

Frantically he sped down the corridor looking for somewhere, anywhere that could offer him sanctuary, even temporarily while he worked out what to do. Skidding round a corner he heard an ominous crash behind him. He found himself facing the lifts, and their lights were on.

Their lights were on! They had power!

He slid up to the lift, colliding with the doors and pressed the call button as another crash, this time accompanied by the sound of splintering wood, echoed down the empty corridor. The dial above the lift doors arced painfully slowly across the display as the lift, and salvation, approached.

Another crash behind him caused him to turn his head as the doors glided open behind him, and Robert fell into the compartment. There was still no sign of the tigers, but he was sure they were only seconds behind. Back on his feet he reached out and pressed the first button his fingers touched. Taking off his jacket and ripping the trainers from his feet he dropped them to the floor and darted back out of the lift round the far corner. He could hear the tigers now, their low growl filling the corridor, their rapid footfalls heavy. He prayed his plan would work.

He risked a quick look round the corner he was hiding behind. The tigers were bearing down the corridor at top speed. Robert ducked back. The lift doors began to close too soon. It wasn't going to work!

The tigers thundered into the lift drawn by the powerful smell of Robert's clothing, their flanks bumping against the doors as they slid closed, only catching Robert's true scent at the last moment. Robert caught sight of Pradeep's eyes staring straight at him as the doors closed the tigers in.

The lift began to move. Robert didn't know how long he had before the doors opened on whichever floor he had randomly selected in haste, so he sped off down the corridor to the lab.

The door to the lab had been reduced to matchwood, splinters lay everywhere and the remains of the door hung limply off one hinge. Robert cleared the debris in a single leap and sprinted as quickly as his socked feet would allow to where the power unit was still plugged in. He ripped it from the wall and every computer in the room went quiet. Robert slumped against the wall.

He needed to check where the tigers were, but he needed a short rest more. While they probably weren't loose on this floor there was a strong chance that the lift had opened somewhere else before he had pulled the plug on the power. He needed to know if he was truly safe or not.

He waited for a few seconds while his breathing returned to something like normal, and his heart rate came down from orbit, then got to his feet. The adrenaline coursing through him made him twitchy but he was able to move around fairly quietly. Robert made his way back to the lifts and looked up at the display. The lift had gone up four floors in the time he had taken to switch off the power. He half thought about just making his way back to the Gate now he had the software the Engineer needed. After all how was he going to convince two wild tigers to follow him to it? If Pradeep had been with him it might have been possible; he could have controlled Vidya somehow maybe, but on his own Robert felt powerless. He would end up as tiger food for sure!

He pushed this notion away; the tigers were his friends after all and had saved him before. He had to find a way.

He looked around himself and saw the metal door to a maintenance stairway. He made the trip up four flights of stairs relatively quickly, only pausing once he got to the door of the fourteenth floor. He put his ear to it, but heard nothing through the hard metal. While he was on this side of the door he was relatively safe. The other side, however, could be a completely different matter.

He pushed the door open a crack and peered through with one eye. From his limited vantage point he could not see a great deal; he could not even make out if the lift was open or closed. He let the door close again.

OK, he told himself, *you have to know.*

Steeling his nerves, he pushed the door open just far

enough for him to squeeze through, then having a brainwave, he pulled the rucksack from his back and used it to prop the door open; this way if he needed to beat a hasty retreat he at least did not have to waste precious seconds heaving open the heavy steel door. He slipped his body through the gap and into the hallway.

Instantly there was a loud crash from the lift, and Robert zipped back in panic. When the expected thump against the door did not come he pushed it open again. There didn't seem to be a tiger, or *tigers* in the hallway. He pushed and propped the door open again.

The crash came again as he entered the corridor, but this time he only flinched. He looked at the lift and a tiger paw, Pradeep's by the look of it whipped out of the lift. Robert started back for the safety of the maintenance stairwell, but hesitated when it became obvious that all that was emerging from the lift was Pradeep's paw and foreleg.

Emboldened, Robert made his way to where he could see the lift doors, but could not be seen by its occupants. The doors had indeed begun to open, but only a few centimetres, just enough for the tigers to push a paw through.

Relieved that he was safe for the time being, Robert stood in front of the lift so he could see inside. Through the slim gap he could see Pradeep pressed hard against the doors, his right forelimb sticking out, swiping at fresh air. When Pradeep saw Robert he growled in frustration. Vidya picked up on this and Robert could see her pacing round in the lift. Robert moved about on the spot to try and see a little more. He caught sight of what was left of his trainers, now just tattered pieces of canvas and plastic. He looked down at his feet. *I hope Eirian has got lots of pairs.*

Robert slumped to ground, exhausted. The mortal danger he had been living with for the past hour or so had worn him out. It had been bad enough when it was just Vidya missing, at least he still had Pradeep, but when he too was lost to his instincts, Robert had not had time to stop and think. He had also been forced to act on impulse and reactions. The parallel struck him as kind of funny as he leant against the wall and slipped into exhausted unconsciousness almost immediately.

Two days left. .

16

Jump

Robert awoke much later with a start. His tiger dreams this time around had been far less pleasant than the ones he had had back in the Lyr, curled up safe against Pradeep. In these he had the distinct impression of being the hunted rather than the hunter, totally lacking in the power and grace of a large cat. Instead he had felt more like a deer, skittish and nervous, spooked by every crack or snap in the undergrowth, until finally he found himself staring into two bright orange eyes, glinting in the darkness.

Heart beating hard, Robert woke up still leaning against the wall. His sense of the here and now took a few seconds to make him remember he was on Earth and not being stalked in some jungle on a far away planet. The feeling of being lost and alone that he had felt in his house before all this had started returned. His situation, if anything had got worse since then. Now, not only was he once again the only person left on the Earth no closer to getting his family back, he had to contend with two fully grown tigers intent on eating him. *Face it Robert, you're up crap creek here.*

He blinked as he looked around. In the time he had been asleep it had grown dark. He checked his watch; it was nearly 6am. He'd been asleep for most of the day and night.

He looked across at the lift, but was unable to see any more than a dark patch where the lift doors were. Realising his eyes were pretty much useless in the gloomy corridor he held his breath and listened instead.

Just as he was on the verge of having to exhale, his ears sensitised enough to pick up a low murmur, almost on the edge of his hearing. He struggled against his lungs to hear more. The gentle, rhythmic noise he could hear was the breathing of the tigers, and they still seemed to be in the lift. He allowed himself a heavy sigh of relief. He had not been eaten in the darkness.

He examined his situation over and over in his head. His plan to hold the tigers had worked; they had not been able to free themselves. However, that did not help him get them through the Gate and back to the Lyr. How he was ever going to convince them to follow him back?

He contemplated letting them out and making a run for it, but the tigers were far too quick for him. He'd be big-cat food before he even got out of the building. He considered leaving them here while he went back for help from Eirian, but could not bring himself to knowingly leave them behind.

They were his friends after all, and he wouldn't leave them. And anyway, what could she do? It's not like she was going to have tiger sized collars or leads to drag them back with, or the strength to do so. Where would that leave them? Stranded on Earth, imprisoned in a lift until they died of starvation.

Whichever way Robert thought around his problem he always came back to the same conclusion; he had to help them now, while he had a chance.

His stomach rumbled noisily in the silence of the deserted hallway. It had been ages since he had had anything to eat. Anything to eat. *Hmm, I wonder…*

He got up and peered out of the window in the hallway to the street outside. There were no streetlights on, the only illumination being the moon and stars. Not nearly enough to see by. He needed to find some light.

Robert made his way back to the lobby, touch-feeling his way down fourteen flights of stairs, both hands on the handrail, and sliding his feet along the steps till they came to the edge and found the flat of the next one down. It was a slow process, and it was over an hour before Robert found himself back in the main lobby of the building. Here the large glass doors let in a little more light and Robert was just about able to see the reception desk. He made his way to it, and opening the drawers fumbled round for what he sought. He was rewarded when his fingers closed around a cold, hard cylinder of gripped metal. His thumb searched for the on button, and a second later the lobby was lit by the beam from the torch.

'Yes!'

He swept the torchlight toward the door, followed to where the beam fell and pushed his way through the plate-glass doors. He could see the footprints Pradeep had made earlier, and began to follow them. In a few minutes he had made his way to the junction where Pradeep had left him but instead of heading back to the Gate, Robert followed Pradeep's diverted tracks.

Two hours later, just as day was breaking, Robert hefted his stuffed rucksack up the stairs. It was slowly getting lighter with each turn of the flights, as he dropped chunk after chunk of its contents onto the stairs. He finished his task by dropping the final item onto the floor in front of the lift with a wet, slapping sound.

Almost immediately the noises from within the lift changed. No longer sleeping, the tigers were alert. Robert heard them pacing around in the lift, stopping at the gap in the doors to sniff the air. What was on the other side was having the desired effect. It was time to put the second part of his plan into effect.

Taking the steps two or three at a time he made his way to an office on the third floor that overlooked the street outside.

Once the door had been wedged shut from the inside, he reached into his rucksack and, retrieving the power unit, plugged it into the wall. His heart rate leapt when the lights flickered into life. He had just let them out.

Fifteen minutes later Robert heard the tigers on the floor he occupied. He hoped the tigers would be too distracted with the entire contents of the butcher's shop to sniff him out. It had taken Robert most of the rest of the early morning to lay the trail of steak, chicken, and anything else he could fit into the rucksack, from the Gate to the office. He had had to go back to the butcher's twice in order to obtain more food for the tigers, and even then he had had to lay the trail fairly sparsely. He only hoped that their keen senses were too concerned with seeking out the next treat to focus on him. He would know soon enough.

He heard the tigers padding down the staircase, their footfalls reverberating around until they stopped. Robert held his breath and closed his eyes.

A minute later he heard the tigers move off once more, down to the second floor and below. He let out the breath in his body as quietly as he could. Now, to see if the next part of the plan would work.

He leant carefully out of the window and waited, looking at the chunks of beef dotted along the sand out of sight. He saw the massive orange heads of the tigers glide out from the entrance toward the meat. Instinctively Robert retreated back into the office, before peering over the edge of the windowsill with one eye. He saw the wide backs of the tigers and for a moment could not tell them apart until Vidya's white foreleg came into view. At least they were still together.

Robert began to let out a loud sigh of relief, before clamping his hand over his mouth, stifling his exhalation for fear of the tigers hearing it. He was in luck. They seemed engrossed in the food he had laid down.

He watched as they both fell on top of a rather fine looking piece of steak, neither willing to let go of the morsel in their mouths. The tigers continued their tug of war for a few moments until the steak tore in two under the pressure. Vidya seemed to have won the lion's (or rather, tiger's) share of the meat. Robert thought himself lucky that it was not him down there being shredded.

After that the tigers seemed to be relatively fair with the trail, one taking one piece while the other trotted ahead to the next and so on. When they were safely out of sight and had been gone for nearly fifteen minutes Robert reckoned it was safe for him to follow them at a distance.

He unlocked the room he was in and made his way down the stairs to the lobby, where once outside the building, he could see the tiger's tracks heading off in the right direction toward the Gate, and he hoped the safety of the Lyr.

He judged the tigers would be moving at a slowish walk, so he followed at a moderate pace; he had no desire to get too close to them yet.

He went over his plan again. The final part of it relied on the piece of meat he had in his rucksack. His one chance of getting them back to the Lyr, where he hoped they would return to normal, depended on them falling for the same trick twice. It had worked once with his trainers and he just hoped that the tigers didn't realise they were being conned a second time. It wasn't much of a plan; throwing a chunk of steak through the Gate, but it was all he could come up with.

He realised he had inadvertently closed the distance between himself and the tigers a little too much for comfort. He might have been within a margin of safety, but had no way to be sure. Just in case, he held back for a few moments before setting off again.

After another thirty minutes of slow walking he approached the final corner before the Gate should come into view. *Nearly there.* Looking round for a hiding place, he spied the roadworks from nearly twenty-four hours ago. The solid metal machinery seemed the perfect place to watch from. He stopped behind the digger and chanced a look round. The tigers were just over halfway to the Gate from where he was, their attention still focussed on the pieces of meat he had laid down.

He watched as Vidya tore at the half chicken, while Pradeep walked toward the next piece. *It was now or nev...* Robert never got to finish his thought, as just as he was about to round the corner and sneak along the pavement, Pradeep stopped dead, and lifted and turned his head.

Robert's immediate thought was that he had been discovered by the male tiger, that he had got over-confident and had blown it now, at the very end. His fear and frustration were replaced with terror a second later when he saw a large, semi-transparent form emerge from a small alley near the Gate. It looked like a huge slug like creature, and Robert's blood ran cold at the sight of it. Pradeep's words came back to him. *It was a Glass Mollusc!*

And it was the most horrible, nightmarish thing Robert had ever seen. Like most eleven-year-olds he had seen the odd scary film with some scary effects, some of which had caused him the occasional sleepless night, nervously wide awake under his duvet. But all the scary things ever paled next to the sight that now lay before his eyes. After all, scary things in movies were only ever special effects; make believe monsters that could be put away when the credits rolled. 'They aren't real,' his Dad had told him, and 'There are no such things as monsters.' But his Dad was wrong, really really wrong. This was no special effect. There were monsters, and they were real, the bad dream thing in front of Robert was testament to that.

The nightmare of living flesh was over ten feet long, shaped like a cross between a slug and a worm; long and thick, with body segments covered in large bulbs of flesh. The whole creature was almost completely see through, its lumpy skin resembling the frosted windows people put in their bathrooms.

The thing sat, pulsing slowly, so that where Robert could

see through it the view was distorted, the image breaking and reforming in a flowing pattern as the Mollusc moved slowly toward the tigers.

Robert could see no discernible features on the creature. It had no recognisable eyes, ears, mouth or face of any kind. Neither did it have any limbs. It was a giant mass of solid, see through flesh.

Robert remembered Pradeep's and Eirian's description of the Glass Molluscs that Ballisargon kept as pets, servants and his army, and he went cold inside, gripped by an almost overwhelming fear far greater than the one he had felt facing the tigers.

'Mollusc pellets,' he swore to himself under his breath.

The single thing in the whole situation in his favour was that it did not seem to know he was there. The Mollusc appeared focussed (though given the thing had no eyes, how could you really tell?) on the tigers. Robert saw Pradeep let a chicken fall from his mouth as the male tiger sensed the danger up ahead. Seconds later Vidya also dropped her meal, and drew her mouth back in an angry snarl.

The Mollusc shuddered along its length, leaving Robert wondering what it was doing for a moment before he realised. *It doesn't work here,* he thought in response to the creature's attempt to Move. *So what does?*

The answer was obvious. Forget Lyr based solutions; use the Earth's technology, even if it was in the form of three tons of industrial earth mover.

Robert leapt up to the driver's seat, and in a second had the digger started with a throaty rumble. The tigers looked over at the new noise while the Mollusc, if it cared, didn't seem to react.

Robert trod on the accelerator pedal and wrenched the steering wheel round. The digger responded with a roar of its engine and lurched towards the Mollusc. The tigers parted as Robert powered at the thing that was threatening his friends, Vidya even trying an ineffectual swipe at the thick tyres as he passed them by.

Robert let out a whoop of victory as he drove the digger straight into the Mollusc, the stubby prongs of the scoop digging into its tough jelly-like flank. The Mollusc reacted by shaking violently, trying to dislodge itself, but it was stuck fast. The digger pushed the bucking Mollusc along in front of it, the sand piling up in a heap as the grotesque payload squirmed helplessly, the engine whining hard with the extra weight. Robert reached down and hauled on a lever, lifting the scoop and the Mollusc a metre off the ground, then two. The shift in the Mollusc's centre of gravity caused it to tumble into the scoop with a wet, tearing sound as the prongs were ripped from its body by its weight.

He drove for a few more seconds until he had cleared the path to the Gate for the tigers, but they stood still, eyeing him, the machine and the Mollusc very warily.

Why weren't they advancing?

He switched off the engine, the whole digger shuddering as it stopped, and carefully stepped off it toward the Gate. He flicked his eyes back up to the Mollusc, but it wasn't going anywhere, trapped as it was in the digger's scoop.

Robert looked back at the tigers. Free from the threat of the Mollusc, even if they did not completely comprehend the strange hard beast that had saved them from it, Pradeep and Vidya became aware of the prey that they had been denied earlier. Slowly they began to walk toward it.

Robert saw the change in the tiger's body language. No longer were they afraid of the digger. They were back to being the hunters, the top of a food chain where boys ranked somewhere near the bottom, just above a fawn perhaps.

'Crap!' Suddenly Lyr expletives did not seem up to the job. While he had been on the digger Robert had almost forgotten the threat posed by the tigers. But now the Mollusc was neutralised the tigers were once again his number one problem. A problem with eight sets of claws and two huge mouths, either one of which could swallow half of him in one bite.

He reached for the rucksack and tried to unlock the clasp, but found his hands refusing to work again. Desperately he tore at the material, but it refused to give. He couldn't get the meat out.

The tigers continued their slow, deliberate advance toward him. By now he could hear their breathing, a low rumbling noise that made him need the toilet. He gave up on the rucksack, and slung it back over his shoulder. Slowly he began to back towards the Gate, all the time keeping his eyes on the tigers.

He chanced a quick look over his shoulder to see how far away he was. Barely five metres. Then he realised his mistake. The tigers saw his distraction and broke into a run. Robert heard the change of pace and knew what was happening without having to look back. He began to run too.

His feet slipped on the sand before they gained purchase. Behind him he could hear the tigers. They were much much faster than he was, but the Gate was so close. He pelted full speed toward it, and leapt into the air at the same time as the he heard the tigers leave the ground behind him.

17

Keep On Running

Falling free in space, tumbling head over heels, Robert hurtled through the Gate. An instantaneous lifetime passed as he felt the light years fall away in a second. Distance was meaningless in the in-between world of Folds and Gates and for an instant Robert existed in both places at once; the Earth and the Lyr, his physical form stretched to infinitesimal thinness as he was pulled and drawn through the Gate. His perceptions were skewed, pulled out of true by the passage between worlds, and he was sure in the momentary hiatus of real-space he fell through he could see creation spread out before, below, above and all around him. The vastness of the Universe spilled out, tiny swirls of lights playing and dancing before his eyes.

He reached out a hand, which stretched out the seemingly impossible distance to scrape the edges of the firmament. *It would be so easy to just nudge it a little*, he thought. Then he saw the impossible; another hand reaching into the void. He quickly retracted his own, and watched as the hand swirled around the heavens, picking up and arranging suns and planets as if to some grand design.

Robert fell out of the other side of the Gate, and landed

on his front, the impact winding him. Remembering what had been following him he barely had time to roll out of the way before the two tigers barrelled out of the Gate and landed in a snarling orange and black heap of legs and tails a little way in front of him.

Coughing and wheezing Robert got to his feet, not for a second taking his eyes off the tigers who were slowly separating themselves. They untangled their intertwined bodies, rolled away from each other and carefully, and to Robert's eye slightly warily stood up and faced him.

'Pradeep? Vidya?' he asked carefully and quietly.

The tigers narrowed their eyes in puzzlement and looked around themselves, at each other, then back at Robert. If he had not been terrified that they were going to pounce on him again he would have found the synchronised nature of their movements amusing. Instead he was reminded of the single-mindedness they had exhibited on Earth, when they seemed to act as one creature with two bodies.

'Are…' his voice cracked and deserted him before he found the resolve to try again. 'Are you two OK?'

This time the tigers seemed to have heard him because at the sound of his voice their ears flicked forwards. Vidya opened her maw and Robert took a step backwards.

'I… think… so…' said the female tiger. 'Pradeep? How are you?'

'Um… fine… I… think,' said the male tiger slowly and deliberately. 'What… happened. The… last thing… I remember is… Robert saying something about… something being here and then… then you were there,' the tiger indicated to his sister, 'and then it all feels like not a dream exactly… but something else. Something more basic, more instinctive. I can't quite explain it.'

'I know what you mean,' replied Vidya. 'I can remember it all… the hunt and the fight and… and trapped and the Mollusc and then running and then being here again.'

Robert's fears evaporated at the sound of the tiger's voices and he could not stop himself running toward them and hugging them both round the neck. Hot tears of joy and relief ran down his cheeks as he jabbered into their fur, 'OhmyGodIwassoscaredyouweregoingtoeatmeI'msogladyou'r ebothbacktonormal.'

The tigers meekly accepted Robert's thanks, and even though the ferocity of his hugging was beginning to hurt, they felt they owed him more than they could ever repay. 'It's OK,' said Vidya gently.

'I felt so vulnerable when I lost you both. I really thought I was going to die.'

'Well, we're back in control now,' said Pradeep.

'But *where* exactly are we back in control?' Vidya asked. 'Shouldn't we on the Bridge? This is open Lyr.'

For the first time since falling through the Gate the three of them looked around. Vidya was right. They should have been back on the Bridge. Instead there was sand everywhere, rising on all sides, obscuring the view in every direction.

'Where are we Pradeep?' asked Vidya.

Pradeep closed his eyes and raised his head. For a second or two his ears twitched, and he drew in a large breath of air through his sensitive nose. His eyes shot open in alarm. 'We're in trouble is where we are.'

'What? Why?' asked Robert. 'So Eirian's Gate brought us back to the wrong part of the Lyr. We'll just have to walk for a little bit again.'

'Come on now Robert, do you think the Engineer would make such a mistake?' asked Pradeep.

Vidya grasped what Pradeep meant. 'We didn't come back through the same Gate,' she said very quietly.

'So who's Gate did we go through then?'

'Who else in the Lyr do you think has the ability and power to create a Gate?' the female tiger continued.

Robert did not have to think very hard to work out the answer to that question. The colour drained from his face and his throat went dry as he realised who had set up the second Gate.

'Right,' said Pradeep. 'And if you think that's bad, guess what else he has planned for us.' The tiger motioned to the edge of the gentle rise the three friends were at the base of.

As if on cue half a dozen large shapes appeared at the top of the bowl. Half a dozen large clear slug-like shapes, evenly spaced round the top of the low circular rise, effectively hemming Robert and the tigers in.

'See, I told you we were in trouble,' said Pradeep.

'What do we do?' wailed Robert.

'We Move. Now.' said Vidya.

Robert did not need to be told twice. He looked with his mind at the Folds the tigers were already executing, and copied them. Space bent for the three of them, and in an instant they were gone.

Just over two thousand metres from where they had left the six Molluscs, Robert and the tigers re-appeared, the sand shifting slightly under the newfound weight of one young boy and two adult tigers. All three of them were breathing deeply with the effort. It had been a very large Move indeed, one of the largest the tigers had ever completed, and certainly the furthest Robert had ever Moved in one go. All three of them felt the effort acutely.

'Are... we... are we... OK?' Robert puffed, recovering his breath.

Pradeep inhaled through his nose once more. He was silent for a second before he said, 'No.'

Vidya scanned their surroundings, 'There, just over that small rise.' She indicated with her white forelimb.

Robert looked, and saw the six Molluscs just over half a dozen metres away. 'But how...?' was all he managed to get out before his instinct took over and he Folded space a heartbeat behind the tigers, and all three of them Moved again.

The three friends appeared once again, only this time the distance travelled somewhat shorter than the first Move.

'How... did the Molluscs... follow us?' Robert asked as he caught his breath. 'I thought you said they couldn't Move very far. We Moved *miles* that first time, there's no way they could have followed us.'

Vidya and Pradeep looked at each other. Robert had articulated the question that both of them wanted an answer to. 'I don't... I don't know Robert,' replied Vidya, also out of breath. 'They cannot Move that far.'

Pradeep sniffed the air once more. 'And we cannot stay here. Look.'

Vidya and Robert looked where Pradeep was gesturing. Just over a handful of metres away were the six Molluscs that seemed to be matching them Move for Move. 'Come ON!' Pradeep shouted at them both as all three of them vanished together.

This time the Move took them barely a kilometre, fatigue forcing them to travel a lot less further than they all wanted to. The air shimmered gently as they arrived, only this time within a tight circle barely five metres across of the six Molluscs.

'Not... possible...' gasped Pradeep through huge lungfuls of air as he took in the scene around them.

The six Molluscs began to shake and shiver gently along their length in preparation for a Move. Robert could guess where they intended to Move to. Right where the three of them stood. He closed his eyes and Folded space. The tigers looked at the Move Robert was planning with their minds. It was the entire remaining distance to the Bridge, much much further than they had first Moved when they were fresh.

'No... it's too... far,' said Vidya. 'We *can't* Move that far. We're too tired.'

'NO YOU'RE NOT!' shouted Robert. He slapped both the tigers hard across the muzzles and blinked out of existence.

Furious at Robert the tigers pursued him across the massive expanse of desert he had Moved. How dare this boy hit them when they were trying to save him!

Robert appeared a few metres from the edge of the lake he had swum across a few days ago, saw the tigers appear nearby, and promptly collapsed to the ground unconscious. His gamble had paid off; he had made the tigers angry enough to have the strength, even if only momentarily, to follow him to the Bridge. They were puffing and panting extremely hard, but they did not fall over. Fuelled by what they had eaten on Earth, they still had the strength to stay on their feet, even if those feet were at the bottom of very wobbly legs.

Pradeep scanned the horizon while Vidya rushed to Robert's prone form. The male tiger looked, listened and smelled as hard as he could, but could detect no trace of their pursuers. The Molluscs would not venture this close to the Bridge, and Robert had known that. He had saved them all. Again.

Vidya lowered her massive head next to Robert's. His breathing was extremely rapid and shallow, and he was shaking. He had not had the benefit of any real rest on Earth; he had been in mortal danger from the tigers for most of his time there, and had not eaten at all or slept properly, and the last Move had been too much for his already over-burdened system. 'We have to get him to the Engineer,' she said. 'I'll take him to her.'

'It's too far to Move,' replied her brother. 'And you'll never walk there in time.'

'I'll Move it alright,' stated Vidya. 'He got us to the safety of the Bridge, I'll get him to the safety of the Engineer.' Vidya walked over to Robert and gently picked him up with her huge jaws. 'If'll vee ukee,' she managed to say as she vanished, taking Robert with her.

Pradeep looked up at the Bridge, the top of it scraping the sky. He hoped his sister was right, and it would be OK. He rested for a few moments, gathering his strength for the Move he would make up to the top of the Bridge, when he saw a figure at the base of the stairway pillar, waving at him.

It was Roen.

He Moved to the edge of the lake, next to Pradeep. 'Vidya told me you were here.'

'How is Robert?' he asked.

'I believe he has exerted himself more than his body could take. The Engineer told me to bring you straight to him. He's very weak. Are you strong enough to complete the Move?'

If Vidya had had enough strength in her to get to the top of the Bridge with Robert, and Robert had had enough strength to drag them both to the base of it, then Pradeep certainly had enough energy in him to make it to Robert's side. 'Of course, I'm a tiger, aren't I,' he said bluntly as he vanished.

Roen shrugged his shoulders and looked across the lake, back to the base of the stairs. He was not a tiger and the two Moves he had completed; one from the top of the Bridge to the bottom and the second across the lake had drained him almost completely, leaving him with no option but to swim and then climb.

At the top of the Bridge, Robert lay in a bed, numerous wires connecting him to a variety of machines that monitored every aspect of his system. His heart rate was still erratic, and more than once his breathing almost stopped completely, causing the three figures gathered at his bedside to actually stop breathing, at least until Robert started again.

'He pushed himself too far to save us all,' said Vidya. 'We should have known what we were capable of without him having to prove it to us.'

'He is a remarkable young man,' said the Engineer. 'He is becoming very adept at proving us all wrong on a great number of things we all believed.'

The three of them were silent for a few seconds, before Pradeep asked, 'Will he be alright?'

The Engineer closed her eyes and said nothing, before

nodding her head gently in affirmation. 'Yes, he is physically safe now,' she said opening her eyes and looking at the tigers. 'My machines will keep his body alive until he regains his...' she turned her head at a noise from the bed. Robert had coughed.

He opened his eyes, struggling weakly against the fatigue. 'We... did... it?' he asked.

'No, *you* did it, Robert,' replied Vidya. It was all Robert heard before he slipped back into unconsciousness.

18

A Hard Day's Night

'Can you remember anything about what happened to you on Earth?' the Engineer asked Vidya as she reached for Robert's rucksack from where it had fallen when they arrived several hours previously. Vidya said nothing, and continued her pacing round in small circles in the living area. She had been doing it ever since she had returned to the Bridge and found out that Robert was going to be alright. In the intervening time Robert's condition had improved, and although he was still out cold his brain patterns showed he was asleep rather than in a more dangerous form of unconsciousness. The Engineer tried a change of direction, 'He's going to be alright you know. He's just exhausted.'

Vidya continued to ignore her. The Engineer picked up the rucksack which left a distinct damp red spot of congealing blood on the stone floor as she lifted it up. 'Tch,' she said, spying the mess distastefully. 'What *is* in here?' She opened the clasp and flicked the top back, only to be hit with the strong aroma of meat. 'Auw, ugh! Wait a second while I dispose of this.'

Upon the Engineer's return with the memory stick, Vidya had at least stopped her unsettling pacing, and was sitting in her distinctive sphinx-like pose on one of the rugs. Initially the Engineer thought that the tiger had settled whatever had been on her mind, but one look at her paws showed her that she had been wrong. Whatever the issue was, it was still to be resolved, as Vidya's claws were out and she was absently pulling at the rug with them, slowly shredding it in the process. Gently, the Engineer sat in her armchair, just across from Vidya.

'I still don't understand how the Molluscs were able to match us Move for Move,' said Vidya her voice worryingly controlled and even. 'I've never heard of them being able to cover such distances in one go.'

'That's because they weren't,' replied the Engineer, who was actually thinking, *That's not it.* But whatever it was, Vidya would, she hoped, get to it in her own time. For now all the Engineer could do was to answer the tigress's questions in the hope of prodding the real problem from her. 'When you two disappeared from Earth I swept the Lyr looking for the distinctive signals your minds give out. It didn't take too long; after all you were back to your full mental capacities, and you shone like twin beacons on my screen. Of course, I still couldn't see Robert, but had to assume he was with you.'

'Of course he was with us,' Vidya shot back, her mask of control slipping for an instant.

The Engineer was taken aback by the tone of her voice. She had never heard Vidya sound that angry before, and it scared her. Not for herself, but for everyone else. Her own voice shaking slightly, the Engineer continued with her explanation as best she could, 'It was at your arrival point I saw the six Molluscs. You see, Ballisargon knew where you were going to arrive; it was his Gate after all, and he also knows a great deal about the tigers of the Lyr, mainly from the numerous encounters with your grandparents, so he arranged for there to be a welcome party of Molluscs waiting at the limit of your capabilities to Move.

'He planted the sets of Molluscs in the areas he knew you

would arrive at on the journey between his Gate and the Bridge. I guess the plan was to get you confused at the Mollusc's apparent strength so that you would tire yourself out in futile Moves, eventually ending up in a position where you had no more energy to fight them with. There were three more groups of Molluscs waiting further along, and I think that if Robert had not managed to get you two angry enough for that quite astonishing Move, Ballisargon would have succeeded.'

The mention of Ballisargon seemed to be the mental trigger for Vidya. Her tail thrashed wildly, and she dug her claws deep into the floor, through the rug and sinking into the floorboards. Her forelimbs twitched with barely controlled anger and her eyes hardened into twin pools of deep, dark jade. Her whole countenance changed at the sound of Ballisargon's name. Her animal side manifested itself again, not in the same way it had done on Earth, but in a far more dangerous way, with intelligence and purpose driving it. The Engineer realised she had made a mistake in recounting the Move and Ballisargon, but she had to try to help Vidya. She was her friend after all.

The Engineer opened her mouth to say something else, but Vidya began speaking, a low, deep throaty rumble in her voice that chilled the Engineer's blood. 'Our grandparents,' she said deliberately and slowly. 'They had the right idea, all those years ago. I'll finish what they started, before your interference with the way of things. I'm going to hurt him. Fatally. I don't care what I may have promised in the past, he is going to die.'

The Engineer raised a hand in protest, partly in her own defence and partly in that of Vidya's grandparents. 'I hardly think you're being fair, Vidya,' she said. 'After all they chose not to remove Ballisargon, knowing the consequences.'

'Which you told them would happen! How do we *know* what will really happen if one of us… removes him?' All signs of control had now vanished, and Vidya was openly very angry. 'Listen to me. I am going to kill him for what he nearly made us do to Robert. If it had not been for his quick thinking we would have killed and eaten him! After my promise to her!'

The Engineer struggled to maintain her composure. In any conversation where one party becomes angry it is always difficult for the others not to do so too, but she just about managed it. 'Her leaving was not my fault, regardless what you might think; I just did as she asked. And if you want someone to blame for Earth, then blame me. I should have realised what would happen to you both. It's my fault.'

'There you go again, hiding the truth behind your skewed view of the way the world is. Ultimately it's not your fault, it's his. And I'm going to hold him to account for everything he's done. We're not meant to be this way, eking out an existence on the fringes of the world when we used to be its guardians.'

'I can't condone this Vidya. You will bring greater sorrow through your actions.'

'Oh don't worry, your precious principles will still be intact. I'm not asking for your permission or blessing. I'm telling you what to expect. I've had enough of "not acting".' Vidya got to her feet and with her tail slung low between her back legs, swishing angrily from side to side she began to walk out of the room. 'I'm going to see Robert. I've wasted enough time here, and it's time Pradeep had a rest. He's been with Robert ever since we got here, and it's my turn to look after him.' She rounded the corner to Robert's bedroom and disappeared, leaving the Engineer alone in the living area.

Eirian sat in her armchair, slowly turning the memory stick over in her hands.

Vidya did not mention her conversation with the Engineer to her brother when she joined him at Robert's bedside. Instead she inquired as to Robert's state.

'He's still asleep at the moment. Judging by his brain

patterns, if I'm interpreting these things correctly, he not even dreaming.'

'I failed him Pradeep, and *he* saved us, and now he's paying the price for my failure.'

'Don't be ridiculous,' said her brother, 'we couldn't have guessed what would happen on Earth. And remember, it affected me too. OK, it took a little longer, but in the end, by your logic we *both* failed him. I have to say I don't feel like a failure for being affected by a whole planet! It was just too big for us, that's all.'

'Too big…' She echoed her brother's words but not his sentiments. 'You mean that whatever we had done we would have failed.'

'No, I don't think so. I just think there we stopped being Lyr tigers and became Earth tigers. No fate, no destiny, just circumstance.'

'And what about Robert's fate?'

Pradeep, who had known Vidya all her life also knew when something was bothering her. She was not normally sullen and fatalistic. 'C'mon Vid, what's the matter?' he said with genuine concern. Pradeep rarely used the contraction of his sister's name. It was a sign of his obvious distress that he had dropped his normally formal but friendly tone of voice and speech.

'…' began Vidya before changing her mind. 'It's nothing. I guess I'm just not used to failing,' she lied. 'It's made me think that we're not invincible after all.'

'I never claimed to be, but then again, I haven't got your rep as the Mollusc Killer,' Pradeep said, some of his usual jocularity returning.

Vidya managed a weak smile at his humour. 'Good old dependable Pradeep. Always there to make me laugh, even when all I want to do is cry. Is that really my rep?'

Pradeep gave her a sideways look and just shrugged, nonchalantly. 'People like their heroes, or heroines I should say. We did good today Vid, and one blip that wasn't even our fault is no reason to beat yourself up.'

Vidya said nothing. She just sat on the floor next to Robert's bed, looking at him, lost in her memories of what had happened on Earth, and thoughts of what she was going to do to the one she held responsible. 'I'll take over watching him now. You need some rest.'

Pradeep nodded his assent to his sister's request and stood up, stretching his front legs out in front of himself, then arching out his rear legs one at a time before giving his head a quick shake. 'Vid…' he began.

'I'll be fine Pradeep,' she replied rather too curtly.

Pradeep did not need his keen senses to tell him that his sister was lying to him. Or at least not telling him the whole truth. Nevertheless he did not push the issue. He knew well enough that she would confide in him eventually. As Pradeep left the bedroom in search of a warm rug to curl up on he could not shake the feeling that it would not be soon enough.

Vidya stayed sitting upright once her brother had left, watching Robert sleep his dreamless sleep. Her conversations with the Engineer and her brother had not gone at all well. She had soured their returning friendship, and was sure that Pradeep knew she was not telling him everything. Which was true. But how could she confide in him that she was planning murder? Hunting prey or killing in self-defence was one thing, but to set out to kill another living being was something quite different. It went against everything the tigers had been taught by their parents. But she also knew that Ballisargon had been allowed to get away with his crimes for too long. It was not enough to just help Robert get his family back. There would be other worlds where other families would be destroyed because of Ballisargon.

She cursed the Engineer for her weakness all these years. If she had wanted to, *really* wanted to, Vidya was sure she could have engineered a way to stop Ballisargon. *After all hadn't she built the engines of this and numerous other worlds' downfall?* Surely she could build something to stop him. And even if the Engineer did believe Ballisargon's threat that any who toppled him would become him, Vidya certainly did not, regardless what her grandfather had told her.

Eirian was sweating profusely, her charcoal suit grubby and unkempt. Her normally well-pressed blouse hanging out of her trousers; tie long since discarded and her jacket thrown in a crumpled heap in one corner of the room as she worked hard on the Bridge's systems.

She had sat in her armchair for nearly an hour, trying to work through the possible consequences of Vidya's stated intention. If she refused to load the software into the Bridge then there was no way the tigress could ever get inside Ballisargon's Keep, regardless of how angry she might be. But if she did that then Robert would never get his family back, and she would be breaking a promise she had made to him.

She remembered Vidya's words. Eirian knew she had said them in haste, but they still bit deep, much deeper than Verun's earlier attempt to wound her.

She *had* tried opening another Gate to Earth for them to return through, but Ballisargon was too strong. Frustrated and sickened Eirian had had to give up, pressed on by the need to prepare the Bridge's systems for the software she hoped Robert had found while there was still time. So she was willing to get involved, but even that had gone wrong.

Was this all she was capable of, mistake after mistake, error heaped upon error? Memories of Zinan came unbidden to her. In the first few weeks of Ballisargon's dominion they and the tiger's grandparents had tried to fight back against him. She thought she had succeeded in regaining his trust, and together they had attempted a direct assault on Ballisargon. Zinan had even succeeded in usurping control from Ballisargon for a brief period of time, donning the control rings she had been forced to craft. It had all looked so hopeful. Ballisargon seemingly defeated and powerless, while her regained husband set about returning the Lyr to its normal state. How wrong it had gone.

The memory stick turned over in her hands.

In the years since, Eirian had vowed not to involve herself in the affairs of the Lyr. She had done enough damage, lost enough friends to that hopeless cause. She had built the Bridge as one final act of defiance and hope, but even that had turned sour.

For nearly one hundred years Eirian had watched, uninvolved as the Lyr and its people, then other worlds had slowly fallen to Ballisargon. She had removed herself so thoroughly from all real contact with people that she had forgotten her loss, buried under the weight of time. What had started out as an act, the feigned indifference she had to practice hard at, had become her so completely she had trouble telling them apart. That was until Robert had entered her world.

The boy from Earth, his fury and drive to regain his family burning out of him, so like her in the first days. He had been too much for her practised ethics to cope with. Eirian had doubted she was doing the right thing ever since she had become aware of Robert's arrival; surely teaching him the Move and sending him to Earth meant she had gotten involved, hadn't it?

And here she was now, contemplating what Vidya had said. Contemplating getting involved again; once more taking up the fight which had cost her so much. She turned her thoughts over and over in her head, and the memory stick over and over in her hands, her face reflected in its polished metal covering, her deeply lined features staring back at her, almost accusingly.

Eirian knew what she was going to do.

Shaking off the memories of a few hours ago, Eirian came back to the present, and returned to her work, the sweat from her brow mingling with a tear that had risen from the corner of her eye. She wiped it away with an angry flick of her hand.

She would not again succumb to the despair and isolation she had felt for over a century. Eirian had been given a second chance to put things right, at least for one family, and she was going to grasp it with both hands.

One day left.

19

The Man's Too Strong

Robert stirred in his bed and opened his eyes. Immediately Vidya was by his side. 'Are you alright?' she asked gently.

Robert moved his head from side to side, trying to look around himself. He was puzzled as to why he was in bed with a spaghetti of wires attached to his head, chest and arms that pulled at him whichever way he shifted. He mumbled softly in response to Vidya's question and looked over at her. Her eyes were full of concern; the flint that had been there when she was arguing with the Engineer gone completely.

Robert reached out a trembling hand, which Vidya cradled in her massive white paw. He croaked a 'Hello'.

'Oh thank heavens you are alright,' she said. 'Don't try and speak anymore. I'll go and get Pradeep.'

'And… Eirian,' Robert whispered.

Vidya could not help but let her paw fall when Robert mentioned the Engineer, but he was still too weak to notice. She closed her eyes and nodded once silently.

Vidya left the room to get Pradeep. He could go and fetch the Engineer.

Pradeep was curled up on a rug in the living area, snuffling quietly as his huge chest rose and fell gently in rhythm with his breathing. She padded round behind him and laid a paw softly on his shoulder. Pradeep recognised the touch of his sister and opened his eyes. 'What is it?' he asked. 'Is he awake?'

'Yes. At last.'

'That's fantastic. I know you've been worried about him since we got back. Maybe now you and the Engineer can put whatever disagreement you've had behind you.'

'You knew?'

'Of course. You don't really think you can hide something like that from me do you? OK, I'll admit I don't completely know what it was about, but I can have a good guess,' her brother replied.

'…'

'You know that what you want to do won't achieve anything, don't you?'

'We only have her word for that.'

'And our grandparents. While the Engineer's motives are no doubt honourable they are still her own, but I don't know how you can question our family.'

'It's not a matter of doubting them, it's just that maybe things have changed since then. I don't know. All I feel is that we have to do *something* about Him. We can't go on living like this. We don't deserve it.'

Pradeep was silent for a few seconds, then said, 'I agree with you that something must be done, and yes, we maybe have spent too long hiding and letting Ballisargon rule unbound, but what you're thinking is not the way.'

'You're starting to sound like *her* now.'

'I think the Engineer's opinions have changed. Ever since Robert's arrival she's been different, almost the person our grandparents described to us. It seems to me that something's awakened in her again, something she'd forgotten. She would have never sent someone to Earth to get something to *help*, even a week ago, would she? And right now, I bet she's fixing the Bridge to help Robert. She's *involved* again.'

'That still doesn't excuse all those years of letting Ballisargon do as he pleased. How many people have suffered because of her cowardice?'

'And you think she doesn't know that? In her mind everything she's done has led to more suffering. I don't know if I could live with myself if I carried that burden with me, yet here she is helping us once more. OK, it's taken decades and one determined boy for her to realise this, but I really think that we will have the chance to sort this place out. With her help of course.'

'So, what do you want me to do?'

'*I* don't want you to do anything. Hell, don't even do it for Robert. You have to want to make your peace with her.'

'Go and speak to Robert, Pradeep, I'm sure he'd love to see you. I need some time to think on my own.'

Pradeep brushed the side of his muzzle along Vidya's shoulder and said, 'Just don't take too long, eh?' before he padded off.

For the second time in a few hours the Engineer's living room was host to someone who had a lot to think about. Vidya sat with her eyes closed remembering everything she had been told by her grandparents about Ballisargon, and how he could never be toppled by force. *How else could they get rid of him then?* Truly Vidya did not know the answer to her own question. While her wit was quick and she was very intelligent, deep down, at the core of her being she was a tiger and had trouble seeing a resolution to the problem of Ballisargon that did not involve physical violence. Still, she trusted her brother, and if Pradeep had confidence in the Engineer then maybe she should too.

Even so she struggled to bring herself to make the trip to the Engineer, each step she took weighed against her instincts. Eventually, she stood behind the Engineer as she worked. Vidya had walked so slowly that her approach had been almost silent, and the Engineer had not noticed the tiger, engrossed as she was in her efforts. Vidya waited for a minute, still fighting the urge to turn away and leave her to it. In the end she had to give a small cough to announce her presence.

'What?' the Engineer said as she looked over her shoulder. 'Oh, Vidya, hello,' she said without rancour.

The Engineer was a dishevelled mess, her normally immaculate self reduced to a shabby state of affairs. Her eyes were red-rimmed and tired looking. It was obvious to Vidya that the Engineer had been working non-stop since she had walked away in anger, and that she had most likely not slept since before they left for Earth.

'Hello,' the tigress replied. 'Pradeep says we should talk. He thinks I'm wrong.'

The Engineer stopped what she was doing and turned to face the female tiger. 'Shall we sit? I'm exhausted and in need of a rest, so your timing is, as always, impeccable.' She moved to one of the seats in her control room, while Vidya sat herself down on the cool floor. If it was uncomfortable then she did not show it. 'I'm not going to tell you that you're wrong. You view the situation in your own way, and I in mine.'

'Still seeing everyone's point of view?'

The Engineer half-laughed. 'It's my way I'm afraid. I've been trying to stay uninvolved for so long that I have forgotten what it is like to know something with absolute certainty. In a way I envy you your sense of right and wrong. But I think it is time I told you something that may change your perspective on Ballisargon and his disposal.

'Back when he first came to this world, from goodness knows where, and after I had freed Zinan from his prison with the help of your grandparents we, Zinan and I overthrew him.'

'I wasn't told this,' said Vidya.

'I know, and neither was Pradeep. Your grandparents swore to me that they would never tell anyone the details of what happened, just the outcome. Zinan said he'd take the control mechanism for himself to put things back, to make things right again… But Ballisargon had altered them somehow… almost from the moment Zinan put them on he became different… he changed from the man I had loved into something else, something horrible. He told me that he no longer needed any of us and that he now knew what real power should be used for…' the Engineer broke off.

'I don't understand,' said Vidya.

The Engineer took a deep breath, exhaling heavily, then another, steeling herself against what she had to say next. 'I realised that Ballisargon had tricked us. I tried to talk to Zinan, convince him he was being used somehow, but it was no good.

'I spoke to Ballisargon in his cell. He laughed at me, telling me now I knew the consequences of my actions against him. Days went by. Zinan was as bad as Ballisargon had been, talking of conquering worlds and crushing all opposition to his rule. Worse even. Ballisargon had at least been working to a plan, whereas Zinan just used the power on a whim. Hundreds of people lost their lives as he tested the limits of his power. If it had not been for your grandparents I am sure I would have died too.

'In the end we grew desperate. Your grandparents and I attacked him in an effort to remove the rings. It was a furious fight, in the end we bested him, but not without everyone suffering grievous wounds. I saw the extent of the damage the rings had inflicted on Zinan. Even in the few days he wore them they rotted him from the inside, just hollowed him out until he was little more than dust and bones. Without the power the rings channelled to sustain him his final moments alive were…

'And then, there was Ballisargon standing before us as he picked up Zinan's discarded fingers and removed the rings. He had set us all up, just to prove to us that he could not be confronted.

'So you see, Ballisargon cannot be stopped by ordinary physical means. He's too clever to just fight. You may think you're winning but you're not; he's too good at playing all the angles and he's had nearly a century to plan for such an attack.

'Even touching the control rings causes you damage. They rot your body and your spirit. Those rings are plagued somehow. I have never been able to fully understand how it happened. You cannot fight him physically and come away unscathed or unaltered. Even the brief seconds your grandparents had contact with the rings affected them for months to come.'

'But there must be a way.'

'In nearly one hundred years I have not found it. For now, we can content ourselves with helping Robert, can't we?'

Vidya thought about Robert and his family, and of her binding promise to take care of him. While she wanted to stop Ballisargon, that was not Robert's fight. He was here to get his Dad and sister back, and she would honour herself by helping him. She nodded. 'We'll find a way when this is over.'

The Engineer smiled, 'Always the tiger, eh Vidya?'

'You bet,' she said, rising to her feet. 'Now come on, let's see how Robert is.'

Robert was better. While Vidya had been speaking with the Engineer he had recovered, and was sitting up in bed fully awake and pestering Pradeep with question after question about the situation. Pradeep eventually had to admit that he did not know where the Engineer was, but that he thought she was working on the Bridge with the software that Robert had retrieved from Earth.

'Yes I was,' said the Engineer, breezing into the room with Vidya at her side. Brother and sister exchanged a look that told Pradeep that, while all was not completely resolved between his sister and the Engineer, they had at least come to an agreement somewhere in the middle and things were back on track with helping Robert.

'I was asleep?' Robert asked.

'Sort of,' replied the Engineer as she moved to Robert's bedside and started removing the sensors that were still stuck to his head. 'You weren't exactly in a coma, and you weren't exactly sleeping. The effort of the day on Earth then the necessity to Move with such rapid frequency took a severe toll on your body. You collapsed at the foot of the Bridge after Moving just shy of eleven kilometres.'

'There goes my record,' said Vidya. 'I am not sure I am going to be able to best that. Ever.'

Robert smiled. 'I don't remember dreaming anything. How long was I out?'

'About half a day,' said the Engineer. 'You woke sooner than I anticipated. I expected to have the Bridge's systems upgraded by the time you came round. Still, I am nearly done; another hour or two at the most. How do you feel?'

'OK,' replied Robert. 'I think I should feel worse than I do, but I feel fine.'

The Engineer and the tigers looked sceptical.

'Honestly, I do. OK, I don't want to have to do another Move like that again, but I'm alright.'

The Engineer nodded. She finished unsticking the sensors from Robert's head and arms, leaving him to remove the ones from his chest, while she retrieved a clean set of clothes from a cupboard. 'Oh yes, and you'll need *another* pair of trainers. I understand that your last pair took some severe punishment from our mutual friends here,' she said, good humour infecting her voice.

The tigers looked, if not sheepish, then certainly embarrassed. 'You promised you wouldn't mention that again, if we didn't,' said Pradeep.

'Sorry, Pradeep. You won't hear another word about it from me.' The Engineer turned to and gave him a knowing wink. 'Now, these are just the same as the last set of clothes, so I know they'll fit.' She shifted to address the tigers. 'C'mon you two, let's leave Robert get dressed.'

Robert took the clothes, glad to be out of bed. He made a face when he thought about the fate of the previous pair of trainers and how close he had come to sharing it. As he put them on and tied the laces he felt oddly re-assured. The sensation of something tightly fitting on his feet, encasing them and protecting them made him feel safe. He hadn't noticed it before, but as he thought about it he felt braver with footwear on than in bare feet or socks.

For the next hour or so Robert recounted the events on Earth to the tigers. He started from where Vidya had disappeared, up to where all three of them had barrelled through the Gate.

The tigers expressed their gratitude to him for saving their lives, both on Earth and back in the Lyr. 'I think we're more than even now,' said Vidya.

The Engineer appeared at the door to her control room. 'Done,' was all she said.

'We're ready? We can go now?' asked Robert, his mouth suddenly dry.

'Yes. I have to instruct you in a few matters before you set off though,' replied the Engineer. 'Come on,' she said as she headed outside

Robert and the tigers followed the Engineer out onto the open platform of the Bridge. The wind still blew the clouds along, but the surroundings looked different. The Engineer took out a small telescope from her jacket and extended it. She held it up to her eye and peered into the distance.

Robert followed the direction the Engineer was looking and could see a dark smudge on the horizon. Darker than the rest of the sky it looked out of place. 'Is *that* Ballisargon's Keep?'

'Yes,' replied the Engineer. 'Here, take a look for yourself.' She passed the telescope to Robert.

Robert looked at the telescope in his hands. It was the

kind he would expect to find on an old sailing ship; solid and made of brass. Shrugging, he held it up to his right eye, while closing the left. In the far distance he could see the darker patch of sky more clearly, and at the centre of it a building of some sort. He looked harder, concentrating on what he was seeing.

Robert could make out what appeared to be a large, rectangular towerblock covered in what looked to be mirrored glass. Ballisargon's Keep, the very heart of his dark power, looked like a skyscraper glinting faintly in the red light of the Lyr.

Robert lowered the telescope, pushed it closed with both hands and handed it back to the Engineer. 'That doesn't make any sense,' he said.

'I have never been able to bring the Bridge within spying distance of the Keep, so as far as I know it's looked like that for nearly a century. Still, it's not what it looks like that is important. You need to get to it, so I've pointed the Bridge toward it. That will make it easier to get to.'

'How *do* we get to it? It's miles away.' Robert said.

'Ah, here's the clever thing about the Bridge, Robert. You, or rather I, just point it at something or somewhere I, or someone else wants to go, and you just walk off it. The Bridge does the rest. After all, the Bridge wouldn't be much of a bridge if it didn't go anywhere, would it?'

'I suppose not. So we just walk to the end and what, we'll get to Ballisargon's Keep?'

The Engineer nodded, while the tigers looked sceptical.

'Be careful around Ballisargon's Keep,' she cautioned. 'It's a tricky place that will try to confuse you. Don't let it. Once inside you'll need to use this to free your family.' She handed Robert a piece of chalk.

'How is this going to help?'

'When you find them, just draw an outline round your family and they will be freed from Ballisargon's control.'

'Like on the telly, in the police shows.'

'Yes, if you like.' The Engineer raised an eyebrow. 'Just draw round them, and they will no longer be in Ballisargon's power. Then, get them to hold onto you and the tigers and use the Rook's Move to escape. I'll be watching the outside of the Keep for you, and as soon as I spot you I'll transport you back here.'

'How does it work? The chalk I mean?'

'The chalk is not really chalk at all. Well, OK, it *is* chalk, but the chalk is really just a substrate for the nanoscopic signal disruptors that are embedded in it. A circle, or any complete line around a person will interfere with the flow of energy from the person to the generators, making the system think that they are all used up. The system then releases the person. Or at least that's how it was built to work.'

Robert nodded. He grasped about half of what the Engineer had said, but trusted her to know what she was talking about.

'Ready?' she asked.

Robert looked at Vidya and Pradeep, who nodded back at him. 'I guess so,' he said.

The three of them set off down the Bridge. Robert strained and narrowed his eyes to see if he could see Ballisargon's Keep as he had through the telescope, but it was no good. All he could make out was the same darkening in the sky. Whether it was it a trick of the light, or only his imagination Robert couldn't be sure, but he was convinced that the dark patch in the sky that lay before him and the tigers had grown blacker, as if it knew they were coming and was preparing for them.

When they reached the edge, Robert turned round to look at the Engineer. He could see she had a hopeful smile on her face. The Engineer waved at him, and Robert heard her shout goodbye and good luck. Robert turned back toward the edge of the Bridge. He looked down at his feet, his toes poking over the edge, hundreds of metres up in the air. Below him the lake that protected the Bridge sat still and placid. *At least if the Bridge doesn't work we'll have a soft landing.*

Robert took a deep breath, and looked at the tigers by his side. 'Dad, Elisabeth, please hang on a little longer. I'm coming now.' He closed his eyes, and raised his right leg out in front of himself. The tigers both lifted a foreleg in readiness. Then all three of them, tigers and human took a step forward out into empty space.

20

The Masterplan

Eight tiger paws and one pair of trainers hit solid ground. What they didn't know was that they were being watched on eight different screens in Ballisargon's control room; three on each tiger and two on the boy.

A scrolling set of graphics updated him on all non-visual information regarding the three of them: heart-rate, respiration, blood-oxygen level, brain-waves (alpha and theta) and dozens of their bodies' other autonomic systems. Ballisargon's Keep had alerted him the instant the three intruders had materialised, and he had wasted no time in Moving himself to his centre of power where he could see what was happening.

And he was not happy with what he saw.

The boy and his pets had made it through everything he had put in their way so far. Not only had the three of them conquered his Mollusc on Earth they had also somehow escaped from the dozens he had scattered throughout the Lyr as well. And now they were in his Keep. Ballisargon was almost as impressed as he was annoyed. How much more trouble was this irritating little brat from that pitiful planet going to cause him? There was only one way to find out, but first he had to get rid of the tigers.

While Ballisargon was confident that the tigers were no match for him, he was not about to test the theory; he remembered what had happened to Zinan, and had no desire to share his fate. Much better to confuse them first; throw them off balance. Then he would be able to overcome them much more easily, and, once they were safely out of harm's way (specifically, his) he could deal with the little boy.

Unaware of their observation, Robert and the tigers opened their eyes after stepping off the Bridge, and looked round themselves. Even with the exterior of the Keep looking the way it had, Robert was not prepared for what he saw. The three of them stood in a plain white corridor, with very ordinary looking wooden doors stretching down either side of it. The corridor branched off to the right and left a little way ahead, and was lit all the way along by fluorescent tubes.

Robert was reminded of his Dad's office; modern design and sparse furnishing with the barest minimum of flourishes. He could hear a faint humming and felt the gentlest breath of warm air on his cheeks.

'I don't like this place. It has no *smells*,' said Pradeep. 'Even the desert has scents and aromas carried on the air, but this place has nothing. All there is is this light breeze, and that doesn't smell of anything.'

'It's *air conditioning*,' said Robert almost not believing what his own senses were telling him. 'I thought Ballisargon was like this huge evil or something? How has he got air conditioning?'

'Beats me,' replied Vidya, 'but I suggest we don't waste time wondering about it. Come on, let's find your family and get out of here. Any idea which way to go?'

'Not the faintest, but I suggest we stay together. I don't fancy being in here on my own,' said Robert. 'How about we start trying these doors, and see where they go?'

'Sounds as good a way to start as any,' said Pradeep. 'How about this one?' He pointed at the nearest one with his forepaw.

On the pair of monitors that kept him under close scrutiny, Robert walked up to the door. In his control room Ballisargon twitched an index finger. When Robert tried the handle; it was locked. He turned to tigers and shook his head. Ballisargon allowed himself a small smile as the boy moved to the next door, and after another twitch of a ringed finger, also found that one locked. This might be easier than he expected.

For well over three hours Robert and the tigers made their way down corridors, trying every door they found. Ballisargon, who had grown bored of locking the doors just before the boy got to them bulk-locked every door in his Keep after the first five minutes, and sat back to watch the amusement. He enjoyed seeing the tigers' grow more unsettled as the hours wore on; they were definitely thrown off balance by the clean, bright environment they found themselves in. He also took some pleasure from the boy's growing demoralisation with every locked door.

'Why don't I try breaking one down?' he heard the female tiger say over the speakers. 'They don't look too strong to me.'

Go on then, just try.

'No, it's probably best not to. After all, I don't want to draw attention to us,' replied the boy. Ballisargon had to stifle a laugh. Maybe it was time to up the stakes a little. He held his index and middle fingers together on both hands, and made shooting motions with his hands. Up ahead, unseen or unheard by the three creatures on his monitors, the corridor shifted, and a door snicked open.

Robert looked at his watch. They had been walking and checking doors for over half the day and he was tired. 'I need a rest for a few minutes,' he told the tigers.

Vidya and Pradeep acquiesced to his request, and lay themselves down on the carpet tiles. All three sat there in silence for a few moments, until Pradeep said, 'I still think this place has too few smells. You can't tell where anything is. Even our scent seems to get carried away by this infernal *air-conditioning*. We could have been walking round in circles for all I know.'

'I know what you mean,' said Vidya. 'It's so *sterile* in here, like there's no life or energy. I wonder why Ballisargon has it like this?'

'I don't know,' said Robert honestly. He had been thinking the same thing since they had arrived. What he been expecting, he didn't know, but it had been something very different. 'Anyway, c'mon, let's get back to it. I don't like being in here any more than you do, and the quicker we can get out the better.' He got to his feet.

The tigers did the same, and they set off the way they had been heading down the corridor.

A camera switched angles so that Ballisargon could view the all three of them in one shot approaching the open door in the dead end corridor just ahead of them. He leaned back in his seat. This should prove both interesting and enlightening.

The camera watched as Robert pushed the door fully open, and walked carefully inside. Instinctively he reached along the wall and was not surprised to find a light switch. He flicked it on and the room was bathed in the same artificial glow as the corridor.

Inside was a bank of computer screens, each one displaying a semi circular graphic with a twitching pointer on it and a series of characters from a language that made no sense scrolling up the right hand side. Robert pondered what he was seeing. *A gauge of some sort? What could it be measuring?* All at once he realised what the displays were for, what they were measuring. He remembered what Eirian had told him about Ballisargon. It was energy! The whole room was monitoring the generators she had told him about.

Even before he could stop himself Robert punched the screen. It didn't give in the slightest, let alone break. Instead his fist bounced off it with a dull, glass knock. 'Son of a…' Robert nearly swore, partly at Ballisargon, and partly at the pain in his knuckles. He turned in disgust from the monitors and made his way back to the tigers. 'There's nothing here that helps us,' he said in a monotone, as he walked past them.

Displayed on Ballisargon's screens, they left the room and headed back the way they had come down the corridor. Ballisargon clenched his right hand into a fist, twice in rapid succession. Taking a left hand turn all three figures exchanged puzzled looks when they saw in front of them a dead end corridor with a door at the end, ajar and the blue-green glow from computer screens seeping through the open doorway.

'We must have got turned round somehow,' the female tiger said. 'Let's try the other way, but just to make sure...' She flicked out one of her sharp claws and, with a ripping noise, gouged a deep scratch into the wall before they turned and left. If he had been so inclined Ballisargon would have been offended at the wanton damage to his Keep. Instead his eyes widened at the sight of the claw effortlessly tearing through the wall. He realised that he had been right to stay put while he disorientated the tigers. He did not want to be on the receiving end of that! Much better to confuse them before facing them.

He turned back to the screens to see the companions this time take the right hand fork away from the computer room. They then took the next left then another right. Ballisargon ensured, with a couple of deft flicks of his left hand, that the next corner they rounded had them once again facing the same door. The male tiger padded up to the scratch his sister had made only a minute before.

I suppose now is as good a time as any to make my move.

'This can't be right,' said Pradeep narrowing his eyes and inspecting the scratch. There could be no doubt; this WAS the same corridor. 'How is it that we keep coming back here when every time we take a different route? It doesn't make any sense.'

'Of course it doesn't make sense to you, you stupid animal,' said a slow, deliberate voice from behind them. 'Only I understand the true nature of what is after all *my* stronghold.'

All three of them turned round, very slowly. In front of them stood Ballisargon; the Stealer of Worlds, Desecrator of Civilisations, Master of the Glass Mollucs, and after his conquests, Lord of the Lyr.

Robert was struck by how *ordinary* Ballisargon looked, after all he had heard about him. He was dressed in a plain sand coloured suit. The only thing that looked out of place were the rings on each of his fingers and both his thumbs. They were all a dull silver colour, hardly reflecting the harsh strip lights overhead. Again, Robert wasn't sure what he had been expecting, but it wasn't this.

'Don't move, Robert,' cautioned Vidya.

'Yes Robert, best you stay still.' Ballisargon sounded like he was offering friendly advice, not making a threat. His slate grey eyes narrowed; Robert could feel his gaze boring into him, through him as if he were made of glass. 'Your Father and I have had a few chats about you, like how it was that I missed you, and so forth,' Ballisargon continued is his slow measured manner.

At the mention of his Dad, Robert couldn't help but react. It was not unnoticed by the tigers.

'Careful, Robert,' urged Pradeep.

'Yes, do be careful, Robert, after all you wouldn't *THIS* to happen,' and with a flick of Ballisargon's hand, Pradeep disappeared.

Now it was Vidya's turn to react. The tigress narrowed her eyes. 'Bring. Him. Back.' Each word was spoken with death hovering around its edge.

'I don't think so,' replied Ballisargon, and with another flick of his hand, Vidya disappeared. He turned to Robert. 'Now, maybe we can talk uninterrupted, man to man, so to speak.'

Robert was left unprotected by the impossible disappearance of his friends. He had no choice but to comply with Ballisargon's request.

'Shall we retire to my throne room? It has seats.'

Robert felt a whoosh, and a vacuum open and close round him almost in a heartbeat, causing him to gasp. He was now standing in Ballisargon's throne room. His place of power, from which he ruled the dozens of worlds he had conquered.

'Please, sit.' Ballisargon gestured to an office chair, which rolled toward Robert, under Ballisargon's control.

Robert sat. Ballisargon's throne room was decorated just like the corridor they had left. Stark, blank walls of muted pastel colours, with fluorescent lighting. Wooden fire doors, and double-glazing sat in the panel walls, while hard wooden veneer desks, with painted metal legs sat on the nylon carpet tiles. In one corner, in front of two huge windows that looked out over the Lyr desert, sat a desk with three large, flat screen monitors, cordless keyboard and mouse on it. Ballisargon walked behind the desk, and sat down so he was silhouetted by the red-brown daylight that poured in through the glass.

'This doesn't look much like a throne room.' Robert tried to sound confident, but he was quite afraid. This wasn't going the way he had expected it to.

'Yes, you're right, I suppose. My throne room, and the rest of my Keep in general take their form from the energies of the people I have powering my generators, and their images and thoughts get imprinted on it. As I currently have your world's population working my generators, my domain resembles them, and their world. Surely Eirian explained this to you?' It was the most Robert had heard Ballisargon say so far. His voice was quite deep, strangely melodic, but had no accent that Robert could discern. 'Still, I am not without some control of my own.'

Ballisargon clicked his fingers. The room and everything in it immediately changed; from the bland nondescript office environment to what Robert took to be that of a feudal Japanese palace. The partition walls were gone, replaced with wood and paper screens illuminated from behind by flickering lamps; the chair Robert sat on became a tatami mat, and Robert was taken by surprise to suddenly find himself sitting on the floor. Ballisargon sat on a similar mat behind a low table on his raised dais. The computer had gone, replaced by a neat bundle of papers. Even their clothes had changed; Ballisargon wore an elaborate kimono with intricate designs stitched into it, while Robert found himself wearing a shorter coat and fitted pants. Oddly, thought Robert, neither of them wore anything on their feet.

'What do you think?' asked Ballisargon, from his vantage point. 'An improvement? Perhaps something else.' He clicked his fingers again and the room changed once more.

This time the room became brilliant white with the paper screens replaced by heavy marble walls. Robert now found himself sitting on a simple wooden folding chair while he wore a light, white tunic and leather sandals on his feet. Ballisargon wore a laurel wreath on his head and his kimono was gone, replaced with a deep purple, almost dark blue toga. The mat he had been sitting on was also gone, replaced with a large marble throne inlaid with what looked like gold and ivory.

'A little too archaic for my tastes,' Ballisargon said as he clicked his fingers once more. Now Robert found himself sitting in a church pew, while Ballisargon sat on a large carved wooden throne wearing long, heavy looking white robes inlaid with gold and crimson. He was holding a sceptre in one hand and had a mitre on his head.

'No, I don't think so,' said Ballisargon and clicked his fingers again and again and again, over a dozen times in under a minute.

With each click the whole room changed instantly into another style and architecture from Earth's history, and each time Ballisargon was the dominant point of focus in the room, while Robert always found himself dressed in markedly poorer clothing. He found himself struggling to keep up with the rapidly changing environment, and eventually had to close his eyes, as he felt like he was going to be sick trying to keep up with the rapid changes.

After a short period where Ballisargon had not clicked his fingers, Robert opened his eyes again.

Where the desk and computer had originally been, now sat a massive oak table, with a carved wooden chair behind it. Candles burned in holders along the length of the table. Where there had been the concealed lighting, there were now torches and censers, their acrid smoke filling the air. Robert saw doors replaced with vast curtains, and the windows had become huge tapestries and oil paintings depicting the Lyr landscape they now concealed. Once again Ballisargon's clothes had changed from the sombre suit to a set of pantaloons, a doublet and a cape. Robert was now dressed in a rough leather jerkin and a pair of loosely woven pants.

'Better? I think so,' said Ballisargon, honestly. 'I don't really care for your world's ways. Why have any of your history when I can use something from your fiction. So much more rewarding than what you laughably call a past. All that fussing and worthless work you pitiful creatures do. Your empty little pointless lives, never knowing the heights you could attain. Satisfying yourself with so little, even in the ones you appoint as your leaders.

'You are so small,' he continued, 'I shall be glad when I have exhausted you all and replaced you with a more

...dynamic race.' Ballisargon sounded almost sorry for himself.

'Well, I don't want everyone back,' said Robert, 'I just want my Dad and sister. It's why I've come all this way, and I won't go home without them.' Robert had no idea how he was going to make the last part happen, but he felt he had to say it.

Ballisargon leaned forward so his elbows rested on the table in front of him. He clasped his hands in front of him, but instead of interlocking his fingers over one another, Ballisargon folded them *behind* each other, so they rested inside his clasped hands rather than on the outside. The action of interlocking his fingers this way was so smooth it looked second nature. He stared at Robert.

'Indeed. And are you sure that is *all* you came here for? After all why bring the tigers if all you wanted was your family?'

Robert felt an itch in his head as Ballisargon spoke, near the base of his skull as if someone was tickling his brain gently.

'They said they wanted to come and make sure you didn't hurt me,' replied Robert as politely as he could. After Ballisargon's display of power he wanted to do nothing that would anger him. 'I really just want to go home.'

'You know, that almost sounds plausible. Do you remember how you felt those times when you were alone in the dark, the burden of responsibility that had fallen to you through a fluke of chance? It wasn't fair was it? After all, if all the other people had been careless enough not to leave someone behind to come and get them, why should you have to? Maybe I could…'

This time as Ballisargon spoke Robert found it hard to concentrate on what he was saying. The feather in his head had become fingertips, poking and probing around. Robert blinked twice and rubbed his eyes with his fists trying to shake the feeling.

'Something wrong, Robert?' Ballisargon asked rhetorically.

Robert instinctively reached for his necklace. As soon as his fingers touched the cool metal the fingertips were removed from his head. Ballisargon narrowed one eye in suspicion.

'Please. I just want to have my family back and get out of here.'

'I have to admit that I believe you, despite myself,' said Ballisargon, unclasping his hands and spreading them out on the table before himself in a gesture of conciliation. 'I expected you to say as much, so I took the liberty of freeing them when you first arrived in my Keep. Saves so much bother if I just give you what you want so you leave and cease to be a nuisance to me. I have much larger concerns than one irritating little boy and his family.'

Robert tried not to look resentful at Ballisargon's comments about him and family. Instead he cast his eyes downward and uttered a very quiet, 'Thank you.'

Ballisargon stood up from behind the large table. 'You know Robert, this is the longest single conversation I have had with another individual for nearly a decade, and loathe though I am to admit it, I am actually enjoying it. I have to say I am impressed that you made it this far, even with all the help you've had.' He stopped speaking for a moment, then continued 'In fact, I think you may actually be interested in the plans I have for your species.' He wagged a single finger at Robert conspiratorially.

The tone in Ballisargon's voice indicated clearly to Robert that he would have little say in the matter whether he wanted to know or not. He thought it best if he played along until Ballisargon made good on his promise.

Ballisargon clicked his fingers once more, and Robert felt the familiar whooshing sensation of being Moved under someone else's control. When his surroundings settled down he found himself standing in a room very similar Eirian's control room, just lacking the keyboards.

'Now, watch this,' Ballisargon commanded to Robert. 'You must have been wondering how I Moved your entire planet's population in one go, when you and your tigers can barely Move yourself. Oh, and you're also probably wondering why I don't have any of those clumsy keyboards that Eirian insists on using. Well, the answer to both those questions is right here.' Ballisargon wiggled his fingers indicating the rings that adorned each one. 'These give me a level of direct control unimagined by her and her inelegant machinery. Would you care to try one?'

Ballisargon removed the smallest ring from his right little finger and proffered it to Robert. Robert stared at the small perfect circlet of metal held between Ballisargon's finger and thumb. He began to reach out to take it when something inside him cautioned against it. 'No thank you,' he said as politely as he could.

'Your loss,' Ballisargon sighed as he put the ring back on his finger.

'But that doesn't explain how you were able to Move everyone on Earth at once though. Eirian said that your machines aren't that powerful and can't take that many people at once.'

'Ah, but they can, young Robert. I have hardly been idle in my time here in the Lyr. Since their creation decades ago the generators have housed some of the finest minds to have evolved in the galaxy. They have been powered by poets, artists, doctors and of course scientists. And it those scientists' great works that have been put to practical use here at my disposal.'

'You've used cleverer people than yourself to upgrade your machines.' It was a statement, not a question and Robert was appalled.

'Why yes.' Ballisargon was almost nonchalant in the way he dismissed Robert's revulsion. 'Do not think that I am that different to thousands of others across hundreds of worlds. And besides, it is not as if your world is any different, so there is no need to look so shocked Robert. The only way they differ from me is in the scope of their plans. Too concerned with their own personal power to make use of the real power their station grants them.'

'And I guess you got them to make you the rings as well.'

'These?' Ballisargon wiggled his fingers. 'No, these were a lover's final parting gift from Eirian, to better allow me the delicate touch of control I would need.' Ballisargon gave a small shake of his head. 'Dear, sweet, foolish, trusting Eirian. Shoulders of giants, and all that. Anyway enough smalltalk. Watch this carefully.'

Ballisargon flicked his left hand up and away while the right twitched almost imperceptibly. On the screen in front of them an image of a brown and white planet, obviously not Earth, came into view. 'A world I passed over some years ago. The dominant sentient race were not compatible with the generators I am afraid. Too dull-witted.' Ballisargon offered in the way of an explanation. 'I suppose you would consider them lucky in that regard,' he said humourlessly.

Ballisargon's gestures became more precise as he zoomed in on a large landmass filled with green. The more Ballisargon zoomed in the more the seemingly single block of green broke up into discrete spots, until there were just six present on the screen.

'A family unit, if I remember correctly. This particular race has three genders and lives in organisational units of six. Something to do with their feeble religious beliefs, I think.'

Ballisargon grabbed the thin air with his right hand. The six spots vanished from the screen with such speed that it caused Robert to gasp out loud. 'Where… where are they?'

Ballisargon grinned, and flexed his left hand. The planet zoomed out again until it was a speck on the screen, then he opened his right hand. The six green spots re-appeared on the screen, only to dim to nothingness straight away. 'There they are. Or rather, were. Like most lifeforms they cannot survive in space for very long,' he said matter-of-factly.

'Why did you do that?' Robert had trouble containing his anger and confusion.

'Because they were of no use to me. Because I could. Because I felt like it. A dozen different reasons and none in particular.' He turned and looked down at Robert. 'Now do you understand the nature of the power I command? What is the point of a few frog-people scrabbling and grubbing purposelessly around in muddy pools, barely aware of their own lives, let alone the potential of the Universe around them? To them I would appear as a god, and what better existence for a people than to serve God?'

Robert said nothing and could not stop himself from looking down, once again humbled by Ballisargon. Then he realised something. 'But you still need us, Earth people I mean,' he said, able to look up at Ballisargon and meet his gaze for a second. Then he immediately regretted what he had said.

Ballisargon was silenced by Robert's directness. Usually people were cowed into submission by him and his overt displays of power. There was something more to this boy after all. He idly wondered why his attempts at examining Robert's thoughts had failed, and that maybe he should keep the boy around for dissection.

Robert collapsed inside himself at his direct question to Ballisargon. He was convinced he had undone the promise Ballisargon had made to him with his bluntness, and had sealed both his and his family's fate, along with that of the tigers.

Instead Ballisargon replied in his ever-present measured tone, 'Yes, yes I do. Although you are not the strongest species I have ever encountered you are by far the most populous. I have never seen a world with as many people on it as yours. That fact alone secured your fate. Let me show you.' He flicked both hands up, and the display changed to what Robert assumed was an external view of the Lyr, the screen now filled with a red-brown disc. 'Ah, home,' said

Ballisargon confirming Robert's suspicions.

'You see Robert, I realised a long time ago that I was reaching the limits of the Move in securing power for my generators and that I needed to find new sources of energy. However, I was constrained by the location of the Lyr. Although the generators provide me immense power, it is not limitless, and I cannot reach much further than your world.

'For years the question vexed me. I predicted I had barely fifty years of power left, and that was not enough. I have too much to do to lose momentum before I have barely started, but here I was constrained by the very world that gave me the scope to realise the Plan. How could I extend the range of the Move? How could I get to the people I needed? Then it occurred to me that I was approaching the question from the wrong direction.'

Robert looked puzzled. He had been following Ballisargon's logic and could see no way out. In Ballisargon's situation Robert had decided that he would have had to use what remaining power he had left more wisely, as to extend its life, possibly until he found a replacement and no longer needed it. But then Robert wasn't Ballisargon.

'I realised that if I could not Move any more people to the Lyr, I would have to Move the Lyr to the people.'

Robert's eyes went wide with surprise and his mouth fell open at the scale of what Ballisargon had just said. 'You want to Move…' he could barely comprehend the massiveness of what Ballisargon was saying, 'the whole planet?'

'Indeed. All that was required was a sufficiently large source of energy.'

Robert remembered the trouble he had had Moving the boulder on the Bridge, and that had barely weighed a couple of kilograms. 'But it must weigh millions of tons!'

'Trillions,' stated Ballisargon. 'So you see my need for your world. Seven billion batteries is enough. Of course it will all but exhaust them all, so I have had to plan this very carefully. The generators have perhaps another twelve hours before they are fully aligned with your people. After that, we Move.'

'But what about my family?'

'Oh yes. Forgive me, I had almost forgotten. I will release them to you now.' Ballisargon clicked his fingers again, and Robert found himself back in the throne room.

A man dressed in a t-shirt and jeans and a teenaged girl wearing Elisabeth's clothing stood waiting for them when they arrived. 'Robert?' his Dad asked as Robert appeared. 'Is that really you?'

'DAD! Elisabeth!'

'Now, as I have things to do, if you agree to leave immediately, I will let you all live, even your bothersome tiger friends.' It sounded like it was going to be Ballisargon's one and only offer. Robert took it.

'OK. Let Pradeep and Vidya go, and I'll leave you alone from now on, and never come back. I promise.'

Ballisargon smiled like a serpent, his dark eyes almost black in the torchlight. They glittered with his power. Ballisargon moved and sat on his throne. 'On second thoughts, perhaps not.'

Before Robert could even react he saw two Glass Molluscs appear in the throne room. They Moved over his Dad and Elisabeth, and in a heartbeat all four of them had disappeared again, only this time his Dad and Elisabeth had been INSIDE the creatures.

The tears came without him noticing, the shock of what he had just witnessed tore his insides out. The unstoppable feeling began in his stomach, turning it over before it moved up to his chest, transforming itself to anger, his heart pounding. It grew to fury as it continued upwards knotting his throat into a tight ball, before it burst into his skull and out of his mouth with the scream of violent rage.

'Noooooooooo!'

He was running without thinking, fists ready to do some damage to Ballisargon, but before he had made it even a single metre across the room Ballisargon waved a hand, and Robert disappeared just like Pradeep and Vidya had done.

Ballisargon let out a large breath as his calm demeanour slipped away. His hands began shaking and he felt sweat bead on his forehead. He breathed in and out deeply as the adrenaline worked its way through his body. In an effort to calm himself and slow his body he let his hands fall into his lap with his palms up one on top of the other; the ends of his thumbs touching together to make a closed circle.

As his mind calmed he remembered how afraid he had been when he had learnt that Robert and the tigers had breached his Stronghold. But in the end he had been able to exert enough self control to overcome them all. Barely, but he had done it nonetheless. Then once the tigers had been removed he had not been able to resist showing off to the little boy from Earth, flushed as he was with his seeming success over his bodyguards.

Ballisargon continued to sit on his throne and allowed his mind to wander freely, following whatever course it chose, connecting and free-associating. He had seemingly dealt with the threat the tigers had posed with little effort. He almost laughed to himself when he thought of how scared he had been of them, but the ease with which he had Moved them out of his way had surprised and gladdened him. He thought about the years of hiding from the original tigers and their descendants.

He should have gone after them all, the whole troupe of them when that she-tiger killed one of his Molluscs. Instead he had hidden in his Keep. What a coward and a fool he had been all these years. They were nothing; he knew that now. He was Lord of this world, and they would all suffer his vengeance.

Smiling with new confidence, he sat back and thought how best he could dispose of them both. After he had thoroughly examined Robert of course.

21

Changes

Vidya padded round her cell a couple of more times knocking her claws against the solid steel bars again in frustration. Across from her in an identical prison was Pradeep, who had sat down a full ten minutes before, and even now was watching her through the bars with an expression of good mannered exasperation.

'Oh Vidya, will you sit still,' he admonished gently. 'We both know Ballisargon has no real power over him.'

'Yes, but Robert doesn't know that, does he? We should have told him who she was, who *he* is. We waited too long, Pradeep. Ballisargon can still use his feelings for her against him.'

'We didn't get the chance; I mean since he arrived it's been non-stop. I thought we'd find the opportunity when we got to Earth…' Pradeep trailed off with a shrug, then continued, 'But Ballisargon doesn't know who she is, and if Robert doesn't then Ballisargon can't make the connection. In a way his ignorance is a shield.'

'I suppose so,' said Vidya, listlessly. 'I just wish he'd get here, that's all.'

'He'll arrive,' said Pradeep confidently. 'You're not doubting his abilities, are you?'

'No,' replied Vidya sternly, 'But we were wrong not to tell him sooner. As soon as he gets here, I'm telling him. Everything.' Vidya finally sat down.

'I can't disagree there...' Pradeep began to reply, when suddenly both his and Vidya's surroundings changed radically. Where a second ago the walls had been smooth, featureless concrete they were now made of thick bamboo, tightly bound together, with twine forming a cage that rested on the earthen floor.

'Interesting,' said Pradeep. 'I wasn't expecting *that.*'

'Me neither,' said Vidya. 'I wonder what it means?'

Before either tiger had a chance to answer the question, the prison changed again. The bamboo replaced with iron bars and solid stone. A set of shackles led from the wall to a large iron hoop around each of the tiger's necks.

'Mmm, nice,' remarked Vidya, kicking the chain that bound her to the wall. 'Pradeep, what is going on?'

'Beats me,' replied her brother. '*He* must be doing it somehow.'

Once again, before Vidya could reply the room changed again. And again and again and again. Each change altered the structure of the prison, but not the fact it was a prison. It cycled through stone walls, wooden slatted panels, solid steel cages, earth pits and even, bizarrely, a force field of some sort that left the tigers hovering suspended in mid-air unable to move.

Finally after a blitz of different types the reality around the tigers settled down into large, cube-shaped granite boulders with coarse mortar between them forming the walls and the bars of the cells becoming rusted, but still formidably thick, iron.

Eirian stood at the window in her living room on the Bridge, staring at the wind driven clouds passing silently by outside as they had done for nearly a century now. She was worried. Worried about Robert, and what she had done.

Still, it was too late now. She had done all she could think of to help, and had to hope it would be enough. After a moment longer of reflection she thought she sensed something.

Involuntarily her head jerked up and over her right shoulder as if in response to a distant sound that only she had heard. Her eyes narrowed in concentration. The sudden movement of her body shook her from her contemplation. She headed outside for a look.

Before she had made it to her doorway everything changed. Suddenly she was no longer dressed in her business like attire, but in the garb of a geisha. Her suit was replaced with a fine kimono tied at the back with the obi and on her feet, which were encased in white socks, were a pair of black lacquer shoes. Even her face was painted; she could feel the tightness of the dry pigment on her skin.

Interesting, she thought. *I wasn't expecting that.*

She looked about her and saw that the whole of her living quarters had also changed. Paper screens replaced brick walls, and tatami mats sat where the chairs had been seconds before.

Like the tigers, Eirian barely had time to register the alteration to her clothing and environment when it changed again. The kimono disappeared replaced with a longish woollen tunic, fastened at the shoulder with a brooch. She scanned her living area again, half expecting the changes that had occurred to it. She was not surprised to see marble walls and oil lamps in place of the delicate, decorative paper screens.

I wonder how many more times he'll change things?

Her question was answered moments later when everything shifted once again. Eirian endured the next dozen or so changes with good humour. She was now fully cognisant as to what was occurring and waited for Ballisargon to get bored with showing off. Finally one set of clothing and building seemed to be settled on. She ended up dressed in a medieval maid's smock and bonnet. Where the windows in her home had been, large tapestries now hung, showing the same view as before, but rendered in cloth and weave. Electric lighting was gone, transformed into hanging torches and lamps.

Eirian returned to her chair, now a functional three legged stool and sat down once more. That something monumental had happened was certain, what that something was and what it portended exactly, was less so.

Out in the vastness of the Lyr desert the Betrothed continued to wend their way, dragging their burden along with them beneath the ever moving clouds.

Their encounter with Robert several days previously had given them cause to think that Ballisargon's time was at hand. Never in their century of suffering had they encountered a single being who had openly defied Ballisargon save themselves, and they had paid a heavy price for their transgression. Collectively they had decided that the boy would not share their fate if they were able to do anything about it. Consequently, they had been making the long journey Keepward since their meeting with the defiant little boy.

As they approached the perimeter of their former master's stronghold they also sensed a change. Like the tiger's prison and the Engineer's dwelling, their tattered clothing changed, altering rapidly according to Ballisargon's will. In those moments of his distraction they found a new resolve. They sensed the shift in balance as Ballisargon redirected his focus onto Robert. In his desire to overawe the boy he had made a mistake; Ballisargon had let slip the hold he had exerted over them for so long. Ballisargon had thought himself so clever when he had corrupted their bodies and spirits using a variation on his control rings. His declaration that they would 'forever be his brides now,' as he had placed the cold, corrosive metal hoop on each of their ring fingers would prove to play a part in his undoing.

The will that controlled the power that had, for nearly a century, flowed through these rings was now removed. However, the energy itself still poured into them, and in its turn into the Betrothed.

Immediately the women's aspect began to change as they felt some of the strength they had once commanded returning to their bodies. They began to stand more upright, their clothing repairing and cleaning itself. Cracking and popping sounds from within them indicated that their heavily abused and broken bodies were healing too.

Together they strode forward, united in their desire to repay Ballisargon for his decades of degradation and humiliation.

Their time was at hand.

22

Subterranean Homesick Blues

With a rush of air, Robert materialised in a cell, deep in the underground bowels of Ballisargon's Keep; his momentum carrying him headlong toward the facing wall of the cell. He was just able to realise what had happened to him as the wall rushed forward in his field of vision, and stop himself. Instead of a painful collision he slowed himself enough to cushion his impact with his arms.

The tears came as he rested his head against the cold stone and remembered what he had just seen. His body began to shake, and his throat tightened with the heavy sobs of sorrow. Inside he felt totally empty, as if someone had removed his insides and replaced them with a knot of frozen air that ate away at him.

His family was dead.

With a scream, he turned and ran straight at the facing wall, not bothering to stop himself when he smacked into the unyielding stone. He collapsed to the ground, not caring enough to catch his fall in any way. He could not be bothered to hold the weight of his body anymore and crumpled heavily to the floor, hitting his head on the hard stone; but he did not care. He barely felt the pain of the impacts; his senses deadened by grief.

He lay on his side, staring out unseeingly across the floor. His body was wracked with huge sobs, snot and tears mingling as he curled up into a ball and cried his eyes out. His breathing was ragged and laboured through his constricted throat, and although he tried closing his eyes he could not stop himself remembering. Remembering losing Pradeep and Vidya. Remembering seeing his Dad and Elisabeth engulfed by the Molluscs, and remembering how easily he had been bested by Ballisargon. And the Engineer; could what Ballisargon have said been true? If so, how could he trust her now?

What an idealistic, stupid idiot he had been to believe them all. Had he really thought he could bargain with Ballisargon, the Stealer of Worlds, and Master of the Glass Molluscs? It had seemed so easy when the Engineer had explained it to him, but now everything had gone wrong. Everything he had done had turned sour. Not only had he failed to free his Dad and Elisabeth, but he had got them killed. As well as losing the rest of his family, he also had no idea what had happened to Vidya and Pradeep. He was completely alone on an alien planet, with no hope of rescue or escape; his most likely fate was to be put into Ballisargon's generators, where his energy would be used to power the Move of the Lyr Ballisargon had planned. Robert felt utterly hollow. Completely defeated.

He lay on the floor for what felt like hours; he was completely exhausted with no fight left; after all what was there to fight for? The tears went and came again in cycles. Robert wondered how much water there could be inside him, he had cried so much. In the end he submitted to his sorrow, closed his eyes and let himself cry. Eventually, his worn out body and mind fell into a fitful sleep.

But that offered him no respite from either his sorrow or his anger. His dreams were filled with images of times he had spent with Elisabeth and his Dad. Times spent on the beach during the school holidays when he and Elisabeth had buried their Dad in the sand, breakfasts his Dad had made for them both, Elisabeth listening to music in her room while Robert tried to do his homework.

In his slumber, Robert's hands moved instinctively to his mangalsutra. At the sensation of the cold metal, he mumbled an apology in his sleep to his Mum for failing her, as his dreams slowly changed to include her.

She was sitting at the kitchen table in their house, eating some of her husband's dosa's. She finished her meal, put the knife and fork tidily on the plate, folded up her napkin and pushed the plate away from herself. Finally she looked over to where Robert should be standing from her point of view.

'Well, don't just stand there gawping, Robert. Come and sit down here,' she patted the chair next to hers at the table, indicating that her son should join her. 'I want to tell you a few things you need to know.'

Robert, who realised he had been standing there with his mouth wide open shook himself into movement. He did as his Mum asked and sat down next to her. 'How?' he began; then, 'I dreamt about you earlier.'

'I know. Now Robert, our time together will be shorter than I would like, and far briefer than I know you would wish, so I will be quick. First let me say that I am extremely pleased to see what a fine and handsome young man you've grown up into. And you keep such excellent company. That makes me happy. What makes me less happy is the situation you are currently in. It is not of your making, it is the way this must go. However, you are not as lost as you think you are.'

'I don't understand. How can it be any worse? I couldn't rescue Dad and Elisabeth, and have even lost Pradeep and Vidya. I've failed.'

'Now now Robert. When did I ever teach you to think that way? Use your head; I know you've got brains. What do you remember from your encounter with Ballisargon?'

Robert looked puzzled. How could this help? Still, his

Mum had asked him, and he always did what she asked of him. 'Well, I remember Pradeep and Vidya disappearing.'

'Go on,' his Mum pressed gently.

'And then he talked about his plan to Move the planet. He seemed angry at people and then he said he'd let us all go.'

'Yes?' she encouraged.

'Then Dad and Elisabeth were there, and then... then he...' Robert could not finish.

'What were your Dad and Elisabeth wearing when they were taken? Can you remember that?'

Robert thought hard. Then it hit him. *They had been dressed!* He said as much to his Mum, then, 'They couldn't have been dressed, because Tairn had been wearing Dad's clothes, and Elisabeth's college top was still in the washing machine. It couldn't have been them in Ballisargon's throne room as their clothes were still on Earth. It wasn't them!'

Robert's Mum nodded.

'But what about the Engineer? How can I trust her after what Ballisargon said?'

'You trusted Eirian enough to risk coming here, didn't you? So what if Ballisargon and her have a history she did not tell you about? You more than most people should be aware that it is how you are that people should judge you by, not what mistakes you may have made. And as for Ballisargon, he may not always tell the truth, but when he chooses to I am sure it is more powerful than any lie.'

Robert pulled his mouth ruefully to one side. What his Mum had said was true, and he'd really known it all along. He did trust Eirian. He told his Mum as much.

'Good. Now, stop all this crying and feeling sorry for yourself. You can still rescue your Dad and Elisabeth. Find Pradeep and Vidya, they're here to help you; they always have been. Get our family back. I know you can do it Robert, I've always known.'

'How? How can I get out of this cell? I don't even know where I am, let alone where Vidya and Pradeep are.'

'I am afraid I can't help you with that, you'll have to figure that out for yourself. I have to go now; our time is done. I would wish you good luck, but I know you'll succeed.'

'No, don't leave again Mum,' Robert implored. 'I miss you so much.'

'Don't worry Robert, everything will be okay. You'll make me proud,' his Mum said as she got up and walked toward the back door that led out to their garden. She stopped just as she reached the door, and looking back over her shoulder as she opened it said, 'And Robert, it's alright to let it hurt a little less as time passes by.'

With that she stepped through the open door and disappeared.

Robert woke still lying on the floor in his cell. His face was wet where he had been crying in his sleep. His eyes felt red and swollen, and his throat was raw. His Mum had helped him a second time, just like she had protected him when he was asleep on the Bridge. He now knew that his Dad and Elisabeth *were* still alive somewhere in Ballisargon's Keep. Possibly connected to the generators, but they were still alive. And they needed him. His Mum had told him that much, and he was not about to let her down.

Resolve replaced despair and Robert got to his feet to have a look round his cell. A really good look round his cell. His first real examination of it since he had arrived there. If he was going to escape, he needed to find out as much as he could about it.

All four walls, the floor and the ceiling were made of massive granite blocks and there were no windows in the cell. The only portions of the whole thing that were not solid stone were two small iron grates barely the size of Robert's hand, one in the centre of the ceiling and one directly underneath it in the middle of the floor.

Robert walked and rapped his fist on each wall in turn, then on the floor. Each time he was rewarded with a dull knock. *Blimey, they're a bit thick.* He was too short to reach the ceiling, but reckoned that it would be no different. What Robert did not know was that there wasn't anything on the other side of the walls, as there was no other side of the walls, only the endless stone bedrock of the Lyr desert.

The cell was lit by a torch on each wall, flickering gently. *Odd. There must be a breeze coming from somewhere.* He looked up at the grate in the ceiling, then down at its twin in the floor. He crouched down and put his hand over it. He could feel a gentle breath of air passing between his fingers.

He let himself fall back from his hunched position and sit down on the floor. He crossed his legs, rested his chin in his hands and thought.

If there is a breeze blowing through the grates, then they must lead to the outside. Logically, if the breeze seemed to be blowing toward the grate in the ceiling then that must be where the air is being driven to, and the way out.

He looked up at the ceiling and thought about Moving as far upwards as he could. He examined his surroundings with his mind, trying to establish how much space to Fold, but he could not get a firm idea. His fatigue had dulled his mind and he was struggling to concentrate. How far would be far enough? He had no idea. Still, he had to give it a go. He got to his feet and began to concentrate on performing the Move, when his watch beeped the hour.

He looked down at it. It was eleven o' clock, well past his bedtime. Robert had been here a few hours, if his watch was anything to go by. However, his fitful sleep earlier had not rested him at all, and he suddenly realised how tired he still was. He reckoned in his present state he could probably Move about ten metres before he collapsed, less if he had to Move through lots of stone and earth. Barely more than his house was high. *Probably not far enough.*

Robert walked to one of the corners of his cell and sat down. He set the alarm on his watch for midnight and closed his eyes.

Sleep came quickly.

Sitting in his throne room, Ballisargon was still wondering how to dispose of the tigers. He couldn't face them directly, that much was certain. Even if he had been able to Move them out of the way earlier, he thought that was probably more a case of catching them by surprise rather than too much skill on his part, and no part of Ballisargon wanted to face two forewarned tigers. The Molluscs then. Let his pets deal with them. After all, they were *only* tigers and there were only two of them, and he had so many Molluscs at his disposal. He sat back and chuckled to himself. He was going to enjoy this.

'Am I dreaming I'm meeting you?' Robert asked Tairn.

'You are dreaming we are having this conversation, yes, but I am meeting you here in your dream,' replied Tairn, smiling enigmatically.

'What are you doing in my dreams? I thought you were going to keep well away from me.' Robert stated.

'Well, yes, I was going to keep well away, but you seemed to need a little help, and as you'd been so good to me earlier, I thought I'd repay the favour. You can't Move because you don't know how far upwards you need to go, correct?'

'Yes,' replied Robert. 'It could be a metre or it could be a hundred for all I know.'

'Well, I know,' said Tairn. 'And better still, I can show you.' He pressed a button on the device he had used to send Robert to the Lyr, and Robert saw the cell shrink away, him and Tairn still sitting inside it. The cell became smaller and smaller in the darkness that surrounded it, until it was barely larger than a sugar cube of light, hovering in the pitch black all around it. Above it Robert could see the rest of Ballisargon's Keep laid out before him. The scale was too small to make out details but he could see all the other rooms of the Keep. The throne room at the very top of the tallest tower, the other cells, scattered throughout the darkness, and a very large room that seemed to go on forever.

'Wow,' said Robert under his breath. Ballisargon's Keep was enormous, and he was a very very long way underground. Far too far for him to have Moved earlier. If he'd tried, he would have materialised in the middle of the earth. He didn't want to think what that would have done to him.

Tairn pressed another button, and the view rushed back at Robert, seeming to zoom back into the cell, where he once again saw Tairn sitting before him. 'So, now you see where you have to go,' said Tairn.

'It's a long way up,' said Robert. 'But I think I can make it.'

'That's a good lad,' said Tairn. 'Now, I have to be going. I really have been here too long. Luckily Ballisargon is currently distracted trying to think of the best way to dispose of your tiger friends without exposing himself to danger. You'd better hurry.'

Robert thought he could hear a faint beeping sound that grew louder with each passing second. Eventually, it filled his entire world to the exclusion of everything else. 'What is that?' he asked Tairn before he woke up, but Tairn had already disappeared once more.

BEEP-BEEP-BEEP-BEEP went Robert's watch on his wrist. Robert opened his eyes, and looked down at the watch.

His thoughts returned to him and he remembered where he was. He pressed a button on the side of the watch, and it stopped its alarm. He got to his feet, shaking the last remnants of his slumber away from himself. The hour of sleep had rested him significantly. He now knew all he needed to. His family was still alive, and so were the tigers. Ballisargon was distracted by his cowardice and there were only a few hours left before he would begin his Move of the Lyr. And now Robert knew how far he had to Move to escape.

He remembered Eirian's tutelage on the Bridge and how the Move worked. Intelligence, strength and determination all fed into his ability to Move. Robert certainly had the wit, and his sleep had rested him. That was two of the three. Now he just needed the force of will. Robert thought of everything Ballisargon had done; to his family, to the tigers, to Eirian, to the Lyr and to the Earth. On top of that he let all the small slights of school pour upon him at once; all the put-downs by the teachers, the name calling and hurt he experienced. All of it, all at once multiplying in his mind. He hid nothing from himself. He needed everything. Wave after wave of frustration and anger crashed through him, feeding his growing determination.

He felt strong and powerful.

Flexing his hands into fists at either side of him, his gaze bored through hundreds and hundreds of metres of stone and earth above him, at his destination.

And he Moved.

The final day.

23

Don't Come Around Here No More

Robert materialised in the lowermost chamber of the Keep as he remembered it from his dream. He appeared half a metre above the floor, and fell to the ground, only just managing to stay on his feet, the surprise of materialising in mid air throwing him off balance slightly.

Not bad for a Move of over a kilometre through solid rock though, he thought to himself when he realised he had overestimated the distance, if only by a fraction. *Better to be half a metre too high than too low.*

The massive Move he had escaped from the cell with had been taxing. Pulling two separate points in space together through that much solid matter had not been easy and it left him puffing a little. Robert drew a deep breath, eager to get some oxygen into his lungs, and immediately began coughing violently, expelling the thick, foul air from his body. It tasted sweet and sickly at the same time, like rotted honey mixed with sour milk and worse. He gagged at the taste it left in his mouth, spitting and snorting to try and clear it from his body. Just one lungful felt like it had coated his lungs with its pollution.

Pulling the collar of his hooded top over his nose and mouth, Robert drew an experimental breath slowly through his nose. The awful smell was still there, but at least this time it was lessened by his makeshift gasmask.

The room he found himself in was easily ten metres on each side, and lit by the torches that now seemed to provide the only form of illumination in the Keep. The walls and ceiling glistened in the flickering light, as if wet with something, and against one wall was stacked a collection of crates and barrels. In the very centre of the room was a large circular pool of some kind, like an oversized garden pond. Robert could see the surface of the pool, but could not see what, if anything was in it.

He carefully reached toward the wall nearest to him and touched the glistening wetness. His finger sank up to his knuckles into a soft jelly-like substance which, to Robert's surprise, was warm. Intrigued, he did not immediately remove his digit. He had been expecting it to be cold and clammy, but it wasn't. He drew his finger in a line down the wall, cutting a trough through the jelly. The stuff responded almost immediately, flowing into the gap Robert's finger had left, sealing it as if it had never been there.

Robert watched in fascination. Now he noticed the other odd thing about the jelly. There was a rhythm in it. It was quite weak, almost imperceptible, but there was definitely a pumping sensation passing through the warm, thick jelly-like goo that he had his finger in.

Realisation came almost too quickly, and his eyes went wide with fright as he pulled his finger out of the living substance that covered the walls. It stuck to Robert's finger and stretched like elastic as he pulled his hand away, before snapping cleanly off his finger and back to the wall with a wet, smacking noise. Hastily checking for any trace of the stuff and being relived when there did not appear to be any, but still wiping his fingers robustly on his jeans, Robert resolved not to go sticking bits of his body into any unknown substances or areas ever again.

He began to picture the Keep, and as the image of it came

into focus in his mind's eye he found his concentration wandering, causing his mental map to go fuzzy on him. He tried again, but the same thing happened. Robert gave it a third go, but it was no good. He had to know what was in the pool.

OK, one quick look, NO putting a hand into it, and then I'm off. I've wasted too much time here already, what with the stuff on the walls.

He made his way to the pool in the centre of the room, and peered very carefully over the edge. The pool, which seemed to be the source of the awful smell, was wide and circular; Robert estimated nearly five metres in diameter with a gentle slope leading into it from the floor. It was filled with a clearish, yellow-white liquid; as Robert leaned slightly over it he could see almost to the bottom. Its depth was difficult to judge and there were no ripples on the surface.

Dotted all around the pool's interior were small, semi-transparent spheres, roughly the size of a football. Inside each sphere, through its thin membranous wall Robert could see movement. Not a lot of movement, not very quickly or often, but movement nonetheless. The clear footballs looked very much like the single celled lifeforms Robert had seen through a microscope in biology class, but sort of crossed with a jellyfish. He counted twelve of the amoeba like things in the pool, all moving inside their sacs.

Robert shuddered deep inside himself, the living footballs making him feel queasy and scared at the same time.

That's it, pool or not, I'm off.

Curiosity satisfied he imagined the Keep, but as he focussed on his destination he saw another Fold occurring, its destination the same room he was in! He shivered from the sensation as he felt the space around the pool begin to shift, as it did when he Moved.

Something was Moving, and it wasn't him!

Not wasting any time, and certainly not wanting to be in plain view when the whatever it was arrived, Robert sped away from the poolside and behind one of the stacks of crates. Once safely out of sight, he peered through a gap at the space by the pool the Moving thing would appear in, taking great care not to back into the slime-jelly on the wall behind him.

The air at in the room began to shimmer, the way Robert remembered from hot summer days. The heat haze effect began to grow. It started out roughly the size of a settee, and it did not stop there. A few seconds later the shimmering had swollen; now seeming to take up as much space as his Dad's car. Whatever was Moving in was big!

Robert watched transfixed. The shimmering seemed to bend in on itself as the air was pressed into shapes it was not meant to take. The effect was incredible. Bent and forced, the space by the pool looked like it was cracking or splitting apart. Dark fissures and rents appeared, hovering in mid-air, before disappearing with a deep cracking sound, like a glacier splitting. The light from the torches split into rainbows in front of him, prismed out by the pressure it was being put under.

A shape became discernible out of the abused space, the air seeming to thicken and congeal out of a cloud of swirling fractal tendrils where the thing was appearing. It grew darker and darker, until all of a sudden, the thing finished its Move and was whole and complete and in front of the pool.

It was a Glass Mollusc!

The sudden appearance of the creature that he thought had killed his family caused Robert to stumble backwards. Instinctively, he put a hand out to stop his fall, and it hit the soft, warm jelly and sank into it up to his wrist. He almost screamed at this point, only just stopping himself by clamping his other hand over his mouth.

Nearly hyper-ventilating with panic, Robert tried to wrench his hand away from the wall, but it did not seem to want to give up now it had claimed him. The moist jelly clung to him much harder and longer than before as he tried to heave himself free. Pulling with all his strength, it finally gave up and snapped cleanly off his hand, and back into place on the wall, where it wobbled gently. The sound it made was loud enough to echo round the pool chamber for a second, and Robert's eyes snapped back to the Mollusc. If it had heard, he was in real trouble.

However, the Mollusc seemed oblivious or uncaring to the noise he had just made. It just sat at the poolside pulsing slowly.

Robert wanted to shut his eyes and take the sight of the creature in front of him away, but it was too late for that. Images of the Molluscs were already burned into his brain from his previous encounters, and no amount of eyes-closed would change that. Better then (if the damage was already done) to try and learn something about the thing in front of him while he had the chance, and it did not know he was there.

He kept his eyes open, and fixed on the Mollusc. Slowly, as if it was in pain, the creature approached the pool. It moved in a cross between flowing and oozing, seeming to seep into itself, bulging out in the middle, before pushing out the front of its body, narrowing along its length, like a worm that was too liquid on the inside.

Once it had got half its great bulk in the pool (which end was the head?) the Mollusc began to shudder, its clear flesh quaking. Robert watched, his hand still clamped over his mouth in case he lost what little self-control he retained. *What was going on?* Then, through the semi-transparent body of the thing Robert could see something moving inside the animal. He could not tell what it was; he was too far away, but he could see *something* progressing along the Mollusc's length, until it disappeared from sight below the surface of the liquid, into the half of the Molluscs that was in the pool.

The Mollusc sat motionless for a few more seconds then heaved its massive transparent body back up the slope and into the room once more.

Now free of the thick liquid the Mollusc began to Move

again. Watching it disappear was almost the exact reversal of the thing's appearance. It grew less and less distinct as the air shimmered around it, until it was gone again with a faint sound, as the volume of empty space it had left behind rushed to be filled.

Happy that he had survived, mostly by concealment (but hey, it still counts, right) and once again curious, now almost to the point of bursting, Robert emerged from his hiding place and ran to the edge of the pool. Peering carefully over the edge, he looked inside again.

The sacs all seemed to still be there, so what had happened? Just to be sure Robert counted them all once more. One, two, three… he began; ten, eleven twelve… Robert trailed off.

Thirteen.

There were thirteen of them now. One more than the last time. A new one.

The Mollusc had given birth.

24

Welcome to the Machine

Robert was overwhelmed with the desire to get away from the spawning-pool, the living jelly and the egg sacs. He needed to put as much distance between him and the events he had just seen, and fast. He brought the memory of the layout of the Keep to mind and Moved. But in his haste he did not take care to determine his arrival point and he materialised in what appeared to be a banqueting hall, and not the prison cells.

What had gone wrong? He pictured the Keep as he had seen it in his dream, mentally looking at where he had been (without thinking too hard about what he had seen there) and where he thought he was going. Then he spotted his mistake; he had been remembering the Keep from the angle he had seen in, and had not adjusted his mental picture to the direction he had been facing when he Moved. *Stupid! Stupid! Stupid! So much for control!*

He spun the map in his mind. This time he saw the prison area much more clearly, and in a heartbeat he was there.

Vidya and Pradeep felt Robert approaching before he arrived. They both got up from their sitting positions and moved to the edge of their cells, muzzles almost touching the hard iron bars.

'Robert!' exclaimed Vidya. 'You're all right. We were beginning to get worried.'

'Well, Vidya was beginning to get worried,' Pradeep clarified. 'I for one, never doubted you'd get here.'

'Oh, it's so good to see the both of you again. I thought Ballisargon had killed you both or something, then he seemed to kill my Dad and Elisabeth, then I was like in a stone cell and I dreamt about my Mum and then Tairn, and then I escaped and I saw a Mollusc give birth and now I am here to free the both of you.' He was almost running out of breath as he finished.

Robert made his way to the cell with Pradeep in it and took hold of the bars in his hands, as if to pull them out. 'I'll get you both out, just hang on.'

Before Robert could do anything, Pradeep said, 'That really won't be necessary Robert. You see,' and Pradeep Moved, 'we are quite capable of freeing ourselves,' and Pradeep was standing next to Robert, outside the cell.

Vidya Moved next, appearing on the other side of Robert to Pradeep. 'We have been waiting for you,' she said.

'I don't understand,' said Robert. 'If you could free yourselves at any time why didn't you come and get me? And why didn't you go and get Ballisargon?' Robert sounded angry, confused and hurt. He had suffered Ballisargon's cruelty and seeing his family die, even if it was a lie had broken his heart. 'I mean, you just *sat* there all the time I was with Ballisargon and in prison!' Robert felt himself getting angry again, his hands curling up into fists, ready to pound on the tigers.

'Now, it's not like that,' said Vidya gently. 'Yes, we could have freed ourselves at any time, but no, we could not have rescued you. We didn't know where you were, and Ballisargon's Keep is very large. Us Moving around looking for you would have certainly alerted him, and that would have been the end of you, and most probably us. While we are tigers, we are not super-feline. We only have a limited amount of power at our disposal, while you...' she trailed off.

'Look, Robert,' said Pradeep as comfortingly as he could, 'we have a lot to tell you. About us, about Ballisargon, about you, and your Mum.'

'Stuff we should have told you earlier, but events kind of ran away from us,' Vidya qualified Pradeep's statement.

'My Mum? What has she got to do with this?'

The tigers looked at each other. Pradeep gave a short nod to his sister, and Vidya spoke for the both of them. 'We appreciate that you must have more questions than you can possibly think about, and for now I think most of them will be answered if we tell you everything from the beginning.'

Over the course of the next hour, Pradeep and Vidya explained to Robert all about Ballisargon and the Betrothed, and what they had meant when they had called him 'more than others'.

'But I'm not more than others, I'm just an ordinary boy,' Robert interrupted.

Vidya shook her head, 'No Robert, you are the son of Kshama. Our sister.'

Robert recognised the name from his time on the Bridge and Telain. 'But my Mum's not called Kshama. Her name was Reena.'

'Kshama was her tiger name. She took the name Reena when she assumed human shape.'

Robert looked over at Pradeep who nodded his head. 'You see, many years ago Kshama decided to leave the Lyr and travel to another world, seeking adventures and glory. She assumed human form with the help of the Engineer, and left the Lyr. She indeed found what she was looking for; great adventures and much glory, but one day she found herself talking to a man, and much to her surprise and shock, found herself falling in love with him. They married and lived in happiness for a while. The man already had a daughter, and Kshama was shocked one day to find that she was carrying his child. A boy. She had not planned this at all.

Eventually her son was born who she gifted a tiger name to, and grew up to be the eleven year old who came to the Lyr to rescue his family.'

Robert's mouth was wide open, and he was clutching his mangalsutra very tightly indeed. 'Rajat,' was all he said.

'Pardon?' asked Vidya.

'Rajat. It's my middle name. I had always thought my Mum had given me it as a reminder of her heritage.'

'And she had, but not completely in the way you thought. It's your tiger name,' said Pradeep. 'You see when we learned of your birth from Kshama, all three of us realised that you would need protection. Kshama gave you another name, a human name, and bequeathed you her mangalsutra knowing it would hide you from Ballisargon if he came to clean your world, and when it seemed that he had indeed done that, Vidya and I waited for your arrival.'

'So, I'm what, half tiger?' Robert asked incredulously.

'Not exactly,' replied Vidya. 'Remember how we became on Earth. Because Kshama grew more human the longer she stayed in human form you have inherited the *essence* of her tigerness. You are human, but you are more than that. You posses the potentiality of tigerness by dint of your heritage, and it seems to be manifesting itself now here in the Lyr. You are in essence one of us, but you are more than either of us.'

'We are truly sorry we couldn't tell you earlier,' she continued, 'we had no desire to hide this from you, but we had to wait until you were up to coping with the information. Imagine if we had told you the full story from the beginning. Most likely you wouldn't have believed us, and even if you had, it would have only hindered you. We saw your necklace, and knew you were our nephew, but we weren't sure what to do about it until we had spoken to the Engineer. She counselled that we should go with you in your search for your family to watch over you. After that, it was just a matter of tagging along with you while you became what Kshama always knew you would become. She would be proud, as we are both proud of you.'

'However,' interjected Pradeep, 'you must realise that while you are here in the Lyr you have abilities far beyond those of mere tigers and humans. And you must be careful how you use them. While they will render Ballisargon powerless over you, you must still be careful.'

'But if I'm this 'more than others' shouldn't my arrival have been prophesised or something? Shouldn't I be the one to stop it all?'

'Get real Robert,' said Pradeep. 'If we'd told you that there was this all powerful prophecy that you were destined to come here and stop Ballisargon, I'm guessing you'd have just sat on the Bridge waiting for it to come true all on its own.'

'I s'pose,' Robert mused. 'If I was this chosen one kind of thing I would only need to hang around, do nothing and Ballisargon would just, I don't know, die of a heart attack or something.'

'Unfortunately we live in the real world,' said Vidya, 'where there are no prophecies and if you want something done, you have to work hard at it.'

'So, what happens now?' asked Robert. 'What do we do?'

'You tell us, Robert,' said Pradeep. 'After all, it is your family you're here to get back.'

Robert remembered the image of the Keep Tairn had shown him, and a vast room, so large it could have held everyone in the world. 'I know where we're going,' he said, his voice tinted with steel.

Pradeep and Vidya exchanged a nervous glance. This was uncharted territory for them, their role as guardians lessening as Robert grew in confidence and ability. All they could do was guide him as best they knew. If what he was about to see was too much then the whole endeavour could end very badly indeed. If Robert lost control they would be powerless to stop the inevitable rampage and slaughter.

'Follow me,' he said. And vanished.

Robert appeared at the foot of one of the generators. Laid out before him, stretching as far as he could see were hundreds, thousands, millions of people lying on steel plates, each connected a neat bundle of fibre-optics. He looked up to see similar rows of plates reaching upwards until the darkness hid them from view. The air was thick with the smell of chemicals.

Pradeep and Vidya appeared next to Robert the very instant he Moved again, this time upwards, as far as he could see. The sight that greeted him when he re-materialised on one of the steel plates was exactly the same as the one he had left behind. An impossibly huge field of people lying down, stretching out before him, and above and below him. He closed his eyes and Moved back down to the ground, where the tigers were waiting for him.

Robert ignored them for the time being and walked to the nearest person, a young man, in his mid-twenties. He was dressed in the clothes he had been whisked away from the Earth in. Judging by his white uniform, Robert guessed he was a cook or chef of some kind.

The man looked unconscious, but underneath his eyelids Robert could see his eyes flicking rapidly back and forth. The man was breathing quickly but not very deeply and occasionally he twitched in his induced slumber.

Carefully and slowly, Robert reached out a hand as if to touch the man. His fingers neared the body when Pradeep asked, 'Do you know him?'

Robert turned his attention back to the male tiger for just a second, but it was enough.

The young man's eyes shot open and he grabbed the sleeve of Robert's top.

'WHA!' screamed Robert in panic, as he felt the man pull him.

'Hooo..?' the man began, 'Hoo… urr… yoo...?' His words were badly slurred as if he was drunk, or drugged. 'Wurr… umm… aiii?'

Robert fought against the man's grip, pulling and tearing at the fingers that held tight to his clothes, hitting the man's hand in an effort make him let go. 'Jesus! Get off me!' he shouted.

The tigers stood motionless, unsure how to help Robert without injuring the other person. Robert continued his struggle, but even in his fugue state the young man was significantly stronger than he was. He pulled again, and Robert was dragged even closer.

'Wott… izzz… thizzz… plays…? Waiimm… aiii… heeerr?' The young man started to try and get off the metal table he lay on. Robert continued to hit the man's hands, his blows becoming harder and more desperate. By now the man was almost sitting upright, even if he was swaying heavily.

Vidya couldn't sit by passively any longer. She lunged at the man's arm with a perfectly placed blow, knocking his grip loose of Robert's clothing, but tearing through the man's sleeve and scratching his forearm deeply in the process. It was a price she was willing to pay to free Robert.

Disconnected from Robert by the force of Vidya's attack, the man sank back to the metal plate, returning to the state he had been in before Robert had gone near him, only this time with a set of long scratches visible up his forearm through his tattered sleeve.

Robert caught his breath. 'Thanks. For. That. Vidya,' he puffed. 'He was. So strong, it. Was really scary.' Then Robert noticed the wounds that Vidya had given the man. 'How hard did you hit him? Will he be OK?'

'Yes, they're not deep, so he won't bleed to death or anything. And anyway, I hit him just hard enough to make him release you. I didn't want to break his arm. Or worse.'

Robert looked at the young man's arm again, and was just glad Vidya's aim was as good as it was.

'Why did he do that?' asked Robert, almost to the vast sea of people that stretched out before him as much as to the tigers.

'We, uh, that is, I, um, I don't know,' said Pradeep.

Robert turned to the male tiger, and narrowed his eyes, staring at Pradeep. Pradeep found himself staring back at his lost sister; a gaze he could not knowingly lie to. 'You're lying,' said Robert, without really knowing how he knew. He just did.

Pradeep looked away in shame, then back at Robert. 'Yes. I thought it better you didn't know what was happening to everyone.'

'Why,' asked Robert, genuinely hurt that his newfound uncle would conceal anything from him, especially after what he had said to him earlier.

'It's just that, well, everyone here is awake. They can feel everything that is happening to them. Feel their lives draining out of them into Ballisargon's generators. Every little pleasure or hurt they ever experienced is being sucked out of them.'

Robert felt his stomach turn over at what Pradeep had just told him, and could not stop himself from being sick. 'It's horrible,' was all he could say in between the retches. 'I never guessed it would be like this. What about my Dad and Elisabeth? Are they here somewhere?'

'I don't think so,' continued Vidya. 'Remember Ballisargon said he had been speaking to your Dad about you. I think they're probably both still alive. Ballisargon may be amoral, but he isn't stupid. He knows you weren't stolen along with all the others, and if he thinks he can find a way to use you to his advantage, he will use every means he can. He's most likely holding them in a cell somewhere so he can question them some more about you.'

Robert thought for a moment. So his family weren't here. So what? All that meant was that they were not having to go through what everyone else was. Everyone else... But Robert didn't care about everyone else. Did he? He had come to the Lyr to get his family back.

But what about Peter? He must be in here somewhere.

And Peter's Dad, Mr Lau. And Peter's Mum and brothers, and all of his family. Maybe he could get them out. But then what about all the people that Peter knew, all his schoolfriends? Even if Robert somehow managed to get Peter back to Earth it wouldn't be much of a life for him without everyone he knew, or that knew him. The more Robert thought about it the more people he realised he would have to release: Peter, his brothers and *their* friends, Peter's parents and *their* friends which led Robert to want to free *their* relatives and *their* friends until eventually he would have to free...

Robert felt in his pocket for the piece of chalk that Eirian had given him. He pulled it out of his pocket and with it came the Te piece Telain had given him. He inspected them both, as if he held the weight of the world in his hand. He picked the Te piece and placed it carefully back in his pocket. That would certainly come with him out of the generator room. That left the chalk. It was far too small to release even Peter and his family, even if Robert could find them all within the seven billion people that were laid out all around him. It was hopeless this way.

Robert closed his fingers around the chalk, tighter and tighter until he felt it crack in his grip. He continued squeezing it.

'What are you doing?' exclaimed Vidya. 'You need that.'

'No, not this way. This has to be stopped,' Robert said. 'This is wrong.'

'Careful, Robert,' said Pradeep. 'Keep your emotions under control. It's all about control. Remember what we told you.'

Robert opened his hand. All that was left of the chalk was a fine white powder, no good for anything. He tipped it out of his hands, wiping the remnants of it on his jeans. 'I'm going to get everybody out.'

25

Won't Get Fooled Again

Robert blinked out of the generator room before the tigers even had a chance to react. 'He's got too good at doing that,' said Vidya to her brother.

'I know what you mean. I'm struggling to keep up with him now,' replied Pradeep.

'Then we'd better get to him. You saw how he reacted there. He's going to need us now, more than at any time before or to come.'

'I hope we're up to it,' said Pradeep before he and his sister followed Robert's scent, Folding the same space Robert had only moments before. When they appeared they found themselves in a small torch-lit room.

Robert had his head poked round the only door out of it, and sensing the tigers' arrival drew himself fully back from the open doorway. He still did not look happy. 'He doesn't seem to know we've escaped,' he told them.

'You mean *yet*,' Pradeep qualified.

'Fine. Then we can still take him down if we surprise him,' Robert stated returning his attention through the open door at Ballisargon. He hadn't planned on having another confrontation with the Master of the Glass Molluscs, but that was before the generator room. Even if his family probably wasn't there, what he had seen had changed his mind. Ballisargon had to be stopped and everyone had to be put back on the Earth. End of story. On his own, Robert had been no match for the Stealer of Worlds, but now back with Vidya and Pradeep once more he felt heaps better. This was their best (and let's be honest, only) chance to really do something.

He turned back to the tigers once more. 'Can you two kill him? I mean before he has a chance to summon any Molluscs or anything?' Robert was deadly serious and both tigers knew it, the steel in his voice obvious.

Pradeep began to bluster a reply, the shock of Robert's request making him almost speechless.

'Oh come off it,' Robert sneered, leaning in toward Pradeep. 'You didn't seem to have much trouble wanting to kill me back on Earth I seem to recall. He jabbed his thumb into his chest, 'And I'm family!'

'Careful, Robert,' warned Pradeep very slowly and very deliberately. 'I know you're angry and everything, but…'

'YOU'RE… You're damn right I'm angry.' Robert had trouble keeping his voice low enough not to carry into the throne room. 'It's alright for you two, you've both known exactly what was going on the whole time. Me, I've had to work it out for myself. And what I've worked out is this: I want this to end, and I want my family back,' he said, repeatedly balling his hands into hard, white-knuckled fists. 'You agree with me, don't you Vidya?'

Vidya met Robert's gaze, but only for a second before she turned her head away from her nephew's unrelenting stare. While she agreed that surprise was always their best advantage, and she had to admit that in a straight fight one ageing man was no match for either her or Pradeep, she was troubled by Robert's request. She remembered her dream and the Engineer's warning against trying to kill Ballisargon, and the potential consequences of making the attempt. Then she remembered how she had nearly killed Robert, Kshama's son and her only link to her lost sister.

Vidya had promised herself that she would rid all worlds of Ballisargon's stain, but she had also promised her sister that if she ever got the chance, she would do anything and everything to protect Robert. She weighed the balances of breaking either promise in order to keep the other. This wasn't as simple as agreeing to speak to the Engineer again. Breaking either of these vows could have big, deadly and quite likely fatal consequences. If there was even the slightest chance that the Engineer was right, then Robert could get seriously hurt or even killed if she tried to kill Ballisargon. Eventually she replied, 'No Robert, I don't think I do.'

'What? Why, I mean, but I thought you'd, after Earth and everything, I thought,' Robert couldn't find the words.

'You are partly right. After what happened on Earth I did want to kill him, regardless of what we had promised ourselves, or Kshama. I wanted to kill him very badly. And painfully. But I spoke with the Engineer, and she, well let's just say that killing has been tried before.

'You see, we all made a promise, Kshama and the both of us, a long time ago before you were born. Having the power we do is a great responsibility. Either of us could tear Ballisargon limb from limb, and tempting though that is,' Pradeep glanced at Vidya, 'we won't. We all promised only to kill for food. To be aware and to do anything else would make us murderers.'

Robert absorbed what Vidya said and let himself calm down a little. In the few days he had come to know and trust her he had learnt a lot about the proud tigress. About how whatever else she may have been or have done, she never betrayed herself no matter what. If Vidya could settle whatever had passed between herself and Eirian in her desire to help him and still not violate her promise to herself then who was he to ask her to do otherwise? Thinking more rationally about the situation he realised that Vidya was right. All three tigers had made a promise, including his Mum, and even though she was gone he felt bound by it. It was the right thing to do and Vidya and Pradeep had been right to stay constant to it.

'Okay,' he said slowly, nodding his head partially in agreement and partially in thought. 'So what can we do then? We've got to stop him, and I'm not leaving without Dad and Elisabeth and everybody else. How about you two, I don't know, just knock him out or something, like you did with that guy in the generator room? That'll be different to killing him won't it? We can take him back to Eirian then. She'll know how to stop him and get my family back.'

Vidya and Pradeep looked at each other. Vidya half-cocked her head and made a 'what do you think' face at her brother. Pradeep replied with a 'that sounds like a plan' face. 'You got it,' Vidya said to Robert.

Robert returned to the door and eased it open enough for the tigers to squeeze through. Ballisargon was seated at the large wooden table on the raised dais Robert had last seen him on. He was bent over a heavy-looking leather bound book, seemingly lost in its pages.

'Pradeep, are you ready for this?' asked his sister.

'I'll be there when it goes down. Don't worry about me, I can look after myself.'

'OK then Robert. Let's get your world back.'

Ballisargon still had his head bent over whatever he was reading and had not noticed their entry.

So far so good.

Robert watched transfixed as the tigers slinked round the perimeter of the throne room, their bodies flowing with liquid grace as they padded silently, each paw placed softly in front of the other with deliberate care. Each of the tigers' movements was a mirror image of the others, and Robert felt the memory of being hunted by the single purpose they had become back on Earth force its way back into his mind. All of a sudden he wasn't sure of his plan. The fear he had felt then returned, turning his stomach over on itself. Only this time it was a fear for the tigers themselves. He watched them close the gap between themselves and Ballisargon, whose attention was still directed at the book on the table in front of him. Robert wiped his hands on his jeans and tried to swallow, but his throat was dry. From his hidden vantage point he felt like he was watching a repeat of something on television he had seen a long time ago, and couldn't quite remember the end of but knew it wasn't going to be good.

The tigers' controlled patience had paid off; they were now within leaping distance of Ballisargon. Robert watched, powerless, as his feelings of unease grew stronger. The tigers had stopped moving. They crouched, backs arched, their hindquarters tense with power. They were going to strike any second.

He saw Vidya look over at Pradeep, who nodded. Robert felt sick with unease. It *wasn't* going to be different. Just not killing Ballisargon wasn't going to stop the bad thing he could feel coming from happening.

The tigers began nodding a count to each other.

One.

He felt for the mangalsutra around his neck. It seemed to weigh a ton. His Mum would not want him to do it this way. Something was about to go very very wrong.

Two.

This was not how it should happen. He and the tigers were better than this. He understood that now. He had to stop it.

Thr…

'Stooooop!' he shouted, causing the tigers and Ballisargon to look over at him as he rushed from his hiding place.

Ballisargon looked seriously irritated at the sight of Robert once again in his throne room. Then, spotting the tigers he looked less annoyed and more surprised. His composure returned as he rose to his feet. 'I see I need to upgrade my prisons. Still, it's not like you'll be going back to them any time soon,' he said, trying to sound uninterested in the three figures who stood defiantly before him.

Ballisargon clicked the fingers of his left hand, and four Glass Molluscs appeared between him and Robert and the tigers. 'I'm sure you three can work out how this bit goes,' he said as he sat back down to watch the show.

Even though they lacked any form of recognisable sensory organ anywhere on their transparent exterior, the Glass Molluscs certainly seemed to be able to tell where their prey was. Within seconds of their summoning all four turned themselves toward the three allies, and began their advance.

Two of the Molluscs moved down the small flight of steps from Ballisargon's throne towards Robert, leaving one Mollusc per tiger. The Molluscs moved the same way Robert had seen earlier in the spawning pool. Not exactly flowing, not exactly oozing, but something else. They closed in on Robert and the tigers with a slow wet noise, leaving behind a sticky trail of mucus that steamed gently, and reeked of the rotten milk and honey smell.

'It's another trick, isn't it?' Robert called to Vidya. 'Like with my Dad and Elisabeth?'

'No this time they are real, boy,' replied Ballisargon.

'He's right, I'm afraid,' said Vidya. 'But don't worry, Pradeep and I will handle them. Pradeep? Pradeep?'

Vidya looked across at her brother, but he was backing away in terror, the fear evident on his face. This was the one thing he could not face. His nightmare.

'I can't say it's been a pleasure meeting you all, but it certainly will be watching you die,' mocked Ballisargon.

Pradeep had been right about the Molluscs; they could sense what was around them, and now they were sensing his fear. Their kind had learnt from the encounter with the adolescent Vidya and were wary of her, but the other tiger *felt* afraid, and they knew it.

A pair of the Molluscs Moved. In a flash they were either side of Pradeep, about two metres apart. Robert saw the Move and saw where the Molluscs had ended up, but the way they Moved did not make sense. Remembering the Mollusc in the spawning pool and how laboured its Moves had been he struggled to reconcile it with what he had just seen. This time the Molluscs' Moves had been almost as graceful and instantaneous as either himself or the tigers, with none of the stress or strain on the arrival point he remembered. Pradeep had seen it too, but was too terrified to do anything about it. The Molluscs sat pulsing slowly, gathering their energy ready for the strike. Robert felt the Fold occurring in the room. Pradeep was about to be killed.

'VIDYA!' screamed Robert. 'We have to help Pradeep.'

Vidya looked at her brother, helpless against the two Molluscs, then back at Robert. What she said next nearly broke her heart, 'Robert. He is going to have to… to look after himself. We can't risk it. We... we have to finish our business with Ballisargon.' Tears formed in her green eyes as she spoke, almost unable to complete the last sentence.

'What?!' Robert was incredulous. 'He's your brother!'

'And you are Kshama's son!' It was the first time Robert had heard Vidya shout. Then, in more measured tones, 'You have to complete what you came here to do. Pradeep will have to defend himself.'

Robert looked back at Pradeep. The Molluscs were looking stronger by the second, their pulsing increasing in frequency, the Fold almost complete. *No!* he thought, and Moved.

He appeared right next to Pradeep and grabbed the tiger round the neck before he could react; Robert's fingertips barely touched each other on the other side of Pradeep's huge throat but he just about closed the circle of his arms. Pradeep was an awful lot larger than a boulder, but Robert had to try. Vidya was wrong. Pradeep was in no state to help himself. Robert had to do it.

He Moved, pulling Pradeep with him just as the Molluscs Moved themselves in for the kill.

The volume of space that Robert and Pradeep had been

occupying barely an instant before was filled. Two Glass Molluscs materialised in it, their bodies mingling in a confusion of clear flesh. For a second they spasmed violently, shuddering in agonising death, their conjoined bodies and brains unable to comprehend what had occurred. Then they stopped moving. Cracks appeared along the region where they had merged and spread across their new single body before it split apart into dozens of fragments.

Robert appeared in an antechamber, his trembling arms only just still encircling Pradeep's massive neck. He let go when he saw that they were safe, for now.

Pradeep was still lost to his terror of the Molluscs, his legs twitching and his orange eyes wide and brittle.

Robert shook Pradeep's shoulder, 'Pradeep! Come on, we've got to get back and help Vidya.'

But it was no use. Pradeep was too far adrift in fear to respond.

Robert took a deep breath, and slapped Pradeep across his nose. Hard. He also took the precaution of Moving backwards a couple of metres, just in case.

The two remaining Molluscs in Ballisargon's throne room realised that they were alone with the female tiger, the only creature to ever kill one of their kind, and that the odds were very much in their favour. They turned their attention to her, sliding slowly across the floor, conserving their energies for the killing Move that was to come.

Without Pradeep's calming, reassuring presence there to steady her, Vidya suddenly felt very isolated. And frightened. While it was true that she alone in the whole of the Lyr had defeated a Mollusc single-handedly, that victory had been out of anger and fury and the need to protect Pradeep. Now she faced two of them, and no Pradeep. She felt the doubt in herself begin to creep in.

She chanced a glance over at Ballisargon. He was still seated behind the large table, a broad grin on his face. It was obvious to her that he was enjoying this. When they made eye contact Ballisargon couldn't resist blowing her a kiss, as if to say goodbye. Maybe she wasn't strong enough to beat them. Maybe she would lose this fight.

Vidya drew a deep breath through her moist nostrils; the rancid scent of Mollusc filled her lungs and head. She may have been about to die at the hands of the small and petty creature that called itself Ballisargon, but she was not going to do so without a fight. She would do what she could to get Robert the time he needed to work out a way to beat Ballisargon once and for all.

Vidya saw the death of the two Molluscs that had been threatening Pradeep and knew what was to come next. She assumed a defensive posture; head low, back arched, her powerful back legs ready to propel her at whichever Mollusc had the nerve to attempt to harm her. She opened her mouth to reveal her fearsome teeth, and her claws unsheathed themselves from her pads. She was going to go down fighting to the last breath.

With a slight flick of her tail, and the barest hint of a narrowing of her eyelids, Vidya Moved.

Robert's smack across Pradeep's nose seemed to do the trick as Pradeep's eyes focussed on Robert.

'ROWRR!' The tiger roared in pain and anger. Finally the claws on his forepaws emerged as he swiped at the air in front of him. 'What did you do *that* for? Again!'

Robert, who was breathing heavily in fear of losing his innards said, 'We have to get back and help Vidya. You were in no fit state to do anything, and I had to get you to listen to me, and, well it worked last time didn't it?'

'Yes, well. Don't do it again. It *hurts*. Now, tell me quickly what the situation was when you Moved me out of the Molluscs' way.'

'Vidya said I was to ignore you and concentrate on stopping Ballisargon.'

'She was right, but you were also right to save me. Vidya is the toughest fighter I know, but she's no match for two Molluscs. She needs me now the way I needed her all those years ago…' He looked down at his paw. Its claws were still out. It had been so long since he had used them, the doubt and fear had always been too strong, the scars too deep. He had carried the debt to his younger sister for so long. But here, now, was his chance to repay it in full. 'Come on, let's go get them.'

In the throne room Vidya re-appeared for the fifth time in as many seconds, breathing hard. She couldn't understand it. Normally the Molluscs were spent after a single Move, but this pair were matching her almost Move for Move. Every time she Moved they were a heartbeat behind her, forcing her to Move again almost instantly. She had never had to Move so hard or so fast in her entire life. Even the flight to the Bridge had not been as hard as this. Her body was nearing failing point; her heart struggling to keep her brain fed with enough blood to concentrate on performing the Moves that the Molluscs were demanding of her. Her head swam as she felt her mind slipping into unconsciousness, darkness beginning to creep in around the edge of her vision.

The toll the Moves were exerting on her showed externally as well. Twin streams of blood ran from the corners of her green eyes down her massive snout, like tears of red rage and frustration. Blood poured freely from her nostrils, pooling on the floor wherever she appeared. Her legs threatened to collapse under her own weight any second. She was at the limits of her strength, and still the Molluscs came. They were too strong for her. Too much.

No! She would not give in to these things; they would not beat her, not while her nephew needed her. If Robert fell to Ballisargon then all that was left of sweet Kshama would fall with him, and Vidya was not going to let that happen. Shaking her head violently to clear the blood from her eyes and nose she roared her anger at the Molluscs, a defiant challenge to them to try and take her if they could.

The next sensation she felt however was not the remembered agony of a Mollusc's touch, but a deep and reassuring calm. Vidya looked to her right to see her brother standing by her shoulder, followed by Robert who appeared a few metres away from them, safely out of range of the Molluscs' immediate threat. Vidya smiled a big cat smile.

Pradeep hadn't forsaken her after all. Buoyed by his arrival Vidya knew that the battle had turned in their favour. Two Molluscs against one tiger was not very fair, but two Molluscs against two tigers was a different story. 'A little help here, Pradeep. The Molluscs are getting smart. And strong,' she said, almost jokingly.

'Certainly, what seems to be the problem?' Pradeep picked up on the change of mood in his sister almost immediately.

Ballisargon, however, hadn't. 'Oh, right, the big scaredy cat come back to save his little sister, has he?' he said, rising from his throne in readiness.

'Actually,' Pradeep replied to Ballisargon, 'it's a case of balancing the odds, more than actual *saving.* You see, Vidya isn't exactly what I would call your average damsel in distress. She's more than capable of looking after herself, provided the situation is relatively fair, so that's what I am here to do.'

With that both tigers Moved just as the Molluscs attempted to engulf them. This time instead of appearing in the same space, the Molluscs appeared a metre or so apart.

The Molluscs did this again and again and again in vain. Each time the tigers were a fraction of a second ahead of them. Robert lost count after the tigers had completed over a dozen Moves in three seconds, a blitz of orange and black. However, as fast as the tigers were they did not have limitless energy and sooner or later they would get too tired to keep evading the Molluscs. Then it would be all over.

Robert turned his attention to Ballisargon during the next

wave of Mollusc attacks, and saw that his hands were not still while he held them clasped behind his back. His fingers twitched and flicked with an intensity Robert had not seen even when Ballisargon had been using them to work his systems. When the tigers re-appeared he shouted to them, 'I know how the Molluscs are doing it. Ballisargon is giving them the energy. That's how they're able to keep up with you. He's *helping* them.'

'Well, I think it's time we gave him and them something they're not expecting then,' said Pradeep. He looked at Vidya, who nodded her assent.

Both tigers disappeared again leaving the Molluscs and Ballisargon momentarily confused. Ballisargon spun round trying to see where the tigers were so he could send the Molluscs to them. He completed his full circle to see Pradeep and Vidya re-materialise *on top* of a Mollusc each. Eight sets of tiger claws sank into Mollusc flesh. Not to wound, just to take hold of. And the tigers Moved.

A heartbeat later the tigers, with their passengers, re-appeared high outside the Keep, in the cloud swept sky of the Lyr. As fast as eight sets of claws had sunk into the Molluscs, eight sets of claws were retracted, and the tigers vanished again, leaving the Molluscs with nothing holding them up except the thin air of the Lyr. Outside of the range of Ballisargon's assistance the Molluscs had no energy to Move themselves to safety, and plummeted through the red sky.

Vidya and Pradeep re-appeared in Ballisargon's throne room. They looked at Robert, then at each other. The tigers each lifted a forepaw off the ground and fist bumped them together in success. 'Told you I'd be there,' said Pradeep to his sister.

Ballisargon, was not impressed, and sighed. 'If I must do this again, then I will.' He raised his hands and with a flick of his fingers Folded space to Move Pradeep and Vidya back to their cells. Instead of disappearing though the tigers Moved themselves out of the way.

'What?' exclaimed Ballisargon. 'Bothersome beasts,' and he flicked his hands once more.

Again, the same result. Pradeep and Vidya Moved out of the way before they could be struck by Ballisargon's Fold.

'How is this possible?' Ballisargon said disbelievingly.

'Do you really think you are faster than us?' Pradeep replied. 'We are tigers and we are beholden to no one, least of all a small and petty man. We react and Move before you even realise what you are trying to do. Your limited knowledge of the Move has no power over us. We will not allow it to.'

'So be it. If I can't touch you two at least I can still imprison him!' Ballisargon gestured at Robert, who disappeared. 'There. Now, how best to deal with you pair?'

The next second Robert reappeared standing exactly where he had vanished from. He was smiling. 'You were right, Pradeep,' he said. 'It is all a matter of control.'

'WHAT?! How? He's just another human!' Ballisargon was angry.

'No,' said Vidya, 'He is more than others. He is one of us now.'

Ballisargon recognised the words as Vidya said them. One who was more than others. It *was* this boy! A bead of sweat formed on his forehead, and his breathing quickened. He could still win this fight if he kept his nerve.

He flicked three gestures in rapid succession at Pradeep, Vidya and Robert, all of who were nowhere near the Folds' effects when they arrived. They had all Moved. Just half a metre, but it was enough to avoid the energy that crackled from Ballisargon's fingers. Ballisargon flicked his hands again, with the same results. Even before his fingers had finished their movements, Robert and the tigers had performed their Rook's Move. Now Ballisargon began to panic. Faster still he flung Folds at all three of them. This time he seemed to have caught them, because they obligingly disappeared from his throne room.

'Ha!' he said to himself, feeling satisfied that he had indeed won.

Crossing his arms he went to sit back down, only to find Robert standing in front of him.

'Boo!' said Robert before vanishing again.

Pradeep and Vidya were next to appear, one tiger either side of Ballisargon. They let vent a huge roar that chilled Ballisargon to his bones before leaping at him, only to disappear at the very last instant before contact.

Unable to stop his reflex action, Ballisargon raised his arms to shield himself in fright. When the impact did not come he carefully lowered them to see Robert and the tigers standing defiantly before him.

'Had enough yet?' Robert asked. 'We can do this all day, every day if that's what it takes you know.'

'So, you have some talent,' Ballisargon sneered, straightening himself up. 'But you know nothing of real power. Let me teach you, and together we can rule this and all worlds. You've seen what I intend to do. Help me complete it.'

'No thank you,' said Robert politely. 'I have enough to do trying to keep my room tidy. I don't want to think how messy a world would be, and I am satisfied with what I currently have. I don't need a world. Anyway, what's the point being the ruler of a set of empty worlds?'

'Ah, but they wouldn't all be empty. I think you'd find that I left behind all the animals; the fishes, the horses, the cats and dogs, the birds. Everything but the people.'

'In fact, I consider what I do to be a great service to the planets I clean. I am ridding the galaxy of the scourge of wasteful and destructive species such as yours. Just imagine all the future lives that would be saved with the removal of the cause of all the wars and conflicts. All the problems I have resolved and the lives I have saved on a hundred worlds, including your own. No more petty fighting over things that ultimately are pointless. No more small minded vindictiveness or exploitation of the weak by the strong.' He sounded confident, sure of the rightness of his argument. 'I will homogenise the whole galaxy and clean it all.'

Robert paused. He hadn't expected Ballisargon's arguments to make even the smallest bit of sense, let alone sound reasonable. Ballisargon sensed the confusion and conflict in Robert and continued: 'The generators are primed with your species. They will provide us with the power we would need to Move the Lyr to a new galaxy. Think of the good you could do if you were ruling a world. It would be run as you saw fit.'

Doubt flashed across Robert's face, Ballisargon seemed to have a point. Robert looked around at Pradeep and Vidya for help. Seeing them he realised the flaw in Ballisargon's argument.

Freedom. They were both free to do as they wanted, they were the masters of their own lives, just as he was of his.

'No,' said Robert. 'Just because you believe that your power is more important than the lives of everyone else doesn't make it right. You reckon that you've saved lives and worlds, when in fact you have destroyed them. People should be allowed the choice, and you don't offer them that. It's wrong.'

'I thought you'd say something like that, boy,' said Ballisargon, the earlier warmth in his tone frosting over to a glacier in an instant. He was no longer grandstanding his vision of the galaxy to Robert. Now he was all business again. 'How about money then? I have riches you can't possibly imagine. You could buy yourself a mansion. A castle!' *Was Ballisargon beginning to sound desperate?*

'My Dad gives me my pocket money, and makes sure I don't go hungry and we have our house. I don't want money.' Robert just kept letting Ballisargon make his empty promises. He was not about to be fooled by them.

'You really are quite predictable,' sighed Ballisargon, his disappointment with Robert evident from his face. 'A shame.

I had hoped you would be astute enough to see the best offer of your life when it was presented to you.'

Robert and the tigers looked incredulous. Surely Ballisargon wouldn't have wanted Robert as apprentice and heir? 'No, really,' he continued, while Robert and the tigers continued for their part to look unconvinced. 'Still, not that it matters unduly. I may not have been able to tempt you with power or wealth, but I do know of something I can give you that you want. Quite possibly the thing you desire most in your little life.' Ballisargon's voice had lost its self indulgent sorrowful tone, swapped out for a definite air of subtle menace. His whole face broke out into skull-like smile. Very quietly, making almost no sound at all, he mouthed one word.

'Mother.'

Robert looked up, his eyes burning bright with memory. Mum. The one thing in the world he wanted. The one thing he would give anything for.

Behind Ballisargon's shoulder a curtain parted, and a woman walked out. She was dressed exactly how Robert remembered her from those last few days, her face kind and sad at the same time.

Pradeep stood open mouthed and seemingly rooted to the floor in surprise, while Vidya took one involuntary half-step forward and gasped 'Kshama!' before she caught herself. Only Robert showed no reaction.

He felt it begin in his stomach, turning it over before it moved up to his chest where his heartbeat quickened. It continued upwards knotting his throat into a tight ball, before it burst into his skull. But this time, he controlled it. He was master of his own skills now. He looked hard at the woman in front of him, and saw the mangalsutra around her neck. Instinctively, Robert reached for the one that hung round his own neck and found it still in place.

Pradeep and Vidya walked up to stand either side of Robert like praetorian guards. Vidya whispered, 'Robert, are you alright?'

Robert knew it was another of Ballisargon's lies. Deep down he *knew* that his Mum was dead and that Ballisargon could not bring her back no matter how much Robert wanted it. The mangalsutra proved that. Nothing was more important to him in the whole world than the memory of his Mum, and Ballisargon had just made his final mistake. If all The Stealer of Worlds had to offer was empty promises and futile attempts at bribery then he was truly without power over him.

Robert strode towards Ballisargon, now unafraid. 'Not Robert anymore,' he said to Vidya; then turning his attention back to Ballisargon he spoke as he walked, 'I am Rajat, son of Kshama, nephew to Pradeep and Vidya, and you have threatened me and my family for the last time. How dare you try to use my Mum against me.'

Ballisargon was taken aback. He had not expected the boy to fight back like this. He started to step backwards as Robert continued to advance. In panic he flicked a desperate Move toward Robert, who just blinked out and in again as it passed through the space he had occupied.

'Is that the best you can do? I'm not afraid of you anymore. Your Molluscs are no threat to us, and your control of the Move is no match for our skills.'

Us? Our? thought the tigers as they looked at each other in confusion. They were having as much trouble as Ballisargon in understanding what was happening.

Robert performed three Rook's Moves in rapid succession, each one taking him forward a metre or so closer to Ballisargon until he was standing right next to him. Robert reached out to take Ballisargon's cape. Ballisargon saw the spark of fire in Robert's eyes and jerked backwards to avoid Robert's grasp. All he succeeded in doing was to stumble into one of the censers, spilling red-hot ashes over his cloak.

Ballisargon spun in panic and shouted as his clothing caught fire. In a second he was a conflagration as the rest of his clothes caught alight. The Stealer of Worlds began to scream, a high shrill scream of panic. Robert had to take a step back for fear of being burned himself.

Ballisargon windmilled round, swatting at his limbs as he tried to extinguish the flames that licked at his arms and legs, but all he succeeded in doing was to fan oxygen into the fire, making it worse. He could feel the heat beginning to burn his skin through the clothing. He fell to the ground, rolling in a vain attempt to quell the human inferno he was rapidly becoming.

'Let him burn,' said Vidya. 'It's no more than he deserves.'

'No,' retorted Robert quickly. 'No one deserves that.' He Moved and grabbed one of the heavy curtains to his right and pulled hard. It came off its fixings with a satisfying tearing sound. Moving back to Ballisargon, who by now was screaming in terror, Robert threw the curtain over him shouting at him to lie still. Robert put out the fire before it had inflicted too much damage, but had still had time to burn away Ballisargon's hair and eyebrows. Realising what Robert had done, Ballisargon rolled onto his back to face his nemesis and saviour.

'How...? How did you see through my illusion?' he sputtered. 'How did you realise it was a trick?'

Robert just smiled, the kind of smile a large cat would make. 'Tigers just know,' he replied.

Then Robert's eyes grew harder, the glint of fire growing to an inferno. 'And unless you want to find out what else tigers can do I suggest you send my Dad and sister back to our house.' His voice had a deep rumble in it, not unlike a growl.

'Harumph,' went Pradeep. 'And everyone else?' he reminded, looking up at Robert.

Robert thought hard for a second. Would the world be as good a place if *everyone* came back? He thought back to the humiliation inflicted upon him by various kids in his school. Did the world *really* need them back? Then he thought that they would have families that would miss them if they didn't all go home. The world was meant to have everyone in it, and it was not for Robert to decide that they should not be.

'And everyone else,' Robert added, not taking his eyes off Ballisargon.

Ballisargon trembled under Robert's unflinching gaze, feeling himself begin to burn under the weight of fire in Robert's eyes. He could no longer meet Robert's stare and turned his eyes away in defeat.

'Yes.' He said it very quietly. He was utterly beaten by this boy, this tiger in waiting. This was why he was afraid of tigers; they weren't scared of him like regular people and animals. They were ferocious and awesome, sleek and magnificent. They were proud creatures who were their own masters.

The fire left Robert, and he looked down at Pradeep and Vidya. They looked back at him and smiled. 'I think we can handle Ballisargon from here,' said Vidya.

Robert let go of Ballisargon and walked away from him. He turned to Pradeep and Vidya.

'Yes, you get back to your family. We'll make sure Ballisargon doesn't cause any more trouble for you. Which you won't will you?' Pradeep growled at Ballisargon.

Ballisargon curled up into a ball on the floor of his throne room, whimpering while the tigers began prowling round him.

26

Take The Power Back

Ballisargon lay on the floor curled up in a tight ball; his hair and eyebrows had been completely burnt away, and where his clothes had caught on fire he had large patches of red raw skin. His cloak had protected him somewhat from the fire, but only the boy's swift intervention had saved him from being completely burnt alive.

So, they let me live. That was a mistake.

He could hear the boy and his pets talking some small distance away, but did not doubt that the tigers were keeping a very close watch on him. He decided to chance a look, and carefully opened one eye halfway. Even this tiny movement was agony as his skin was still burning in pain from the fire that had nearly killed him. He winced at the pain, but managed to stifle the gasp that leapt up his throat and threatened to betray him to his victors. From his limited vantage point he could make out the two tigers just over a metre away, the female one with the bleached right paw if he remembered correctly. Both of them were staring at him very hard.

'But what can we do with him now?' he heard the male tiger, Pradeep he believed it was called, say.

His sister, Vidya if his memory served him correctly

replied, 'I still think there is value in a permanent solution. Even if I can't kill him, surely the Engineer will be able to deal with him?'

'Perhaps, although I think she may never have planned for this moment.'

'Regardless of that, I still think she'll have the best idea what we can do.'

Not a chance.

At no time in the conversation between themselves did the tigers take their eyes off Ballisargon, even for a single second. The discussion about what to do with him continued for a few moments, during which time Ballisargon slowed his breathing and calmed his mind. If he was going to escape from this, and that was certainly his intention, then he needed to think. And possibly a distraction of some sort.

He could not chance what he had planned with the three of them concentrating on him so intently. Even if the tigers would not feel the Fold occurring before he had time to complete it, the boy certainly would. He had proved himself more than a match when it came to control of the Rook's Move, and he would never be able to escape with the boy watching over him. But if Robert were somehow concentrating on something else, then he reckoned he would have the split second he needed to evade him.

The conversation about him died down, causing him to wonder what had changed. He flicked his gaze over to the corner of the room where it seemed the other three were now looking.

Ballisargon could barely see past the forms of the tigers, but it seemed to him that there were three human forms standing in the shadows at the very edge of his throne room.

Now?

He began to draw a deep breath as slowly as he could, opening his mouth wide to make as little noise as possible on the inhalation. However, he was not prepared for the pain that opening his mouth would cause, and this time he could not stop himself from crying out.

He felt the female tiger's eyes on him in a heartbeat. 'Well, it looks like he's awake after all.' Ballisargon heard the tigress say.

'And been listening to everything we've been saying no doubt,' the male tiger concluded correctly. 'Not that it matters, he's beaten. You did it Robert.'

That's what you think.

Ballisargon saw no point in continuing his clandestine observation of the events in his throne room, and spoke, very quietly to confirm what Vidya had said. He watched the tigers pad over to him, and disappear from his limited field of view. He assumed that they were standing at either side of him; a fact that was confirmed when he felt a huge and heavy paw press on him and roll him onto his back. He opened his other eye to see the tigers staring down at him.

'C'mon, get up,' Vidya ordered.

Slowly and carefully Ballisargon moved his traumatised body into a sitting position. Each centimetre he lifted himself caused pain to shoot through his entire frame as he shuddered slowly upright. Not that the tigers seemed to care. They were as oblivious to his obvious pain and suffering as he would be to theirs. He almost admired them for that.

Now upright Ballisargon could see who it was that had distracted Robert and the tigers, and inadvertently caused him to give himself away. In the corner he could see three women; the three women from his past. The Betrothed. Only now they were healed and whole again, the ravages of the decades wandering the Lyr swept away, replaced with the beauty that had drawn him to them in the first place.

Too hasty first time. Think. Turn this round somehow. Ah, of course...

'No, not you, not now! It can't be!' he mock-exclaimed, hoping he had not overdone it. But the tigers seemed to fall for it.

'Friends of yours?' Vidya sneered into his ear.

Moving as one, the three figures took a step forward into the light, revealing themselves to the rest of the room's occupants. Three women, each looking very different to the others, and each dressed in a vibrant colour strode into view. One wore deep blue clothing, another wore bright red, and the final woman was dressed in lush greens. They all walked towards Robert and the hunched form of Ballisargon. 'Thank you, Robert, son of Adam and more than others,' they said in unison.

As soon as he heard the words, Ballisargon saw realisation spread over the boy's face. 'Are you… are you the Betrothed?' Robert asked the three, almost not believing the words as he spoke them. 'You're better.'

'Indeed. He no longer has power over us thanks to you.'

'Me? How?'

'When he was demonstrating his control over the Lyr. His hold over us slipped for a moment only, but it was enough for us to shake his bonds. Now we have come to claim what was his and restore the natural order to this world.'

So, that's when it happened. Such a little lapse, such large consequences.

The three women reached toward Ballisargon's fingers and grasped the rings he still wore.

'Wait, don't touch those!' shouted Vidya.

'Fear not Vidya. These hold no danger to us.' The three women each lifted their left hand and displayed a similar ring on their wedding finger. 'We have long since grown immune to the evil that lurks within them.'

Ballisargon felt his former servants' hands about his own, and felt their firm hands start to slip the control rings from his fingers. He made a show of trying to resist. 'No, you can't!' he wailed pitifully, until he felt the large claws of Vidya in his back.

'Let them take them,' the tigress growled.

Ballisargon dropped his head, as if in complete defeat and held his hands up to the Betrothed. They stripped his fingers of the rings, just as he had hoped they would.

Take them, they won't do you any good.

The Betrothed held the ten rings in their hands before slipping two each onto their fingers. Ballisargon kept watching Robert intently.

Not yet, he's still on guard.

The woman in the red clothing stepped away from her companions and proffered a ring to Robert. He balked at it, but she reassured him that all was well. 'It is safe for you. What was once corrupting within it has been removed. You may take it with no fear.'

Ballisargon watched as Robert carefully and slowly extended a tremulous hand to the woman in the red clothing, and gingerly lifted the ring from her outstretched palm. He held it up to one eye, peering through the hole, while rolling the ring between his forefinger and thumb. 'Is it really safe?' The woman in the red nodded.

Robert looked over to Vidya and gestured toward the ring with his eyes, silently asking her if he should accept it completely. Ballisargon looked over his shoulder and saw the female tiger shrug a 'I guess so'.

He watched as Robert, seemingly emboldened by the tacit approval of his friend, slipped the ring onto his index finger, where it hung loosely. 'It doesn't fit,' the boy said rather obviously.

'Maybe you'll grow into it?' Pradeep observed dryly.

'Be *serious*, Pradeep,' Ballisargon heard her whisper to her brother.

That's it, keep joking tiger.

Robert turned back to the woman in the red, who said, 'In time Robert, I am sure you will come to fathom the nature of the ring. When you do it will be open to you as a means of empowerment. Then it will fit.'

You should live so long.

Now?

Yes.

Ballisargon's plan had worked. Seemingly stripped of the last remnants of his power and control by his one time victims, the boy no longer viewed him as a threat. This was the chance he needed. The attention had shifted from him, much in the way that the boy had distracted him earlier.

Even stripped of his rings he was not without a failsafe control mechanism. Ballisargon had been astute enough to realise that one day somebody might very well overcome him and all his defences, and as such had implanted into his brain a small device that functioned in a similar manner to the control rings, albeit over a much more limited range; kilometres instead of light-years. Still, he knew it would Move him far enough to escape and take his revenge safely. Closing his eyes, Ballisargon drew in a deep breath, this time not caring who heard him, and Moved.

He appeared in a completely enclosed chamber deep within his Keep. There were no doors or windows in any of the walls, and the whole room was several dozen kilometres underground, safely out of the range of Robert, the tigers or even the Betrothed. Ballisargon had had nearly a century to prepare for any eventual defeat, and he had not been idle in that time. The room contained a duplicate set of control rings he had had fashioned; not even Eirian knew they existed, and Ballisargon slipped his fingers eagerly into them.

Immediately his clothing restored itself and his hair and eyebrows regrew, the livid burns he had received fading to nothingness in seconds. His posture straightened as his body healed. He cricked the final stages of his recovery out of his neck with a small grimace. Now he would have his revenge.

Flicking his right hand angrily, a screen flickered into existence, its display showing the throne room with the Betrothed, the tigers and the meddlesome little boy all standing looking frantically around themselves. Ballisargon guessed they were trying to work out where he had gone.

Here's something else to think about.

His left hand jabbed at empty space and he clenched it

into an angry fist. Fifteen Molluscs appeared on the screen in the throne room. He clenched his right fist and fifteen more appeared. That should do it, he reasoned, and with a nonchalant brush of his left hand, sat back on the chair he Moved into the room to watch the fun.

The tigers sensed the incoming Molluscs fractionally too late to react and were engulfed instantly. Pradeep barely had time to register Vidya's white paw sticking awkwardly out of the body of the Mollusc that contained her, twitching in agony before she disappeared, absorbed completely by the cold hard flesh. Pradeep's senses went blank as he too died.

Robert and the Betrothed fared no better as the Molluscs appeared. Robert Moved violently once, twice and a third time trying to escape, but for some reason he was unable to relocate himself outside the bounds of the throne room, and three more futile Moves later he appeared in a corner, heaving lungfuls of air into his wracked body. He willed himself to Move one more time, but was too tired. He saw the horrible, clear flesh of the Mollusc as it approached him, slowly and purposefully. He tried to raise an arm to protect himself as the Mollusc swept over him, filling the corner with its malleable body. He went limp and died.

The Betrothed attempted to Move the Molluscs out of the throne room the second they appeared, but the rings they wore no longer served them. They were powerless to stop the slaughter of the three individuals who had freed them from Ballisargon's wrath. They stood back to back in a circle as the Molluscs finished off the tigers and Robert before turning their attention to them. In a second, it was all over.

Ballisargon leant back in his chair and let out a stream of laughter. It was high and loud, and he continued laughing for a very long time afterwards.

27

The End

Darkness. Without form. Void.

'Would... would he really have done all of that?' Robert asked, his face ashen and his body trembling in shock at what he had just witnessed. It was not every day that you got to watch yourself die pointlessly and painfully, and it had shaken him badly. He turned away from the blank, black display screen. 'I think I'm going to be sick.'

'He would have done all that just for starters,' said Yu-Lin, the Betrothed in green, who was a short Chinese woman in her mid-thirties. 'After he had finished us all off he would have been free to do as he pleased. With your planet's population back under his control he would have rampaged across the Universe, unopposable.'

Robert looked back at the Betrothed, then at the empty display screen again before finishing up looking at the tigers. Pradeep and Vidya sat on their haunches, eyes wide open with shock and fear at the massacre they too had just seen.

'But it's all... surely we would have had some chance?' Vidya asked. 'Even if it is all just in his head.'

'Why would you?' asked N'ptha, the powerfully built

African woman dressed in the loose fitting red clothing. 'He is little more than dreaming for the moment, and for now at least, he is mostly directing what occurs in those dreams. He would expect to best us all.'

The tigers and Robert turned to look at the prone form of Ballisargon, lying on a bed. His burns had gone, healed by the Betrothed, and his hair and eyebrows had been restored. He looked asleep, and although his state of unconsciousness was much deeper than that, his eyes moved rapidly underneath their closed lids.

'But if he's dreaming, won't he wake up?' asked Pradeep. 'And be very angry when he does and finds out he hasn't killed us all.'

'No,' replied Kaori, the final Betrothed to speak. The blues of her clothing matched the deep cerulean of her eyes. She was short, round and smiled gently as she spoke. 'He does not have that much control over what occurs inside his head any longer. We are not allowing it.'

'You?' asked Robert, turning to face the three women. 'You're controlling him?'

'No.' This time is was Yu-Lin who replied to the question. 'We are directing his rehabilitation.'

'You mean his *punishment* surely?' queried Vidya slightly surprised and slightly angrily. 'After what he has done he deserves to pay.'

'And he will,' said N'ptha. 'What good would merely restraining him physically do? It has been proved not to work. All we would accomplish would be to delay his eventual escape, and resumption of his Plan.'

'So how will this rehabilitation work then?' asked Pradeep, glaring at his sister as soon as he saw her open her mouth to say something as he had said 'rehabilitation'. 'What will it achieve?' he added, still looking at Vidya, only now his expression was conciliatory.

Kaori replied, 'Over time, at our direction, he will be shown the eventual, logical outcome of his Plan. The extreme he would find himself at if he continued unchecked. Then we can demonstrate to him that he was wrong. For now however, he must remain immobile while he dreams.'

'A prisoner in his own mind.' Robert said it so chillily that even Vidya shuddered at the image. 'But what will you do now that you have the controls to his generators and machines?'

'We don't have enough of the control rings to work all the machines to the degree that Ballisargon could,' said Yu-Lin indicating the four rings they had given Robert and the tigers. 'But we have enough to put things right here. You Robert, along with Eirian and the tigers will ensure through your possession of the remainder that we will never be able to abuse them.'

Vidya still felt sceptical about something, but she wasn't sure what it was. Then she had it. 'But what is to stop you making more rings? Completing the set.'

'We do not know how,' said N'ptha matter-of-factly. 'The only two people who know the art and science of the generators are him, ' she indicated in Ballisargon's direction, 'and Eirian.'

'Well he's no threat now,' said Pradeep, 'and I doubt that the Engineer would want to create any more rings,' he finished, hoping that Vidya would agree. She half shrugged her shoulders in partial acquiescence, not wholly convinced.

'Anyway Vidya,' said Kaori, 'even if we do abuse the little power we need to control Ballisargon, we could not withstand an assault by two tigers both armed with control rings of their own.'

'Yeah,' Robert added almost cheerfully. 'Now that the rings are no longer dangerous...' he paused as Vidya narrowed one eye before continuing, 'in *that* way, you'd have nothing to worry about. About stopping the Betrothed I mean, if they ever tried to abuse the power.'

Vidya considered this for a moment. Pradeep and Robert were both right. There did seem to be enough balance in the situation to ensure nothing would go wrong. Even if the Betrothed did succumb to temptation and begin dominating the Lyr in the way Ballisargon had done, she knew that her and Pradeep could stop them if they had to.

'And anyway-' began Yu-Lin before Vidya cut her off mid-sentence.

'Don't worry, I'm convinced. You three need the rings you've kept to keep *him*,' she emphasised, 'under control, but you've relinquished enough power to stop yourselves ever becoming him. For our part, we will guard the remainder,' she indicated Pradeep, who nodded his assent, 'and help the Engineer rebuild the Lyr to its former glory.'

'Go to Eirian and tell her that her vigil is over. The Lyrne are a free people again; they no longer need her protection. She can lay down her burden,' said N'ptha.

'But what about Robert,' asked Pradeep, echoing Robert's earlier thoughts. 'He can't stay here, his family will miss him. We've got to get him back home.'

N'ptha glided toward Robert, indicating the ring she had presented to him earlier. He followed her gaze down to his hand, and realising she was asking him for it, handed the ring over once more. N'ptha held the slender circlet of metal up to her eye, peering through it before handing it back to Robert. 'There. It has enough power within it now to Move you back to Earth.'

Robert slipped the loose fitting metal back over his index finger and clenched his hand into a fist to stop it from falling off. 'What, so I just think about Moving back home, and this thing'll do the rest?'

'More or less,' smiled Yu-Lin.

Robert gulped and looked at the tigers. Going home meant leaving them for good. He'd never ever see them again. He opened his mouth to say something. What exactly, he wasn't quite sure, but after everything they had experienced together, goodbye did not seem enough. 'I...' he began before the tigers bounded over to him and pressed their huge heads into his tummy.

'Go on, we'll be fine,' said Vidya. 'You've got your family waiting for you. And besides,' she began to sniffle, 'if you drag out the goodbye Pradeep will only start crying.'

'Hey, I will not,' Pradeep said, tears beginning to form at the corners of his large orange eyes.

'You've made her very proud,' said Vidya. 'You truly are her son, and we are equally proud to call you nephew.'

'I am sure you'll do wonderful things with your life Robert,' said Pradeep.

Robert, for his part said nothing. He was trying to be the strong tiger his Mum had been, and Pradeep and Vidya were. And besides, they both knew what he was thinking. Putting it into words was unnecessary. He held them both for a very very long minute, breathing in the smell of their soft orange fur, feeling the power hidden beneath it in their large frames, feeling the warmth against his face. Eventually he broke away from them so he was standing upright again. 'Better move back a bit,' he cautioned, 'I have no idea how much room I'm going to need.'

'Farewell Robert,' said the three Betrothed, speaking as one again.

'Goodbye and good luck, ' he replied. He looked back to the tigers, who just nodded.

Robert closed his eyes, feeling the cold, hard metal of the ring around his small finger. In his mind he pictured his bedroom, in his house in his road in his town in his county in England on the Earth going round the sun in the solar system that was part of the galaxy that lay light years from where he stood now in the Lyr. As soon as the connection between the two places was made in his head, Robert felt space Fold around him, and he was gone.

He opened his eyes to find himself on his bed, fully clothed. He looked at the clock, which showed it was Wednesday morning, the very day he had woken up to find everyone gone, and when it had all started. *Had no time passed at all then?* he wondered. More importantly, was his family back?

Robert jumped off his bed, disturbing the slumbering Catanooga, and ran to the bathroom, pushing the door open without a second's hesitation. His sister, who was moisturising her face, began shouting at the top of her lungs at him to get out.

Delighted, Robert dashed out of the bathroom and hurtled down the stairs, nearly slipping twice in his enthusiasm. He shot into the kitchen, colliding with his Dad who had his head buried in the fridge.

By now Robert was laughing and whooping with joy that he had his family back. Elisabeth and her hours in the bathroom. Dad and his surprise breakfasts. He was overjoyed.

'Whoa, calm down there, Robert,' his Dad said firmly. 'Sit down and tell me what all the excitement is about?'

Robert barely knew what to say. Did his Dad not remember anything of the time he and Elisabeth had been Ballisargon's prisoners? Just then Elisabeth came down the stairs, her hair in a tangle, and moisturiser dripping off her chin.

'Dad, that little...' she began.

Robert's Dad raised his hand gently to silence Elisabeth. 'I know. He barged in on me too.'

'But he KNOWS not to disturb me in the bathroom, doesn't he?' she whined.

'Yes, yes he does. I will deal with it, Elisabeth. Now go back upstairs, you're making a mess on the kitchen floor.'

Elisabeth looked down at the pool of moisturiser that had collected at her feet, back at her Dad, then glared at Robert. 'Little...' was all Robert heard as she stomped back upstairs.

'Now Robert, do you want to explain all your careering round the house? What's got into you?' his Dad asked patiently.

'I...' Robert began but the words died in his mouth, unspoken. How could he tell his Dad what had happened? And anyway, he wouldn't believe him even if he did tell the truth. Robert's head fell slightly, averting his eyes from his Dad's. 'I don't know,' was all he could mumble.

He felt the heat of tears begin to form in his eyes. After all he had done, he was still just Dad's Robert. He wasn't a tiger anymore; he was just Elisabeth's little brother, and he would have to go and apologise to her.

'I'll go and tell Elisabeth that I'm sorry,' he sniffled.

'I think you should,' his Dad said sternly. Then more softly: 'Here, dry your eyes first.' He handed Robert a tissue.

Robert blew his nose hard, and wiped away the hot salty water. He could still taste the tears in the back of his throat, but he had stemmed their flow. He turned and headed out of the kitchen.

'Oh, and Robert,' his Dad called after him. 'Thank you for rescuing us. Elisabeth and everyone else don't remember, but I do. It's funny; your Mum always said you'd make her proud, though I never understood what she meant till now. You truly are the tiger she knew you would be.'

Made in the USA
Charleston, SC
07 July 2014